SIGN OFF

SIGN OFF

JON KATZ

BANTAM BOOKS
NEW YORK • TORONTO • LONDON • SYDNEY • AUCKLAND

This is a work of fiction. Names, characters, places, and incidents are either the product of the author's imagination or are used fictitiously. Any resemblance to actual persons, living or dead, or locales is entirely coincidental.

SIGN OFF

A Bantam Book / February 1991

All rights reserved.
Copyright © 1991 by Jon Katz.
Book design by Glen M. Edelstein.
No part of this book may be reproduced or transmitted in any form or by any means, electronic or mechanical, including photocopying, recording, or by any information storage and retrieval system, without permission in writing from the publisher.
For information address: Bantam Books.

Library of Congress Cataloging-in-Publication Data
Katz, Jon.
  Sign off / Jon Katz.
  p. cm.
ISBN 0-553-07123-8
  I. Title.
PS3561.A7558S5   1991
813'.54—dc20   90-46206
                                                         CIP

Published simultaneously in the United States and Canada

Bantam Books are published by Bantam Books, a division of Bantam Doubleday Dell Publishing Group, Inc. Its trademark, consisting of the words "Bantam Books" and the portrayal of a rooster, is Registered in U.S. Patent and Trademark Office and in other countries. Marca Registrada. Bantam Books, 666 Fifth Avenue, New York, New York 10103.

PRINTED IN THE UNITED STATES OF AMERICA

BVG   0   9   8   7   6   5   4   3   2   1

To Paula, who wasn't sure, but hung in there anyway.

CHAPTER ONE

NEWS ALERT

*P*eter Herbert got to the phone on the second ring. The digital clock on the night table read 2:45 A.M. He flashed on the pinpoint lamp that cast a beam by the side of the bed but wouldn't shine into Barbara's eyes.

"Mr. Herbert?" said the calm voice on the other end, waiting patiently for his confirmation. The two words were enough to quicken his pulse and jolt him awake. He knew the voice well.

"This is USB News, Operator Five Hundred. This is a news alert. Can you confirm?"

"I confirm. This is a news alert at two forty-five A.M."

Peter hung up and ran into the bathroom, filled the sink with ice-cold water, and plunged his face into it. He sprinted back to the phone, sputtering.

Barbara rolled over. "You macho jerks," she groaned. "Do you all have to rush in there like Mel Gibson?" She didn't expect an answer.

Peter began dialing.

"Is it the end of the world?" Barbara asked.

"No," he said. Their understanding was that if the alert wasn't World War III or the end of the world, he didn't have to waste time telling her about it. It was never good news—that she knew.

"I'll put some coffee in the thermos," she said, climbing out of bed. A grudging wifely gesture. Domesticity was not her forte.

Sam Adelson's News Alert Paging System was erupting at almost the same moment. Carol rolled onto her back, cursing. "Oh, God," she said. "Who's dead?"

Adelson muttered that he didn't know who was dead. Either somebody important was, or a lot of unimportant people were.

The pager didn't beep; that would not have been urgent enough for the people who put on television news. It blasted an earsplitting honk, like the klaxons in old submarine movies, and didn't stop until Adelson dialed Operator 500 at network headquarters and gave his name. This was to make sure nobody ignored the page. Not that Adelson, vice-president for news, ever would.

Like other network news executives, he bitched about the pagers constantly, and loved them. The noise they made was really a declaration: *I am a big cheese at the most influential news organization in the free world, and if anybody thinks he can come up with better dinner-party chat, let him try it.*

The telephone would have caused much less fuss, to tell the truth; it seemed to work well enough for Peter Herbert. But the pager was more fun. If an occasional concert or play was disrupted by network executives racing up the aisles honking like geese, that was a part of the myth, the excitement. Let doctors beep discreetly. They spent their days in offices, looking down people's throats and up their behinds. USB newspeople went off like World War III, taking everybody in earshot with them.

Adelson peered at the alarm clock. He would wait a few minutes, then call Herbert, whose show, *Morning in the U.S.,* was next up. The bastard would have barely logged any sleep before he would have to hop back into his silly little Toyota and speed toward Manhattan.

Looking out his window across 68th Street, he wondered again why anyone, especially someone with Herbert's hours, would voluntarily live in New Jersey. Adelson had a ten-minute cab ride from his apartment to the studios on the Lower East Side. He would beat Herbert by almost half an hour.

Adelson leaned over and kissed his wife. She would awake to find him gone, but she would know where he was. It was the third time this year, and this was only early February. Adelson figured he had enough time to stop at Dunkin' Donuts and pick up provisions for the control room crew. A few dozen dough-nuts bought lots of goodwill.

Great, Adelson thought. He could feel the adrenaline, the physical charge. Big stories were good for everybody—for advancing careers, for fattening budgets, for bolstering morale. He hoped this was a monster of a story. He hoped somebody had blown up half of Europe.

Peter's car phone began warbling as he pulled out of the drive-way. That would be Adelson, he thought. Possibly Brookings, the USB News president, but generally Brookings called only if Adelson was out of town. Calling Peter directly would violate the chain of command, something Brookings disliked.

Thank God he didn't have to use the News Alert Paging System anymore; Barbara would have chopped the pager to bits by now—maybe him as well. Brookings had granted a special exemption from NAPS—the acronym was someone's idea of a joke—after Peter complained that it frightened his children. The kids were only six and nine, he objected, and they thought the house was being robbed whenever the damned thing went off.

Brookings had agreed to Peter's being contacted by phone, but he was clearly annoyed at the exception. It was bad form, Peter knew, to bring family into these things. Family was your problem, not the news division's, and if you wanted to play in the big leagues and get a big-league salary, you did what you were supposed to do.

The story looked to be huge; he probably wouldn't get home for days.

Like most of his peers, Peter enjoyed thinking of himself as a cynic. But big stories still excited him as much as the first one had fifteen years earlier, when a bus crash in Asbury Park had killed twenty people. He remembered racing to the accident scene, interviewing the survivors and relatives of the dead for his newspaper, scrambling and writing for three days and nights, describing the gore. The rest of the world was put aside for however long the story lasted.

Most people went through their work lives without ever experiencing the delirious exhaustion that followed a big story, when the final edition was out or the broadcast over. Like most newspeople, he'd become addicted to it. Peter loved to leave them behind—the sleeping suburban stockbrokers, lawyers, and academicians, awaiting the morning rush. *His* work couldn't wait.

But the fear was also unique. Big stories were opportunities, but they were land mines as well, always capable of blowing up on you. An eerily quiet annex to USB News, the subdivision where public affairs and religious programming were based, was populated largely by former producers who'd made bad calls under fire.

"Herbert," he snapped, picking up the car phone.

"You at the Meadowlands yet?" came Adelson's familiar Brooklyn bray.

"Not quite. You at work?"

"No, I'm at the Dunkin' Donuts. You take your coffee light, right?"

"Sam, there's coffee at work. The cafeteria will bring up food. You don't have to drag your drippy disgusting bags into the control room; you almost blew out the director's console last year. The story sounds good, doesn't it?"

"Yeah." Adelson sighed happily, then collected himself. "But it's going to be a tough call on your part. Be real careful, especially about going with a special report. Screwing up one of those is the last mistake you get to make at USB News. What's your ETA?"

Peter ignored the jibe. "I'll call when I get to the tunnel approach, before the phone goes dead—about fifteen minutes, I guess." He hesitated, wanting more guidance. But even though

Adelson was his friend, he was also a vice-president; he had not managed that by putting his head on other people's blocks.

Adelson provided no reassurance. "Good luck. See you in the control room. If you lived in the city, you could've been here already."

"That's why I don't. See you soon."

Patricia Flannery responded the way she always did when the pager went off in the early morning. She jumped out of bed, pulled on her Nikes, grabbed her book of telephone numbers, and charged out of the apartment. She left a cat hissing, the pager blaring, the lights on, and the door unlocked. Mrs. Gianetti, the octogenarian who lived down the hall and never slept anyway, happily took $50 a month to be part of the news business and come in to put things in order, giving Flannery crucial minutes when she most needed them.

Flannery hit the street running, turned right, and barely acknowledging the sparse predawn traffic, dashed half a block into the USB lobby, up the elevator and into the main newsroom. Elapsed time: just under five minutes from the pager's first honk. She smiled. This was a new record, handily beating the old one of 5:21. If the sight of a tall, angular woman rushing through the newsroom in her bathrobe and running shoes, clutching a thick leather-bound book, struck anyone as odd, it wasn't apparent.

Of course there were already ample distractions. The red bulbs mounted in every room in the vast building were flashing, signaling a news emergency. Flannery had noticed that the blue network vans, parked in bays near the main entrance, were idling, ready to move.

Taking things in quickly was Flannery's job, and she was extremely good at it. As chief booker on *Morning in the U.S.,* she was supposed to lure guests on to her show before her rivals could snare them. She and her staff—the Body Snatchers—were justly considered the best in television news. She'd once been accused of virtually kidnapping a murder witness right out from under the federal agents guarding him, by pretending to be a federal prosecutor. Peter told her that she would have made a great one.

Moving to the new apartment building across the street a few months earlier had given her a tremendous jump on the competition, cutting nearly half an hour off her response time. Her counterparts were going crazy trying to figure out why she was first by an even wider margin than before. Once they realized what she had done, they would probably find apartments closer to their studios too.

Flannery scanned the newsroom desks to see which looked busiest. These were the minutes that really mattered, critical time, something the men she was watching never seemed to understand, so intense was their preoccupation with visas, phone lines, and transmitting devices. Her eyes were drawn to the Foreign Desk right away. Eight or nine frantic producers were all screaming into phones, ordering satellites, moving crews and correspondents around. The blue light above the newsroom's main entrance was also flashing, meaning that the Special Assignment Team—SAT—had been activated.

She came up behind an assistant foreign editor, but he was on the phone and waved her away. The Foreign Desk coordinator was screaming into another telephone; so was the chief of correspondents. She glanced at the clock, felt panic. Seconds mattered.

Climbing onto an empty chair, she cupped her hands to her mouth and aimed toward the foreign editor, waiting until he'd slammed the phone down.

"Fuck!" she screamed.

Bob Anglin turned toward her in shock. God, she thought, will men *ever* stop being surprised when women curse?

"What's the story, Bob?" she yelled.

Two minutes later she was upstairs at her desk in the *Morning in the U.S.* newsroom, with an assistant setting down the first of what would be a half-dozen cups of scalding black coffee consumed before 9:00 A.M. Flannery had her phone book open in front of her, a receiver cradled in her neck, a bottle of imported throat spray from England within reach. She would be screaming for at least three hours.

She glanced up at the huge clock. Peter would be in any minute; she had to have something to give him. *Kissinger,* she thought. I'll give him Kissinger. She grabbed her book and flattened it at the dogeared "K" tab.

★   ★   ★

When the pager began blaring in Danny D'Amato's apartment, the young woman he had met at a party the night before jumped out of bed with a shriek. Her scream frightened D'Amato's aging and ill-tempered dachshund, Naughton, who rushed over and nipped her on the calf.

It took D'Amato several minutes to call the network operator, get the pager shut off, calm everybody down—especially Naughton—and tend to the girl's slight wound. He thought her name was Vicki, although he wouldn't swear to it, and leaning over her long legs to press on a Band-Aid, he was tempted for an instant to smother the pager under the mattress and crawl back into bed with her—but tempted only for an instant. He could have sex anytime; big stories sometimes didn't come along for months.

"It's just a scratch," he said, reluctantly letting go of her leg.

"What the hell was that?" she asked anxiously. "I thought the building was on fire."

D'Amato pulled his pants on and slipped the pager into his pocket. "It's the news pager. It goes off whenever there's a big story. It's so loud that you can't miss it even if you're in the shower. All the executive producers have them."

Vicki was an editorial assistant at one of the fashion magazines, he remembered. Smith, or was it Sarah Lawrence? She wanted badly to get into television, and he thought she would be just right for it: bright, neurotic, attractive, obsessed with her future.

Her anxiety seemed to ease. "I didn't know you were an executive producer," she purred.

He opened his dresser and began pulling out underwear. "I run the Special Assignment Team—we call it the Crash and Burn unit. It goes wherever the story is. I'm going to have to say goodbye now, and I really am sorry, because I had a great time. I'll call you when I get back. Stay as long as you want. My daughter Bobbie will probably be up before you are, and she'll make you a cup of coffee. You'll like her. She's a great kid."

D'Amato's reputation as the sexiest man at USB News

puzzled the other men. He was short, muscular, Mediterranean-looking, but hardly a movie star. Still, women went on and on about his charm and warmth. He didn't entirely understand it himself, but he accepted it.

He checked his travel kit, a leather pouch stitched with the network's blue eagle logo. It was in order, holding a battered passport, $3,000 in cash, police credentials for a dozen major international capitals, a company American Express card, and clothes for two days. Anything else he needed, he could buy at the scene.

D'Amato decided to head straight for Kennedy Airport. If things happened in their usual sequence, Brookings would activate his unit within minutes.

What might have happened, and where, mattered little to D'Amato. Other producers and editors sat around for hours after work analyzing the ramifications of this story or that; D'Amato forgot what he'd been covering the second it was over. What mattered to him was getting there ahead of everybody else, getting his equipment past suspicious customs and border people, and sending pictures to New York before anybody else did.

To that curious end, he had committed innumerable acts of daring, cunning, bribery, and personal courage. He had learned to sleep standing, or to get along without sleep. Risking imprisonment to smuggle videocassettes past authoritarian cops was routine. He had been harassed, beaten, and shot at; he had witnessed unspeakable acts of deliberate and accidental brutality.

When he thought about it, which happened rarely, he supposed that he did it for the company, which for twenty-five years had paid him more than he ever thought he would make, sent him to almost every country in the world, and given him a full-time substitute for marriage and family life, which he had never been much good at anyway. It was a good deal all around.

David Nab was awakened by three loud knocks and one soft one on the door of the co-op on Central Park South that he used whenever he came into the city from Connecticut.

That would be Farmer, his assistant, using the code they had worked out to make sure the wrong person didn't get in.

"It's a little after three," Farmer called out, letting himself in. "The London flight leaves Kennedy at five. The briefing folder is in your attaché case. The bike is set up in the exercise room in front of the television."

Nab stood and stretched. It was early for him, but not that early. He believed that rising before dawn was a major reason he was worth $800 million. That, a series of smart takeover decisions, and the $40 million nest egg Dad had set aside before his private jet had splattered all over a mountainside in Colorado.

Although, given a few breaks, Nab might have made it even without Dad's lumber interests and mines. He was bright enough to have excelled at the Harvard B-School and to have built his inheritance into a small empire that included hotels, computer chips, and enough real estate to rival the square mileage of Delaware.

The bothersome part was that he was smart enough to be taken more seriously than he was. Nab had been envious and impressed back when Donald Trump began making speeches about foreign policy. What did Trump know about foreign policy, he had grumbled to his wife. Nab had been all over the world a dozen times. And he had some interesting ideas about how to get things done—look at what he had accomplished by the age of forty-four. But nobody cared what successful businessmen thought. Except for Iacocca, who could probably be President; that's what happened when you plunked yourself in the middle of every other car ad on television.

Nab knew that the media had a lot to do with how people like him were regarded. Reporters might be slobs, bugs, petty little parasites—he certainly had never met any who could run anything—but when they started quoting someone in *The New York Times* and putting his picture in *Newsweek,* one thing led to another. A congressional committee might want to hear your views on economic policy. A governor might ask you to head a task force. Nab couldn't remember being more depressed than when Trump had showed up at the Russian Embassy to meet Gorbachev. And he'd had to watch it on TV in Connecticut.

Nab climbed into gym shorts and a sweat shirt, walked into

the living room, and mounted the electronic exercycle that followed him wherever he went and would shortly be traveling to London.

To call it an exercise bike was an understatement; it was more like a leisure-time complex. The machine clicked itself on as soon as Nab climbed onto the seat. His pulse rate flashed on the digital readout before him, along with the time, total calories expended, and a message strip that welcomed him aboard by name. Yesterday's stock quotations flowed across the top of the screen. A reading stand protruded from the handlebars; clipped onto it were fresh copies of *The Wall Street Journal, The New York Times,* and the *Financial Times* of London. On the left, a telephone stand, complete with message pad and private line, was within arm's reach. Nab never spent more than half an hour on the machine, but there were people not far from the apartment who would have been quite content to live on it for a week or two.

He skimmed the front page of the *Journal,* flipped through the *Times*'s first section, and yelled to Farmer to turn on the television.

Farmer came out of the kitchen with a tray holding a goblet of orange juice, a silver coffeepot, a thin china cup, and a bowl of fruit. He attached the tray to a special mount on the right side of the exercycle. On his way back to the kitchen, he punched on the television, putting the channel switcher next to the telephone on the stand.

Nab looked up as a Glenn Ford movie suddenly yielded to the USB News blue eagle and the hourly headline service provided throughout the night. He felt a shiver at the back of his neck as he listened. He was a news freak, had been ever since the weekend he'd spent as a teenager glued to his television set watching Walter Cronkite guide the country through the Kennedy assassination.

He continued to stare at the set, lost in thought. Farmer had to ask twice if he wanted more orange juice. The exercycle beeped softly, signaling that his pedal rate had slowed below the pace required to burn 350 calories. Nab didn't hear it.

He looked up USB's trading code and punched it into the Quotron terminal bracketed onto his cycle. It almost instantly flashed a short business profile of the company—its latest stock price, dividends paid, earnings per share. USB was trading at $125, down from a fifty-two-week high of $160, a big drop.

He scribbled a note to Farmer on the memo pad, asking him to locate the story he had read somewhere that week about Wall Street concerns that the network was not being well managed, that costs were too high and revenues slipping. He wanted to read it on the plane to London.

He reached for the telephone. Harold Wallace loved London, and even a high-priced attorney wouldn't mind being awakened for a quick trip there by private jet. It would be worth his while.

CHAPTER TWO

PETER'S CHOICE

*N*abih Patel, Peter's deputy, sounded even more cautious than usual.

"What we know," he told Peter on the car phone, "is that the Associated Press is reporting—and they're emphasizing that this is unconfirmed—that there's been some serious incident involving an American naval vessel docked in Lisbon."

"Portugal—that could mean anybody. The Libyans or Iranians or the Palestinians—right?—if it's a terrorist thing. Where does this come from?" asked Peter, still a bit groggy.

"Stay cool, Peter. The AP is quoting unnamed Defense Department officials," said Patel. "According to the Foreign Desk people, the navy is scrambling all over the Atlantic. And they're hearing from the Portuguese government that an American ship has been heavily damaged. Maybe—repeat, *maybe*—even sunk. There's a lot of activity at the Pentagon, too, the Washington bureau says; the Joint Chiefs showed up. Not enough to go on yet, though."

Peter tucked the phone in his neck, glancing at the dashboard clock. Three A.M. Less than three hours before air time. What, he asked, about the existing lineup, scheduled to include a full half hour on the homeless with live remotes from several cities, plus a panel on crack and interviews with the authors of three hot new diet books?

Patel guessed what he must be thinking. "We can't scrap our lineup, Peter. There's not enough to react to. We'll get ready, in case something materializes for a special report, but we need a lot more concrete information before we even do that."

Peter wasn't convinced. "We wait for official confirmation and it'll be too late to do much. *Something's* going on. Maybe we should kill the old stuff and get ready to jump."

USB News regulations were clear about such situations: There had to be two reliable confirming sources before a story could be aired. So far he had only half of one.

Yet the logistics of his program were daunting.

If a naval vessel had, in fact, been sunk by someone—especially if there was heavy loss of life or the possibility of retaliation—Peter had to cancel the existing schedule and loose the show's guest-getters, Patricia Flannery's bookers, on all relevant parties. They would need naval and congressional responses, intelligence types, diplomatic experts, public reaction from around the country, representatives of whatever foreign country was involved. He would have to call in extra technicians and producers to prepare maps and graphics and edit the tape that would come flowing in by satellite. To do it right, to pull enough people in, he would have to set things in motion immediately.

But the consequences of screwing up were daunting, too: If the story didn't pan out—after all, even the AP wasn't sure—he would have three yawning hours of airtime to scramble to fill. And if he ordered a special report on the supposed sinking and it turned out not to have happened, or it proved to be a minor incident, Brookings would get him. In forty years USB News had never aired an inaccurate special report.

Peter, wrestling with modern technology and with the journalist's lifelong addiction to coffee, held his steaming thermos in his left hand and the car phone in his right, steering down the mostly deserted suburban highway with his elbows.

They were career-makers, these wee-hour judgment calls. Adelson's Law Number Eleven: *You can enjoy a big success in television, then fail, but you can never overcome a big failure and then succeed.* To overreact seriously could be expensive and embarrassing, a sign you lacked poise and common sense. To underreact, resulting in another network's getting there first, was a sign that you lacked a future. You had very few minutes to call it, either way.

"Nabih, hammer those donkeys in Washington for some answers. If a navy ship has been sunk, families have to be notified; there's got to be a chain reaction triggered. What about our bureaus in London, Madrid, Tel Aviv, Cairo? Call them—make sure they're not sitting on their hands. Try Miami, San Diego, and Norfolk—have them check the navy's home ports. If it's true, there must be chaplains running around. They'd have to get that giant military morgue in Delaware ready, wouldn't they? And call the Resource Center and get navy and defense technology experts in."

The network's Resource Center maintained contracts with dozens of specialists, from medical to meteorological; whenever major news broke, they appeared almost magically, to guide producers and writers through the story. Every executive producer had hair-raising stories to tell about errors that would otherwise have crept on to the air.

Patel knew the stakes involved as well as Peter did—better perhaps, since he had watched a half-dozen or so executive producers hit the wall at high speeds during his nine years with the morning program. Patel, in fact, had invented the program's ritual control-room exorcism as each executive producer got cut down: He would yell "Flameout!" while on the monitor the techs ran an old tape of an airplane with a nose camera spiraling into the ground.

Producers were like baseball managers, Patel had figured out. Even though the network never actually fired anyone outright, you could spend the rest of your career so deep in the hole—working on the weekend news or serving as deputy to some faraway bureau chief—that you were never heard from again.

"I'll do that, Peter. But it's too early to blow out the show." Patel sounded a last cautious note.

They hung up while the Toyota made its way through a series of overpasses that turned mobile-phone conversations to earsplitting static. Peter took advantage of the lapse to gulp coffee. He needed the caffeine to kick in as he pondered the possibilities.

When the car phone warbled again a few moments later, Patel had more to report: USB's Tel Aviv bureau was quoting Israeli intelligence sources as saying an American warship had, in fact, sunk off Portugal with considerable loss of life. The bureau was saying the Israelis were "solid" about that much, but could provide few further details. The London bureau, added Patel, said its sources were also confirming an incident, but had no other information. Whether the supposed sinking was an accident or the result of an attack remained maddeningly unclear. USB's Pentagon staff had information that whatever the incident was, it involved a new ship. One producer had also talked to a navy chaplain who said, off the record, that the navy expected many casualties—*scores* was his exact term—and that extra chaplains were heading for Norfolk.

Peter tried to listen to his gut. He had heard considerable talk in his career about "golden guts" and "news guts," how many a brilliant judgment had been made by trusting one's gut, although he wasn't precisely clear in which part of the body the gut resided.

"All we know for sure," Patel summarized, "is that some admirals went rushing out of a cocktail party in Washington, that the Joint Chiefs are up early today, and that the navy is on alert in the Atlantic and the Mediterranean because something happened in Lisbon, but we don't know what. It could just be a collision, Peter. If you toss out the lineup now, we'll never be able to get a show put together in time if this thing—whatever the hell it is—fizzles."

Peter hesitated. What had been drummed into producers' heads a hundred times was: better to be late than to be wrong. Both of them knew that Patel's ass was covered, but Peter's had a giant bull's-eye on it.

If he made so colossal a misjudgment, Peter would be made an example for years to come. His name would be synonymous at USB News with dishonor and incompetence; subsequent producers would commit to memory the sad saga of the bright producer on the move who aired a special report that wasn't right and scrapped three hours of carefully planned programming for a crisis that never materialized.

But something serious had happened to a navy ship and, according to the Washington bureau, to a relatively new one. New ships aren't supposed to sink, thought Peter, unless somebody sinks them, not with all their high-tech safety gear.

For once, he felt his gut was sending him a message.

"Blow out the show, Nabih. Cancel every segment. Let's prepare to do the whole three hours on the sinking. Tell Flannery to blanket everybody on the navy, its technology, the works. Have her get a terrorism panel ready, just in case. Tell her to get a Body Snatcher ready to hit the ship's home port once we find out where it is. Have her send somebody to the airports to stand by. We may need lots of relatives tomorrow. And tell her to find some sailors and officers back here from duty in the area. There must be hundreds."

Patel signed off, leaving Peter anxious. If the Israelis thought something had happened, and the AP thought something had happened, and the Joint Chiefs were meeting, then something *had* happened, he reassured himself. But he had to know *what* before he could interrupt regular network programming. Special reports had enormous impact. They were a signal to the country, sometimes to the world, that USB News believed something of crucial importance had occurred. Stock prices had been known to plunge within seconds of the appearance of the special-report graphic, even before anyone knew what it was about.

The Toyota zipped through the Lincoln Tunnel and downtown, doors locked against the increasingly aggressive hookers who would hop in and proposition drivers from their own back seats. Peter thought of them as colleagues on the overnight shift.

He dialed Patel again. He was close enough now for the car phone to work quickly and clearly. "Nabih, can you patch me through to Brookings? He needs to know now that something is going on."

"Not necessary, Peter. He called a couple of minutes ago. The National Desk called him—wouldn't you know it? Even scooped the Foreign Desk. Nobody dick-sucks faster than Holman. Brookings seemed a little irked that we hadn't called him."

"How irked?

"I'd say seven out of ten. But he can't kill you in the

middle of a news alert, can he? And think what he'd do if he knew you'd blown out the whole show."

Peter chortled. Fuck it. It was too late to worry about Brookings now.

He pulled into the news division garage and backed into his reserved parking space, perhaps the most cherished perk the network offered. Less than three hours to go. He clipped his ID to his shirt pocket as he jogged toward the building entrance.

"Morning, Mr. Herbert," said the security guard, a young Sri Lankan named Sanjih, who slipped every executive producer in the building a resumé every month or so. The kid was lucky to have gotten a job inside the building; sooner or later somebody would give him a clerk's slot. Lots of people in the news division had started that way; that was why 50 percent of the building's security guards had graduate degrees, according to personnel. Herbert sometimes pictured the slight guards attacking intruders with their book bags.

He sprinted up one flight to the cafeteria, where the staff was already struggling to accommodate the technicians and producers pouring into the building. The bored cafeteria staff was delighted when a big story broke in the middle of the night. Vats of coffee and juice and trays of toast and eggs—including the famous thirty-second Emergency Omelette—were shuttled back and forth between the cafeteria and control rooms all night.

Peter waved to the overnight cashier, who'd already spotted him loping down the hallway. "Coffee, two toasts wheat!" she shouted. By the time he'd reached the cash register his food was waiting for him. He snapped out his account number. News executives were presumed to be too preoccupied with affairs of state to get in line and pay, so their secretaries settled up once a month from petty cash.

He took the special elevator used to ferry newspeople to their studios during emergencies; the rest of the time it was the private preserve of Jack Thomas, known in the division as The Anchorman, also known (although never in his presence) as the 800-Pound Gorilla, Jack "I'm-Just-a-Million-Dollar-a-Year-Reporter" Thomas, or just plain Damien.

An endless, carpeted corridor led past the cavernous studio used for elections and specials, past dressing rooms, past humming control rooms, now dark except for the video monitors that flickered everywhere, all the time. At the end of the long hallway, behind a flashing ON THE AIR sign, was Studio 38— Peter's age.

The door in front of him seemed almost to glow. Whatever bullshit arose during the day—bureaucratic politicking, budget fights, ratings troubles, anchor feuds—there weren't a hundred people in the world who did what Peter was about to do.

As he reached for the door, nodding toward the security camera and waiting for the click, he took a deep breath. Even through the reinforced steel he could hear the shouting inside. Not for the first time since the telephone had rung an hour earlier, he felt fear. Every day you could blow it, especially on a day like this. But he shook it off.

Let's go, he thought. Cover yourself with glory.

A news alert meant that every executive in the building had to report to his office and stay there. You couldn't even go to the bathroom without calling the special operator. It would not do to have the leadership of the news division urinating while historic events were in the making.

Stepping into the control room was like being in the cockpit of a 747 hurtling out of control. More than a hundred monitors jammed one wall—satellite feeds, local stations, Washington and London bureau lines, graphic display banks. A dozen consoles were lined up in front of the wall, with hundreds of multicolored lights and buttons and switches that controlled the lighting, sound, and cameras.

In the middle of the room was a raised platform—a throne for the executive producer and his deputy. Glassed-in work stations for the producers, crammed with headsets, telephones, and small monitors, lined the back of the room.

Jamie Webb, the director, was hovering over his personal console, ordering up graphics, testing camera angles. Sam Adelson, preoccupied, waved as Peter came through the door. He had wired his short round body into the telephone bank that connected the studio to the network's fifty-one bureaus.

In the open area known as Pamplona, Patricia Flannery sat surrounded by a cluster of her Body Snatchers, each with a phone in the curve of her neck. Pamplona was where the Body

Snatchers held their ground during live interview segments, facing the producers' wrath if the anchor asked a stupid question or the guest smiled dumbly and said no, I have no idea how the hospital is handling those fifty victims from the train wreck, that's not my department.

In a business where responsibility seemed fluid at best, here it was refreshingly simple: anything that went wrong was the Body Snatchers' fault. Tough as they were about bludgeoning people into appearing on the program, they lived in terror of an executive producer who could, with one sentence, dispatch them to an office job for good. Once, a supposed eyewitness to a hotel fire that killed thirty-five people had come on live from Mexico City and begun babbling hysterically about Jesus. He'd ranted for twenty seconds before they could cut him off, and the booker, ashen, had fled the control room and the building before Peter could say a word. He never saw her again. She'd wound up as a news assistant in children's television, Flannery later told him.

Peter tried to look relaxed as he waded into the control room. Let the damn thing break, he prayed, seeing the frenzy he'd unleashed. Let it happen.

Patel came up to him, grinning. "God loves you this morning," he said. "The Washington bureau just called to say the Pentagon is confirming that a heavy cruiser—the *Providence,* out of Norfolk—burned and sank off Lisbon this morning. They're not giving any more details. I think it's still too vague for a special report, but it's your ass. Your wishes?"

Peter tried not to look as relieved as he felt. But before he could quite take in the information and respond, pictures suddenly and unexpectedly began appearing on the monitor showing the London satellite feed. Except for Flannery's cursing at some hapless congressional aide, the room quieted.

The pictures were confusing at first. They were shot at night. A faint flashing red light became visible through the dark. "It's a chopper," Jamie Webb said softly. The audio tech next to him nodded. Both men had been in Vietnam. The red light came closer in the monitor, making sharp streaks on the tape, like the slow-shutter photographs of freeways taken at night. Then the outlines of the helicopter, picked up by floodlights, became clear.

"It's a carrier," said Adelson. "This is our crew—Jeff Sven

was on assignment on the *Kennedy*. It's gotta be them. They must be transmitting from the ship. Holy shit."

They saw the helicopter land, the U.S. NAVY stencil clearly legible on the side. A swarm of people in white helmets ran toward it, crouched low, many carrying stretchers and first-aid boxes. The helicopter touched down; its doors slid open. Crew members peered out, squinting into the floodlights. A body was handed out to two medics, the face dark, one arm dangling. At first Peter thought the injured man was black; then he realized that he was horribly burned.

"Shit," Adelson whispered. "I hope the poor bastard isn't still alive."

Seconds later, bodies wrapped mummylike in gauze were handed down to the corpsmen. It was impossible to tell if the victims were alive or dead. Peter kept watching the monitor anxiously; these pictures were too grisly to use. He looked at the clock, then back to the monitor. C'mon, c'mon, he thought, give us pictures we can use.

The camera panned up to a second helicopter landing behind the first and the scene was repeated, except that a handful of sailors, wet and dazed, climbed out under their own power. Two more lifeless-looking bodies were handed out on stretchers. Then the monitor went black. Peter jumped out of his chair; Webb stood up, turned and slapped Peter's open palm with his own. These pictures were about to become enduring images for millions of Americans.

Adelson was pointing excitedly at the bank of monitors: the other networks' screens were still running old movies or public service programming—raccoon shows, Adelson called them, because no one else was awake to watch them. The pictures coming into USB News were the first from the scene on anybody's satellites, which meant it was not only a great story, it was *their* great story. Webb yelled at the videotape bay to check the quality of the pictures, and the techs scrambled to crank up the New York, Washington, and London studios, all of which they would surely need. The babble erupted into a roar.

Through it, Peter heard the squish of Flannery's throat spray and her voice, pleading. The tone was usually reserved for families of tragedy victims, people it was awkward to bully. The trick was to persuade them, without actually saying it, that while you were devastated by their loss, your job depended on their willingness to share their moments of grief with four or five million strangers.

Flannery put her call on hold and switched to another line. "Look, you piece of shit, this is the last time I'm ever going to be fucked by Defense. The Secretary has gone on NBC first the last two times, and it's our turn, and if he doesn't appear on this show first this very fucking morning, he will never appear on it again. And the next time you want to peddle some Under Secretary to brag about some swift new tank that fires silver bullets, I'm going to tell you to stick it right up your ass. Is that clear?"

Peter was thinking that she could hardly have made herself clearer when the red telephone on his desk flashed, the one linking him to the newsroom. It shouldn't be ringing now. Could there be some additional emergency?

"This is Peter Herbert. What's up?"

"This is Debbie Schorr, Code Twelve-twelve, Foreign Desk." Peter had never heard the name. He couldn't remember if she was using the correct silly-ass code or not. Each executive had one for use during major stories, to avoid a hoax.

"Sam Seplow is on the line from the *John F. Kennedy,* off Gibraltar," she went on. "He's the first correspondent we've heard from. He says the *Providence,* which was on a week-long goodwill visit, exploded and sank within minutes. He says that it appears to have been an engine room explosion, and not the result of sabotage or hostile action. He says there are at least a hundred and fifty dead, probably more, and he claims this is from Admiral Joseph Calderone, commander of the battle group that included the *Providence.* He says he's seen most of the bodies himself, and that the report is absolutely solid. The dead and the worst burn victims are being taken to the *Kennedy* to be transported to the army's burn center in West Germany. The crew transmitted the pictures from the ship, only the Admiral doesn't know it. Go with it, he says."

Peter turned to the news assistant bringing fresh coffee and told him to tear down to the Foreign Desk and confirm that Debbie Schorr was a real person, and to do it within three minutes.

"Let's go, Jamie," Peter yelled over the din, clapping his

hands together and flashing Patel a look of triumph. "We're going to get on the air first with these pictures. Let's do a special report—five minutes."

The room exploded. Buzzers blasted in the studio and in the control room to signal the staff that a special report was imminent. Flannery jumped up, shocked. Jamie Webb raced out into the studio; Nabih Patel rushed to the writers' room; Peter yelled to a news assistant to find Don Leeming, the morning show's anchor, and tell him to get ready to go on.

Stagehands struggled to get the black backdrop up while the camera people kicked cables out of their way to move the cameras into position. The lighting director scrambled up a ladder to open light banks with a long pole.

Behind Peter, two cameramen tore through the control room toward the studio. Webb called up the special-report graphic—the network's eagle logo with the words SPECIAL REPORT in brilliant red—on the standby monitor.

Leeming burst into the studio, flailing to pull his jacket on. A technician raced alongside, trying to clip a wireless microphone to his tie and the battery to his belt. A makeup woman trotted behind them, ready to powder the anchor's clefts and crags. Webb was shouting for camera one to focus on the anchor chair, which Leeming suddenly slid into. An audio tech was screaming for sound checks.

In the announcer's booth off the control room, Peter saw Harry Ebener, the show's announcer, rush into his seat, his tie askew but his makeup perfect; visible or not, he took his appearance seriously. Over the special audio line heard only in affiliate-station control rooms, Ebener began repeating his urgent warning over and over: "Attention all stations. The network will air a special report at four-fifteen A.M."

Webb turned to Peter. They began communicating in the special language they had learned to use amid the chaos of big stories. Webb crooked his finger, a question mark. Peter held up three fingers.

Webb turned back to the microphone that connected him to the technicians on the floor, the cameramen, and the anchor. "Three minutes. Three minutes to air. Let's check sound and light."

Patel tapped Peter on the shoulder.

"Peter, if you can move it up one minute, you can cut into the West Coast at the scheduled commercial break. Then, when we update later for California, there's a clean break."

Peter nodded. He threw a wadded-up paper at Webb's back. The director turned and Peter held up two fingers.

Webb nodded, turning back to the microphone. "Two minutes. Videotape! We need five seconds of tape. Can do?"

The voice-box squawked back. "Two minutes? No way, Jamie, no way! It's crazy—"

"Do it, baby," said Webb.

"Is the copy ready?" Peter asked Patel, who was on the line to the writer.

"It's ready, Peter, but we don't have time to get it on prompter—"

"Fuck the prompter. Leeming can read it off the paper. Get it to him. Now!"

Patel yelled into the phone to get the copy to Leeming. The sound man gave Webb the thumbs up; so did the lighting tech. Leeming looked into the camera, squirmed to get comfortable. Peter, never particularly fond of his anchorman, warmed to him now. Most anchors would be nervous, whining that they hadn't had enough time, didn't know enough, didn't look good enough. But Leeming was an old newshound, always ready to run.

Peter waited.

He sipped from a coffee mug locked into its special spill-proof holder, conscious of everyone watching him while he tried to look calm. If you weren't a cop in the Bronx, or Chuck Yeager, you had few opportunities in life to look cool under fire; this was one of them.

Adelson headed downstairs to watch from the main newsroom. "Good luck, Peter," he yelled on the way out.

Peter's direct line flashed red. Patel picked it up. "The clerk says Debbie Schorr is for real."

"Go," said Peter.

He suddenly heard Leeming's voice in his headset. "Peter? Jamie? Anyone on earth? I have no copy; want me to make it up?"

Peter opened his mouth to scream when he saw a news assistant dive underneath Leeming's desk and hand him a script. She would remain there until the special report concluded.

Peter also noticed the tall, immaculately dressed figure of Julian McCallister, executive vice-president of USB News, gliding into the control room. McCallister had maintained his usual perfect timing—just right to bask in the glow of a success, too late to share in the blame. He was never off by more than a few seconds.

"Announce," yelled Webb. In five seconds the central monitor, showing what was being fed out onto the network, abruptly went to black and the special-report graphic appeared. Peter felt his heart thudding as Harry Ebener's baritone broke into the network's programming. Did I cause this to happen? he asked himself.

"This is a USB News special report. From New York, here is Don Leeming."

Leeming looked perfect: calm, grave, as authoritative as if he had been on the story for hours. "Good morning. An American warship visiting Lisbon, Portugal, exploded and sank last night. The *U.S.S. Providence,* a four-year-old cruiser, went down with a, quote—heavy—unquote, loss of life, says a Defense Department spokeswoman.

"USB correspondent Sam Seplow, reporting from fleet headquarters in the Mediterranean, says the warship, equipped with the latest radar technology and weapons systems, sank within minutes and that casualties may climb over a hundred. According to naval officials, the sinking was the result of an explosion aboard the ship, not the result of an attack. Portuguese rescue ships and helicopters have rushed to the scene, joined by rescue vessels and planes from other U.S. Navy ships stationed in the Atlantic and Mediterranean."

Leeming looked perfectly composed, but over his headset he could hear shouts from the control room. It sounded as though Jamie Webb and Peter Herbert were screaming for pictures, but when he glanced over at the monitor, he saw only his own face. He frowned almost imperceptibly; pictures were everything.

Leeming was right. Peter *was* screaming at Webb, and Webb was screaming into his mike: "Now, fuckers, now, now, now, now!" The editor in the videotape bay was yelling something back, but no one could hear what.

Leeming's face faded suddenly from the monitor, replaced by the first pictures from the disaster scene to appear on American television: five stark seconds of bandaged sailors and bodies wrapped in plastic bags being lifted from helicopters onto the floodlit deck of a ship.

Webb brought his clasped hands up over his head; Peter blew him a kiss. So far, the other networks' monitors were still showing reruns, which meant either that the story had been mishandled and Peter's career was over, or that they'd walloped the competition.

"We will of course bring you reports as they come in," Leeming said, signing off. "Full coverage will begin on *Morning in the U.S.* starting at six A.M." He'd barely finished when one of the other networks broke in with its own special-report graphic.

The control room staff cheered, touching off muttered curses from Flannery, who had traced the Portuguese ambassador to the United Nations to a New York City apartment and lured him to the telephone. "Mr. Ambassador, what you need to understand is that USB is right on the way to CBS and what makes perfect sense is to stop here first. We work cooperatively all the time. How about we just stay on the telephone and I'll get a limousine started so that it will be there by the time we hang up. We can pretape you here in the studio and then drop you off at CBS. They won't mind. It's a courtesy; we do it for each other all the time."

Peter slapped Patel on the back. It was a clean kill. First report of the sinking. First pictures from the scene. First details of the incident. Across town, his colleagues were picking up flashing red phones and listening to enraged vice-presidents demanding to know what the hell was going on.

The telephone from the main newsroom flashed. "You ate their fucking lunch," Adelson yelled to Peter. "Good move, putting up the 'fuck you' graphic." It was Webb who had thought of inserting the USB News logo over the carrier pictures. That meant that USB would be credited if the pictures were stolen, but more important, it would rub their competitors' faces in their defeat.

"Don't forget, Peter," Adelson reminded him before hanging up, "that tomorrow night is the anniversary party for Brookings. I don't care if the Russians are invading—you got to be there."

Peter groaned, mostly for show. No USB executive in his right mind would miss the party marking the fourth decade of the reign of Elliott Brookings, president of USB News. But tomorrow seemed a long way off. "Nabih, pick up the earphone and listen to those guys to make sure they have the same stuff we do," he said calmly. "We won't be cheering so loud if some other network's going on to say the whole story is a bummer."

Peter felt Julian McCallister's soft hand on his shoulder. "Pretty aggressive, Peter, but don't you think you might have waited for second confirmation, as the standards call for, before you scrapped your whole lineup? We're not supposed to luck out here, my friend. We're supposed to know."

Peter turned around wearily. He was about to reply that the other networks were going with the same story when the light on his direct phone line from Brookings flashed. McCallister, standing between Peter and the telephone, picked it up.

"Morning, Chief." Peter noticed sudden fatigue creeping into McCallister's voice. "Yes, I thought so. Tough call, but you're right, the right one, since we beat the competition. Thank you. That's very kind. I'll tell Peter as well.

"Brookings," he laughed. "He says, 'good job.' " McCallister smiled sweetly and left.

The control room quieted, tension draining from the room. Everyone had his own way of unwinding and refueling before the show. Webb kept a huge rose-quartz crystal in a drawer. He held it in his palms so that he could soak up the calming feeling of the inner earth, as he explained it. Some of the techs took out their "stress-paks," Styrofoam picnic coolers stocked with wash-cloths packed in ice. Whenever they could, they pressed the cold cloths against their foreheads.

Flannery and the Body Snatchers, on the other hand, gulped pots of black coffee. The point was not to remain calm, she constantly exhorted her staff. The point was to stay juiced, so that when you got people on the telephone, you simply willed them on to your broadcast.

The switcher, who pushed the buttons that switched from camera to camera and put the pictures on the air, dropped to the floor in a yoga position. Harry Ebener, trapped in the sound booth for the duration of the news alert, sucked at squeeze bottles of honey to soothe his raspy throat. Peter felt it inappropriate to acknowledge tension, so he sipped coffee heavily lightened with cream.

After a ten-minute cool-down, during which Peter was tickled to see that the other networks still hadn't managed to air any pictures from the scene, Webb and his crew drifted into the studio to set up. Peter wandered out to join them. Christ, he thought, we haven't even gotten to the show yet.

He held up a yellow lineup sheet, a signal for Flannery and Webb to join him in one of the greenrooms. Flannery reluctantly hung up the phone and collected her book. The quiet, lavishly appointed rooms were used to make VIPs and movie stars comfortable before their appearances. Many important behinds had rested there.

"Hi, Patricia," said Peter, smiling. She had been on the phone continuously since he'd arrived; these were the first words they had spoken. He barely noticed the bathrobe anymore; it was standard attire during breaking stories now that she'd moved across the street. She looked wild-eyed, frantic, as if he were some threatening alien she had to appease.

"Well, Peter. We have Kissinger first," she announced, pausing to let her coup sink in. Henry Kissinger was the big hit on major foreign stories because he was the expert most likely to be quoted on foreign affairs. The wire services would all mention *Morning in the U.S.* in their reports on what Kissinger was bound to say about the need for U.S. military strength abroad.

After celebrities like Kissinger, the second most quotable guests were high administration officials, followed in rapidly declining order by members of Congress and by the legions of professional pundits tucked away in New York and Washington think tanks and universities. If not for morning television, scores of Soviet watchers and terrorism experts would have remained totally obscure.

"We've got Kennedy, Biden, Bradley, so far from Washington," Flannery continued. "Wait, Kennedy is in Boston; he'll go to the affiliate." Webb made a note to set up a Boston remote.

"All Democrats," said Peter.

"We have requests in to Simpson, Dole, and Hatch," she said quickly, "but we haven't heard yet."

"Look," Peter said, "this happened last time. Brookings will be up my ass if we have three Democrats trashing the administration. You can't balance a Kennedy with some shnook from an institute in Georgetown. Dig up a fucking Republican, okay?"

Flannery excused herself to tell one of her staff to pull out the stops for a fucking Republican. She was back in less than a minute, her bathrobe dragging the floor behind her. Peter smiled. She was crazy, he thought, but there would be stacks of Republicans available within half an hour.

"We've got an affiliate setup in Norfolk near the base, but the navy won't let us in until the next of kin are all notified," she went on.

"How about off the base?" he asked. "There must be a newsstand or diner where people hang out, no?"

Flannery nodded and headed for the control room again. Peter and Webb ran through the first hour: the newsblocs, pictures from Portugal, Washington bureau reaction, remotes from the base in Norfolk, Kissinger, congressional comments, remotes from Florida, where other navy ships were based.

"This fancy stuff you're trying to do is going to add up to some pretty hefty bucks," Webb pointed out.

Peter dismissed Webb's caution with a wave. In other businesses the boss was the one who fussed about money, but executive producers at USB News were not conservative about covering stories. Peter remembered Adelson's Law Twenty-four: *No executive producer ever got fired for going over budget.* Certainly not if he had the first pictures of the sinking of the biggest American warship since World War II. Webb went to fuss with the stagehands and Peter went back into the studio.

The broadcast itself seemed almost anticlimactic. Kissinger rumbled on about the need for an American presence abroad. Flannery had, in fact, come up with not one but three Republicans, and they and their esteemed colleagues from across the aisle went at it over the issue of military deployment of warships for a good eight minutes.

By eight, live reports were coming in from Washington, Portugal, and various points in the Mediterranean. An ample stream of academics and specialists then provided what producers called "blah-blah."

Peter was pleased, though in truth he did not have much reason to brag. In television, what mattered was a gutsy but surreptitious camera crew aboard the *John F. Kennedy,* serendipitously assigned for a feature on new naval technology, and Patricia Flannery's throat spray.

He was already framing the compliments for his staff in the memo he would write, with a copy to Brookings. It was not likely that he would write a note saying: "Dear Staff: We did well this morning. None of you had nervous breakdowns and Patricia Flannery now lives so close to the studios that all she has to do is roll out of bed to get guests."

The network press office had already delivered the wire reports citing Kissinger's comments made on the program and crediting *Morning in the U.S.* with the first report of the sinking. McCallister was quoted in the AP report saying it had not been an easy call, but one you sometimes had to make in television.

At 9:00 A.M., Jack Thomas, the evening anchorman, took over the coverage from his own studio downstairs. The stress-paks came out again and so, finally, did a relieved Harry Ebener, who dashed for the men's room.

Out of the studio and into the control room came Don Leeming in full glory, a deep-voiced, elegantly dressed study in how authoritative and attractive one could look in late middle age.

Leeming and Peter had a pleasant but detached sort of relationship. With multiyear, multimillion-dollar contracts, anchors were small companies in their own right, and no producer could really tell them what to do.

"Morning, bo-bo," yelled Leeming, reaching toward Peter's crotch. Peter bent forward suddenly, shielding his genitals with his hands. It was one of Leeming's little jokes, this crotch-grabbing. It infuriated Peter, but he never quite knew how to ask another man to please not grab his penis.

"All set for the kudos, Peter? You know the brass were all watching. I'm sure you'll tell them it was your brilliant producers, making us dummies look good. Hope we *did* look good." As always, the threat was implied. If the show got into trouble, the manual was clear, the precedent ample: First the producer got it, then the anchor. Adelson's Law Number Two: *Shit flows downhill.*

"You were very polished with Kissinger, Don," said Peter.

He went downstairs to conduct the planning sessions for the next day. The story would be pretty much over within two or three days, unless the President decided to invade Libya or something. Afterwards, a comfortable hotel suite awaited—he wondered if it would be the Plaza or the Parker-Meridien this time. The suites had become something of a USB News tradition. After hammering away for days on a big story, executive producers were entitled to a bit of rest and room service. Besides, he had to be reasonably alert for Brookings's damned party. He doubted he would fit in more than a catnap tonight.

As he walked back through the control room and down the long hallway, he passed the greenroom where he had met with Flannery and Webb. Flannery was lying on a couch, sound asleep in her bathrobe, her phone book still clutched in one hand. One of the Body Snatchers was draping a blanket over her.

CHAPTER THREE

MURROW'S SHRIMP

She fussed with the perfectly neat knot in his tie and he flicked a nearly invisible piece of lint from her black silk blouse, the way contentedly married couples do as they wait to greet their hosts.

Barbara permitted herself a last mutter, in the elevator, at having to face what was sure to be another dreary, self-congratulatory USB News social function. Peter muttered back that the last one he had badgered her into attending had been nearly a year ago.

"I'm ready," she said glumly. "I'll be sure to tell Jack Thomas that it is no overstatement, in my view, to say that his documentary on the deficit was the most extraordinary contribution to public policy since the Magna Carta. And of course I'll make every effort to eavesdrop on the other wives to be sure that none of them is saying anything detrimental to your interests. I'm excited, Peter—I am. I just love an evening with these folks, shoes off, lying on the carpet by the fire, smoking a little dope, listening to Otis Redding."

They had squabbled good-naturedly about coming. After he'd worked nearly forty-eight straight hours on the *Providence* story, she contended, it was insanity for him to go to a party. She was even more annoyed when he told her he would be staying in the city again tonight after the party so that he could get to the staff meeting that had abruptly been called for 9:00 A.M. tomorrow. That would mean three days since he had been home. People would understand, she insisted, that he was too exhausted to celebrate.

"Quiet, hussy," said Peter as the elevator rose. "These people are paying for you to work on the great American novel in your cozy little study. Be grateful."

There was no door to be answered. The elevator opened directly on to the broad, white-carpeted foyer of the Park Avenue duplex. Down the hall, toward the living room, black-jacketed waiters could be seen scurrying back and forth. Peter sniffed and smiled. "Barbara," he exclaimed happily. "They're here! I smell them. The Murrow Shrimp."

Peter and his friends called them Edward R. Murrow Memorial Shrimp, in recognition of their reliability, refined good taste, and hallowed place in the history of broadcast journalism. They used the term only among themselves, of course. Publicly, they were as respectful toward shrimp as were all the other executives at USB News, given that shrimp were the dietary staple of their leader, Elliott Brookings, in whose honor they were gathered.

Drifting over to one side of the gleaming living room, Peter and Barbara joined Sam Adelson and Philip Barnard, producer of the network's jazzy new magazine show. They stood watching in bemused fascination as the caterers scrambled to put the finishing artistic touches on a HAPPY 40TH ELLIOTT message painstakingly constructed, shrimp by shrimp, on a bed of ice chips, arugula, and seaweed.

"Just think," Barnard murmured, "how many thousands of brave crustaceans have given their lives to honor Elliott Brookings and advance Julian McCallister's career."

Adelson, considerably older and wider than the other two, snickered discreetly, took an impressive swig of Johnny Walker Black, and gauged whether he was out of earshot of the closest USB executive. He looked toward the buffet tables. "Didn't these shrimp begin their careers in London during the War? During . . ." Adelson paused and cupped his hand to his ear.

"The *great and early days of broadcasting,*" finished Herbert and Barnard, on cue and a bit too loudly. Even though he had worked for a different network, Murrow had become the Chairman Mao of network news, his legacy constantly invoked, his name a talisman that could simultaneously inspire the troops and fend off real and imagined enemies.

"All of us—seafood included—salute the smart job you guys did on the *Providence* sinking. You got the division off to a great start on the story, and D'Amato's pictures were unbelievable," toasted Adelson. Peter bowed his head modestly and Barnard smiled perfunctorily. He was not into admiring other people's work.

They had gathered this evening—Herbert, Barnard, and Adelson, more than 150 other USB News correspondents and executives, a substantial number of the famous faces that beamed into tens of millions of homes each day, and thousands of Gulf shrimp—to honor Elliott Brookings's fortieth anniversary as president of United States Broadcasting's storied news division. In network television, where news division presidents fell like Yankees managers, such a string was unprecedented, and no one in the room would have wagered a nickel that it would ever be repeated.

There had been talk of staging this celebration at the Four Seasons (Peter had argued for the New York Aquarium) but Julian McCallister, Brookings's deputy, had fought for the right to mark the event in his own apartment, with due homage to Brookings's high-protein obsession.

Brookings was devoted to shrimp, and grateful for it. He attributed much of his good fortune—his full and distinguished shock of white hair, his lean body and flat stomach, his golden radio baritone, his legendary rise through the ranks—to his having consumed at least a few shrimp almost every day of his adult life.

There were trays of cold shrimp with cocktail sauce in Brookings's office, continuously refilled by USB News Food Service attendants. Silver buckets of shrimp graced the center of the vast rosewood conference table at USB News' weekly staff conferences. When Brookings traveled to USB's domestic and foreign bureaus, cases of air-freighted shrimp beat him there, dispatched by two doting secretaries who had become extraordinarily knowledgeable about the creatures' life spans, mating habits, and optimal survival environments.

Brookings's shrimp obsession, Adelson noted with considerable relish, had brought about significant changes in Julian McCallister's own lifestyle. Adelson referred to McCallister, his long-time competitor, as the Unluckiest Deputy; it was McCallister's unhappy lot to serve one of corporate America's most enduring executives. Nobody who remembered the Midwest-raised McCallister from his early days at the network could recall any fondness for seafood at all.

But McCallister had plunged into shrimp lore with a zeal equal to the most devout Talmudic scholar's. He read books about shrimp, frequently discussing with Brookings the distinctions between Gulf and Atlantic and Mediterranean shrimp. He acquired exotic samples, having them flown in from fishing ports around the world to share with Brookings. And the eastern wall of McCallister's Park Avenue living room was a veritable monument to shrimp this evening.

As Peter had tried to explain to a skeptical Barbara, this was not just another of Julian's endless round of dinner parties. This marked the fourth decade not only of Brookings's leadership but of USB News' own unrivaled position. It was one of the premier information-gathering institutions in the world, and Elliott Brookings had guided it from its very beginning.

McCallister had personally designed the floral arrangement that spelled out FORTY MORE!—and formed the network's blue eagle logo—in orchids, irises, and mums. Before it rose an ice-chip mountain from which protruded fat pink beauties flown up that afternoon from the Florida Keys.

"The most insincere floral arrangement in the history of plants," fumed Adelson, glowering at it, then at the shrimp. "If there was a God, the smelly little things would rise up and attack Julian. Shrimp have always hated hypocrisy."

"If there *were* a God," offered Adelson's wife, Carol, joining the group, linking arms with Barbara, "wives would not be dragged to these insipid events."

Adelson had as much trouble as Peter did, luring his wife to corporate occasions. And when they did come, Barbara and

Carol (who analyzed securities on Wall Street) made little effort to hide their contempt for the intrigue and old-fashioned boot-licking that were essential ingredients of almost every television career.

Peter caught Barbara's eye and jerked his head toward the napkins, which he knew would fuel her exasperation. Arranged along the edges of the buffet tables, they were imprinted with the corporate motto Brookings had mounted on the office wall behind his desk: NEVER BELIEVE THEM, NEVER FEAR THEM, NEVER ASK THEM FOR ANYTHING.

"Who's that quote from, Patrick Henry or somebody?" asked Peter, who'd never been sure.

"Solzhenitsyn," Adelson said matter-of-factly. "I asked Elliott once. *The Gulag Archipelago*. But it serves pretty well for television, too, doesn't it?"

Their host, satisfied that shrimp, flowers, and napkins were being appropriately arrayed, was heading toward them. Peter leaned behind Barbara, pretending to pick another thread from her blouse. "This is McCallister, remember?" he hissed. "Number two in the news division. Wife is a decorator. Be nice."

But McCallister had spotted the television reporter for *Variety* standing beyond them and veered away without a word, a missile locked on to a fresh target.

"You have to admire Julian's honesty," Barnard observed. "He doesn't even pretend we're important."

"All we do is work for him," said Peter. "Compared to somebody who can *write* about him, that barely counts at all." He put his Diet Coke down on a passing tray. At thirty-eight he'd found that drinking at night made him too drowsy either to drive home to Jersey or to pop out of bed with the vigor he would need to deal with any problems that came up on tomorrow morning's show, then stay awake through the mysterious emergency staff meeting.

"What was that telephone call you took, Sam?" he asked. "Any news?" There was a tension in the room, Peter thought, that went beyond the usual office politicking. Several people, looking purposeful, were scuttling back and forth to phones in the next room.

Adelson shrugged. "Something's going on with the company; the stock is in play. The corporate heavies are ricocheting around like billiard balls. It's so rare that they actually have anything to do."

Tomorrow's meeting suddenly made more sense. "Is that what this staff meeting is about?" Peter asked.

But Adelson shrugged. "Not for me to say," he said importantly. "Mostly because I don't know."

Barbara was about to point out that if there was really important business going on, perhaps it made all the more sense to go home and get some rest instead of standing around McCallister's palazzo past midnight, reflecting on shrimp. But she knew that her argument would prove futile.

Instead, she and Carol scanned the crowd, nudging each other. Their bewilderment at the people their husbands worked with made them kindred spirits, despite an age difference of almost fifteen years. Barbara told Peter that she liked Carol Adelson because she was the only wife of a USB executive who had allowed her hair to go gray.

"This is better than a movie," Carol whispered. "Look at Donna McCallister working the network execs. Now that's a good corporate wife."

Carol sighed. "This makes fifty-five." Barbara looked at her quizzically. "The fifty-fifth consecutive news division event, over the eight years Sam and I have been married, at which no one but you has asked me a single question about myself or my work."

"Not true," interrupted Adelson, coming up behind them. "Brookings asked you just last year how the children were doing in school."

"Forgetting," she shot back, "that we don't have any."

Their cluster, from which emanated considerable cackling, was drawing curious, sometimes hostile stares from some of the others awaiting the guest of honor.

" 'Heaven knows its time; the bullet has its billet,' " quoted Peter in his deepest baritone.

"That wasn't Murrow," Adelson decided. "Shakespeare?"

"Umm, no, it was Sir Walter Scott," said Peter. "Although Murrow *would* have said it, I'm sure, if he'd thought about it. Your point. That's six and two, still my favor. I'm thinking Le Cirque."

The rules of the game, invented by Peter and named The

Wisdom of Murrow, were simple: Either he or Adelson recited some pretentious quotation; the opponent had to guess whether Murrow actually said it or not. Whoever reached ten points first won lunch at the restaurant of his choice.

Barbara and Carol were laughing, but Adelson looked around, as he always did when they played this game, to make sure no one important was within hearing.

Adelson saw himself as mentor to and protector of the two younger men, Peter and Phil Barnard. Peter particularly needed protection, given the beating his program was taking in the ratings and the press lately. Peter was tall and serious-looking, with dark hair curling over his collar and the first signs of paunch at his belt buckle. He didn't make it to handsome, but he was intelligent and credible-looking, the way people would want a youngish family doctor to look.

Adelson had nicknamed him Family Man because Peter was always droning on about his artsy wife and adorable daughter and son and faithful dog and their various antics, and because there were hardly any executives at USB News with actual families. Certainly there were no others who got into a Toyota at the end of every workday to drive through the Lincoln Tunnel to New Jersey.

Adelson had been incredulous and contemptuous when Peter had announced that he and Barbara were moving to New Jersey, a place Sam saw as dangerously unhip, occupied primarily by carcinogenic substances and accountants. Peter could not tell him the truth, which was that Barbara had insisted they put as much space as possible between their family and the politics and parties of USB News. Peter had argued with her at the time, but the fact was he felt considerable relief when he got a few miles beyond Manhattan, particularly these days.

Despite his unhelpful residence, Peter had the requisite share of ambition, most of it centering on USB's *Evening News* broadcast, for decades the most-watched news program in America. But at USB News, ambition was relative. Phil Barnard, who ran the trendy *TGIF* show, had much more of it, although a different variety. He made no secret of his conviction that he was destined to be a major film producer, with USB News a station stop en route to the Coast.

He was the prettiest man in the room—in most rooms. Peter kidded him about being the National WASP Poster Boy—riveting blue eyes, blond hair swept back, aquiline nose, miracle slenderizing metabolism.

Barnard's career track was perhaps the least predictable of the small and elite group of USB's hotshot executive producers. His family's tradition was diplomatic, not journalistic, Barnards having joined the diplomatic corps all the way back to the end of the Civil War, during which his great-grandfather led a heroic and successful charge against the Confederates through the woods at Spotsylvania. He was the first male Barnard in memory to leave Washington, although the family's diplomatic tradition had propelled him as far as Georgetown, where he'd graduated with honors. His parents could scarcely believe a Barnard was in television; neither could he. His father, a retired assistant secretary of state, never referred directly to his son's work—Philip's two brothers were posted in Rabat and La Paz respectively. But Barnard never doubted for a moment that he had made the right choice.

He would have been the first to acknowledge his own self-obsession. No one, Adelson had once told him, could love him nearly as much as he loved himself. Barnard had laughingly agreed. Plenty of women seemed willing to try, however: the combination of terrific looks and the power to put people on television was sexually lethal. Peter and Adelson called him Hootchie-Kootchie Man, in honor of the Muddy Waters classic.

Barnard had long ago shed his wife, explaining candidly that it had taken him only a few months at USB News to realize that maintaining a relationship was a major impediment to landing your own show. His wife had begun complaining almost immediately about his grinding schedule, and when push came to shove, she was shoved. She was out the door, friends observed, before she knew there was a problem. Now, Barnard boasted with relief, she was remarried, to an orthodontist who never scheduled patients after 5:00 P.M.

Sam Adelson, their boss, was a round, balding, profane, sweaty Brooklyn street rat in a suit. He was unapologetic about his belly, nurturing it with a steady flow of soda, saturated fats, and nitrites. Without the pin stripes, he could just as easily have been driving a cab or running a newsstand, so thick was his accent and belligerent his demeanor.

His childhood years as a Jew dodging Irish and Italian kids dedicated to making his nose bleed had prepared him well for the murderous infighting of network television. While he sometimes lacked the brilliant conceptual strategies of a Julian McCallister, there was no one better in a quick, dirty skirmish.

Since he was the executive responsible for all of USB's news operations, his phone rang whenever an airplane failed to clear a mountaintop or some crazed fanatic took aim at a hapless head of state. USB News was his whole life; he was fiercely proud of it and of himself for working there. And he had done it while harboring a dreadful secret he had shared with no one but his wife: He loathed shrimp.

Peter and Barnard had not dared tag him with a nickname, at least not to his face. But there could be only one choice: Company Man. They meant it as a compliment.

"How are the kids . . . uh, what the fuck are their names?" Adelson asked Peter, losing patience with himself. He always blew this business of appearing interested in people's families. He accepted it as something he was supposed to attend to, but he had trouble enough keeping the names of USB News' 1,500 employees straight, let alone their mewling brats.

"Dick and Jane," Peter said, deadpan.

Carol elbowed her husband in his substantial middle. "Goddam it, Sam. You remember the name of every Dodgers pitcher in history who won more than twenty games, but you can't remember the names of Peter's and Barbara's kids? It's Ben and Sarah, for God's sake."

Adelson looked shocked that anyone would compare children to the Dodgers, but muttered an apology.

The elevator opened, prompting a last-minute flurry as some wayward shrimp were restored to their places. McCallister beamed at his handiwork, then darted for the hallway. So respectful a silence descended upon the room that it could mean only one thing: The Chairman himself had entered. There was no more eloquent testament to Elliott Brookings's importance than the appearance of this patriarch, a.k.a. The Founder.

In his eighties, the Chairman was a figure of myth and legend. Peter had seen him only a few times in eleven years, most recently when he had arrived by limousine for a news division lunch with the prime minister of India.

As the aura around him had grown, the protocol for dealing with the Chairman had come to resemble that involving the House of Windsor. One did not approach him unless invited to; one never spoke first. On rare occasions, correspondents and producers received his distinctive notes, on creamy Tiffany stationery, praising stories or programs. These were cherished and, after a suitable grace period, framed.

The Chairman passionately believed that the news division should be completely independent and insulated from corporate affairs. This practice, he candidly admitted, brought so much prestige and influence that the rest of the network could make boundless profits from airing as much junk as it wished.

The Chairman—now slightly stooped and balding, but tanned and vibrant-looking—was ushered into McCallister's living room, where he sank into a wing chair and was promptly engulfed by a cloud of division presidents and aides and some of the glamorous correspondents and anchors with whom he sometimes dined.

There was some carping in Wall Street circles these days that with broadcasting under stiffer competition, it was time for USB to look beyond its golden years, perhaps even to seek a successor to the Chairman. But this was not an argument that carried much weight in a company expected to post profits of close to half a billion dollars this year.

It was time for Brookings to appear, but his dinner with Prime Minister Thatcher at the British Consulate was obviously something that couldn't be rushed.

Peter, fighting his mounting fatigue, looked up to see the beautiful face of Linda Burns looming toward him. She was the newest correspondent on Barnard's program, and both Peter and Adelson had spotted the two of them coming in together, but quickly separating to work the room.

Her hiring had been controversial: She'd been plucked straight from a Home Shopping Channel in Raleigh, North Carolina. But Barnard had defended her against the howls of USB's entrenched traditionalists, who sat like crows on a barnyard fence, cawing reproachfully whenever they felt the sacred standards of USB News had been violated. Linda Burns, Barnard had insisted, had three years' experience as a weekly newspaper reporter before she'd joined the Home Shopping Channel. Besides, the camera—as television people put it—loved her, her porcelain complexion framed by chestnut hair. That, plus several carefully produced profiles of serious artists, diplomats, and politicians, had enhanced her image considerably.

"Ah, Peter," she said, offering him a firm handshake. "I'm a great admirer of your broadcast. I thought the coverage of the *Providence* sinking quite extraordinary. I would hate to be in charge of the *Evening News*. What is left for them to do?"

Peter mumbled his thanks.

"I've been planning to drop you a note about your segment last week on child drug addicts. It was one of the most powerful I've ever seen. Closing on that long shot of the boy lying down on his hospital bed and shutting his eyes—was that your idea?"

Barbara and Carol exchanged "oh, brother" glances, but Peter glowed. "Why, thank you. It's very kind of you to mention that. You know, I fought for weeks for that segment."

"Honestly?" Burns said in apparent wonderment. "You had to fight? I almost burned breakfast because I couldn't stop watching it."

"No kidding," interjected Carol Adelson, eyeing Burns's leggy, aerobicized body. "I wouldn't have taken you for the hot-breakfast type. Bacon and eggs and hash-browns?"

Burns raised one perfectly shaped brow, then drifted away toward Barnard and the shrimp.

Adelson was watching the vice-presidents swarming around the Chairman and buzzing in anticipation of Brookings's arrival. "Forty years Brookings has been in that job," he said. "That's incredible for broadcasting. That will never happen again."

His wife agreed. "And even if it did, it wouldn't be anyone like Elliott. There are no more of those."

"Brookings is unique, all right," Peter put in. "Last year we were doing this consumer segment about a voice-activated door—you know, the door's programmed to open at the sound of your voice. It was Don Leeming's segment—he loves to anchor the technology stuff. We rehearsed for a half hour, and then the segment comes on and pompous old Leeming goes up to the door and says 'Leeming!' and the door does nothing. So he says 'Leeming!' again and the door still does nothing. This goes on about three more times, and we have nothing else to put in there—we're

coming up on the newsbloc and it's a three-and-a-half-minute
hole. Leeming is looking like a deer caught in the headlights of a
car and he's signaling to the floor manager to get out of it, but I
have nowhere to go and I'm in his ear telling him to tread water,
we'll go to a commercial as soon as we can. So the red phone
rings and I pick it up and it's Brookings.

"There's this pause and I hear Brookings say, 'Herbert, I
was awakened by a nightmare this morning.' I've got the phone
in one ear, Leeming going nuts on the monitor, and the producer
is about to open her wrists in front of me, and I say, 'Oh, really,
Mr. Brookings? Tell me about it.'

"He says, 'My nightmare is a strange one. It has the anchor
on the morning program in my news division talking to a door,
and the door doesn't seem to be hearing him, and this is going
on for what seems to me to be hours and I start wondering if the
broadcast is under the supervision of anyone with the compe-
tence and responsibility of a flea. And I am shocked, when I call,
to learn that you are there, on the scene, in control, and the
anchorman is still repeating his name to the door and the door
still isn't hearing him. And the way I'm going to get rid of my
dream is, I'm going to rub my eyes and look at the television and
if the man is still talking to the door when I do, then I will
conclude that this is not a dream but the real thing and I will
come in and personally tear your throat out.' And he hangs up!
Classic Brookings, right?"

Adelson shook his head, his belly jiggling with laughter.

Barnard had returned to the circle. "Well, anything can
happen on your show, Peter, right? Maybe that's why the ratings
are down farther than the Knicks are this year."

Adelson snorted. "If I believe half of what I read in the TV
columns, Phil, your glitzy little show is good for half a season,
after which you'll get knocked off by a sitcom about lesbian
single mothers."

Peter appreciated the defense, but Barnard's dig stung because it was true: Peter's program was losing viewers the way
his retriever shed fur. Whereas Adelson's retort, while well-
intended, was inaccurate: Barnard's show was being greeted by
critics as if it were a new Salk vaccine.

Where was Brookings?

Barbara, who did not like Barnard or find his gibes amusing, anxiously checked her watch. It took at least a half hour to get home to Glen Ridge, assuming the Tunnel's toxic fumes hadn't ignited. Peter looked ready to collapse.

But Julian McCallister was sweeping excitedly across the room toward the door, a signal that Elliott Brookings had concluded his private chat with Thatcher and was ready to review the troops.

The crowd broke into cheers and applause as the tall, elegant man entered, nodding and beaming. Peter, as always, was fascinated by Brookings; he'd clearly come from some other age, but Peter could never figure out which one.

Elliott Brookings was the only president USB News had ever had, a television record for continuity. At sixty-eight he was believed to be planning retirement in two years, but that was not the sort of thing he would discuss with anyone. His reserve and detachment were fabled. No one in the news division had ever seen his Fifth Avenue apartment; outside of network functions, none of them had ever socialized with him at all. He watched every minute of every broadcast the news division aired, spotting and avenging all errors of fact, judgment, and taste. He never looked the other way at a mistake, never winked at sloppiness, was never understanding about or interested in the reasons for error.

Brookings would not have seemed out of place in Buckingham Palace or the State Department. Adelson, who had somehow gained access to pictures of baby Brookings, claimed the man was born looking distinguished. His very posture was a tremendous boon to USB News. Ever impeccable in his Savile Row suits and shoes, he could face congressmen, Presidents, and heads of state as an equal.

Brookings glanced over at the shrimp monument shining across the room and smiled graciously. The crowd around him instantly became an entourage, following him to the buffet, leaving Peter's cluster behind. "You always have to allow McCallister and the veeps fifteen minutes of slobbering," said Peter. "Then the serfs like us will go over and lick whatever remaining bits of boot have been missed." The crowd around Brookings applauded as he devoured the first shrimp of the night. Soon, Adelson groaned, the endless round of toasting would begin.

Barbara caught Peter's eye and pointed to her watch. "I've got to go," she said. "You at least ought to get to your hotel and sleep, if you haven't the brains to come home." She knew Sam would try to make Peter stay, which was no big deal to these people: The news division retained some rooms at the Parker-Meridien every night of the year, for news emergencies or social ones.

"I have to leave soon," he said to Adelson, who began shaking his head vigorously. "I'm a wreck, and I have to get some sleep before this damned meeting."

"No way you go before Brookings at least sees you're here," Adelson protested. "Forget it. There are some things you've just gotta do."

But Peter was growing increasingly bleary-eyed.

"This is just another kind of work," he complained to Adelson. "Everybody has to talk to everybody else in the room at least once and seem genuinely thrilled to see him. I'm just not creative enough."

Adelson put one arm around Peter's neck and pinched his cheek. "Work on it," he advised in a whisper. "For the money you make, you can find something to say to these shitheads for an hour a month. It's part of corporate life."

Adelson and Barnard moved off to join the adulatory circle around Brookings, and Barbara put her arm through Peter's.

"Why do I always get the feeling that I'm a crasher at these things?" he mused. "I've been here more than ten years."

Barbara looked around to make sure no one was listening; she had absorbed at least that much of USB's corporate culture. "Oh, you're different, there's no doubt. It's almost imperceptible to the naked eye, but you're just a step slower than most of these people. I'm not sure that your teeth are as sharp as theirs."

"And theirs grow back when they're broken. Do you think it's genetic?"

"And situational. You have distractions, like a marriage and these pesky kids. Keeps you from devoting quite as much attention to your work as perhaps is expected. Nor do you have a properly loyal ally in your wife. And to demonstrate the point, it's time for me to slink home to New Jersey, before our nanny passes out. Sweetie, you look so tired. Can't you skip the meeting tomorrow and come home? I mean, I know all this is crucial to the public's understanding of the great issues of the day—"

"Knock it off, Barbara," Peter said dully. "It's something I've got to do. Let's just say I don't have as many options as you do."

She kissed him on the nose and smiled sympathetically, snatching a cheese puff off a passing tray and heading for the coat rack. "I know," she said. "We just miss you out in Joisey."

CHAPTER FOUR

STAFF MEETING

*P*eter lowered his face into the hotel room sink, which was filled with cold water and spiced with a bucket's worth of ice cubes. It helped a bit, but he knew he couldn't really snap out of this kind of exhaustion without a lot more rest.

Marie, his secretary, had awakened him after a few fitful hours of sleep—it was the only rest he'd had in nearly two days—to make sure he got to the meeting on time. She'd arranged to have room service bring fresh orange juice, coffee, and whole wheat toast to his suite. He also took a moment to skim *The Los Angeles Times, The Washington Post, The Wall Street Journal, The New York Times,* and *The Times* of London, which Marie made sure were delivered every morning to his door, no matter where his door was, at home in New Jersey, on the road somewhere, outside Bar Harbor in the cottage the family rented every August.

Even the papers were now reporting that the the sinking of the Navy cruiser was an accident. But the explosion's toll had been horrific: nearly two hundred killed, scores seriously burned.

Morning in the U.S.—thanks to Danny D'Amato and his Special Assignment Team—had continued to score on the story, with exclusive pictures of the fire aboard the ship and a biting report on how the ship's supposedly crackerjack high-tech alarm and fire-prevention control systems had failed. The show had been first with footage of heroic navy divers plunging into the water to rescue injured sailors, and with stunning pictures of the charred ship rising bow up, like the *Titanic,* and sliding below the water. The stuff was so strong that over two days Peter had netted two calls from Brookings, who reported that the Chairman himself had called with congratulations.

It was a sweet feeling. Peter never felt safer than when he had performed well on a big story. It was about the only time in the television news business that you really *could* relax. Now Peter could go home and sleep for twenty-four hours. He would be off the clock: free from fears of competitors, ratings, affiliates; done with irate anchors, scheming vice-presidents, and temperamental producers.

I just have to get through this mysterious meeting, he thought. Normally, Brookings would have made a point of excusing him after a big story, but Brookings had insisted that every vice-president and executive producer be present.

There was just time to dial home first. Peter had something to be grateful to Danny D'Amato for, besides great videotape from Lisbon: It was the peripatetic Special Assignment Team chief who had taught him to call his children every day, if only to say hello, no matter where he was in the world or what he was doing. D'Amato had once called his own daughter, Bobbie, from a Mujadeen camp in Afghanistan under fire from strafing Russian helicopters, patching the call through on a wireless radio.

"Hey there, stranger," Barbara answered. "Are you as bushed as you sound?"

"Yeah, I guess I am." He yawned. "How are the kids?"

"Great," she said. "They tried to watch all your shows. You know, Peter, despite the razzing, your coverage *was* terrific. The pictures were very powerful. You probably saw worse."

"Yeah. I wanted to say hi to Ben and Sarah. They still around?"

"Yes. I told them you would call. When will you make it home?"

"I should be there about noon. This meeting must be important. Some people think Brookings is retiring, but I don't buy that. Barb, he called twice to congratulate us on our coverage. And listen to this—last night he told me the Chairman had called him at home yesterday."

"Praise from The Founder himself? I hope Brookings is having the telephone receiver dipped in bronze." Barbara didn't want to belittle Peter's moment, but she couldn't resist a poke. She had never been big on cult figures, particularly corporate ones. "Well, I hope the meeting goes okay. I wouldn't put any money on Brookings retiring, though, Peter. They'll have to pound him out of there with a jackhammer, unless McCallister gets some tainted shrimp into him. Love you. I'll put Ben on."

"Hello."

"Ben. It's Dad."

"I know that."

"How you doing?"

"Fine."

"What are you doing in school today?"

"Turning in my Mayan harvest project," Ben said. "Mom and I built a Mayan village last night. We made rows of corn with yellow clay and built a temple out of Legos. Then we had Mayans harvesting the corn."

"What did you use for Mayans?"

"G.I. Joes. And the head priest was a Teenage Mutant Ninja Turtle."

Peter wondered how the teacher would react to a Mayan farmer with hand grenades, but he knew better than to raise the issue of historical accuracy. "Great, Ben. Have a good day. I'll be home this afternoon. Put Sarah on, would you?"

"Daddy?"

"This is Gossamer Wump."

"No. It's Daddy. I know your silly voice."

Rafael Miranda pushed his linen-covered cart toward the USB News conference room. The cart, almost as long as Miranda, was laden with the normal provisions for a news division staff meeting. As senior man on the executive dining staff, Miranda—by union contract—had the prestigious job of setting up for and serving Mr. Brookings and the news executives. This had given him, over the years, an inside track on many of the world's major events. Miranda was curious this morning, however; this was not one of the division's regularly scheduled meetings. Something, he told the food service manager, was up. Might it be related to those rumors, which had reached even the food service, that someone was buying up USB stock?

He backed into the room and flipped on the light switch, pulling the cart in behind him. The soft, recessed ceiling lights flickered on, reflecting in the huge rosewood conference table that reminded Miranda of a ship, solid and gleaming.

He unlocked the matching rosewood cabinet and took out the translucent china, each cup and plate embossed with the network eagle, then set twenty-one places, as requested on the order sheet sent down by Brookings's secretary.

Plugging in the teapot behind Brookings's leather chair, he made sure to pour in distilled water from the refrigerator. Mr. Brookings drank only Hemming's British, freshly brewed.

Reaching under the cart, Miranda pulled out of the portable oven trays of croissants, sweet rolls, and muffins, placing them at intervals along the table. From the refrigerator compartment he took pitchers of fresh orange juice and bowls of fruit. He slid the coffee urn onto the serving table and plugged it in.

He'd almost forgotten the stationery. From the lower drawer of the cabinet, he counted out twenty-one legal pads and an equal number of pencils, all carrying the network logo, a far more tasteful eagle than any that had ever flown. He set them at each seat, pulling every chair back exactly half a foot.

And he saved the most delicate preparations for last: He would have just enough time to return with the two bowls of shrimp before the executives filed in. This last-minute meeting had necessitated a string of hysterical calls to the food service's supplier, but the icy crates had arrived at the loading dock as Miranda was leaving to prepare the conference room. He carried white cotton gloves in his uniform pocket, always, so as not to leave fingerprints on the gleaming surfaces of the silver shrimp bowls.

Peter staggered in at 8:45, red-eyed, and sat down next to Buzz Allen of the *Evening News,* who was poring gravely over the morning story lineup sent in by each of USB News' domestic and foreign bureaus. Peter was greeted by a brief congratulatory babble, led by Adelson.

He was pleased but dazed. He had slept for six of the last forty-eight hours, nourished mainly by mounds of cheeseburgers and cold pizza, gallons of coffee and diet soda, and last night's party fare. He had a headache, a dreadful taste in his mouth, a burning stomach. A Big Story Hangover, it was called.

"Do you have time for this meeting, Julian?" said Adelson, resuming the enthusiastic needling of McCallister he'd been forced to suspend during Brookings's party. "Who's manning the news division? I've just been reading about your journalistic heroism in the *Daily News*. Which was even more remarkable than they know, because in the two hours I was up in the control room Tuesday, I didn't see you at all."

McCallister smiled tolerantly. "It's hard to see when you're burrowed into a bag of doughnuts, isn't it, Sam?"

"Grab a paper, Peter," Adelson called from across the table. "Have you read about the brilliant job Julian did over the last two days covering the sinking of the *Providence*? It's in all the TV columns. Say, didn't I see you there in the control room? But you obviously weren't working on the story or I would've seen your name mentioned, so what the fuck *were* you doing in there?"

McCallister yawned elaborately. "Got anything good for tomorrow, Peter? This isn't the Academy Awards, you know. We can only bask in glory for a morning or so."

Peter couldn't play. He thought only of getting home and crawling into bed. Besides, he knew McCallister wasn't really playing; the *Providence* was yesterday's triumph. McCallister, Adelson had warned Peter, had opened last week's hush-hush executive powwow with a cutting dissection of *Morning in the U.S.* as a show firmly rooted in the '50s, one that wasn't meeting the snappier competition from the other networks.

Buzz Allen chuckled, looking up from his cables. He had endured the same drill with McCallister a hundred times, not to mention the legendary gamesmanship of anchorman Jack Thomas. He leaned over to Peter. "Executive producers who get their names in the paper don't last long, do they?"

Peter wasn't surprised, or even particularly irritated, by

McCallister's glory-snatching. Good clips were vital to corporate careers. McCallister had told Peter during one of their rare and uncomfortable lunches that you couldn't depend on reporters' diligence and love of truth; they needed a lot of help.

If he thought too much about McCallister and the way he worked, Peter knew he could easily come to dislike the man intensely. The career implications of that were frightening to contemplate, so he tried not to think about him much at all.

McCallister personified the new breed of media executive: affluent, well-educated men and women who did their pulse-taking at brunches on the West and East Sides, at dinner parties in Northwest Washington, and in and around the canyons of L.A. If the hard-bitten, cigar-smoking newsman had ever existed, Peter thought, he certainly existed no more. Socialite journalists were too busy sun-drying tomatoes and brewing decaffeinated espresso to notice that farmers were being booted off their land or that Mexican immigrants were overwhelming health clinics in Texas. Not that Peter wanted to romanticize the TV old-timers, either; their idea of a good story was a car hitting a train. It seemed sometimes that there wasn't any group at USB News that Peter quite felt part of.

McCallister had another ominous quality beyond his appetite for media manipulation and social networking. He had picked up what was now an almost casual habit of betrayal. His wake was littered with the bodies of ex-friends, aides, and colleagues he had found it convenient to discard or blame for one reason or another. One of Adelson's Laws was that in times of trouble no television executive's lips could form the words *I was responsible.*

The low-grade hostility and ceaseless maneuvering that accompanied any gathering of USB News executives was, in fact, beginning to penetrate Peter's mental fog. Even when they were sitting around the conference table with their morning papers, trading supposedly jocular jibes over coffee, these people were always probing, skirmishing, parrying.

Even Adelson was no saint, thought Peter. Adelson viewed corporate bloodshed the same way Peter's daughter viewed killing animals, however: It was okay if you *really* needed the food to live, but not okay for sport.

"Julian," said Adelson loudly, "what's this meeting about anyway? I mean, as Brookings's loyal deputy, you must know."

The usually unflappable McCallister flushed, more in anger than in embarrassment, Peter thought. But McCallister said nothing.

Patrician demeanor notwithstanding, McCallister had grown up the son of a police detective in a grim immigrant neighborhood in Cincinnati. Adelson's humble youth was not so dissimiliar, but they preferred to emphasize their differences.

McCallister had left Cincinnati and his six brothers and sisters far behind—first, sitting out the Vietnam War at UCLA's film school, then working his way up through the ranks of one of L.A.'s hottest independent film production companies, and then—seeing Hollywood as too risky and unpredictable—shocking his friends and colleagues by quitting after ten years, heading East against the flow and into the news business, where he had again defied the odds and prospered. McCallister had gambled wisely, and not as recklessly as it might have seemed. His production instincts, his feel for music images and graphics were first-rate, even by Hollywood standards, but in USB's stuffier news environs, they sparkled, catching even Elliott Brookings's cautious eye.

McCallister took pride in being polished, polite, fashionably well-tailored. Adelson, overweight and rumpled, wore like a medal of honor the personality and outlook of the Brooklyn Jew and everything he took it to mean: toughness, smarts, loyalty. Hardly anyone in the news division knew that Adelson had a master's degree in English literature from Princeton, and about the only time Peter could make him squirm was when he threatened to reveal it. Peter thought it inevitable that the two would someday fight to the death, probably when Brookings retired. It would be a main event, the pit bull versus the afghan hound, as one wag had put it.

Buzz Allen was different, an Eagle Scout who took seriously USB's public palaver about truth and fairness and obligation to the public. At thirty-nine, Allen still looked like the college football star he once had been—USC, Peter thought, although he could never keep straight the difference between USC and UCLA. Right now Buzz seemed quite absorbed in his reports of the congressional brouhaha that had erupted over how an engine-room explosion could sink a state-of-the-art cruiser.

"Peter, we've got a report running tonight that says a ten-dollar seal on one of the boilers caused the ship to sink," he said with quiet pride. "It's a great story. A piece of plastic that you can buy in a hardware store for a ten-spot sinks a three-billion-dollar ship."

Peter shook his head in seeming wonder, although his interest in the sinking was already ebbing. It was a Washington blah-blah story now, and the follow-ups would be political and technological and dull.

There was more interest in the room, he noticed, in a story no one at the table was covering. Everyone was poring over the business sections this morning, not usually the first section these people scanned. The rumors of an attempted takeover of USB were getting good play.

Peter, too, had read the story in the *Times*. Harold Shurken, the media analyst for Roberts & Carroll, an investment banking firm, was quoted as saying that "broadcasting has been living in a fairyland for years." The takeover rumors signified that "reality has arrived." Shurken had specifically mentioned that costs were known to be out of control at USB, especially in the news division, where the budget had risen by nearly 70 percent over the last five years. "Too often, broadcasting has felt it is immune from the restructuring that has been sweeping American business," the analyst had lectured. "Now the company will have to demonstrate very quickly that it can move to control spending and give stockholders a fair return on their investment."

Tough stuff, thought Peter, watching Adelson take in the same story along with his first Classic Coke of the morning. But Peter was skeptical. USB was not only profitable, it was a national institution. What did Shurken mean, that the company had to "demonstrate" that it could control costs? To whom? The Chairman and Founder still owned a third of it. Peter couldn't imagine him sitting by while somebody bought his network as if it were a fast food chain.

Peter took one of the cups of coffee Miranda was pouring from the silver pot. Everyone understood that after working for two uninterrupted days and having to endure last night's soiree, he would be useless at extended conversation. Glassy eyes aside, though, he didn't look much more unkempt than usual. Since college he had worn the same uniform: chinos, a blue oxford-cloth shirt, a red knit tie, and navy blazer. Fashion intimidated

Peter—everyone seemed to know more about it than he did—
and he had taken himself out of the competition.

Everyone watched the clock, monitoring attendance as meeting time approached. Brookings wasn't tolerant of lateness, so
staff meeting protocol was rigidly observed, even by flamboy-
antly maverick producers. You were in your seat by 8:55 so that
you could have your juice and croissant and coffee before Brookings arrived. The door was locked as soon as he walked in. Only
a call or visit from the Chairman had ever been known to delay
him.

"Julian," said Adelson politely, "I was leafing through some
old newspapers the other day, and read about what an incredible
job you did covering the Kennedy assassination. Apparently
they're still talking about it over at the *Times*. And it was all the
more miraculous, considering that you were, what, fourteen?"

McCallister yawned and returned to his paper. "And you
were already over the hill."

Though no one had ever imposed a seating arrangement,
producers and top management always planted themselves on
opposite sides of the table, in tacit recognition of their natural
enmity. The creative types—the executive producers, front-line
centurions in television's bloody trenches—sat facing the windows. Philip Barnard was the last of the producers to arrive, as
was his habit. He'd brought his customary French mineral water,
placing it conspicuously on the table.

"How do you know goats from France haven't pissed in the
streams that stuff comes from?" Adelson asked suspiciously,
eyeing Barnard's bottle.

"Well, Sam, that shows how little you know about health.
Goat piss stimulates potency," Barnard said calmly. "Turns you
into a rampaging sexual animal."

"You ought to sue then," shot back Adelson. He found the
very notion of bottled water anti-Semitic.

Barnard eased into the chair next to Peter's, patting him on
the back and murmuring a few compliments about the *Providence*
coverage, even though Peter doubted he had gotten up early
enough to watch it. Barnard was bored by news, and made
no secret of it except when Brookings was around. Peter
felt the usual stab of envy as Barnard slipped his lean frame
into the chair. It was too much to bear, thought Peter, for

Barnard to be that good-looking and smart *and* to have a hit show.

Making it as an executive producer these days meant much more, Peter was learning, than it once had. Making it now meant you'd come up with *au courant* graphics, new theme music, and a set ordered up from wizards in L.A. It meant you'd demoted or bumped off the show some of the troglodytes who had lived in the hidden recesses of USB News for years, expensively savoring past triumphs. And it meant you'd come up with a knockout idea for a show, one explainable in fifteen words to an ad agency, to affiliates, to network executives, and to television reporters, not to mention viewers.

Peter had never been judged this way before. He had come out of USB News bureaus, the way executive producers traditionally had, up the chain from Houston to Detroit and Washington. Making it in the bureaus meant getting good pictures to New York quickly and getting the script absolutely right all the time. He'd had to prove that he was smart, decisive, and hard working, and for most of his career that had been more than enough.

But times change, as Adelson had lamented at lunch with Peter a couple of weeks earlier. It was now quite possible, Adelson had observed, to be very good and not be good enough. You changed with the times or you went the way of all big creatures who couldn't adapt. Sometimes, Adelson said, Peter seemed to want to run the world; others, he behaved as if he ought to be running a bookstore in Maine. The warning was delivered with Adelson's legendary concrete-block subtlety. If Peter wanted to be Papa Walton, Adelson had told him, he could fucking well go to West Virginia and run the morning program at some station in Wheeling.

They had ended the lunch laughing. So what you're telling me, Peter had said, is that if I would only dump my wife and abandon my kids and move back into Manhattan, I could pay the requisite amount of attention needed to pump up *Morning in the U.S.* Adelson had said that was a little crudely put but not far off the mark: Peter didn't have to do all three, but any two would help.

Peter yawned again, looked at the clock. He scribbled a note to Adelson: "Difficulty is the excuse history never accepts." He crunched it into a ball and rolled it across the conference table.

Adelson studied the note, scribbled something, and tossed it back.

"Roosevelt?" he had written.

Peter wrote back: "No, sucker. That really was Murrow. Score is 7 to 2."

Rafael Miranda walked along the table refilling coffee cups. The time was edging toward nine. While the producers bantered, sipped coffee, doodled on their legal pads, and read the papers, the executives across the table, with no time to fritter away, read memos, clicked at their calculators, dictated letters into portable tape recorders.

Barnard's entrance had roused Grace Viola from the novel that she had daringly pulled from her briefcase a few moments earlier. She was the new vice-president for Finance, but reading a novel, along with being one of the first women to join the top ranks, marked her as an oddity. Even the executive producers, who reveled in their freedom from corporate strictures, would have been wary of bringing a book to a staff meeting.

As the keeper of the budgets, Grace Viola was the producers' nemesis, and they had all pretty much ignored her in the three months since her arrival. Only Adelson had taken Viola to lunch. Her presence, he advised, was a symbol of change, and he counseled his fellow executives to take her more seriously. They hadn't, and two empty chairs separated her from the nearest person at the conference table.

Women had advanced considerably in recent years at USB News, but the all-too accurate joke that made the rounds at women producers' lunches was that whenever real decisions were reached or real money changed hands, there were still always three middle-aged white men in the room.

Viola had been glaring up from her book at Barnard ever since he'd plopped his mineral water on the table. At first, Peter had thought she was staring at *him,* since he was sitting next to Barnard. Then he was surprised to see Barnard suddenly look away.

When Barnard wouldn't meet her gaze, Viola spoke up. "Mr. Barnard," she said quietly, "since you haven't returned my phone calls, perhaps you can tell me now when we can meet to discuss your London expenses."

The room stilled. Even the fidgety vice-presidents paid attention. Budget people did not challenge news producers, certainly not in public.

Barnard, too, seemed astonished, then infuriated. "I'm rather busy these days, Ms. Viola," he said icily. "I have a show to air every week; sometimes I don't have the time it takes to add up the cost of my newspapers and paper clips."

"How about the cost of your hotel suites?" she shot back, this time to gasps.

Adelson got up and hurried over, depositing himself in the empty seat next to her. "Grace, Phil and I will sit down together this week. We'll get back to you, okay? This is not the time." She looked back at Barnard—Peter thought her gaze could burn a hole through the rosewood table—and slowly picked up her novel, with just the slightest trace of a smile on her face. Barnard looked rattled; the vice-presidents began clacking and rustling again.

Whew, Peter thought, that was a message well-delivered.

While Viola resumed her reading, everyone else was beginning to squirm. It was 9:06. Brookings was officially late, and Brookings was never late. The vice-presidents began staring nervously at his empty seat.

Peter emerged from his reverie long enough to wonder what was up. He scribbled another note to Adelson on the same crumpled paper: "Must be trouble." Adelson read the note, nodded imperceptibly, palmed it, folded it into tiny squares, and ate it. Peter was watching and his face began to contort with laughter, causing several vice-presidents across the table to look at him curiously.

Peter alone had noticed Sam's habit of eating sensitive notes, something Adelson said he'd picked up in California, where he'd once scribbled a note calling a colleague a faggot and tossed it into the trash. The station manager always had his secretary comb through the garbage for just such incriminating evidence, and Adelson had almost gotten fired as news director. Peter hadn't quite believed it the first time he'd seen Adelson fold a sheet of paper into tiny squares and slide it into his mouth. He'd made Peter swear never to tell. Paper was harmless, he assured him, and anyway, job security compensated for any minor health risk.

At 9:20, Elliot Brookings, pipe clenched between his teeth, opened the door and walked to the head of the table. He carried a sheet of paper; he had some sort of announcement to make.

He reached for the tea that appeared magically at his elbow, no matter where he was. He took a sip, scanned the faces around the room, and nodded. "First of all, I would like to commend all of you—Peter, Julian especially—for the splendid job we've been doing on the sinking of the *Providence*. Congratulations. I've also sent a telegram to Dan D'Amato and the Special Assignment Team commending them on the superb pictures they were able to obtain."

For Brookings, that was lavish praise. Now he got down to business. "Gentlemen . . . and Grace." He smiled, nodding to Viola. He could never quite get the introductions right since she had infiltrated the all-male hierarchy.

"I apologize for being late. I was delayed because I was on the telephone with the Chairman. I want to address two points this morning. It is imperative that you digest what I'm telling you.

"First, the reports that the company faces a takeover threat are true. Because of federal laws regarding the way such information is communicated, I have been asked by the network's attorneys not to go beyond the statement I have just made. There is a takeover threat, and it is possible the network may have to take defensive measures to strengthen its ability to remain independent. I do not yet know what those measures will be."

Adelson began to say something, but Brookings silenced him with a gesture. "It is also important that you all realize that things may change. The Chairman feels that while the news division will continue to receive the necessary funding to continue the highest-quality work, we will have to take a harder look at our spending. We will have to restrain ourselves in a way we have never been asked to before. The threat is real, and the company's efforts to combat it will be just as real. I need not tell you that the prospect of a real estate conglomerate running this news division is unthinkable.

"I am sure I can count on each of you to help. Grace Viola will be meeting with you to find ways of managing our costs more effectively. I am sure she will have your full cooperation."

Brookings looked pale and grave. The Chairman's phone call had been a rough one, Peter concluded.

"I hope I do not need to remind you," Brookings went on, "that you are expected to cover this story in precisely the same way you would cover any major national business story—completely, fairly, and cautiously. I am sure you all have questions, but this is not the time. I need your patience and your support, and I know I have them."

Brookings stood up and left the room, avoiding even casual eye contact. The vice-presidents, Viola included, looked startled and quickly filed out of the room. Brookings had not consumed a single shrimp.

Allen mumbled something about getting some stories assigned and rushed off. His broadcast was the next scheduled to air.

McCallister seemed confused, an unusual state for him. He lingered a moment in the conference room and exchanged troubled looks with Adelson, then trailed after the vice-presidents.

Peter and Barnard both turned to Adelson.

"What does that mean in English?" Barnard asked.

Adelson reflected. "Nothing much. Nuclear winter, maybe. The end of intelligent life as we know it."

"Could we all go to lunch together?" Peter wondered, breaking the ensuing silence. You didn't need to be much of a newsman, he thought, to notice that the earth had just moved.

"Not such a terrible idea," said Barnard. "Maybe we have more in common than we think."

"Oh, you do," said Adelson, struggling to recover from the shock that had left him uncharacteristically quiet. "You're all lunchmeat."

CHAPTER FIVE

THE
SANITY
CLUB

*A*t first glance Tony's Pub and Pizza could have been mistaken for a newsstand or, as Phil Barnard suggested, a men's room in a small-town bus station. A dozen tables were jammed into a kitchen-sized space. No credit cards were accepted at Tony's; no fern could have survived the lack of natural or artificial light, the heat and smells from the kitchen.

Barnard was not enthusiastic. "Where do they get all this cigarette smoke these days?" he wondered, sniffing. "They must buy it and ship it in."

But it seemed an inviting shelter from the gray February chill outside, and a refuge from the bomb that had just been detonated over their heads.

"You'll be all right, Barnard," sniffed Adelson, "once you

get over the shock of finding something other than plants to eat."

Peter struggled to squeeze into the ten inches or so between a chair and the Formica table. "In a place like this," he observed, "the pizza *has* to be outstanding." But no one was really thinking much about food.

Barnard shook his head. "I don't believe it. I saw Elliott Brookings' mouth move, and I heard the words, but it was like they hired somebody to play him. I can't square the man with what he was saying."

"It reminded me of that old movie," Peter agreed, "where the President comes on television to announce that the country has no choice but to surrender to the Martian invaders."

"Maybe we're overreacting," Barnard said hopefully. "Are we overreacting, Sam?"

They looked at Adelson in mute appeal. Peter could practically hear his reassuring words: Just relax, Adelson would say; watch expenses for a while. The company and its high-powered lawyers would sort everything out and things would return to normal.

But Adelson was not offering reassurances. Watching his friend and boss, Peter reflected that he had rarely seen more than three moods in Adelson: wisecracking, philosophical, or outraged. He had never seen him at a loss for words.

Adelson called for a scotch and water, though Peter had never seen him drink at lunch before, either. Peter didn't dare drink—he would have fallen face-first into the pizza—so he ordered more coffee. This would be his fourth or fifth cup of the morning, and despite his fatigue, it was beginning to take effect: the caffeine and adrenaline from the meeting were working to pump him up. Barnard ordered a frosted glass of beer and the three of them sat quietly until the drinks arrived. Adelson was collecting himself.

"Well, I'm not going to bullshit you," Adelson said finally. "That was a heavy speech. I can only guess what it did to Brookings to have to say it."

"But Brookings isn't saying it's over, is he?" Peter asked. "He's just preparing us for the battle, right?"

Adelson, the color returning to his cheeks, harrumphed. "You hotshot journalists have a great knack for seeing only the stories you want to see. Haven't you been reading the papers? That Wall Street jerk Harold Shurken—he's been in the *Times* every other day squawking about USB and how bloated it is and what a tempting opportunity it is for some efficient managers. Where have you been?"

With my head up my ass, thought Peter, playing big-shot TV producer and missing the biggest story of my own work life. He tried to focus on the two men across the table.

"What we obviously need," said Peter somberly, surveying their discouraged faces, "is a men's caucus."

Adelson looked as though Peter had just stepped off a space-ship. "Men don't have caucuses, asshole."

"Men who are victims do," Barnard interrupted. "There's a gay men's caucus at USB News. And we're about to become victims, aren't we?"

"The USB News Men's Caucus," Peter continued. "We would meet every week in a church basement and help one another survive what is clearly going to be a period of turmoil and stress."

Barnard nodded eagerly. "My name is Philip and I am a man who yesterday was gloating to himself about how powerful and successful he was and today is eating shit."

"And what are the criteria for joining?" Adelson said skeptically.

"First," Peter said, "you have to be eating shit."

Adelson took out his pen and began taking notes on a napkin.

"And," Barnard added, "you have to be one of the twenty-five thousand."

Peter and Adelson both looked at him questioningly.

"This is probably going to come as a shock to you both, but we are among the twenty-five thousand most successful people in the world," Barnard announced. And even as they began to scoff, he went on. "No, really, I've thought about this quite a bit. Research even did a workup for me last year. Listen.

"You factor in heads of state, right? There's about a hundred and fifty of those, give or take some uncertain situations. To be fair, throw in military chiefs, cabinet ministers, heads of secret police organizations—that's a couple of thousand at the most. Take CEOs and owners of the world's two thousand top companies—and two thousand is more than generous. Then throw in the top professional people—if you take the cream, you have no more than five thousand, and I mean the best, the well-known physicians and lawyers and all. Throw in another five thousand political leaders, members of Congress, parliaments, assemblies, that sort of thing. Add the important creative people: film makers, publishers, authors, musicians. Remember, we're talking about people who really influence people. There aren't more than a few thousand on that level."

Adelson, scribbling more figures on his napkin, nodded.

"Now stack us up against all those people," Barnard said, resuming his analysis. "We command large staffs and budgets of tens of millions of dollars. Plus, we control chunks of network television and can reach millions of people and help set our country's agenda and some of the world's, true? So depending on how you calculate it, we might rank in the top fifteen thousand, although I'm not on solid ground there. But we're in the top twenty-five thousand, no sweat."

Adelson snorted. "Maybe Carol will be more respectful. She thinks I'm just some shlump from Brooklyn."

"I sort of lean to her view," said Peter, trying to sound ho-hum. "Listen, I think we should invite Buzz Allen next time we all have lunch. He's an executive producer, and he trains the network's biggest and most unpredictable killer gorilla, so he's clearly one of your twenty-five thousand. And we should invite Danny D'Amato when he gets back from Lisbon."

"You mean D'Amato talks about something besides ground stations?" asked Barnard.

"God, yes. D'Amato can talk about women," Peter said, lowering his voice. "He's always got three or four on a rotation. He sees each one once or twice a week for, say, six months. If they mention exclusivity or marriage, they're out. If they bring more than one night's change of clothes? Out. Or if they answer his telephone."

"Well, we gotta get this guy to lunch," Adelson agreed. "Maybe he can give us tips. I'd like to bottle what he's got. You know him best, Peter—what *does* he have?"

Peter had never been good at talking sex or sports, a failing that had tended to isolate him from other men, so he was enjoying this male-talk. "Well, he's good-looking and he keeps in shape, and somebody told me that he has a trampoline in his bedroom."

"I've heard that, too," Barnard said. "That qualifies him for caucus membership in my book."

"So to be admitted," said Peter, "a man has to be scared shitless and one of the most powerful twenty-five thousand men in the world, and it helps to have a trampoline. What else?"

"He has to be overextended financially," Adelson said. "And he has to have much of his life tied up in his work. Because one of the things the caucus has to do is prepare men for the coming crunch."

"And," said Barnard, signaling for more beer, "it's a place to air grievances."

"They used to call that whining," said Adelson unenthusiastically. "And I doubt anyone would lose too many tears over the likes of us. I've just been hearing about how we're at the top of the heap. Now we're filing grievances?"

"We've got plenty of grievances," Barnard insisted, a bit defensively. "We can be fired at will. If we stumble, we're dead. I mean, companies aren't looking to improve their hiring records of middle-aged white males. We're all scared to death, just like women are, but if *we* admit it, we're weak and unreliable. And none of us have any real options. I've given everything to my work, and I mean everything."

Peter turned to Adelson, whose cheeks showed the flush of scotch. "What would your grievance be, Sam?" he asked.

Adelson, usually leery of too much introspection, surprised Peter by saying mournfully, "I have a grievance about what's going on at USB News." He took a healthy swig from his glass. "It isn't a matter of money, you know. These companies have always been run by cheap, murderous pricks who would slit their grandmothers' throats for fifty bucks. It isn't money." Adelson rarely sounded this deflated. Nostalgia, he often reminded his producers, was necessary only for losers.

"I'm a little older than you guys," he went on. "I remember the Golden Age of Television. I saw Sid Caesar and Jack Benny. I remember the Golden Age of Radio—wonderful comedy, and mysteries. I even remember the Golden Age of Magazines: *Look, Life, The Saturday Evening Post.*

"When I got out of college I had the damnedest time figuring out which Golden Age I wanted to join. I wanted to take pictures for *Life,* or be a foreign correspondent for *Time,* or be Charles Collingwood—that sweet fucking voice; he borrowed it from God, my mother used to say. Maybe Hollywood, I thought. All kinds of work in Hollywood—even Faulkner and F. Scott Fitzgerald worked in Hollywood for a while."

Adelson looked up from his scotch. "So you guys, you make a lot of money, you travel around, you *are* among the twenty-five thousand success stories of the era, but I gotta tell you something. This is the Golden Age of Chickenshit. That's my grievance."

There was a long silence. Barnard turned to Peter and said suspiciously, "What about you, Peter? We're getting soused and pouring out our souls, and you're sipping coffee and taking it all in."

"I have lots of grievances, don't worry."

"Well, let's hear them, asshole," said Adelson, recovering. "You got us into all this touchy-feely shit."

"Well, I don't think these people—whoever they are—should be able to tear up the contract," said Peter. "I've been with USB more than ten years. I've seen it as the place I planned to work the rest of my life. We had a deal: I would work hard for them and they would give me enough money to buy a house—"

"Your little slice of the American dream in New Jersey," Adelson interjected.

Peter nodded. "And college for my kids, and doctors if I get sick, and some comfort when I'm too used up to work anymore. We've got an agreement, USB and I. Somebody can't just come in and rip it up. That would be a major grievance, as far as I'm concerned."

"The answer, my friend," Barnard said, "is pissin' in the wind."

Peter ignored the sarcasm.

"Phil is right; none of these are grievances you can do anything about," said Adelson with a shrug. "We don't know if the people we made our deals with will even be around next month. Whatever six-billion-dollar combine takes over USB won't give a rat's ass about our grievances. I vote to disband the USB News Men's Caucus."

He straightened, deliberately looking at the clock, abruptly altering the mood at the table. "Don't let me stay much longer anyway. This is no time to get sloshed. I've got to meet with Buzz Allen at one; he's been struggling with Jack Thomas about the 'editorial direction' of the *Evening News*."

There was no misunderstanding the implications of a dispute like that. Thomas was ridiculed behind his back for his carefully crafted folksiness—he kept a Bible on his desk and was often seen studying it when reporters arrived for interviews, although rarely at other times. For every possible news development, he had a pointless down-home animal analogy about hound dogs or possums. Getting out a newscast was "like wrestling a panther at midnight"; White House reporters were like "bees falling out of a hive." But Buzz Allen's contract ran for three years and was worth about three quarters of a million. Thomas's ran for ten years and was worth at least $15 million.

Then Adelson, looking mysterious, sternly asked if they could keep a secret. "Really, guys," he said, "you have to swear on everything that's holy, 'cause I could get hurt for just knowing this."

"I swear on my kids," said Peter.

"On getting Michael Jackson on my show," said Barnard.

"Okay, but if a word of this ever gets out, I will hunt you two down and beat the shit out of you." He confided that Buzz Allen and two of his senior producers had sneaked into Jack Thomas's office a few months earlier and unearthed his list of folksy sayings, which he kept tucked inside his Bible. They had, Adelson told the riveted producers in a whisper, changed the names of the animals all around. This had caused a series of incomprehensible anecdotes to appear in various newspapers and magazines.

The others began laughing hard enough to attract stares from adjoining tables.

"Let's see," he mused. "There was the llama with two humps, the camel that honked like a goose, the pig as mad as a woodpecker in a cigar store. The amazing thing is that no one, absolutely no one noticed—not Thomas, not the reporters. We always held our breath, waiting for some cracker to call up and say 'What the fuck is going on there?' But I realized that real crackers wouldn't be caught dead saying that shit anyway."

Peter felt safer. Things couldn't be that bad if he was sitting here joking about USB News with these two powerful, confident men.

They were still laughing a few minutes later when the proprietor came over to take their pizza order. Adelson, patting his eyes with a handkerchief, told Tony to make three pizzas—one plain, one with everything, and one with sausage. It was Adelson's habit, no matter what restaurant he was in, to order for everybody, as if he feared there wouldn't be enough to eat.

"This is like a Paul Mazursky movie, isn't it?" said Barnard, when the first pizza had arrived and everyone was pulling at strings of cheese. "You know, like the one where the women sit around and talk about their problems. Maybe," he added tentatively, "we should schedule lunch now and then until this all blows over. Instead of meeting in a church basement. A lunch club. A Sanity Club."

"Don't count on this blowing over soon, Phil," Adelson cautioned. "And don't kid yourself about lunch either—we'd run out of war stories in about two weeks. Men don't do intimate lunches, even if they like the idea in principle."

They agreed, nevertheless, that the Sanity Club should meet again, with Allen and D'Amato as fresh recruits, though not the following week; Barnard was going back to London to hear the music that he swore had finally been written for his program. And Peter was considering a trip to Los Angeles to review graphics that might help his broadcast's declining ratings.

Adelson seemed bothered. "You guys better be cautious about trips now. And watch yourself with this London business, Phil," he warned. "Grace Viola's people are on your tail like a heat-seeking missile. You guys would be making a big mistake by underestimating her. You know, Brookings has invited her to the winter meetings in Santo Cristo next month, and that's the first time a finance person has ever been allowed in."

Barnard flared. "Fuck her!" he thundered. "Can you imagine, an executive producer at USB justifying his expense accounts to a bean-counter like that? Let the little snot come after me; I'll have her ass. Does she think I'm the first producer who ever junketed to London?"

Adelson clucked. He was well acquainted with Barnard's temper; producers dreaded screenings where he would throw coffee cups, cassettes, and careers around the room if displeased.

"Just a little warning, that's all. These are getting to be tricky times."

"Poor Sam," said Barnard, dismissing Adelson's caution with a wave of his hand. "He's just jealous because he has to stay behind and comb Brookings' tweeds."

Adelson, never much of an Anglophile, shrugged and changed the subject. He'd done his best.

"I'm going to drop," said Peter. "For a while there I half-forgot that I've been up for forty-eight hours looking at pictures of burned bodies."

Adelson leaned over and thumped him on the back. "It's good you haven't completely forgotten," he said. "Because everybody else already has."

If there were a better view of New York harbor and the Statue of Liberty, David Nab had never seen it; it was the sort of view only lawyers could afford.

Harold Wallace, senior partner at Brooks, Petrow, Rubin & Burrows, was Nab's oldest and most trusted advisor. They were sitting in the firm's thirty-fourth-floor meeting room, at a conference table that made the one at USB News look like a coffee table. One wall was all glass.

The couple of dozen people arrayed around the table constituted Brooks, Petrow's entire acquisition advisory unit, at the moment the hottest on the Street. Nab was not immune to the pleasure of knowing they were all there to attend to him.

Two discreet but clearly visible metal poles stood in each corner of the room—taping devices, they had all been told. Nab always recorded his business meetings, and so did the law firm. A young man in a three-piece suit was bringing in extra chairs for the attorneys and analysts still arriving.

Nab looked surprisingly alert for a man who had just stepped off the Concorde, his blue suit unwrinkled by the flight. Although he was not flashing a single piece of jewelry, and made a point of not even wearing a wedding ring, there was no mistaking his wealth.

Wallace began the meeting with a nod in his direction.

"Gentlemen and ladies, you all know David Nab, with whom this firm has had a long and close relationship, as it did with his father. Mr. Nab has acquired substantial holdings in United States Broadcasting. There are rumors on the Street, and a few have even appeared in the press, about David's efforts to amass USB stock. The purpose of this meeting is to declare, and then to execute, his desire to acquire control of the company. This is one of the most ambitious efforts undertaken by our firm, and I have assured David that we are up to it. Acquiring a television network involves sensitive issues that we have not previously had to confront. But USB is a national treasure, and it's sitting there like a big fat hen for the plucking."

Wallace opened the leather-bound folder in front of him. Nab sat calmly and silently with his arms folded.

"This is Nab Enterprises' tenth acquisition, but by far the most important," Wallace went on, "so we need to move fast. The stock is in play. I don't want Icahn or someone to move in and gobble it up while we use lawyerly caution and review analysts' reports. David is in the process of arranging financing and plans to start quietly purchasing. USB stock was at one twenty-one this morning. It's worth one eighty anyway, so there's not going to be any screwing around. We have to move fast. But that's for the investment bankers. Our job is to ensure a legal and orderly takeover. We want this one done perfectly."

Wallace did not want to talk openly yet about what was really worrying him. He made a point of studying the personality, history, and psychology of the companies he helped take over. You never bought just a business, he was always telling Nab, you bought a subculture too.

USB was probably the greatest example of the need for that approach. Wallace was much more preoccupied with the political ramifications than the financial ones in this case. USB, especially USB News, was no hotel chain. The media would swarm over the story like angry wasps, because they were a part of it. Congress might easily get involved. He knew a discreet but well-connected public relations firm in Los Angeles that ought to be brought in early. It specialized in helping to diffuse the flak when raiders took over ripe, mismanaged companies; it had prospered through the Reagan years.

The skirmishes ahead were fairly predictable: the fight, the takeover, the trimming of the fat. Usually there was surprisingly little real difficulty in the end, given the disruptions, the lost jobs, and so on. But this time it would be producers and correspondents getting ditched, and you would hear their howls all the way to Georgetown. Wallace thought of Jack Thomas, who played tennis at his club and once had even played a set of doubles with him at the Racquet Club. And of Harry Sommers, USB's famous *Weekend News* producer, a regular at Wallace's Southampton tennis club.

He jotted on his memo pad:

Tennis/Thomas.

Lunch/Sommers.

Council on Foreign Relations banquet with N.

Call Hal Danzig in L.A.

CHAPTER SIX
RESTING

*F*lannery had ordered the sleek black limo with the color television and the car phone to wait for Peter outside the USB building. The driver hopped out to open the door, to the jeers and hoots of Adelson and Barnard, returning from lunch with Peter.

Brookings didn't want his executives driving themselves home after 48-hour story marathons; any tired executive could always get a ride home in a cab or a USB News staff car. But the executive producer of *Morning in the U.S.* traditionally took the perk a step further, borrowing one of the limos used to transport guests to and from the program. Flannery dealt with the limo companies, since she and her staff recruited the guests, and she liked to arrange something special for Peter after a cruncher like the *Providence* sinking.

"I'm calling Grace Viola," Adelson hollered. "I'm going to tell her to look out her window at the boat driving you home. She'll probably try to shoot the air out of the tires."

"Poor dear," Barnard trilled. "You must be so exhausted

from watching all those pictures Danny D'Amato took in Portugal."

Peter gave them both the finger, climbed in, and closed the door before they could glimpse the snack and drink tray that Flannery had ordered. Knowing that he would be getting ready to sleep, she had ordered scones and a pot of decaffeinated tea. Peter, struggling to recover from black coffee and pizza, needed no more food.

He leaned back and closed his eyes, smiling at the sight of Adelson and Barnard waving handkerchiefs at the limo and pretending to cry. "Goodbye, darling," he heard Adelson yell as passersby tried to peer in the window and the monstrous Lincoln swept toward the Tunnel. His Toyota sat safe in the company garage; Flannery would send another, more modest car to bring him back to the city when he had rested for a day or so.

He felt curiously upbeat, considering how the morning had begun. The Sanity Club lunch had blunted the shock, if not the unease, of the staff meeting.

Just as he began to doze off, the car phone alongside the tray began to twitter. It did not have the urgency of what he liked to call a "news ring," distinct in tone, he claimed, from a normal telephone ring. But he answered using his brisk executive voice, just in case.

"Yes?"

"Peter? I didn't wake you, did I? You sound half asleep."

"Oh, you finally left the office." He yawned. "Did you go home to change your bathrobe?"

"No, asshole, I went home to rest."

"Patricia, how quaint. I didn't think you did that," he said.

"I do it in my own way. The deli has delivered a chicken salad, and then I'm going to float for two hours in my vacation house."

Peter laughed. He had never seen it, but Flannery had commissioned a $6,000 bathtub, which she likened to a car wash. Four feet deep, with nozzles along each side, it produced steam and featured a temperature control, a perfumed bath-oil dispenser, and, encased in a waterproof plastic bubble up front, four television monitors. Across the room were stereo speakers connected to the main system in the living room.

When Flannery was depressed or exhausted—and she was

one or the other virtually all the time she wasn't working—she would retreat into her bathroom for hours. Flannery maintained that the tub was her healing sanctuary when she was wrung out from hours of bullying and cajoling, when she couldn't bear the thought of packing and fighting traffic to get to her Vermont cottage. Peter had learned not to remind her that she no longer went to Vermont at all except to open the house for the summer and to close it, that the cottage usually was occupied by her assistants and friends from work.

He couldn't imagine how she had the time or energy for any personal life. Yet at least twice a month, she would pop up at his house in Glen Ridge, loaded with food from a trendy West Side deli, playthings from the hippest little toy shop in Soho, and the latest children's books.

Flannery joked about her domestic incompetence; she even had an adoring deli man down the street deliver her fresh coffee and an oat bran muffin every morning. Peter didn't believe that she *couldn't* make a cup of coffee, but he had no trouble believing that she wouldn't. She worked sixty or seventy hours a week, and at least once a week she was at USB all night. By the time she'd prepared her questions for the anchors and picked up the guests—she insisted on being there personally for all her guests— she figured there was no point in going to sleep anyway, since it was time to start working on the next day's program.

Her reward, he knew, was that she relied on other people to do things for her. Aside from having coffee delivered, she had a manicurist who came to do her nails and toes every week, a hairdresser who made housecalls, and even a masseuse.

Male producers and executives, including some married ones, frequently cornered Peter in the hallways, salivating over Flannery and seeking information about her. Their approaches always made him uncomfortable—he had never found sex talk easy anyway, and Flannery was a close friend. He had learned to shrug enigmatically and move on.

Now he paused, trying to clear his head. There was obviously no news emergency. On the other hand, Flannery knew all too well that he wasn't up to snappy banter, so she probably wasn't calling to say hello.

"Patricia? You okay?"

"Well, it's my birthday. I'm thirty-nine. I didn't realize it until I looked at my horoscope in the *Daily News* and saw the date."

"Happy birthday, Patricia."

"Thanks, Peter. I know you're wiped. I'm sorry."

"What about your parents, your sisters? Didn't anybody remember? There are shitloads of Flannerys, if I recall. We would've invited you out."

"It's okay. I don't know who's called. I haven't been home for two days, and I haven't checked my messages yet. Most of them are probably from agents and publishers pitching guests for the show. We kicked some ass, didn't we?"

He felt a twinge of regret. He had neglected to thank her.

"Oh, Peter. Not only did I realize that today is my birthday, do you know that I also realized today that I haven't had sex in a year? A year! The longest period of abstinence I've had since I was seventeen years old. I can't even remember what making love is like."

Peter normally would have felt embarrassed by such a revelation, but in this case he just didn't know what to say. Especially to Flannery, who could have had sex as often as she liked if she hadn't preferred to book guests.

"Does this make you uncomfortable, Peter? It's a strange thing to say to your boss."

"I don't mind your saying it, Patricia, although it's a little weird to be hearing it over a car phone going into the Lincoln Tunnel. I just don't know how to respond. How do you know it's been a year since you had sex?"

"Because the last time was my thirty-eighth birthday, and the guy was that heart surgeon we had on the show from Santa Barbara. You know, the guy who did that gross operation, putting pig's guts into human hearts or something."

He remembered. She'd spent two frantic days in Santa Barbara; it couldn't have been much of a romance.

"Usually I think—expecially after one of these stories—well, this is the last year like this; after this I'm going to start living like a human. But now, I mean, work's over and I'll spend all afternoon in this stupid bathtub for no reason I can think of except that I have nobody at the moment worth being with. Life isn't going to change for me, is it, Peter?"

"It could change if you wanted to change it; you're plenty

smart and tough enough." But he thought she was probably right: Her life wouldn't change, not without some unthinkable trauma that turned her existence upside down.

"I honest-to-God do not want to end up like this, Peter, I swear I don't. It isn't that I want to have kids or wind up in the suburbs; I'd rather die—no offense. But I just can't take the idea that there's nothing but booking guests."

Peter heard the line turn to static and told her to hang on; they picked up the conversation when the limo emerged into the light on the other side of the Tunnel.

"Patricia. I don't mean to sound patronizing, but basically I believe you're doing what you want. It's a trade-off: You get some things and you give up some. You wouldn't be able to do it if you didn't want to. And when you're ready, you'll stop. If you still can."

"Fuck you, Peter," she said, sounding more tired, less plaintive. "By the way, what about that big staff meeting this morning? Is this takeover stuff for real?"

"Well," said Peter, "Brookings says the company is taking the rumors seriously. But I can't believe they won't fight it off. Happy birthday, Patricia."

"Yeah, thanks."

Twenty minutes later the limo glided down Peter's street in Glen Ridge. Marie would have called home to apprise Barbara of his arrival. He rolled the window down and stuck his head out. Several of his neighbors were taking in the limousine. He would never admit the kick of parading down the street this way. The other commuters would come home, dragging their asses and their briefcases, on the Boonton Line express from Hoboken. USB News producers did not drag their asses anywhere.

Not that the limo made up for all he missed. He usually went to work and came home in the dark. The novel he was trying to read had been open to the same page for three weeks now. When he did stagger home somewhere between 7:00 and 8:00 P.M., he was lucky if he had enough energy left to read a bedtime story. Sarah loved to joke about having to tuck him in when he fell asleep in the middle of *Charlotte's Web*. He certainly never felt alert enough to help Ben with his models or his homework.

Sometimes, on an easy day, he stayed up for a half-hour or

so to talk with Barbara, but usually he only nodded as she gave him the news of the day, the progress she was or wasn't making on her book, updates on the kids. Saturday mornings he slept till noon. He tried every Saturday afternoon to plan at least one family activity: a trip to a museum, ice-skating on the pond, a half-decent children's movie. But there was a compulsive making-up-for-lost-time quality to his afternoons with the kids, a little like the divorced fathers he saw at the zoo, stuffing their children with popcorn and intimacy. He loved his kids dearly and cherished his time with them, but he was never quite up to speed on who their friends were or what the hot new video game was, or the significance of the colorful woven bracelets that suddenly sprouted on their wrists. Because he was away so much, and was so tired when he was home, he and Barbara had made few friends in Glen Ridge, although Barbara had found some other lonely writers to lunch with. The weeks spun by, one indistinguishable from another, except by presidential elections, 747 crashes, assassinations, and terrorist attacks.

Small wonder people like Barnard figured it out quickly and dropped their families.

Peter saw Ben waving from the back door and Sarah yelling, probably to alert Barbara. The Labrador, Eugene, was outside dragging one of his rubber toys back and forth in excitement. The big old house looked especially inviting on a bleak winter day. He was glad Barbara had kept the kids home from school to greet him.

He reached down for the bag of toys that Marie had purchased the day before and stashed in the limo—a model sailboat for Ben, multicolored blocks for Sarah. The kids knew the drill: He would pull up in the big car; they would peer inside looking for the toys; he would deny that he had any and hold the bag behind his back. Then they would pummel, tickle, and chase him until he yielded and turned over the booty.

Barbara, who came into the backyard waving, disapproved of his efforts to ease the sting of his absences with goodies. But the kids were already grabbing his arms, and Ben was getting too strong to be pushed back. They snatched the bag and went racing toward the house.

Sarah stopped, rushed back, and leaped into his arms. "Hi, Daddy! Welcome home. We all missed you. Will you play with me this afternoon—"

"Daddy needs a nap," answered Barbara, peeling Sarah off, giving Peter a hug, and picking up his briefcase.

Peter signed the driver's chit, handed it to him along with a $10 bill, and staggered toward the house. A laundry bag with his dirty clothes had arrived earlier and been dispatched to the cleaners by Carmen, the nanny, who yelled hello from the kitchen window and asked if he wanted any lunch.

"Hi, Carm, but no thanks. What I want is sleep."

Arm-in-arm, Peter and Barbara walked into the kitchen. Barbara poured him a glass of milk. She was in her winter writing gear—an oversized blue TANGLEWOOD sweatshirt, jeans, and Reeboks.

"You're so late. Was it because of the meeting? Marie said the whole place was buzzing. I tried to call you on the car phone," she added, "but it was busy. Yakking with Flannery again?"

Peter swallowed some milk. His stomach would be in turmoil for days. "Just trading gossip," he said vaguely.

Eugene lumbered into the kitchen and put his drooling chin in Peter's lap. The dog would accompany Peter upstairs for the long sleep, and remain immobile at the foot of the bed for as long as Peter was there.

"Mom, do I have to go to school now?" Ben bounced in. "There's only one period left. I just want to work on my new model." He looked appealingly to Peter, whom he knew to be a softer touch.

Barbara shook her head. "No, it's too late to go to school. I thought Daddy would be home earlier. Go play with your model. Where's Sarah?"

"She's building a skyscraper with her blocks, and squealing like a little mouse," he said derisively, heading for the playroom.

Peter noticed the pristine white high-tops. "New sneaks?" he yelled at his retreating son, who nodded and kept going.

"Seventy dollars," said Barbara, "and he won't even play basketball in them. He's afraid they'll get dirty."

Peter yawned, and ran his hands over his eyes. The crash had come.

"Who *were* you talking to on the phone?" she asked.

"Flannery," he confirmed. "She says she's spending her

birthday in the bathtub. Of course, she also complains in the same breath that she'll never find a man. Typically, she never connects the fact that she's not going to meet anybody as long as she spends twelve hours a day at work and four more in her tub."

Barbara looked wary. "Why is she telling you about all this?"

Peter shrugged. "We're friends."

"I wonder sometimes if she's really that conflicted about it all. I think she would do something about it if she were," Barbara said, sounding mildly piqued. "So Flannery already knows what happened in the meeting. How about filling me in?"

Even though Barbara was fond of Flannery herself, he could understand why she resented their constant, unguarded talking. It had never been easy for Peter to talk with Barbara about his work. When they'd met, Barbara had been spending weekends at antiwar demonstrations; she'd yet to outgrow her suspicions of big corporations and the people who ran them. She had never worked in any large institution, let alone a capitalist pressure-cooker like USB. In contrast, Flannery had spent her whole work life in television networks; she shared Peter's weird world and she was reliably, even ferociously, discreet. As much as he had enjoyed lunch with Barnard and Adelson, he would never dare to be as candid with them as he routinely was with Flannery.

"Brookings says there's a real takeover threat," Peter began. "It was so unnerving that even without any sleep, I went out to lunch with Adelson and Barnard to talk about it. We all let down our hair a little. I don't know. Brookings looked and sounded grim," he reflected. "I was pretty shaken up, but I felt better after lunch. The winter meetings are coming up in Florida next month. We'll probably learn more then."

Barbara poured them both some more milk. "A year or two ago it would have seemed unimaginable," she said. "Now it almost sounds inevitable. After years of screwing over everybody else, these companies are now eating each other, aren't they?"

"I still don't see a takeover at USB News as inevitable," Peter said soothingly. "And USB isn't like a cereal company, anyway. There are different issues."

Peter wasn't clear in his own mind how the possibility of a

takeover would affect him; they hadn't actually discussed their prospects much at lunch, he realized, just indulged in some generalized pessimism.

"What usually happens, I think, is that new companies want their own management. Whether the housecleaning would reach down to me, I couldn't really say."

"I'm sure I've gotten spoiled, Peter. We have Carmen to help with the kids, and we have this nice spot to live, and I don't have to hold down a job, so I can spend a lot of time on my writing. I might actually get somewhere with this book. So it would seem perversely appropriate about now for the damn company to get taken over."

She said it offhandedly, but Peter almost winced when he thought of the years of writing, rejection, and frustration that had brought her to the point where she might actually pull it all together and do the book she really wanted to write. Losing that would be crushing for her.

He tried to dispel the gloomy notion. "Let's not get ahead of ourselves; it's way too soon to worry. Besides, I want to rest on my laurels. I was happy about the way we covered the *Providence* sinking, and I'm pissed off that I can't bask a little longer."

Barbara laughed. "You can bask in a warm tub and you can commend yourself until you fall asleep. I will return to my literary labors. Welcome home."

In the playroom, Ben had the schooner's parts laid out in a long row on his work table, and Sarah had constructed a block castle in which My Little Ponies reigned benignly. It was a nice scene, Peter thought, watching them for a moment before lumbering upstairs for some sleep. Barbara had already drawn the shades, pulled down the covers, and laid out a fresh pair of pajamas. He would probably sleep till morning. He switched off the bell on his phone, stripped off his rumpled, ripe clothes, and walked into the bathroom, where, like Flannery, he would find soothing warmth and isolation.

He had proven himself again in a major league arena, and he planned to sleep the sleep of the successful and the secure. Even new managements, he told himself, need executive producers who can make tough calls.

*   *   *

Danny D'Amato's taxi was pulling up to his Soho apartment. His plane had barely landed in Lisbon, it seemed, before Brookings had ordered his unit back. D'Amato had been surprised. It was true that the *Providence* story had fizzled quickly once there was no likelihood of conspiracy, but he'd begged Julian McCallister to let the unit stay a few days, just in case.

McCallister had been amazingly, and unprecedentedly, adamant. The SAT cost $12,000 a day in the field without a single picture's being transmitted, and Brookings was on a rampage— the first budget rampage anyone could recall. If nothing was popping, McCallister had said, then head back.

D'Amato and his zombies had managed to shoot a hundred cassettes in the two days they'd actually spent in Portugal. They had rented a chopper and three boats and taken footage of wreckage and washed-up bodies, flying the tape by chartered jet to London, where it was fed to New York in time for USB News to score a major beat on the competition. The crew had even been chased by a Portuguese gunboat at one point, before anyone was sure what had happened. D'Amato thought Brookings was risking a lot, and he told McCallister so. How could he be so sure there wouldn't be some kind of terrorist link uncovered? Wouldn't that mean U.S. retribution? It had always been USB News' creed to be ready for anything. D'Amato couldn't remember being called back from a story when there was even the slightest chance it wasn't over.

But it was not in his nature to seethe or brood. His motto was: if that was what the boss wanted, that was what you did—a philosophy inherited from his father, who had employed that rule as a vendor in South Philadelphia's Italian market for fifty-one years.

D'Amato senior was intensely proud of his only son, who, he told customers, was in charge of disasters for the USB television network. If there was a hurricane or plane crash or bloody riot anywhere in the world, puzzled customers at Trattino's Meats would hear Frankie D'Amato bragging about it.

D'Amato slapped his doorman on the back, went upstairs, and began fumbling with the key. Naughton was already yipping through the door.

"Bobbie, you're here? Hi, sweetie. I thought you'd be at school."

"Even medical students get a break now and then, Pop. I sure didn't expect to see you back so fast. It sounded horrible. I taped all the newscasts on the VCR."

"Whose stuff was best?"

"Oh, you killed them, Dad—you wiped them. NBC had debris, some oil slicks; CBS got some survivors on the carrier. But *nobody* else had bodies floating at the scene. I'll go load up the tapes."

This was a ritual whenever D'Amato got back from an assignment: sitting down and reviewing all the network tapes. Bobbie watched with him now that she was sharing his apartment. If there was a single shot of any worth that USB didn't have, he would explode, cursing the cameraman or producer in his unit who'd missed it. Bobbie was growing well-versed in the details and images of assassinations and crashes.

The Sanity Club was wrong about D'Amato in at least one important respect: Satellites and women were important, but they almost disappeared next to his daughter. Unfortunately, for most of her life he had been someplace far away. Although he never spoke of it, the guilt was often nearly unbearable. He consoled himself with the thought that the work that had separated them would now enable her to become a doctor.

After the divorce, he had agreed that Bobbie should stay with his ex, that she would have a far more stable life there than he could ever provide. Fifteen years later, he was still supporting his former wife in the house in Silver Spring, but his daughter was living with him again, now that she had been accepted at NYU Medical School.

The arrangement had been awkward at first, given all of his "friends," but he had found a roomier place in the same building, with Bobbie's bedroom at the other end of the apartment from his. She had become friendly with some of his regulars, and she had clearly been relieved to find most of them interesting and intelligent.

D'Amato, changing his clothes in the bedroom, made a note to check his emergency kit and replenish the money he had spent chartering boats and helicopters. He also flipped through his address book and dialed a number.

"Is Vicki there? Dan D'Amato calling."

By the time his shirt was off, she was on the line.

"Hi. I didn't expect to hear from you so soon. I've been watching your network. Great stuff."

"Thanks. The unit was sent home earlier than planned. How about coming over later tonight and finishing the night we started?"

"I'd love it. Just put that buzzer away, and keep your dog out of sight. I've still got the bandage on."

D'Amato laughed at the memory. Talk about breaking the mood. He liked Vicki, though he didn't think she would make the steady rotation. Despite his reputation, he didn't enjoy women in their twenties all that much. They weren't formed yet, hadn't done anything. At his age, he thought, all you could talk about was what you had done. At theirs, it was all about what you wanted to do.

He thought he might take Bobbie out for a Thai dinner before Vicki came. He reserved at least one night a week for Bobbie whenever he was in New York.

He put his exercise trampoline down on the floor and jumped on it for ten minutes to strengthen his increasingly rubbery calves. He remembered winking at Peter Herbert one day and telling him that he had purchased a trampoline. He laughed at the thought of that one making the men's room rounds. D'Amato shook his head. Married guys. They needed to think there was a riotous life to be had out there, and he was doing his part for them.

Adelson didn't get home until almost midnight. They'd had a mid-afternoon scare out of Washington suggesting that some kind of mobilization might be in the works, that there was some suspicion about the *Providence* incident. Then there was a late-night panic prompted by the arrest of two Libyan diplomats in Lisbon, which turned out to be unrelated. And he'd had to listen to that asshole Jack Thomas lecture him for fifteen minutes on the division's responsibility to go the extra mile before he'd noticed the reporter from the *Chicago Tribune* standing a few feet away, scribbling. Adelson was still steaming about it when he climbed into bed.

He was completely exhausted now, as the high from the story and the kudos wore off and the implications of the staff meeting set in. His feet and back ached from standing and running down hallways for two days, and his throat was hoarse.

But he would not rest yet.

Over the years it had become Adelson's custom to make love whenever he returned home from a big story and was reunited with Carol. He reasoned that instead of bitching about his absences, she would come to associate big stories with sex.

Accordingly, snuggling behind her and breathing softly into the nape of her neck, he reached with one outstretched finger for the crook of her bent knee. She stirred a bit and started to giggle.

It was shocking that Brookings had recalled the SAT unit, Adelson reflected, now sliding his palm around and lazily traveling up Carol's inner thigh. They had all been amazed—Brookings included—when Grace Viola banged her fist down on the table at yesterday's staff meeting and told them what it cost per day just to send SAT, before it shot a single cassette.

"That can't be," McCallister had objected, but Viola had produced a computer printout.

Adelson had begun to protest that it didn't matter, but Brookings, looking resigned, had held up a hand and silenced him. That was a silence that portended a lot, Adelson thought now as Carol turned toward him with a sleepy greeting and a smile. He smiled back distractedly and went to work on her neck.

For the first time since her arrival in New York, Linda Burns seemed nervous.

"It's just the Waldorf," said Barnard. "Why are you in awe of it?"

"You wouldn't understand," she said. "I watched Guy Lombardo and all the swells every New Year's Eve with my family. Sitting around the TV in Somerville on some freezing-cold night, it looked like the most glamorous spot on earth."

"It was like Times Square for us," Barnard sniffed, holding the door for her. "Nobody in the city would be caught dead here on New Year's; that was for tourists."

The Council on Foreign Relations was meeting at the hotel to hear three former Secretaries of State argue about trade policy. It was another of those functions that journalists used to wait outside of—drinking bad coffee for hours in hopes of a morsel of news—that had now evolved into an event where the media people outweighed and outshone just about everyone else. The paparazzi ignored the former Secretaries and swarmed around the television news personalities. The anchors of all four networks were expected, as were half of the correspondents of *60 Minutes* and *Nightline*, much of the editorial board of *The New Republic*, and various editors from the *Times*, *Time*, and *Newsweek*.

Barnard might have passed on the discussion but for the fact that Julian McCallister was giving a post-meeting bash in his Park Avenue apartment for Jack Thomas, who had just been elected to the Council's board, and for various other luminaries. For years Thomas had declined to serve on the board, feeling it inappropriate for a journalist, but by now he had gathered so much foreign policy experience and had met so many foreign leaders that he was convinced he had an obligation to share his insights.

"It's hard to believe Julian couldn't let someone else give a party for these stiffs." Burns rolled her eyes as waves of well-maintained but grave-looking elderly men and their overdressed wives headed up the escalators.

"Julian?" asked Barnard, also scanning. "Julian would give a party for the F train if it would write something nice about him. Even now ten thousand shrimp are raising their hands and marching off into steam pots."

They affixed their name tags and sauntered over to the bar of the Grand Ballroom, ornate and cavernous and filling rapidly with the kind of wealth and power that only New York City can amass: CEOs and academics, former National Security Council directors and syndicated columnists, ruthless developers and beautiful hangers-on.

Burns spotted him even before Barnard did. "Look, it's David Nab," she said under her breath. "Let's get closer." She had seen Nab's picture the day before in the *Daily News*, which reported that he was buying USB stock and described him as key to the speculation that USB might be a takeover target. Burns herself found it hard to imagine USB's being taken over, but she also saw no reason not to take a look at one of the people who might be trying it. Or perhaps, Barnard kidded her later, she merely had a soft spot for rich men in the market for television networks.

Grabbing Barnard's arm, she sailed through the crowd toward Nab and silver-haired Harold Wallace, whose name she read on his name tag at about the same time he registered hers and Barnard's.

The attorney stepped slightly in front of Nab. "Pleased to meet you. I'm Harold Wallace. Miss Burns I recognize from *TGIF,* naturally, although I must confess I'm not usually home in time to catch it. Mr. Barnard, of course, is the executive producer."

Burns smiled, flattered. "We just thought we'd introduce ourselves," she said, offering her hand to Wallace and smiling warmly.

Barnard was impressed at the several things Wallace had revealed and accomplished in a few words. A lot of people were recognizing Linda these days, but only someone who had a reason to know would bother to keep track of producers. Wallace had done his homework. Second, Wallace was going to determine if Nab was about to be questioned by two journalists or approached socially, and they weren't getting past him until he knew. And finally, he was making sure Nab knew their names and who they were. First-class, thought Barnard.

"May I introduce David Nab," said Wallace, stepping aside.

"*Such* a pleasure to meet you," said Burns, her smile turning brilliant. "I have seen your picture in the paper more than once, Mr. Nab. Just this morning, I was rereading *A Bend in the River,* and the conversation toward its conclusion, as Salim is preparing to flee the village, reminded me of some of the panic at USB News these days."

Wallace looked intrigued. Barnard nearly snorted, recalling that Naipaul's character bore not the slightest resemblance to David Nab, but he quickly collected himself.

"Salim, who was after all a simple businessman, was changing directions, rather like someone going from commerce to communications," she explained airily. "It's so exciting to change oneself, don't you think?"

"Wonderful book. How do you manage time to reread V. S. Naipaul?" asked Wallace, smoothly deflecting Burns.

Barnard interrupted. "I should answer that for you, because Linda is self-conscious about telling people how much she reads. She needs less sleep than mortals do, I guess. She goes through nearly a book a day."

"Phil, please," Burns protested lightly, punching him on the arm in what was now a well-rehearsed ritual. Burns, terrified of being knocked for her lack of hard news experience, was determined to create a new image for herself. It was Barnard who had suggested reading as many books as possible and always having literary quotations handy, ready to toss off. It impressed people, he said, especially if you were a television person, since no one expected you to read at all.

"It's a pity you're acquiring USB stock," Burns was saying, "because I was telling Phil when I read yesterday's story in the *Times* that you'd make a perfect profile for the broadcast. That would obviously be inappropriate now. Still, I would love to hear your views about the trade imbalance, because I expect to be reporting on that one of these days, and while I've read a great deal about it, I understand that you have a unique perspective."

Nab looked surprised that Burns knew anything about him. But he allowed himself to be drawn aside and expressed himself on the subject for more than ten minutes, outlining essentially the same views he had frequently sent to the *Times* op-ed page without success. Burns looked utterly fascinated.

She was surprised and annoyed when the familiar voice and face of Harry Sommers materialized at her elbow. He smiled and offered his hand; Barnard forced himself to smile as well.

Sommers was an institution within an institution; barely a month went by without a glowing piece in some newspaper or magazine on his impressive tenure as executive producer of network television's most respected weekend issues program. He was always well tanned, and with good reason: For twenty years, he had spent almost every weekend of his life with USB's Chairman, in Maine or in Bermuda, on the Chairman's clay courts, or aboard the Chairman's yacht as it cruised the Greek islands.

Sommers winked at Linda Burns and ignored Barnard and Wallace—an arrogant mistake, Barnard thought, catching the flicker in the attorney's eyes. "David," Sommers boomed, surprising them all. "You owe me a tennis match, you son of a bitch. You beat me last time, but I have a new graphite. I will see you on the court at ten A.M. Sunday, you motherfucker." Nab roared as Sommers clapped him on the shoulder and walked away.

"You see," Barnard grumbled to Burns as Wallace and Nab said farewell and moved to their seats. "We're babes at this. We're children. Harry has already got his nose halfway up Nab's ass. That's the difference between the big boys and us."

But Burns remembered reading that Nab eschewed limos, and she tracked him and Wallace down after the question-and-answer period to offer them a ride home in the USB News staff car, a service available to division executives at official functions. Nab seemed particularly interested in the big black Chrysler, equipped with two telephones and a four-pack television monitor system.

Burns took advantage of the ride to grill Nab tirelessly, though certainly not uncritically, about the Japanese position on exports. They all wound up sitting in the car outside Nab's apartment building for half an hour, arguing about the deficit. Burns and Barnard had agreed that it would have seemed excessive to invite Nab to either of their apartments for a drink, but Burns did ask if she might drop by and ask him further questions. Nab said he would be delighted.

Later, at Burns's new apartment in Turtle Bay, she and Barnard compared notes. They had behaved with meticulous correctness and professionalism through the evening, but Barnard felt turned on by the encounter, and he could tell that she did too. She had enormous sexual energy that seemed to blaze most brightly when the stakes were high. He fell onto the sofa with a drink while she lit the pyramid of seasoned logs that the super replaced in her fireplace each morning.

"Did you really go to school with Harold Wallace's son?" she asked, a trifle suspiciously, tracing the crease in his trousers with her forefinger.

"Did you really read all of *A Bend in the River*?" he shot back, making no effort to hide his all-too-visible response. "Yes, we both went to Trinity. That's why people send their children to those places, you know. If you go to the right schools in New York, you meet everybody."

"I didn't go to the right school," said Burns, slipping off his tasseled loafers. "I was selling electroplated gold necklaces for the Home Shopping Channel in Raleigh, remember?"

"Don't play the simple little girl with me," he said. "You blew Nab so full of helium I'm surprised he didn't float home."

He unknotted his tie, tossed it onto an armchair. "You were great, Linda. I honestly don't think I've ever seen anyone look so interested in trade policy. And the Naipaul bullshit, my God. Was *Bend in the River* really the right book for this occasion, though?"

"Of course it was," she purred. "It was a gamble, but I guessed one of them would know about Naipaul. Important but not inaccessible." She offered Barnard her nape and asked him to unclasp her necklace.

He took his time at it, letting his fingers play along her neck. "Meeting Nab seems to have aroused your interest," he observed.

"These people are sharp," she sighed. "Harold Wallace is the sexist man I've seen in a long time. He gives off this intelligence, and he's sort of X-raying you with his eyes, taking in everything and running it all through his mental computer." She turned, flashing the smile that had made him hire her. "Like you, Philip, except you don't have the distinguished gray hair."

She had it all, he thought, every attribute and every move. She was truly intelligent and hardworking, she had the instincts and moves of a coyote, and she was breathtakingly beautiful besides. He considered himself a shark among lumbering prey, but he knew he had only half the drive and electricity she did.

They were feeling successful and attractive, cagey and buoyant, and they made love enthusiastically on the deep-pile carpet.

Barnard tried to rouse her again in the middle of the night, but Burns said no, she had to be ready for the morning. She had to be in Soho at 6:00 A.M. for a brutal one-on-one with her personal trainer.

Barnard reminded himself to call Steve Wallace, Harold's son, in the morning. Invite him to play tennis this weekend, maybe. Burns made a mental note to pick up some books on trade policy. Then they drifted back to sleep.

CHAPTER SEVEN

DAMN
TED
WILLIAMS

*P*eter had responded to the early-morning phone call from his mother in much the same way he responded to news alerts—calmly, quickly, professionally. He blasted himself awake with a cold shower, called the show to say he wouldn't be in, told the network operator where he could be reached, grabbed his overnight bag, kissed Barbara and then the children goodbye.

He bent over Eugene to murmur reassurances that he would be back and to urge the dog to extra vigilance in protecting the family while he was gone. With Eugene, extra vigilance still wasn't a lot, but he wanted to believe that the dog understood. It was a male thing: Only they—the adult males of the household—understood that women and children needed watching.

By 8:00 A.M. he was striding through the automatic doors of

the Yale–New Haven Medical Center's intensive care unit. It was the fourth time in two years; the last one had been almost exactly a year earlier, also in late February, another worried call on another dark morning. The similiarity between his father's heart attacks and breaking news stories was starting to make him uncomfortable; they should feel different.

He was aware once again, walking past the indistinct shapes in the rooms on either side of the hallway, of the dimmed lights, the whirring and sighing machinery all around him, the distasteful feeling that he had covered this story before.

If this had been a news emergency, of course, he would have had lots of company, lots of support—Patricia Flannery's competent and reassuring strength, Adelson's exhortations, flocks of producers and techs and researchers, perhaps Danny D'Amato dispatching the sleek blue trucks of his Special Assignment Team.

But Peter was on his own now, and he felt even more alone as he recognized his father lying unconscious in a cubicle across from the nurses' station, a respirator strapped over his mouth and a heart monitor beeping theatrically at his bedside.

The sight took his breath away, as it always did. He should be steeled to it by now. He thought he had made the mental adjustment to this unsettling time when parents and kids reverse roles, when it was the child who called to check every week, who issued a stream of cautions and warnings about diet and rest and late-night driving.

Frankly—this was what Peter most hated himself for thinking— he didn't need another crisis; he already had his hands full. And he had never been close to the man lying gaunt and wheezing before him. Before the heart trouble, he had never seen Steve Herbert ill.

He wasn't sure he had even seen him asleep; his father was never one to nap, and Peter couldn't recall ever having walked into his parents' bedroom. Standing there in the ICU, he mourned their lack of closeness, helpless as he was to do anything about it.

He turned to the woman sitting at the desk, recognizing her face, though not recalling her name. "I'm Peter Herbert," he said. "How's my father?"

"Oh, Mr. Herbert, there's a call waiting for you. It's been on hold for half an hour; the caller said he'd wait until you arrived. You also got two telegrams from USB News, but perhaps you'll want to take the call first."

The nurse, a large woman with a blond beehive, seemed rattled by all the attention. Peter, bewildered, picked up the telephone.

"Hello?"

"Mr. Herbert?" asked a voice that sounded young and sleepy. "Hold on, please. Hold on for just a minute. . . ."

"Peter? It's D'Amato. Just got back from Lisbon a few days ago. I heard about your dad. How bad is it this time?"

"Dan. Who was that on the phone? How do you even know about my dad?"

"I had one of our kiddie producers keep the line open. Good training for him. I'm at the office working on the follow-up we're doing on the sinking. I was talking to the Foreign Desk, and Rosenthal told me. Anything I can do, I'll do. Just wanted to let you know I'm here."

Peter murmured thanks, for the call and for the great pictures from Portugal, and assured D'Amato that no, there was nothing he needed.

The first of the two wires the nurse handed him read: ROOM RESERVED AT UNIVERSITY TOWERS HOTEL. ASSUME YOU HAVE CAR. NAMES OF NYC HEART SPECIALISTS READY IF NEEDED, AS ALWAYS, BUT YALIES AMONG THE BEST. BROOKS BROTHERS BRANCH NEARBY IF YOU NEED SHIRTS. MARIE SAYS CALL IF YOU NEED CASH. LOVE, FLANNERY.

"The flowers have been pouring in," said the nurse, gesturing toward the adjacent solarium, lined with elaborate bouquets in tall vases. "We don't allow them in patients' rooms, but we save them for when they move downstairs. We always have such beautiful flowers when your father is here."

Peter tore open the envelope and read the second telegram. OUR THOUGHTS ARE WITH YOU AND YOUR FAMILY. YOU HAVE A LOT OF PEOPLE BEHIND YOU. ELLIOTT BROOKINGS AND THE STAFF OF USB NEWS.

Peter, not normally given to corporate sentimentality, felt a wash of gratitude and pride. Brookings had sent him the same note any employee got in similiar circumstances, yet it *was* comforting to know that all those people were standing by. Anything he might require was a phone call away.

Peter turned toward his father and almost collided with the lanky man in a green scrub suit who was also headed into his father's room.

"Dr. Logowitz, how are you?"

The doctor nodded. Peter braced himself for some remark about his show, which the doctor always seemed to have. "Fine, Peter. How's my favorite morning show? How's Don Leeming doing? I think the chemistry between him and some of the other people is a bit off, don't you?" The doctor offered some other observations, which Peter nodded through politely. The man was treating his father; there was no point in brushing him off.

Dr. Logowitz concluded his critique of *Morning in the U.S.* while peering at the heart monitor and reading Steve Herbert's chart. Then he motioned Peter out into an empty room next to the nurses' station.

"Your mother went down to the cafeteria to get some coffee," he told Peter. "Your father's condition is stable and his vital signs are good, given the fact it's his fourth. He's going to make it, I think."

He put his hand on Peter's shoulder. "But recognizing his age and the fact that he's not really strong enough for surgery, it's just a matter of time. The next one, the one after . . ." He paused and shrugged. "But not this time. If there are friends or family who might want to see him, I'll allow one or two."

Peter walked into the room where his father lay, his face obscured by the respirator mask. His father's eyes flicked open and he gasped something unintelligible. Peter put his hand in the old man's and felt a weak squeeze. It was time for the next stage of the ritual.

"Dad," he whispered, "is there anybody you want to see? Do you want to see Billy?" His father nodded. He always wanted to see Billy.

From his wallet, Peter pulled a scrap of paper with two phone numbers—a local cab company's and Billy Hamlin's. For almost eighty years—since before World War I, Peter thought, before there were many cars on the road, before television or fast food or daddies who played with their kids—Billy Hamlin had been his father's best friend. He made the two calls from the nurses' station.

The familiar voice answered on the second ring.

"Billy. It's Peter Herbert. How are you? Listen, my dad's in Yale–New Haven again. Dr. Logowitz says he'll pull through. Cab's on the way, should be there any second. . . . Sure, I know you can get around, but it's no trouble to call a cab. See you soon." He hung up.

He returned to his father's room. His mother, he knew, would appear shortly, although he was never sure how she guessed he'd arrived. She must have arranged for one of the nurses to fetch her from whatever corner of the hospital she was hiding in. The staff and the family all kept up the fiction that she was resting, pacing herself, but the truth was she couldn't bear to sit alone and see her husband hooked up to all those machines. She was terrified that he would die right there in front of her.

When Peter was a kid, he and his father and Billy Hamlin had driven up to Fenway Park once every summer, the two men springing him from school or camp. At the park they jumped up and down, booing or cheering every pitch, stuffing themselves with hot dogs, peanuts, and popcorn. Peter's father, usually so tired and humorless, was, for an afternoon, a man transformed.

Otherwise, Peter remembered the schools and his neighborhood as drab and lonely places. He could not recall an image from his own childhood comparable to Ben and Sarah romping in their huge yard with their friends. Nearby Yale—its polished, assured students and the intellectual life he fantasized they were living—might as well have been in Kansas.

From time to time he would take the bus over to the campus bookstore and, pretending to be a student, buy cheap keychains and ballpoint pens. During the bitter winters when the dark came early, the gracious campus buildings seemed especially inviting. To most of the people in his neighborhood, the university barely existed, but to Peter it was always proof that there was a world beyond.

He was nearly dozing off when his mother came into the room. She hugged him in her affectionate but weary way and sat in the chair next to his, almost disappearing into its pink vinyl cushions.

"What did the doctor tell you? Is he going to be all right?" Like many women of her generation and background, she assumed that a doctor would tell Peter the truth but not entrust it to her, even though she was something of an expert on heart disease by now.

Gertrude Herbert was a daughter of Russian Jews who'd married the son of Irish Catholics; her husband was descended from a long line of city workers who had a choice between the police force or municipal patronage jobs.

It seemed to Peter that both his parents, defeated by fate and circumstance, had long ago grown too tired to break out of their monotonous lives together. His mother, who'd once voiced ambitions about going to college and doing something with her life, battled her fate with occasional bursts of energy, humor, and vitriol. But born a generation or two too soon, she had never really succeeding in changing it. With no real support from her family or her friends, she now lamented her wasted opportunities, working part-time as a secretary in a drapery business while complaining that life was a difficult and hopeless business.

His father, he gathered, once possessed some ambition to rise in government, perhaps even to run for local office. But the rough-and-tumble nature of the city's Democratic politics discouraged him early, and he settled for the predictable and relatively secure life of the low-level career bureaucrat. Or so Peter's mother had told him—his father had never talked about it much.

His father seemed astonished by Peter's career, remarking from time to time that he couldn't imagine how Peter had risen to such an important position—after all, he had never been an athlete or a dazzling student.

Peter's television career had given his mother a much-needed boost within her quarrelsome family, however. She delighted in inviting her sisters Rose and Ida over for coffee on Friday mornings when the *Morning in the U.S.* credits rolled at 8:55 A.M. and Peter's name hung impressively for long seconds at the end.

Now Peter and his mother remained at his father's bedside for what seemed a long time, hypnotized by the monitor's steady beep and the respirator's rhythmic whoosh, Gertrude sitting quiet and spent in the adjacent chair. They had long ago run out of things to say about his father and his illness.

Peter daydreamed about having a father who was a friend, like those of Adelson and D'Amato. What would he be feeling if that were the case? They were always calling their fathers up, asking their advice. D'Amato's father, Frankie, had spent a morning with Peter in the control room a few years ago, bug-eyed at the monitors, the screaming, and all the glitzy technology, but Peter's father hated to come to New York and had never visited USB. And Adelson's father was a twinkly and lecherous old man who traded dirty jokes with his son. Peter was flabbergasted; he would no sooner tell his father a dirty joke than run barefoot through Times Square.

As for advice, his father was the last person he would think to ask. Yet, Peter wondered, wouldn't he miss him when he was gone? He was sure he would, but was that because he would miss having a father more than he would miss this particular person? The notion deflated him even more than the sight of the motionless man in front of him.

He heard from down the hallway the hacking cough that always signaled the imminent arrival of Billy Hamlin, and looked up to see Hamlin's crumpled face. He still had a wave of thick white hair across his forehead, although he had grown increasingly stooped, and he still had his half-smirk. He never said much, especially to women or children.

"Hey, Peter," he said softly. "Hey, Gertrude."

The old man was born one year after Peter's father but on the same street; they had never lived more than half a dozen blocks apart. Peter thought it impossible for someone his own age even to imagine that kind of history. Adelson was the man he felt closest to, he supposed, but how close could you really be to a man who could fire you, and left no doubt that he would if you fucked up badly enough? When he had to confide in someone, he turned to Flannery, if it was about work, or to Barbara, if it concerned anything else. That's what wives were these days, if you were lucky; they were friends and confidantes as well as lovers. At least his father had a genuine best friend—he had to give him that.

Peter stood up and stepped away as Hamlin patted him on the shoulder. Hamlin leaned over the bed until his mouth was almost at his friend's ear and said, loudly enough to startle Peter, "Steve? Steve? It's Billy. Can you hear me?"

Steve Herbert's eyes popped open. He nodded, and Peter was sure he smiled. The two men stared at each other. "Peter's here, Steve. And Gert. Petey's right behind me."

Steve Herbert looked over at his wife and Peter and waved a few fingers weakly. Peter waved back.

There was a long pause as the two old friends looked at each other, the sounds of the gadgetry calling attention to their silence. In Peter's world, both at home and at work, there was no such thing as a long silence; the ones between his father and Billy made him want to jump up and shake them.

It was Peter's father who broke the quiet, slowly lifting his right hand to pull the respirator mask off his face. He gasped and moistened his lips. Peter moved closer.

"Looking good," he thought he heard his father say.

Billy Hamlin said nothing, leaning closer himself.

"Clemens," said his father, distinctly this time.

"Clemens?" Hamlin repeated. "Roger Clemens. He's pitching tonight. Against the Yankees, Steve, against Guidry. This year, if they bring that kid up from Pawtucket, what's his name?"

Peter's father whispered something unintelligible to Peter, but Hamlin nodded and laughed.

His mother looked to the sky outside the window. Peter walked over to take her hand. "Cursing Ted Williams?" he asked, sympathetically. She looked surprised and guilty, as if he had caught her in some shameful act. Perhaps, he thought, it was completely subconscious by now.

It was accidental, her discovery that cursing Ted Williams would wound and shock the men around her as swiftly as a slap in the face. When she wanted to prod her tired or uninterested husband into some sort of action, or punish him for some show of indifference or neglect, she would damn the one person Steve Herbert vowed would be the last on the planet to hit over .400. Peter's father would redden, speechless and enraged. Invoking Ted Williams had evolved into his mother's almost unconscious response to trouble.

Billy turned around and shushed them.

He squeezed Steve Herbert's hand. "You're looking great, Steve. I'll be back in a day or two. Maybe we can get a game on the cable," he said, and turned and walked out of the room.

"Mom," said Peter, "they've given Dad something to make him sleep. He won't be awake for a few hours, the nurse says. Let me drive you home, so you can rest. I've got a hotel room, so I won't be any trouble. I'll pick you up later. We'll have dinner at the hotel, and if Dad is doing as well as Dr. Logowitz expects, I'll go back tomorrow. We've got this conference in Florida coming up that I've got to get ready for."

Gertrude Herbert nodded. She no longer argued about his staying in a hotel when he came to town. He insisted he did it so that she wouldn't have to take care of him, but they both knew it was because he never wanted to spend another night in that pale-green triple-decker with the peeling paint. A few years earlier she would have complained, pushing him to spend some time with his aunts or cousins. But she didn't have the stomach for fighting anymore.

A nurse glided into the room on crepe soles and told Peter's mother there was a telephone call for her. When she returned she was fuming. There was no mistaking, thought Peter, the look and tone that his mother and her family reserved for only one person on earth.

The call had to be from the Unmentionable One. The dread Nate.

"Mom, was it Uncle Nate?" Her eyes flashed. It was one of the few times he had mentioned Nate in more than twenty years, certainly the first time in front of his mother. Simply uttering his name was such a taboo that Peter still felt a rush of fear.

"It was," she spat. "Calling to check on your father. Very sweet. He abandons a wife of thirty years, but he's quick with a quarter, isn't he? I hung up on him," she said contemptuously. "He can save his quarter and his concern."

"Mom, look. Nate didn't abandon Heddy—they separated. And he's taken better care of her than any judge would make him do—"

"What do you know about it? You don't see Heddy. I've watched my sister for years—no friends, no hobbies; she doesn't go out of the house except to shop. What good is a roof if you have no life under it?"

Peter helped her on with her coat. The anger melted from her face, replaced by fatigue. She was not by nature a hater, and the sustained enmity toward Nate had always drained her.

"Where is Nate?" Peter asked. "I owe him, Mom. I'm a journalist because of him. I'd like to see him."

She shrugged. "He's on Commercial Street somewhere," she said listlessly. "I don't know where, exactly. He was too good for a hardware store." She rubbed her temples, then followed him out of the intensive care unit.

She sat in the lobby reading the *Register* while Peter went to a pay phone and dialed his office.

"Peter?" said Marie. "How's your father? Everybody's calling—Adelson, Brookings, Allen. D'Amato has called practically every hour."

"He'll be all right. Tell everybody I'll be back tomorrow if everything goes okay, and I will definitely make the Santo Cristo meeting." Brookings had scheduled the news division's winter conclave for a resort on the west coast of Florida, a place so ritzy, Adelson said, that it had an unlisted number. "Switch me through to Flannery, will you, Marie?"

Flannery popped on the line in seconds, clearly on the trail of some elusive or powerful guest. "Flannery," she snapped. "Whoozis?"

"Ms. Flannery," Peter said, lowering his voice and speaking slowly, "this is Jon Landau getting back to you about your request that Bruce appear on your program. You know we don't give television interviews, but your letter promising to focus discussions on Amnesty International has changed Bruce's position. He will under no circumstances perform, however."

Flannery was silent—suspicious, Peter surmised, but unsure. "This is Jon Landau?" she asked cautiously, doubting that he was but not daring to blow it if he turned out to be.

"Yes," said Peter, "calling from the Tunnel of Love."

Flannery let loose an impressive string of curses. "I knew it wasn't Landau, asshole. No way Springsteen is appearing on a show with ratings as bad as yours."

"Perhaps more of our fellow Americans would share their mornings with us if you would get off your butt and book some truly significant guests, like Cher or Princess Di," Peter replied. "It's not all that helpful that you can deliver on the Under Secretary of State for Arctic Affairs."

"Fuck you, boss. How's your pop? He must be okay or you wouldn't be pulling your usual dumb jokes. What do you want?"

"Patricia, I need a favor. I want to find out what's become of a man named Nathan Brill, here in New Haven. I just need his

address, nothing else. Don't browbeat him or hurt him. And,"
he added as an afterthought, "don't try to book him on the
show, either."

"Any agenda I should know about?"

"He's my uncle, the family pariah. I haven't talked to him in
decades. Probably never will. But in a way, he's responsible for
my being in journalism—"

"Oh, well," said Flannery. "That should get him a plaque at
the Columbia J School at least. Call me back in fifteen minutes."
She hung up.

Peter drove his mother home, agreeing to pick her up in
two hours, when they would have dinner and return to the
hospital. They had both been through this before. When his
father was awake, they would make excruciatingly banal small
talk, as uncomfortable and unpleasant for him as it was for Peter.
Then everyone would pat everyone else's hand and Peter would
give his father a sackful of paperback mysteries to get him
through his ten days in the hospital. Then Peter would go home.

For the first four or five days, everyone at USB News
would ask him how his father was doing. He would call his
mother frequently, and Marie would check with the hospital
several times a day. By the second week, his father would be
feeling better and preparing to go home, and he and his family
would resume their intermittent, dutiful, and bloodless weekly
phone calls. He wouldn't feel the need to check in constantly. He
knew that bad news travels fastest.

On his eighteenth birthday, Peter's father had surprised him by
carting down an enormous cardboard box from the attic and
dumping it in his bedroom.

"Nate's been sending you subscriptions to this stuff for
years," he said. "Your mother and I didn't think it was suitable
reading for a boy. Now that you're eighteen, it's up to you, I
guess."

Peter had been mesmerized by the trove in the box: years'
worth of subscriptions to *I. F. Stone's Weekly,* dozens of clipped
pieces from *The New York Times,* copies of *The Nation,* the
Realist, Ramparts. His uncle, known in the family as Red Nate,
had stunned them all one day by announcing that he was leaving

his wife of thirty years, selling the hardware store, and enrolling at Yale. His name had never been mentioned since.

Peter remembered poring over everything in the box. He had never heard of Stone, the iconoclastic Washington reporter who tirelessly burrowed through documents for stories while most of his colleagues sat at press conferences. But reading his searing reports on corruption and incompetence, Peter had decided that he would be like that; he would be a journalist.

He drove to a pay phone.

Flannery had the address, of course. Nathan Brill, she said, had popped up right away in the computers of USB News Research. Mickey Grodner had found him in a local newspaper profile of the people behind a militant rent control movement fighting to keep some of New Haven's poorer neighborhoods from gentrifying under pressure from Yale teachers, students, and hangers-on.

Flannery read the piece to Peter. It described the seventy-four-year-old leader of the growing movement, a feisty Yale graduate named Nathan Brill. Brill, read Flannery, had organized neighborhoods, delivered truckloads of petitions, and was credited, even by grudging city housing officials, with helping scores of families remain in their homes and neighborhoods.

Damn, thought Peter, he did it.

CHAPTER EIGHT

BLINDED

Watching the smoking rubble and flashing lights live over the monitor from USB's New York City affiliate, Peter fanned through the possibilities: fire, bombing, accidental explosion, building collapse. There seemed to be too many cops in too many gold-trimmed caps for a simple fire.

Peter normally scanned the other networks, not his own local affiliate, but with the *Providence* sinking having fizzled out days ago, he was bored, alert for anything that might end a string of tedious shows.

New Haven was receding, causing both guilt and relief. Events had different perspectives for people like him, people in the news business. It was nothing to fly to the scene of an earthquake or plane crash or tornado and be gone the next morning, forced to purge the images and focus on something else. He had put the takeover prospects aside along with other old news. That he was also able to do this with his father disturbed him, gnawed at him as he watched the monitors in the darkened room.

He kept returning to the notion that his father's heart attacks had come to be too much like stories—islands, events separate from other events, things to be handled, then left behind. Didn't he have an obligation to deal with this strangely distant man clinging to life in New Haven, to confront the fact that he would die soon?

He thought it might be pleasant for his father to get a phone call—Peter had never called him from the control room, or from work at all, for that matter. He called his parents on Sunday mornings, just before the morning conference call that set up the Monday show. He always phoned them fifteen minutes before the conference call so that he had a natural way out of the strained conversations—not that his father fought to keep them going longer.

But before Peter could pick up the phone, his eye caught a tight shot of an angry-looking young woman whose head was swathed in bandages, her face crosshatched with cuts and bruises. She was earnestly answering questions and had the look, he thought, of a person with a cause. Switching the channel selector on his earphones, he cut away from Don Leeming's dogged interview with a panel of grim-looking scientists worrying about the impending doom to be wrought by the Greenhouse Effect, the media's current crisis of choice. In a few months, Peter thought, it would be time for the this-is-the-worst-pollen-count-in-the-history-of-hay-fever story, an annual favorite.

The bandaged woman was a doctor, according to the title now being superimposed over her picture, and she was standing before what remained of a women's medical center in Queens which offered abortions and other gynecological services, primarily to poor women. She had been addressing an abortion-rights group at the clinic the night before, the doctor was saying, when a bomb went off in a planter in the lobby.

The doctor, whose organization operated fifty clinics on the East Coast, had suffered a minor concussion and lacerations. A staff counselor had been badly cut by flying glass. Twelve others had been treated for minor injuries at local hospitals and released.

"Isn't this the fifth bombing at one of your clinics?" asked the reporter, Cindy Kane.

"No, it's the eighth, and you might recall that a security guard at our clinic in Sarasota, Florida, was blinded last spring in a similar incident. And there have been countless other incidents of harassment—bomb threats, sit-ins, picketers blocking our entrances, blood splattered on clinic walls.''

The camera moved to a close-up of a troubled-looking Cindy Kane, who reported that the Associated Press had received a warning call, two or three minutes before the explosion, from a male who said that a bomb had been set and that the clinic should be evacuated. The sanctity of human life was at stake, the caller said. Police, Kane added, believed the device had gone off sooner than intended.

Peter switched back to USB, took off his headset, and stood up. At the research station, Mickey Grodner pulled off her own earphones and threw the switches that readied her computer terminal before Peter could take the four strides to the rear of the control room. She was always the easiest person to spot in the darkened room, because she glowed; her phosphorescent sweatshirt stood out in the dimness, with USB Research's own logo—lightning crossed with a quill pen and, in large letters underneath, FACT-FINDER. Her fingers were poised at the keyboard.

"Mickey," he said, savoring the rush of activity he was about to uncork. "Abortion clinics. Bombings. Harassment. Start last night in Queens, the Women's Care clinic."

She nodded. "When d'you want it?"

"Two hours," he said. "Thanks."

He could practically see Flannery, whose desk was next to Mickey Grodner's, swivel her ears in his direction. She was at Peter's side almost before he was back in his seat.

"I want in on this, Peter."

"Why?" he asked, puzzled. Bookers rarely got involved in reporting stories.

"Because it's a good story, asshole. And I can help. I grew up in Queens; I can get these people to talk to me. I need to get out of here and away from a telephone for a few days, anyway; I can't stand my bathroom or the control room anymore. I'd love to work on a real story. You can favor abortions or not—I can see both points of view. But these fanatics who blow people up and lure pregnant girls to phony clinics—I hate them. I'd love to nail their balls to a pole. Or, put another way, let me work on this story or I'll nail *your* balls to a pole."

"Convincing reasoning," Peter said. "Okay, but no freelance stuff; you have to join the team. Brookings is still steaming about your kidnapping that goddam hostage from CBS. So you have to play by the rules. Deal?"

"Deal."

Thirty minutes later Mickey Grodner tapped him on the shoulder and handed him the first of many manila folders containing a thick stack of computer printouts, along with newspaper clippings sent up from the library and a confidential file from the Investigative Unit.

"Progress, Peter," she said matter-of-factly. "There have actually been thirteen clinic bombings in recent months, and eight or nine of them seem to fit this pattern—small device, not meant to kill, some advance warning. Our Investigative Unit put together a pretty strong file on this when Senator Ponzio got all that flak for encouraging organized attacks against abortion clinics. They suspected Ponzio and his staff of having ties to some of the more extreme anti-abortion types. There are those in Washington, according to a recent article in *The New Republic,* who think the feds aren't trying very hard to nab the bombers because Ponzio is on the Appropriations Committee. The best way to proceed is to do a nationwide computer sweep. That can cost some money, Peter, okay?"

He waved assent. Within minutes, USB Research staffers in each of the news division's fifteen bureaus would all be scanning data banks, transferring computer files by telephone to Mickey's terminal with its high-speed laser printer. Soon, the files would cover his desk.

He was waiting in Adelson's office when Adelson came to work a few hours later that morning. "We've got to talk," Peter announced. "We're jumping on a great story."

Adelson rummaged in his briefcase and offered Peter a jelly doughnut from the waxed bagful he always brought to work with him. Peter couldn't remember ever seeing Adelson take any business files out of the misshapen, scarred leather case, but he had observed that it provided a constant stream of candy bars, potato chips, and pastries.

"Can I take my fucking coat off?" Adelson said. He knew the signs when Peter got cranked up about a story: He grew feverish, obsessed. His enthusiasm was overpowering and sometimes annoying, especially at the start of the day, before Adelson had even had time to scan the press packet of clippings that were examined daily for signs of advancing and declining corporate fortunes.

"It's this latest clinic bombing—you know about it?"

Adelson nodded. "I saw it on local this morning. What's the big deal?"

"It's the eighth bombing of a Women's Care clinic, and in one of them a security guard was blinded for life."

"That doesn't explain your pacing in my office before I even have a chance to have a cup of coffee," said Adelson, reaching into the bag for his cardboard cup. He preferred the doughnut-shop acid to the specially brewed stuff served up by the news division cafeteria.

"Listen, I put four producers on it this morning, plus Flannery, who wanted in on it. The reason is, Research says a group called Sanctity has been linked to at least one of these bombings and is suspected of involvement with several others. Flannery's buddy in the local FBI office says the group has ties to Senator Ponzio and his subcommittee staff."

Adelson groaned. "Joseph Ponzio? Mister Lawsuit?"

Peter nodded. "I saw the bombing on the local affiliate feed this morning. According to the Washington bureau, and to Patricia's law-enforcement source, everybody in Washington knows that this group is behind the bombings, but there's no hard evidence and since Ponzio is on the Appropriations Committee, federal types are not exactly knocking each other over to bring this outfit to justice."

Adelson sipped his coffee and took a substantial chunk out of a jelly doughnut, scattering powdered sugar over the newspaper that Elaine, his secretary, had the foresight to spread across his desk each morning before his arrival.

"So what you're telling me is that the FBI can't track down the bombers but Patricia Flannery and *Morning in the U.S.* can?"

"I'm telling you I have a gut feeling about this one. I think we may be able to connect this Sanctity group to Ponzio. Flannery's source—I don't know who he is—says a member of Ponzio's staff addressed a Sanctity meeting in Queens a few days ago and congratulated them for carrying on the fight against legalized

murder. He also offered Sanctity some Appropriations Committee office supplies and telephones. The agents assigned to the case
are all pissed off because they think the Bureau is dragging its
feet. I'm here to ask you to crank up the Panzers. I want to use
the Investigative Unit in Washington, I want D'Amato and the
Special Assignment Team here, and I want a few hundred thousand dollars for travel and research."

Adelson quickly calculated the bureaucratic procedures and
struggles. What Peter wanted required the involvement and approval not only of Brookings, but of the law and finance departments, the Washington bureau, and the National Desk, which
viewed such intrusions about the same way Americans had viewed
the attack on Pearl Harbor. The infighting quickly grew vicious
whenever bureaucratic lines were crossed.

They were slipping nevertheless into what Adelson called
their story act. Dozens of times in the last few years they'd stood
shoulder to shoulder, Peter pressing a story idea, Sam prodding
and cajoling, oiling the machinery that would permit it to happen. In television, where no one could work alone, each man
required the other. Adelson trusted in Peter's news judgment and
creativity, Peter in his boss's willingness to fight for him and his
ideas up to the limits of what was possible and to crank up
USB's awesome bureaucracy to the limits of what was practical.
If Peter said it was a story, it was. If Adelson said it couldn't be
done, it couldn't.

"So, the payoff," said Adelson, preparing the twenty-word
summary that defined the extent of most network executives'
attention spans, "would be a story saying a member of Ponzio's
staff, or even the good man himself, supported, encouraged, or
contributed to the bombing of abortion clinics and the maiming
of taxpayers. Has a nice ring to it."

He whistled, which Peter took to be a positive sign, but
went on cautiously. "What exactly do you need Investigative and
SAT for?"

Peter looked down at his notes. "Well, I've got my people all
over the East digging into each of the bombings, looking for
common denominators. I need Investigative to mine its federal
sources in Washington and to run checks on Ponzio's staff and
files and expenditures to see if we can match up any Sanctity

names or spot any travel vouchers to New York, substantiate the agent's claim. I'm also sending Flannery into the Sanctity group."

Adelson's eyebrows went up.

"I know, she's not a reporter. But she wants a piece of this story and she grew up in Queens and says she knows how to talk to people who believe Our Lord sends them out to blow up buildings. She says it's important to her. She's going to come in as an anti-abortion activist who wants to get more involved. Yeah, yeah, it stretches our standards about misrepresentation, but she won't lie about her identity; she just won't disclose her real reason for being there. I need twenty-four-hour SAT camera surveillance of the Sanctity office; there's a chance people coming in and out might give us a clue about what they're up to. Flannery's going in with a transmitter, in case there's any violent rhetoric, so I want people outside."

Adelson assumed what Peter called his Miranda warning look. "Look, Peter, I want you to be real careful. The USB standards flatly prohibit misrepresentation, and Brookings views those standards like Jerry Falwell looks at the Bible. They're not just a guide; they're the word of God—you got that?"

Peter nodded.

"Okay, let's make this happen," Adelson said. "Don't dally; we've got three days before finance will start jumping on me. It isn't like the old days. Viola's a tiger. And before we air anything, we'll have to have a war council with Brookings and the whole bunch. I don't want to see anything popping on to the air that hasn't been lawyered and approved by Brookings. *Capisce?*"

Peter nodded again.

"Zeke Christian owes me," Adelson muttered, reaching for the phone. "I got him four extra hiring slots for his precious Investigative Unit and I have yet to collect. You got a ballpark on what this will cost? SAT will need infrared stuff and research will be using computers all over the country."

"I don't know exactly, Sam, maybe a hundred thousand. Tell Viola one hundred thousand. It'll be worth it. We'll cost it out later."

Flannery had worked hard and spent some money to look this frumpy. She was wearing the plainest clothes she could find—a pleated plaid skirt and a button-down white shirt. She had bought a shapeless black coat at an Army-Navy store on lower Broadway; USB News would reimburse her for it. She had startled her stylist, Eddie at Le Snip, by asking him to tease up her hair. The silver cross she usually wore inside her shirts now dangled outside.

Emerging from the subway and checking the address, she walked five chilly blocks through streets lined with row houses with green plastic awnings and spotless front steps. Despite subfreezing weather and waning daylight, the street was filled with kids yelling, tossing balls, and tearing up and down the sidewalks on high-handlebar bikes. If Flannery had looked over her shoulder, she could have seen the towers of midtown, but she didn't want to do that. She wanted to return fully to Queens, and she knew that in order to do that, she had to think of Manhattan as being as far away as the tower-dwellers thought Queens was from them.

She had fantasized for most of her early life about getting out of here, and she had. Now she lived in a bathtub with a headset growing out of one ear. Never in the sorry history of human life, she often thought, had so many struggled so furiously for the right to live in such tiny and expensive places. If she didn't get out to Jersey to see Peter's kids every few weeks, she thought, she might have long ago turned off the bathroom lights, unplugged the phones, and slid beneath the bubbles. Maybe she could book a partner and a life, she thought, by pretending that her loneliness was a hole in the first half-hour of the show.

She found the address, surprised to see SANCTITY in neon in the window of the storefront, tucked between a dry cleaner's and a karate studio. They certainly weren't hiding. Weren't bombers usually a little more discreet? She was shaking, she realized. *I don't particularly like the notion of abortions on demand,* Flannery told herself, *but these people give really religious people a bad name, and I am going to help fix that.* The thought helped her feel better, more heroic. If this worked, she was going to nail Peter for another raise.

She flicked open her new black vinyl purse and unzipped a side compartment. The transmitter was no bigger than a cigarette case and looked just like one, but any sound within fifteen feet would be heard, clear as a bell, in the control room trailer. She squeezed the device in the middle and heard the sharp click that meant it was sending. Behind her, a battered blue van had parked halfway down the block with its parking lights on and its engine running, as if it were making a delivery. She looked to her right, where a small refrigerator truck with a giant crab painted on its side had parked in front of a coffee shop. Make sure both trucks are in place before you go in, D'Amato had said at least a dozen times. She knew the control room trailer, filled with the sophisticated electronic gear the SAT unit used, would be cruising the neighborhood as well, though it was out of sight. The trailer, which had been all over the world, was as well-equipped as most network control rooms, every nut and bolt designed by D'Amato.

She turned toward the blue truck and yodeled softly and quickly, the way she loosened up her voice every morning before she attacked the telephones in the control room. The truck's emergency flashers blinked twice in the dusk; they'd heard her. Taking a deep breath, setting her face in the grim expression she associated with a fanatic, she pushed the buzzer by the door.

The woman who opened it partway was intelligent-looking, heavyset, with closely cropped hair. She wore a thick gray knit sweater and jeans. The room behind her was small, with about twenty folding chairs set up in a semicircle. A giant SANCTITY flag, blue on white, was draped across the front of the room behind a battered old wooden podium. The walls were decorated with posters depicting fetuses in garbage cans and in plastic bags. Along one side of the room, Flannery saw three middle-aged women making calls on phones set up on an aluminum table.

The woman greeting Flannery wore a big cross—four times the size of Flannery's—and a black pin that said, in white letters: THERE IS NO CONSTITUTIONAL RIGHT TO COMMIT MURDER.

"Yes?" the woman said, sounding wary.

Flannery reached out her right hand and pumped furiously. "Patricia Flannery," she said. "I'm here because I want to be a part of what you are doing."

The woman took Flannery in from head to toe. "I have some questions I'll have to ask you," she said, holding the door open. "Would you like some coffee?"

Flannery, walking in, glanced down at the woman's hand. "Can I ask you a personal question? Isn't that ring from St. Francis in Philadelphia?"

"Yes," said the woman, looking surprised. "Did you go there?"

"No," Flannery said. "No, we couldn't afford private school. But I grew up in South Philadelphia, not too far away. Second and Moyamensing?" This was not, of course, true. But knowing about that intersection had once helped her lure an eyewitness to a mob killing on to the program. Flannery worried briefly that she could be nailed later for lying. But the technique usually worked; people seemed more willing to trust people who came from the same place.

"Really," said the woman, flashing a wide smile. "Down near the Italian Market?"

"A few blocks away," said Flannery. "The Market is at Ninth and Washington. I miss the Italian sausages they sold there." Details, thought Flannery; details and homework make all the difference.

"You *do*?" said the woman incredulously. "I thought they were disgusting."

"Well," said Flannery, "it's not a good sign that we start out disagreeing, is it? You must have loved the Mummers, though."

"I *loved* the Mummers," the woman said, relieved. "By the way, I'm Maggie Shawn. How about that coffee?"

"Oh, I brought some," said Flannery, following the woman and holding up her brown paper bag. "I know you have more important things to spend your money on. But I had to walk so far to get here, I really wouldn't mind sitting down for a few minutes, let my toes thaw."

By 9:00 P.M. Flannery had signed up her fifteenth contributor. Brookings, she thought, would be thrilled to know that one of his staffers was raising money for a group that might be bombing clinics. Flannery's tally was higher, Maggie pointed out warmly, than what the three other women, long since gone home, had managed to bring in all day. Sanctity members engaged in just about every anti–abortion activity there was, Maggie explained. They picketed the private homes of physicians who practiced abortions, hoping to shame them before their families and neighbors. They sent photographs of the dismembered unborn to Congress and to judges; they made countless telephone calls to registered voters.

And they had a policy of "disruptions," about which she was vague, other than to say it was aimed at preventing the activities of abortion clinics; for every hour the clinics were out of operation, she said, a life or two was saved. But she was thrilled by Patricia's aggressive fund-raising, which made everything else possible. And in just her first night!

"Each pledge was for more than twenty-five dollars," said Flannery proudly. "And I'll call them back tomorrow, keep them in heat."

"What?"

"Keep them fervent," Flannery amended. "Forgive me, Maggie, but my father worked on a tugboat. My language isn't always what it should be, I'm afraid."

Maggie laughed and pulled up a chair. "Well, this isn't really a place for dainty ladies. Patricia, your phone work is wonderful. I get the feeling you could sign up a hundred people a week if you stuck with us, couldn't you? You seem to be a born salesman."

"Saleswoman," Flannery corrected. She cursed herself silently; she'd grown so used to correcting the assholes at work that she couldn't help it.

"Yes, yes. Patricia, can I bring up something we didn't seem to get to before? It's usually the first question I ask, but somehow we skipped past it. What do you do? Why are you here?"

The question was calculated to be abrupt, and the fact that Maggie's face was five inches from Flannery's was none too subtle either.

Flannery looked down at the phone lists. "Do I have to talk about this?"

Maggie patted her shoulder sympathetically. "Look, Patricia, you came to us for a reason. Everybody knows our reputation; this isn't the League of Women Voters. We're committed to stopping the murder of hundreds of thousands of babies. Some people think of us as fanatics, as extremists, and that's fine with me. If you believe what we believe, to sit still is a crime against God and man. I need to know who you are and how you came to be here."

Flannery, thinking that Dan D'Amato probably had one foot out of the van by now, asked if there were somewhere they might talk privately. Maggie motioned her toward a small office; Flannery shouldered her purse and walked in.

When they'd settled on opposite sides of a plain wooden desk, Flannery put one hand over her small cross and looked Maggie in the eye, a long, cool stare. "When I was twenty-one, I made love to a man I was infatuated with physically," she said. "I became pregnant. I never told him I was pregnant, but I told my brother, who was furious with me and demanded I get an abortion. He said it would kill my father if he knew about the baby, and he might have been right. My brother was a lawyer, older than me, and he had the money. He sent me to Puerto Rico and I had the abortion. I will regret it to my dying day. I have to tell you, Maggie, there are times when I don't see it as murder, quite. And I have real trouble with the idea of middle-aged male priests telling women what to do with their bodies."

She paused in pain. "But each day that goes by, I regret it more and more. I wish she were alive. I wish that I could have given her up for adoption so I could look forward to someday maybe getting to know her. I'm heading toward forty, Maggie, and sometimes I think I'll never have a child of my own. Maybe it's egotistical, but I just know she would have been something special."

She stopped. Maggie nodded. Flannery took out a handkerchief and wiped away the tears that had gathered in her eyes. She wondered what the guys in the truck outside must be thinking, listening to all this. They would probably be grinning, giving her their thumbs-up, saying "That Flannery, she is something else." She doubted it would ever cross their minds that every word was true.

In fact, the crew in the mobile control room did burst into applause when Maggie reached over to hug her and said, "Okay, Patricia. I know when people are lying and when they aren't."

So you see, Mr. Brookings, thought Flannery, I didn't transgress your glorious standards. I didn't misrepresent anything.

The war council gathered four days later in the executive conference room. At 8:55, Rafael Miranda was distributing coffee, fresh fruit juice, and croissants to Sam Adelson, Julian McCallister, Grace Viola from Finance, John Rosen from Legal Affairs, Zeke

Christian of the Washington-based Investigative Unit, the chief of correspondents, the national editor, the head of Research, Buzz Allen of the *Evening News,* Danny D'Amato from the Special Assignment Team, Chester Cunningham of Standards and Practices, plus Peter and a nervous-looking Flannery, who had never before been invited to such a high-powered USB gathering. Staffers rarely saw Brookings or Julian McCallister outside the annual Christmas party, except on those few occasions when they presented themselves in the control room and stood in the back, making everyone nervous.

A small pile of rosy Gulf shrimp, nestled in a silver bowl of ice chips, was stationed in front of Brookings's seat.

Adelson grimaced at the sight. The smell, he thought, was disgusting.

"Have some shrimp, Sam," purred McCallister as Brookings walked briskly into the room. Adelson had managed to hide his loathing for shrimp from Brookings for twenty years, but McCallister had recently gotten wind of it and had taken to offering him shrimp in Brookings's presence.

"By all means, Sam," said Brookings, looking disapprovingly at Adelson's belly, which rose above the table top. "Be good for you."

Adelson smiled sweetly and popped the uppermost shrimp into his mouth. Staring evenly—but, to those who knew him well, murderously—at Julian McCallister, Adelson swallowed it in a gulp and washed it down with an entire cup of coffee.

McCallister slid the bowl toward Adelson. "Have another?" he said smoothly. Adelson deftly stuck a toothpick into the dish of red cocktail sauce and, with the silver bowl shielding him from Brookings's sight, flicked it. A tiny blob of sauce flew past McCallister's startled face and landed on the wall, just below a portrait of the Chairman. Grace Viola struggled to keep from laughing. No one else stirred.

Brookings sat down and scanned the room, his eyes resting curiously on Flannery, who had abandoned her control room combat jeans and running shoes for a more respectable navy suit.

"Welcome, Patricia. Your excellent work is well known to us and we're delighted to have you. Hope your presence here means you've been willing to abide by our few simple rules."

Flannery looked uncomfortable, then nodded several times,

but said nothing until Peter gave her foot a sharp kick underneath the table.

"Thank you, Mr. Brookings. It's a pleasure to be here. This story is an important one, and I was proud to be able to contribute to it."

Brookings nodded toward McCallister and Adelson—his custom at all USB News meetings, fulfilling some protocol unknown to anyone else—then looked expectantly at Peter, who was about to burst with a pride and excitement that he knew would sound corny if he ever tried to explain them.

"Your show, Peter," prodded Adelson.

At Peter's signal, Rafael Miranda hit a wall button and a screen descended from the ceiling. Marie had typed up some pertinent facts selected from the research material Mickey Grodner was still amassing—it now filled four cardboard cartons—and the show's graphics technicians had transferred them to slides. Adelson's Law Number Eight: *Executives love visual aids and are twice as likely to approve projects that use them.*

Peter clicked the first slide into place:

U.S. ABORTION CLINIC INCIDENTS/CURRENT YEAR
BOMBINGS—9
ATTEMPTED BOMBINGS—3
VIOLENT INCIDENTS—12
DEMONSTRATIONS—63

"We're still at the beginning of the year," Peter pointed out. "This is triple the number of incidents at this time last year. And here's the intriguing statistic," he said, clicking to another slide.

INCIDENTS INVOLVING THE 50 WOMEN'S CARE, INC., NONPROFIT WOMEN'S HEALTH CARE FACILITIES:
BOMBINGS—8
ATTEMPTED BOMBINGS—2
VIOLENT INCIDENTS—10
DEMONSTRATIONS—42

He clicked again; a press photograph appeared of the crumpled-over security guard at the Women's Care clinic in Florida, holding his eyes, blood trickling down to his jaw.

"As you can see," Peter said, "the number of incidents involving Women's Care, a chain of clinics that provides low-cost medical services and counseling as well as abortions, is out of proportion to the overall violence. We believe we have connected this violence to the staff of a United States senator, and we have reason to believe the support is more than moral."

Adelson beamed; Brookings looked grave; McCallister, bored. One of the vice-presidents whistled softly.

"Here's what we've got," said Peter. "First, many thanks to Research and the Special Assignment Team and the Investigative Unit, all of which did an extraordinary job under a very tight deadline. Research ran computer checks through its National Information Bank hookup and also ran down hundreds of news reports on these incidents and scores of others, looking for leads and common threads. They—special credit to Mickey Grodner—found that each of these eight bombings took place on a Sunday night in an East Coast city between ten P.M. and midnight. In every case, callers telephoned the closest Associated Press bureau and used the word *sanctity* in the message. This call to the Philadelphia bureau was typical: 'An explosive device is due to go off in the Women's Care clinic in Germantown in fifteen minutes. Please alert the police, as we value the sanctity of human life.'

"Research," Peter continued, "went through the daily papers in each area for the weeks before the bombings and found that an anti-abortion rally was held somewhere in the metropolitan area the Sunday preceding each bombing. In the case of the Philadelphia bombing, it was held in Cherry Hill, New Jersey." He clicked to a news photograph of the rally, showing a tall, thin, dark-haired man raising two clenched fists in the air.

"This man is Jack G. Fox, about whom we'll hear more later. He is on Senator Joseph Ponzio's staff, an assistant research director on the Health and Human Services Subcommittee, which has held frequent hearings on abortion. Fox is passionately opposed to abortion and travels the country speaking to anti-abortion groups, often substituting for Ponzio when the senator is unavailable. Research has definitely placed him, through local tele-

vision tapes or newspaper reports, at six of the eight rallies held
before the bombings.

"I'm going to turn you over to Patricia Flannery for part
two of this. She's normally assigned to guest-getting, but she
was eager to work on this story, and I'm glad she did—"

McCallister's droll murmur rose from across the table. "This
isn't the awards banquet yet, Peter. Just get on with it, please."

Adelson sputtered, and Brookings tapped his pencil against
the table impatiently, like a schoolmaster quelling minor mischief.

Flannery's voice cracked at first, but she told herself to cool
down and pretend she was talking with friends. "Thanks, Peter.
I'll be brief. I spent three evenings at the Sanctity headquarters in
Queens this week. The group is relatively new on the anti-
abortion front, but one of the most active and extreme. I presented myself as a Catholic with intense views on abortion. The
first two nights I licked envelopes and made phone calls, made
some friends and attended a prayer session. The third night
everyone seemed very excited, and although there was some
discussion and some reluctance, I was invited to stay to hear a
speaker. I had already been told that Sanctity was the one anti-
abortion group in America that does more than talk; it acts.

"Everyone seemed very excited when the speaker arrived.
He was Jack Fox. He talked for five or ten minutes about how
many abortions were being performed in the country, and about
how he and Senator Ponzio were determined to do everything
possible to stop the murder of the unborn. Then he said to them:
'And speaking only for myself, I want to say that your recent
actions here have advanced that end considerably. About twenty-
five children a day have been saved by the shutdown of the
Women's Care clinic, and that is a lot of lives.' "

"We have this on tape?" interrupted John Rosen, vice-president
for Legal Affairs.

Flannery nodded. Peter made a note to write a formal commendation for her USB file. He knew she was presenting an
extremely low-key version of her days undercover. She had sat
up all night with Maggie Shawn, drinking wine and talking
politics and sparring about feminism. Peter was sure Flannery
had come to like Shawn, but she wouldn't say either way.

"What did you do then?" Brookings asked.

"Well, his speech was over and he shook hands and headed

out of the building. Peter and Dan D'Amato and I had agreed
that if anything was said linking the group to any of the violence
or connecting it to Ponzio's office, I would immediately confront
whoever had made the remarks and identify myself as a reporter.
So I followed Fox onto the sidewalk. He turned around to smile
at me, and I pulled out a pocket recorder. I also took out my
USB News ID, identified myself, and asked him how a staff
member working for a United States senator could appear to be
condoning bombings and other violence."

Peter got up and slipped a videocassette into the VCR built
into the wall behind him. First the date, then the USB News
logo appeared, then Jack Fox's startled face.

"You're a reporter? Are you saying you're a reporter?" he
was asking incredulously.

Flannery said she was and repeated her question. Fox pushed
the recorder away and ran down the street and into a waiting car,
which sped away. Peter explained that Flannery's appearance
with a tape recorder was a prearranged signal for the SAT unit to
begin "open filming"; one of the three crews that had been
staking out the Sanctity office had jumped out of its van and
videotaped the exchange. It was also a security measure, he
added, since no one was likely to get rough knowing Flannery
was on camera.

Flannery sat down, and Peter continued: "Patricia attempted
to go back inside the office with the crew to hear the Sanctity
members' side of things, but they had watched the scene with
Fox and locked her out." Flannery, listening to Peter's account,
recalled painfully the look of betrayal on Maggie Shawn's face.

"You never identified yourself as a USB News staffer before
the Fox exchange?" asked Chester Cunningham. Flannery said
no, she hadn't. Brookings and McCallister exchanged glances;
John Rosen was scribbling furiously on a legal pad. So was Grace
Viola.

"I'll ask Zeke Christian to pick it up from here," said Peter,
"and I have to say I've rarely seen more impressive work."
Christian looked irritated by what he viewed as gratuitous praise.
A former army intelligence officer, Christian hated reporters; in a
world of professional talkers, he was invariably stone-faced and
unforthcoming. He put his glasses on and, forgoing pleasant-

ries, opened a folder to read from a report visible only to him.

"We began inquiries, as requested by Sam Adelson this Monday. Avoiding the details of how we operate, we were able to review expense vouchers for the Senate Appropriations Committee and the Senate Subcommittee on Health and Human Services. Such vouchers are public information, but normally take up to four weeks to receive; we were able to obtain them by Tuesday.

"We found, among other things, that Mr. Jack Gorman Fox of Cherry Lane, Bethesda, Maryland, has taken more than forty trips in the past fiscal year. Seven were air or train trips to the cities in which Women's Care clinics were bombed, one or two days before the bombings. We have transportation vouchers and hotel receipts."

There was an approving murmur around the table. Everyone at USB News found Christian dour and odd, but his record was impressive. The unit's Denial Wall in Washington was legendary. It displayed scores of fervent disclaimers from congressmen, lobbyists, contractors, and White House officials swearing they had not put that prostitute on a payroll, bribed that Under Secretary of Defense, or taken that pleasure trip at taxpayers' expense. Despite the Denial Wall, which stretched the length of the unit's closely guarded floor in the Washington bureau, the USB News Investigative Unit had never had to retract or correct a story, due in no small part to Christian's fanatic devotion to detail.

"We also obtained Mr. Fox's military record, by the way. He was trained as an ordnance expert at Fort Bragg, North Carolina, before assignment in Vietnam, where he was heavily decorated and served two tours of duty."

Christian turned a page or two, careful to keep the folder at an angle that prevented anyone else from seeing its contents.

"Our Capitol Hill people say this man rarely does any work for the subcommittee itself. He was a Ponzio appointment. They met through an anti-abortion group Fox founded in Malden, Massachusetts, where Ponzio spoke one night. Fox graduated from Holy Cross, with honors. Football. Trained as an accountant, took a mail-order degree in health care to qualify for the committee work, makes forty-three thousand, five hundred dollars a year. Married, with six children, all living at home—"

"Poor bastard," muttered Adelson without a trace of a smile.

Dan D'Amato took his turn and gave a brief description of what the SAT had been able to film. Operating out of the three trucks, they had all Jack Fox's comments on audio tape. They also had photographs of Maggie Shawn and other Sanctity officials coming and going. The new infrared night scope, originally developed for army jungle fighters in Vietnam, had been an expensive addition to SAT's technological arsenal, he said, but one that had already proven itself.

"What about the esteemed senator himself?" asked Brookings.

"He has not traveled to these places, or at least the government hasn't paid for it if he has," Christian responded. "But he and Fox are close friends. They play cards, they swim together twice a week, and if the senator is having a busy day, Fox even drives him to the pool. We have dozens of pictures of them together, everything from lunch to speeches. There's nothing to link Ponzio directly to any of this, other than his connection with Fox, but it's hard to picture Fox blowing his nose without the senator knowing about it."

"In addition," Peter put in, "he recruited and hired Fox. The strong possibility exists that he is encouraging Fox in this activity and supporting it through government funds."

Brookings nodded. "This is all a little circumstantial," he mused. "I'd like to hear how you plan to present this."

In other circles—banking, insurance, manufacturing—an assault on a United States senator as powerful as Joseph Ponzio would have driven even the hardest-nosed CEO to the edge of panic. But no one sitting around this table thought much about it. Brookings was measurably more powerful than just about any United States senator. Forty million people watched USB News every night, and according to survey after survey, most people who watched it believed what they saw. A couple of years earlier Brookings had ordered a thirty-part series on the *Evening News* called "AIDS: The Truth"; the series was credited with educating the country almost overnight about the new plague. Just that afternoon, the Vice President of the United States had invited Brookings to lunch, but Brookings had passed. It would never have crossed Elliott Brookings's mind to be afraid of Joseph Ponzio.

Peter waited for Rafael Miranda to freshen his coffee and took a sip to keep his throat lubricated. It would not do to go hoarse now.

He took out a red folder. "First, we need to emphasize that we cannot air a story claiming that Senator Ponzio or members of his staff bombed abortion clinics. We recognize that."

John Rosen expelled a rush of air considerably louder than he could possibly have intended, causing chuckles around the table.

"That," said Adelson, "was the best sigh I've ever heard."

Peter smiled, always grateful to Adelson for easing his tension. Brookings might not be nervous about pissing off a senator, but Peter was scared to death. If the story was wrong, he would spend the rest of his career in the basement ordering satellite time.

"The story, which I want to air tomorrow, would simply say what we know.

"One, that a chain of nonprofit women's health clinics has been singled out for a disproportionate share of violence, including bombings.

"Two, that an anti-abortion group called Sanctity held rallies that preceded each and every one of the bombings.

"Three, that an aide to Senator Joseph Ponzio made remarks to volunteers at Sanctity headquarters in Queens that appeared to condone and approve of the most recent bombing of a Women's Care clinic.

"Four, that this aide and Senator Ponzio are extremely close personally and politically.

"Five, that this same aide, whom we will of course name, addressed rallies before at least six of the bombings, and used public money to do so—don't overlook that; that will get the General Accounting Office off and running."

Peter looked across the room. "I don't propose to speculate or draw conclusions. I propose to lay out what we know. I think this advances the story tremendously. I think it will get the FBI off its butt; I think it leaves viewers free to draw the clear conclusion that an aide to a United States senator condones bombing, and I would be proud to air it on *Morning in the U.S.*"

Peter sat down, drained but pleased. He looked over at Adelson, expecting to see the wink that signaled "great job" but seeing instead a warning frown that meant there could be a squabble brewing.

Brookings speared the fattest of the shrimp in the silver bowl set before him, and put it on his plate. Taking a knife, he sliced it into three more-manageable pieces and chewed meditatively. Miranda appeared over his shoulder with freshly brewed tea. Knowing that the shrimp was a stall to give Brookings time to mull the story, all the others used the pause to refill their coffee mugs, butter their croissants, and gird themselves for their coming stands, all of which were pretty predictable and none of which usually mattered much except for Brookings's and Adelson's. And McCallister's, on the rare occasions he felt like taking one.

Brookings nodded to McCallister, who, as his number two, had the right of first reply.

"Interesting story," McCallister said heartily. "I'm proud of you for getting it. Special congratulations to Patricia Flannery, the people in Research, and the Investigative Unit.

"There are, however, some problems," McCallister went on smoothly. "First and most seriously, I am concerned that Ms. Flannery has violated our Standards and Practices. Second, I want to make absolutely certain that we are not airing a piece that implies that a United States senator—even one who is personally repugnant to me—condones violence on the basis of brilliantly gathered but nevertheless circumstantial evidence." That said, the meeting had violated McCallister's attention span. He immediately began doodling on his note pad.

Brookings turned to Cunningham, possibly out of fear he would implode if he didn't have the opportunity to speak. "Chester? Stay calm and tell us why this is a bad idea."

Cunningham took a deep breath and sipped from a glass of orange juice. "Sir, the standards have guided USB News through forty years of unparalleled prestige and respect. They are quite clear. 'No employee of USB News shall misrepresent his purpose or position for any reason. Failure to follow this standard will result in immediate dismissal.' Elliott, I consider that the most important regulation we have, next to the one forbidding bribery. If we make this exception, producers will be lining up outside your door seeking permission to claim they are anything but what they are. These standards are not stuffy old rules; they are the journalistic soul of USB News. I can't imagine any circumstance that would justify their suspension."

Adelson interrupted. "Chester, you've left out the regulation on page two hundred which allows for the president of the news division to grant exemptions from the standards under extraordinary circumstances. Flannery couldn't walk in there and say, 'Hello folks, I'm from USB News. Are you blowing up abortion clinics?' Investigative reporting has always called for unusual methods and it yields unusual results.

"One of these days these people are going to kill somebody, and we might be able to stop it—that's what's at stake here. Patricia didn't lie about who she was; she just didn't volunteer to tell them the whole truth. She told them her reservations about abortion, and she's skillful enough to avoid the truth without violating it. Talking about regulations, I'm remembering some called the Bill of Rights, which are supposed to allow people to disagree with one another without being blinded."

Peter looked away from Adelson, lest one of them laugh. The last time Peter remembered Adelson citing the Bill of Rights was when he accused the Finance Department of thwarting the First Amendment by attempting to monitor the Political Desk's travel expenditures.

Brookings opened up the discussion. John Rosen, seeing caution as the lawyer's role, customarily argued against anything that might land USB News in court, although once a decision was made to air such a story, he would defend it ferociously. He was opposed in principle to this story, he announced, because it involved a number of sticky legal problems. By violating its own standards, USB News was leaving itself open to the charge that it had behaved recklessly and irresponsibly.

Second, there was the invasion-of-privacy issue. It was unclear whether the people in this group were public figures—harder to libel under the law—or private citizens meeting about an issue of common concern.

Then there was the question of entrapment. Sending Flannery into the field under false pretenses might make the company appear to be instigating violence in order to get a story, especially if Flannery had spoken—he was certain she hadn't meant to—against abortion in an inflammatory manner in an effort to win the activists' trust.

Then, too, the danger of libel had to be considered. Senator Ponzio had sued newspapers before and had threatened USB News with lawsuits about a dozen times. Suggesting that he—or anyone associated with him—was connected with maiming or injuring people or planting bombs was troublesome. Wasn't this a law enforcement issue best left to the police and the FBI? Wasn't USB News the wrong institution to infiltrate and expose an extremist group prone to violence?

Finally, Rosen argued, shouldn't USB News bring its suspicions to the police? Wasn't it morally obligated to do so? USB could be open to lawsuits by anyone injured in the future if it became known that USB News had learned something about these crimes and hadn't gone to the authorities.

Peter watched as Brookings made notes on his pad. Rosen had clout; he was thoughtful and articulate, and Peter felt he had scored some compelling points. Whenever anyone argued that USB News's sacred reputation might be tarnished, there was trouble with Brookings.

Grace Viola came next; her comments were to become the talk of USB's hallways for several days.

"I don't want to overstep my bounds," she said, "but I came to USB News to be part of decisions like this, and I appreciate the opportunity. I think this is a terrific story, and I hope it is aired. I for one would not like to wake up one morning and read of another clinic bombing, knowing that USB News could have stopped it and didn't. John, I am not a lawyer but I strongly disagree with you. Peter proposes to lay out some startling facts and let viewers make up their own minds, which I thought was the way it was supposed to work. Nor do I buy your argument about leaving it to the authorities. We all know—especially those of us who are female—that this isn't an issue that keeps the Justice Department awake nights. If people had been bombing New York department stores or government buildings for this long, you can bet there would be plenty of FBI agents on their heels. So not being a journalist or a lawyer, and recognizing that, I hope you run the story and congratulate you on getting it."

Peter blinked. Adelson seemed flabbergasted, and even

McCallister looked up from his doodling. No finance officer had ever commented on a news story. The money-changers might be allowed into the temple, but they weren't supposed to conduct services.

"However," Viola went on as Brookings opened his mouth to respond, "there is something about this story that does bother me, and I am going to be frank about it. When this story was approved, Peter, you told Sam that you estimated it would cost one hundred thousand dollars, and he passed that estimate on to me. As far as I can tell from my auditors, that budget was based on a wing and a prayer, and I am here to tell you that the figure is bullshit."

The head of Research gasped.

"Pardon my language," said Viola hastily. "But there is a principle here that is just as important as editorial integrity, and that's budgetary integrity. You all know that the stock is in play. There are rumors all over Wall Street. I don't know if they're true, but I do know the word out there is that this company can't manage its spending and that the news division is the worst offender. Elliott, when you asked me to come here, you told me there were sea changes coming and that part of my challenge was to make the division understand them. This is as good an opportunity as I'll get. Peter, please understand that you are just one example and I have no desire to single you out or embarrass you. But this isn't a one-hundred-thousand-dollar story. It's a two-hundred-thousand dollar story.

"Anyone who'd taken the trouble to cost out this effort would have learned that in computer time alone, Research spent forty thousand dollars in two days. Three camera crews on stake-out, using infrared nightscopes in vans for three days, will come to almost thirty-five thousand. Four of Peter's producers, each of them flying to a different city, staying in hotels, assigning crews to shoot bombed-out clinics and talk with clinic officials—that will easily run to thirty thousand. And the Investigative Unit—I am not allowed to know all the details, I gather—copied thousands of dollars' worth of federal documents in two days. And I'm not including manpower and shooting costs and staff time, telephones, et cetera. It isn't up to me to say whether it's worth it or not; that's up to all of you. But when you submit an estimate, it matters that it be real. Otherwise, we're not going to have good answers to the questions more and more people are going to be asking us."

Peter squirmed; the people around the table sat frozen. A finance person directly involving herself in editorial policy? Brookings had never tolerated that. And she had again challenged an executive producer directly, in public. Wasn't it also an implicit rebuke to Brookings, this suggestion that USB News had better clean up its act?

Who cared what people said on Wall Street? Who cared what people said anywhere? USB was making plenty of money. You spent what you had to spend to do the story better than anybody else—that was the creed. No one wasted time adding up the cost before the chase. What you did was tally it up once it was all over.

Rafael Miranda passed quietly around the table, placing fresh ice cubes in everybody's water glass. Usually at moments like this, Adelson cracked a joke. This time, if there was to be any response, it had to come from Brookings, who sipped his tea and cleared his throat.

"I know you're all shocked. You needed to be. I'd planned to raise these concerns in greater detail at the winter meetings in Santo Cristo shortly, but this is as good a time as any. Grace is operating under a clear mandate from me to help pull us into the 1990s. She is raising issues we have not had to face for forty years. You all read the papers; you know we have to face them. I love this institution and I know the rest of you do too. That's our motive for looking at things differently. Budgets matter now."

Brookings had to know—perhaps he had even worked it out in advance—that word of this exchange would tear through the news division within minutes after the meeting's end. Adelson, for one, had no doubt that Viola's speech was heartfelt but prearranged, meant to send a message. You did not embarrass Brookings and survive.

Brookings continued, like a Supreme Court justice announcing his ruling. "I take our standards seriously, as you all know. Like John, I am concerned that we came too close to skirting them here. At the same time, and as the standards themselves allow, there are times when every rule must be considered individually and in its own context. I take Ms. Flannery at her word when she says she did not violate the standards by claiming to be something she wasn't. She, instead, failed to disclose exactly what she was. The result is that through her courage, and the Investigative Unit's superb follow-up, we have linked a United States senator to a group which has advocated violence in preventing abortions and which, at the very least, applauds the use of bombs. This is appalling, a gross misuse of public funds and congressional power. This is an important story; we must air it tomorrow. John Rosen needs to lawyer it, and I would like to see the script, as I am sure Julian and Sam will."

Brookings nodded and exited, prompting a noticeable release of breath around the table. Flannery darted from the room—a trapped bird who'd suddenly found an open window. Viola walked around the table to Peter, where she was quickly joined by Adelson.

"Peter," she began apologetically.

"It's okay," he said. "The point is well taken. We never had to do it before, that's all. You might have castigated me privately, though."

"But I had to make the point to everyone else too. You have to understand that at most companies, you bust your budget by more than fifty percent and you're out."

"Be a big boy, Peter," Adelson said. "Grace was just waiting for an example, and you waltzed in. Could have been anyone. Now how about if this graduate ethics class comes to an end? We need to get Leeming to do the voice-over before Brookings and all these fucking people go home, right?"

"Right," said Peter, offering a conciliatory hand to Viola and smiling. "It won't happen again, Grace. But I don't think people will be lining up to take you to lunch in the next few weeks."

"I will take you to lunch today," Adelson gallantly offered. "We'll cab up to Nathan's. I know the maitre d'. He can get me a table and be sure I get extra crispy fries. It'll wash away the lingering taste of shrimp."

The story, broadcast the following morning, was nine minutes long. In order to ensure impartiality, the reaction to the story was turned over to another broadcast, the *Evening News*. So it was Buzz Allen who called to tell Peter that the Senate Ethics Committee was scheduling an inquiry and the U.S. Attorney was investigating to see whether public funds had been spent illegally. By nightfall, the New York City police had raided the homes of six Sanctity members, including Maggie Shawn. The next day, agents dug up the floor of an abandoned Queens warehouse; USB's New York affiliate reported that they found large quantities of materials used in making explosive devices.

The night the story aired, Zeke Christian called Peter at home to say that the FBI had assigned a dozen additional agents to the clinic bombings, and that the director of the Bureau was personally reviewing their progress. Meanwhile, the GAO was checking into congressional travel expenditures.

"Peter," Christian said in a rare display of enthusiasm, "we've got a great headline from the New York *Post;* it's already up on the Denial Wall. It says 'Ponzio Bombed on TV: Zaps Aide.' "

CHAPTER NINE

LONDON

*L*inda Burns was irritated that Philip Barnard was so slow to get up. He must know she had been up half the night, stewing over the profile of her in *Television* magazine, the industry bible, about to go on sale that morning at the newsstand downstairs. That was the major reason she had agreed to stay at his uptown apartment—so he could go out and buy the magazine for her, unobserved. In her own downtown neighborhood he might be seen by someone from USB.

Madison Avenue was humming. Buses, cars, and taxis deposited teenage girls in spring garb—moccasins, white socks, and short skirts—in front of their private school, and the black limos were already lined up outside the funeral home across the street. Burns looked over the funeral crowd, pegged them as gangsters. She dismissed the young girls as twits, the kind she had naturally despised when she was growing up in Somerville, Massachusetts—not that she saw much of them.

The memory gave this morning special meaning. This was the day Linda Burns, queen of the Raleigh cable shopping channel, would be officially left behind, and Linda Burns, serious television journalist and potential superstar, would be born.

"Phil," she grumbled. "Get up, will you? Go see if the magazine has come yet. I can't go out like this—somebody will see me."

Television people worked for years to reach make-or-break moments like this. This was why she hadn't married, wouldn't dream of having kids, exercised ten hours a week, nourished herself on the same stuff hamsters ate, and had staggered home exhausted every night for years. Today she would know if it had all been worth it.

The least her executive producer and lover of the moment could do was remember. God knows they had talked about the article enough. It had almost become a superstitious reflex, her worrying that she would be trashed, that her lightweight past would be dredged up and her momentum stalled. Granting this interview to *Television* entailed considerable risk; if it backfired, she didn't know what she would do.

Barnard and her agent, Marty Hoffman, had orchestrated the interview, and both had reassured her so many times she couldn't hear them anymore. Her fear was something they could appreciate only intellectually. They wouldn't have to go back to a cable channel, no matter what happened to them. For her—for other women, too—the hold on success seemed much more tenuous.

So she had left nothing to chance. She'd had lunch and dinner with the reporter. Phil had taken him to a Knicks game, a movie screening, and to Aurora for lunch, and Marty Hoffman wouldn't even tell her what *he* had done. If Don Kristed trashed her after all that, Phil assured her, he was a singular reporter. Even so, she took nothing for granted.

She had been superb during the interviews with Kristed, she constantly reminded herself. She had quoted from *Foreign Affairs Quarterly* at least twice, from Henry James and *The Washington Monthly*. She worried that she had overdone it, but Hoffman, who had been stroking reporters for thirty years, said you couldn't overdo it.

She was proudest of the point—just after the veal piccata and before the sorbet—when she had leaned back, eyed Kristed coolly, and astonished him by saying, "Dammit, Kristed, if we're going

to be friends—and I feel in some ways closer to you than anybody I've met since college, no matter *what* you write about me,
and I mean that—I want to ask you a question. And if I don't get
an honest answer, I'm going to get up and walk out of this
restaurant."

Kristed had been taking in the stares of the tourists and
hotshots at the other tables, fantasizing for a moment or two that
people thought he and Burns were a couple. Despite his having
seen forty a few years ago, and despite his fleeing hairline and
swelling belly, he had cultivated an intellectual sort of look that
he thought worked well here at the Café des Artistes. True, in
one hour he had to be at Grand Central to catch his train to
Yonkers, which was certainly not where Burns or most of these
other people would be heading. But the people watching didn't
know that, did they?

Now, puzzled, Kristed put down his spoon.

"What is it you want to ask?" he said, pushing his notebook
aside as if to signal that she had his full attention.

She bit her lower lip, seeming to agonize about whether or
not to proceed, and then she shook off the indecision. "Have you
ever thought about doing television? There, I've asked it. I've
asked it straight out." She leaned back and crossed her arms.

Kristed's eyes widened and his face reddened. "You mean—
What do you mean? *My* working in television?"

Burns leaned forward, concerned. "I didn't mean to make
you uncomfortable or put you in an awkward position. Forget it.
It was a thoughtless thing to do. I'm sorry I raised it."

Kristed, fiddling with his napkin, demurred. "No, Linda.
No, hell, I'm asking you enough questions—you have the right
to ask me some. It's just that I'm surprised. No one has ever
asked me that before, at least not that directly. You're probably
joking, aren't you?"

Burns looked uncomfortable. "I'm so sorry. Marty will kill
me for this, for risking ticking you off like this when we were in
the middle of an interview. It's typical that I feel I have to ask the
tough question, no matter what; it's become second nature to
me, even when it isn't politic—"

Kristed shook his hand, looking slightly anguished. "Look,
Linda, no, it isn't an insulting question. Hell, I'm flattered. I take
it as a compliment. Why would I be offended?"

Burns signaled the waiter for more wine. She was a twice-a-week regular; he knew her hand signals. The staff at restaurants like this one had sound instincts about who was going to be a superstar and who wasn't, and they were going with her.

"Because I know newspaper people find television offensive at times, find its values disturbing, as do many of us who work there," she said haltingly. "I envy so much your freedom, your use of language, the fact that your looks don't matter—"

She threw both her hands up over her face. "I'm sorry, Don. That wasn't what I meant to say. Here I go again. I don't think I'll *ever* be able to be as glib as you need to be to make it in television. Of course, I didn't mean to say you weren't good-looking enough to make it on television, although you'd better stop that hairline."

They were both laughing now, warmed by candor and, well, intimacy would not be too strong a word, he thought, although he had been around stars long enough not to have his head turned. But Kristed did not want to lose the intriguing thread of the conversation.

"Linda, you are frank, but that's a refreshing quality in your business. You wouldn't believe how many people try to outslick me—"

"I would believe it, Don. I work with those people!"

"Of course you do. Look, I know I'm not pretty. The question about television is intriguing, though. Others have hinted at it—Julian McCallister, Jack Thomas. It's funny, when we were at the Knicks game last week—McCallister and Phil and I—Phil asked if I had ever thought of doing commentary or media criticism on television. And I said sure, I had to be honest about it, it had occurred to me. I certainly know about the media, about television, why not? But McCallister said that Phil shouldn't put me in that position, that it would seem like a bribe. Then, he put me on notice that if he ever became president of USB News, it would be one of the first things he would try to do."

Burns looked troubled. She pushed her long chestnut hair back from her face and fixed her blue eyes on Kristed's.

"They said that?"

"Yes, and now that you mention it, your agent, the all-knowing Hoffman, has been badgering me for five years to let him represent me in putting together a deal like that. He thinks I'm a natural for television, honest, direct, lots of opinions." Kristed paused. He had never added it all up before, but when he did, it didn't seem all that implausible.

"Can I be honest with you, Don?"

"Why not, Linda? Why break a tradition?"

"Don't do it."

"No?"

"No, don't do it. It would be a big mistake. You don't have the delivery for television. You're a word person, somebody who uses the language. Television would destroy that. Phil's my boss—so is Julian—and Marty is practically my father, but they're trying to kiss your ass and you know it. Even though I'm not yet thirty-five, I've seen that scam often enough to know somebody like you can't be bought that way. What was it Keats wrote in one of his poems? 'You know my face, you know my heart, you know the winds that take the soul and turn it to a barren space.' I *think* that was Keats."

Kristed nodded. He was not into poetry, and Linda could be intimidating, the way she always seemed to have some gem at the tip of her tongue. He would have to remember the Keats reference for the story. Also the anecdote Barnard had whispered— swearing him to secrecy about the source—about her singing arias from obscure French operas in editing rooms late at night.

The waiter refilled Kristed's glass for the third time. Burns was drinking mineral water, as always. Kristed looked down at the table and moved his dogeared spiral notebook back in front of him. He took a sip of wine and smiled.

"I appreciate that kind of honesty," he said. "I also know you're right. I am savvy enough to know when I'm being handled—I think those guys know it too."

Burns nodded her head. "They do. That's why so many people warned me not to do this interview."

Kristed's head came up fast. "With me? Who warned you not to do it? Barnard? McCallister? They'd better not have. I don't do cheap shots, and they know it."

Burns smiled. There would be no fussing over the check. The dinner would simply go on USB's bill, unless Kristed made a stink about it, like those tiresome reporters from the *Times* and *The Washington Post*.

When she got back to her apartment, she would leaf through some of her classics for the right witty quote or line of poetry and send it to Kristed's house the next day.

She had enjoyed the dinner. She even liked Kristed. He was going to be an historic influence in her life—the person who buried the Home Shopping Queen for good. She smiled at him and allowed herself a deep, sweet, long breath. It was harder than it looked; these guys were not dumb, despite the frequency with which they were hustled. One misstep could kill you, but she had not made a single one.

Barnard pulled on a pair of Egyptian-cotton khakis and a white shirt. He skipped the handkerchief, even the hand-loomed sweater, and trundled down to the corner newsstand. Barnard was not into the macho news culture; he thought long hours were for immigrants and idiots, and he loathed getting up early.

"It's here, Mr. Barnard," said the Korean woman from behind the counter. "*Television* is here, and I've saved your ten copies."

"Thanks, Mrs. Kim," said Barnard, for good measure picking up *Time, Newsweek,* the *Times, USA Today, New York* magazine, *Vanity Fair,* and *Esquire,* along with a small bottle of Scope.

"Lot of time to read, Mr. Barnard?" she asked cheerfully.

"Yeah, back to London this afternoon," he said. The woman smiled, and slipped him an extra issue.

"That's a beautiful picture of Miss Burns," she said. "Please tell her for me." Barnard smiled, hiding his surprise. Linda had been to his apartment no more than half a dozen times. But he didn't care if it got out; it couldn't do his reputation any harm. He just hoped the goddam article was all right. Otherwise the next four days with Linda in London would be pure hell.

He waited until he was back in the lobby of his apartment house before taking a good look at the cover of *Television.* There, head thrown back, hair in lovely, stylized disarray, was Linda Burns, her bright teeth in a smile that could melt rocks, her flawless skin set off against a pale-blue backdrop. She was truly beautiful, he thought—something she often said about him. Barnard accepted that he was handsome. He was also conscious of his position; ever since he had been named executive producer of *TGIF,* women seemed to have found him just a little more attractive.

He scanned the cover and, off to the right, saw the line that guaranteed a happy trip: LINDA BURNS: SHE'S GOT A TICKET TO RIDE—ALL THE WAY TO SUPERSTARDOM, *by Don Kristed.* He smiled, leafing through the magazine until he came to a dazzling ten-page spread that included a full-page picture, in sharp color, of Linda running up to the Vice President of the United States with microphone outstretched, looking as if she would tackle him if necessary. The caption on the opposite page, in bold oversized type, read: LINDA BURNS, USB'S NEW SUPER-STAR, DOGGING THE VICE PRESIDENT IN WASHINGTON LAST MONTH. HER TOUGH, INTELLIGENT INTERVIEWS AND NOW-LEGEN-DARY PREPARATION ARE THE TALK OF THE INDUSTRY—AND THE COUNTRY.

He leafed back to the beginning of the spread. There was a picture of her in her network office, the darkened newsroom behind her. On her desk was a pile of books, the only visible one a collection of short stories by Peter Taylor. Her glasses were pushed up on her forehead as she stared at five inches of briefing papers. The headline, spread across two pages, read MEET LINDA BURNS, USB'S BRAINY POWERHOUSE—AND ANCHOR SOMEDAY?

Barnard ran out onto the street and looked up to his ninth-floor bedroom window. He couldn't tell if she was watching or not, but he gave the thumbs-up sign and went back upstairs. He was happy for her. Among television people, Barnard included, success didn't count until they read about it. From now on, reporters profiling Linda Burns would have to go no further than Don Kristed's piece, and they wouldn't.

He didn't even want to think about Jack Thomas's reaction. Young correspondents who got press like that tended to have serious trouble getting airtime on the *Evening News* and invaria-bly ran into contract problems. But Burns was truly star mate-rial, maybe even beyond the paranoid Thomas's power to hurt her. Barnard felt some sadness, too: Her new status would inevi-tably end their affair—so obviously that nothing even needed to be said. She would grow past him, need someone considerably more powerful and connected. He was quite pleased with his own success, but Burns was moving into a new realm, a track too fast even for him—weekends in Aspen, dinner parties in Georgetown, flirtations in Paris.

Barnard enjoyed Burns's company, more than he had expected to. She was very much like him, ambitious, witty, and sharp. He knew that within a year she would probably turn into a monster, a metamorphosis seemingly unavoidable among television superstars. She would leave his show behind shortly, and she would inevitably move up a notch in men too.

Barnard briefly considered leaking word of their relationship to one of the TV gossip columnists before it ended. But he rejected the idea. He didn't want to exploit their relationship.

Still, none of this would spoil their trip to London; she wouldn't turn weird for at least a month or two, after it had all sunk in. He felt a slight twinge of anxiety about London, in view of Adelson's warning. He knew the new theme music for his show wouldn't be ready. But he could always tell Adelson he had rejected the latest offering and sent the musicians back to square one. Burns could just as easily be doing her now-legendary research on Margaret Thatcher, who was coming to Washington in six months, in the USB library. But Barnard doubted anybody would question her, not after this valentine in *Television*. Let Grace Viola make another scene and she would be counting paper clips in the Jacksonville affiliate.

It was killing Linda that she hadn't yet read the magazine. Despite her impatience, she was at first too nervous to read it in the apartment, then too carsick to read it in the cab that bounced up the East Side from one pothole to another. She could hardly savor it on the flight, at least not until the overhead lights were turned off, lest some jerk call up the New York *Post* once the plane landed. If Phil's synopsis of the piece was accurate, though, it had all worked, the research, the short story collections left lying around, the anecdotes about poetry and opera. Barnard kidded her that she was deliberately postponing reading the piece so that she could savor it all the more.

She was grateful to Phil; he had gone way beyond what was required. He and Hoffman had managed her conversion from the self-conscious newcomer with the awful hair to a powerful television presence with just the right image for the '90s—hip and smart and sexy and serious. Now it was hers to blow with some stupid mistake, which she swore not to make.

She promised herself she would be one of the few people in the business who never forgot her friends. Most successful TV people had one person in the world, maximum, that they trusted absolutely, and that person was usually outside the industry. Friendships were hardly possible, not in the way she intended.

Still, it would be wise to be careful about being seen with Phil in London or, after this trip, anywhere else. He was charming enough, but she could no longer be involved with her own executive producer; that would look tacky. If it was true that this piece would launch her career, she'd better cool all relationships for a while, until she could sort out which was the right one. The stakes were higher now; there would be speculation about her private life, and people would be paying more attention. She was sure Phil understood that too.

When the overhead lights went out, she figured it was safe to read. The only allusion to the shopping channel was a mention that she had worked as an announcer in cable, she saw with great relief. The first major article became the bedrock of every one that followed, good or bad; that was one reason she had worked Kristed so hard. She had seen other women in television tagged as ambitious bitches or as former weather girls and beauty queens. It was almost impossible to live such early labels down; now Burns would not have to.

It was a very significant triumph, and by no means undeserved. She had worked like a demon these past few years, getting up at 5:00 A.M. to pore over current literature and classics, to read every newspaper, magazine, and journal she could get her hands on. She went into every interview meticulously prepped. With a coach's help, she'd perfected a serious, even grave on-air demeanor remarkable for someone so young. Goodbye, Cable Queen, she thought as Barnard dozed, and fuck you, Sisters of Mercy in Somerville.

The bureau's driver was waiting outside the customs bay at Heathrow with a sign that said BARNARD. His eyebrows rose when he saw Burns. He knew who she was, but hadn't expected her on the same plane.

They made small talk with the driver on the way to the Connaught, and checked into their separate suites. Burns had insisted; she'd come too far to get sloppy now.

Barnard, like most of his fellow USB executives, loved London, loved these quick excursions. Aside from the fact that he could do some shopping—he had exhausted the few good men's boutiques on Madison Avenue—he considered these junkets the best perk network television offered, a sign of his status, acknowledgment of his hard work.

On the way to the hotel the limo had passed the USB Bureau, an impressive, beautifully furnished town house three blocks from the American Embassy. The network eagle fluttered from the flagpole.

Sometime during the next day, Barnard would stop in to make the obligatory courtesy call on Harry Crockett, the London bureau chief.

With Asia and the Middle East heating up, and the revolutions in Eastern Europe fading from the headlines, Crockett and his seventy-two producers, correspondents, cameramen, drivers, and assistants had less and less to do, so they became especially vigilant about keeping the network brass supplied with shopping advisories. No housewife ever hit a bargain basement with more glee and determination than USB newspeople hit London's clothing and specialty shops. Important visitors expected and got a car and a full-time driver who by now knew the circuit of boot- and shirt-makers. Bureau drivers regaled one another with stories of vice-presidents and executive producers hitting Jermyn Street and Savile Row direct from the airport.

The bureau also cabled visitors lists of current plays and concerts so they could check off their preferences. Restaurant reservations were another courtesy. So was delivery and pickup: If a producer or executive was fitted at his favorite tailor, ordered shirts at Turnbull & Asser or china from Harrods, he could depart secure in the knowledge that Crockett's reliable staff would pick up the items when they were ready, cart them to the bureau, and ship them home. There was never a customs fuss, either. In exchange, all Barnard had to do was find a half-hour or so to sip tea and exchange gossip with Crockett.

Retreating to his own suite, Barnard thought of Burns, of making love to her tonight. That would be an amazing thing to reflect on in years to come: He was shacked up in London with a woman most men could only dream of meeting, a woman whose beauty had struck him immediately when he and Pete Brophy, the USB talent scout and head of personnel, had watched her audition tape together.

Her cassette comprised several minutes from a cable shopping channel and another few minutes of stand-ups from consumer pieces on slow ambulance service in Orlando, but both men had clapped their hands together at the same time. She had passed Brophy's famous jerk-off test, the standard he used to rate women applicants to the news division. First, and this was routine, he'd put the applicant's cassette into the VCR and fast-forward it for ten seconds with the sound off. If something about the woman struck him—"leaped out at him," as he put it—he would replay it at normal speed with the sound on. Then he would look for the jerk-off factor, which was really quite simple, as he explained it: Do you want to masturbate when you watch this woman on the small screen, or not? If you did, you brought her to New York for a closer look.

Barnard found Brophy's philosophy crudely expressed, but he and most of his colleagues also admitted that it was pretty reliable, given Brophy's track record. To tell the truth, he had been aroused himself at the sight of the less polished but already stunning Burns.

After a quick bath he headed down the hall to Burns's suite. He knocked, heard her yell to come in, and was surprised to see her sitting half-naked on the edge of the bed, reading *American Demographics*. Surprised—given her reserve—and pleased.

"Welcome to the shopping channel," she said. She couldn't have come much farther, he thought.

Barnard and Burns had a sweet, grand time in London, free of even the minor hassles that could befall tourists. They strolled through Hyde Park, prowled the Victoria and Albert, hit a half-dozen galleries in Mayfair, and made it to Queen Elizabeth Hall in time to hear some dreamy French pop singer. After the concert, their bureau car was waiting to take them to hear a jazz quartet at Ronnie Scott's.

At Fortnum & Mason, Linda selected jellies, jams, and cookies to send home to Somerville, and a $130 case of filled chocolates for Don Kristed. Barnard picked up a couple of tweed sport coats at Gieves & Hawkes and a raincoat at Harvey Nichols, reported by the bureau staff to be Princess Di's favorite haunt. They saw a new production by the Scottish Opera, and they drank too much wine afterwards at the Café Royal, where Oscar Wilde made his last stands.

Barnard was conscious all the time of being with a beautiful woman, of being eyed and envied. He liked to think, as he gazed across the pillow at her after their efficient but cooler lovemaking, that he had discovered this superstar, created her. She liked to think mostly of the *Times* television writer who was considering a feature about her for the Arts and Leisure section.

On the flight back to New York they talked little. Barnard had a sense of their already having parted; both were anxious to minimize the coming separation. It had not been an intense romance, so there was no reason for a soggy farewell. Probably neither would ever mention their relationship to the other again or, if Barnard was classy, to anybody else.

They separated at Kennedy, and Barnard was amused to note that they embraced briefly, brushed cheeks, and went to their own apartments, Linda complaining of travel fatigue and emotional exhaustion. Maybe a few more evenings together, he thought. Maybe not.

He was relaxed, thus startled, when he arrived at work the following morning and found Grace Viola waiting in the anteroom outside his office.

"Good morning, Mr. Barnard," she said coldly.

"Good morning, Ms. Viola."

"Do you have a few minutes to talk about your trip to London?"

Barnard waved her in.

She looked angry and determined, which Barnard found unnerving. He walked over to the coffee machine at his secre-

tary's desk and poured himself a cup, black. He did not offer
Viola any.

"I want you to know, Mr. Barnard, in the interests of
honesty, that I'm going over to Brookings's office this morning
at ten to turn over the results of my staff's inquiry into your five
trips to London. I don't want you accusing me of being
underhanded— "

"No need for accusations, Viola. It's a known fact about
you," he said evenly.

Barnard knew very little about Viola, in fact. But she needed
to be brought down to size. "All right, Viola, let's have the
results of your little investigation. But I'll be honest with *you*.
This is outrageous, and I'm not going to lie down for it, so your
stuff better be good."

If Viola was about to retreat or apologize, she showed no
sign of it. She sat down at Barnard's conference table and handed
him a sheaf of papers just as Adelson came huffing in, his hair
disheveled, his belly hanging over his belt, tie loosened, shirt
sleeves rolled to the elbow. Barnard, fastidious about his appearance, could never understand how Adelson could care so little
about his.

"I got your message, Grace, and I hope this is as important
as you said, 'cause I'm in the middle of a deal down there. We're
renegotiating Bill Cox's contract—he wants to cover the Pentagon
for two more years—and I just told his agent that we've decided
to fire him."

"Cox?" asked Barnard. "Brookings loves Cox."

"I know," said Adelson, "but in the new climate, he's
unleashed me to get tough in negotiations. Canning Cox is a
great starting point, if the agent doesn't have a heart attack. I've
never seen an agent gasping for breath before," said Adelson,
chuckling. "This interruption may turn out to be helpful. By the
time I get back, the guy will be ready for a transplant."

Viola smiled. "Well, I think this meeting is quite important,
Sam," she replied, handing him a folder of photocopies. "But
judge for yourself."

"I'm glad you're here, Sam," Barnard put in. "This is
pissing me off. This is not high school; I'm not into getting
called before the principal."

Adelson, sensing with a sinking feeling that he was at another of those things-are-different-now meetings, looked over the papers in the folder. They listed $11,000 in hotel charges for suites, storage, room service, liquor, and meals during different London trips, all spent at the Connaught.

A separate sheet catalogued $7,000 in airplane tickets, $3,500 in car and driver costs, $600 in theater tickets, and $3,400 in restaurant costs, obviously reflecting, in some instances, large numbers of people. There were no names other than Barnard's, but an accompanying report stated that during all five trips, Barnard had booked two separate suites.

Perhaps the most damaging document was a letter from the head of Soho Music Studios saying that no theme music had been composed yet and none would be for several more weeks. Or perhaps it was the receipt from Turnbull & Asser, the four-figure amount exactly matching the listing on Barnard's expense form for "props."

"Gentlemen, when I leave here I am going into Elliott Brookings's office, and I am going to show him this report. I am going to request that all of these expenses be disallowed, that you, Mr. Barnard, be given thirty days to repay the company for all of these trips, and that if you do not, that the cost of the trips and these items be deducted from your salary."

Barnard flushed. He tried to look angry but felt unnerved. He had expected her to bug him about his expense accounts, but this confrontation felt unexpectedly formal and harsh. He looked at Adelson.

"Look, Grace, can I be frank?" Adelson said. "Can I speak freely here? I know you're just doing your job. Maybe Phil doesn't, but I know." This was one of Adelson's Mother Hen tricks, ordinarily used to cool off vice-presidents and lead them away from his chicks.

Viola nodded.

"And look, pal"—Adelson wheeled sharply toward Barnard—"how about we appreciate the fact that she came to us first. She could be in Brookings's office right now, you know; she didn't have to do this."

Then he turned back to Viola. "Grace, here's the thing. We all know what's going on. There's takeover talk, the Chairman is getting nervous, and Brookings has put the word out that we have to get serious about money. That's why you landed on

Herbert about his story budget last week. Now dumb-dumb here has given you another lulu of an example. But—we're being frank—this is not the first time this has happened, is it?"

Barnard banged his coffee cup down on the table and stood up to close his office door. The staff was beginning to filter in, and even a whiff of this scene would be humiliating. He jumped into the conversation. "Let's be even more frank, *Ms.* Viola. People have been doing this for forty years. There isn't a network producer, or vice-president for that matter, who hasn't been to London ten times, Paris, Berlin, all over the world. Traveling is part of the job. Seeing the world, entertaining people, particularly our overseas staffs—that's all part of the work. So how is it that I'm being harassed about something that everyone else has been doing for years?" Barnard's voice was rising. His anger was turning to fear.

Viola leaned back in her chair and shuffled her papers, then coolly looked Barnard in the eye. "I am not a hotshot producer. I am not an idea person. I am not a creative sort," she said. "Left to me, this network would shrivel up and die in a month. I came here to work because I wanted to be around creative people like you, because it's exciting and I'd rather crunch numbers here than for a cereal company.

"But this is wrong. This is stealing. This is what people in the government get indicted and go to jail for. Do you understand that?"

Adelson understood, all too well, but he knew Barnard did not. There had always been a sense at the network that its executives deserved to eat well, dress well, travel well. Sometimes the company had to help pay for those things. Barnard hadn't invented that perception; he had learned it. It seemed absurd to equate that tradition with corruption.

Adelson figured the angles quickly. Charming Viola was pointless and impossible. So was flattering her. This was a new entity. He gambled.

"Grace, I'm not going to bullshit you. Even by news division standards, Phil went too far. He's right—we all see these trips as perks and we all find bullshit reasons for going to Europe twice a year, though we're smarter than Phil was and perhaps less excessive. But you are a new reality, a finance person with power, someone serious about costs. This is something we are going to need time to get used to.

"Barnard is a brilliant producer—you sense that yourself—and he is on the verge of having a hit show that could bring tens of millions of dollars to the network. Look, just yesterday *The Washington Post* said *TGIF* was the most exciting television news offering in twenty years. You know what that could mean. Don't get him tossed out for a few plane tickets. I understand what you're trying to do, I get it, but don't push it so far that you win a battle and blow the war."

Adelson was a born negotiator, a natural deal-maker. He instinctively sought the common ground, and years of battling about turf, contracts, and egos had given him sensitive antennae about where the common ground was. Barnard had been relegated to the sidelines, watching uncomfortably as his fate was decided by the people with real power.

Viola mulled it over. She had gone over and over this with her husband the night before. She was uncomfortable in the role of hard-ass, but she also knew she had to unleash a few thunderbolts; otherwise no one in the news division would hear her.

"That's Brookings's call, not mine. If he wants to forget it, something I would recommend against, that's his decision," said Viola. "But I've got to tell you, I think this stinks. It stinks to make up five trips to London and take your friends out to dinner and buy clothes on the company. And it stinks for the company to pay for your affairs."

Barnard clenched his fists. "My affairs are none of your fucking business, and stay away from them."

That was the ballgame, calculated Adelson. Viola had played her trump card flawlessly, something only the savviest executives knew how to do. Brookings, apprised of the expense shading and the Burns business, would never side against her. The bureau had flashed word of Barnard's fling to Adelson, but no one Adelson knew would have confided in a finance person. Viola must already have set up her own intelligence network.

It was time for retreat. Adelson's last appeal would be to Brookings. He might, at worst, make Barnard pay for some of the trips. But there could be no mistaking the signal, or the manner in which it was delivered.

Viola stood up. "I am being direct about this, Sam, so that we all know where we stand. This isn't your money, Mr. Barnard. It belongs to the company and to the people who own stock in it, and people like you are stealing it, helping to make it very likely that somebody will try to take us over. If we don't change things, someone else will do it for us, and you won't like that at all. You both read the papers: The party's over. We have to account for our money now. USB News isn't an independent state anymore. We have budgets these days, just like normal folks."

She collected her copy of the report and left the office, nodding to Adelson.

Barnard whistled incredulously. "What is this, Sam? Am I supposed to quit? Get a lawyer? This is outrageous. I'm being singled out for what everybody else has been doing for forty years. It's what you get back for handing over your nights and your weekends and your personal life and your blood pressure."

Adelson rolled his shirt sleeves up another inch or two. "Don't get on your high horse, Phil. There aren't lots of two-hundred-thousand-a-year magazine producer jobs lying around. Don't do anything stupid. My guess is you *are* being made an example of, and between us, she's got you dead to rights. And what the fuck is wrong with you, anyway? This isn't dinner with the boys—this is hog-wild hubris. Five trips in two months? You and Burns popping up all over London? Is that why your marriage busted up? Because if it is, you're crazy. She's not going to stay with you.

"Listen, you're valuable, and nobody's going to hurt you too badly. Maybe Brookings will go for a warning. Maybe you won't have to pay it all back. I'll try. If you need a loan, you can ask me. You better write him a sweet note explaining and apologizing. This says to me that Brookings wasn't kidding at that staff meeting, and it's not a good time to be arrogant."

He stood up and headed toward the door. "You made another stupid mistake, Phil. You badly underestimated Viola. Sometimes people like you who went to Harvard, never had to worry about getting a car or a girl or a job offer, come to think you're invincible. You can't fix this lady. Okay?"

Adelson turned back, his tone growing conciliatory. He had no trouble being tough, but these producers were his special charges. He knew the battering they took, the precariousness of their successes. It was up to him to keep them fresh and enthusiastic.

"Look, in a few days we'll be in Florida, at the winter meetings. Santo Cristo is supposed to be paradise. And we'll hang around with Peter and the other guys, and we'll sit on the beach and bullshit, and you'll feel better, okay?" Adelson patted Barnard on the back and left, eager to continue his torment of Bill Cox's agent.

Barnard nodded, then went out into the anteroom to pour himself more coffee. London seemed far away. He began thinking about his note to Brookings. Correct. Businesslike. Regretful, but not groveling.

CHAPTER TEN

SANTO CRISTO

*P*eter loved Adelson's rituals. They made him feel part of a team, a feeling he'd known only sporadically in his life. The car had become one of their major shared jokes, Adelson vowing that no matter where in the world USB's meetings were held, he would pick his executive producers up at the airport in a red convertible.

This promise had occasionally been put to the test. In Haiti, Adelson had pulled up in a 1958 Cadillac freshly repainted for the occasion, the original blue still peeking through in spots; in Berlin he was driving an antique Mercedes that looked to Peter like the Nazi staff cars seen in movies.

But Santo Cristo was a snap. Adelson had acquired a brand new Mercedes, which he piloted wearing Ray-Bans, a Hawaiian shirt, and Bermuda shorts. The top could safely be let down, of course, for the news division did not conduct its important business in cold or rainy places. It was too easy to get bored in cities where people had to stay inside all day; a bored television executive was an unhappy television executive. Florence, San

Antonio, Key West, and Nice had been the most recent conference sites.

Two elderly porters jammed the well-worn suitcases into the trunk of the Mercedes and it glided off, stuffed with Adelson's adoptees: Peter, Phil Barnard, Buzz Allen, and Danny D'Amato.

"Should we be traveling together like this?" wondered Barnard—ironically, Peter hoped. "They don't let the President and Vice President fly together. What if the car cracked up?"

"Journalism would experience its greatest leap forward . . ." Adelson paused teasingly.

"Since the *great* and *early* days of broadcasting!" the others shouted in unison.

Peter felt his tattered spirits lift with each passing palm tree. His father's declining health was weighing on him; he could no longer suppress, as he had for several years, the conviction that his father would soon be dead. The *Providence* sinking and the abortion story had both been crash jobs, exhausting and exhilarating at the same time. Now, if he could endure the bureau chiefs' whining about their stories' not getting on the air often enough, maybe he could get to the two novels Barbara had packed for him. That, after all, was the point of the USB News winter meeting, held this year at the Santo Cristo Conference Center on the west coast of Florida—to relax.

Of the men in the convertible, Danny D'Amato was proudest to be there on behalf of USB News. He was a bit too enthusiastic for Barnard's taste. Simple organisms, Barnard called such people. But D'Amato found it natural to be loyal to a company.

For more than twenty years he had fought fiercely for USB, almost routinely risked his life for it. He had never done the same for a friend, though there were always some in trouble, the ones who fell out of favor or were pushed, who were exiled to Brussels or Bonn or the satellite desk, or who resigned abruptly and vanished like cheating mob couriers.

D'Amato would have seen no irony in this. He simply believed that if you worked hard and kept your mouth shut and your nose where it belonged, you were okay. When men he knew got into trouble, it was usually because they overreached, complained, plotted, or got lazy. He was guilty of none of these.

Still, the Sanity Club, such as it was, was the first club he could remember being invited to join. And the first benefit of membership was this convertible ride, the sun on the men's shoulders and Sam Adelson at the wheel.

The ostensible purpose of these meetings was to give news executives and producers a chance to see and meet with the division's far-flung correspondents, bureau chiefs, and producers. The normal script called for the producers to explain their shows' philosophies of the moment. The executives and producers would then pretend to solicit and care about the bureau chiefs' grievances—not enough people, not enough stories getting on, not enough information about what was going on in New York. Then the bureau chiefs would pretend to ask tough questions of the executives and producers, and the executives would pretend to answer them.

Occasionally a bureau chief would get tanked and go at Brookings or one of the producers, but this was rare. Nobody wanted to jeopardize the real agenda, which was to get away from New York, its late-winter sleet and its tension.

"We're really in cracker country," yelled Adelson above the wind.

"How can you tell?" asked Peter. They were passing a roadside stand advertising bear meat and chameleons, and he toyed briefly with the idea of getting Ben and Sarah a chameleon, but Barbara would probably murder it. They were already straining under the burden of seven goldfish, a rabbit, four mice, and of course, Eugene.

"Easy," said Adelson. "This is the only airport we've ever flown into where you see middle-aged white men carrying your luggage."

Peter pondered that. The observation fell into the category of Things That Are True When You Think of Them but That Nobody but Adelson Would Notice.

Peter was tickled to be there, balmy meetings in beautiful places being a major perk. As he took in his companions he guessed they all needed a break. It was impossible not to feel the exhilaration of getting away with something. Besides, the trip itself was a kind of reassurance that despite all the persistent takeover talk, things couldn't be all that grim.

D'Amato leaned forward from the back seat. The sun and the ride were making him drowsy, but he fought to stay awake. "Hey, Sam, the word is, personal sailboats for everybody here. That true?"

Adelson said he didn't know, but Elaine and Harriet had been on site for two weeks setting things up, so anything was possible.

By custom, two secretaries were chosen to oversee each meeting, winter and summer, planning every detail down to the brand of scotch. Each team tried to outdo the previous planners in supplying recreational surprises. In Austin two years earlier, Elaine, Adelson's secretary, had provided every conference participant—there were thirty-seven—with his or her own horse for the three-day session. So far, no one had topped that.

"Individual sailboats wouldn't be smart," said Peter. "Somebody would leak it and the network would look even more wasteful than it already does."

"Even Julian wouldn't leak that," Adelson said. "He'd be afraid they'd stop holding the meetings."

"Julian," said Barnard, "leaks like the *Titanic*. He would rather be leaking than fucking."

Adelson laughed. Dumping on McCallister always put him in a good mood. "Speaking of fucking," he yelled back to D'Amato, "you haven't said anything about your trip to La Paz. Did you fuck any of the lady pilots flying the relief stuff in? I saw pictures of these women pilots in an Air Force recruiting ad. I almost enlisted."

Peter groaned. "How about I tell your wife this fantasy, cowboy? Then you can enlist in the World Eunuch Federation."

D'Amato smiled enigmatically. Although he enjoyed encouraging the other men's fantasies, the truth was that he never talked about his female friends to anyone. He liked the women he saw and would never gossip about them.

Allen was not joining in the chatter, Peter noticed. Word was, he was girding for the imminent breakup of his marriage.

This was so familiar an occurrence in television that Peter, along with almost everyone else, recognized the symptoms right away. It usually happened when men were in their late thirties and early forties. The first signs were withdrawal, secretiveness, and unpredictability—coming in late, leaving early, popping in to work on weekends. The next phase was irritability, alternating with a sudden openness. Adelson's Law Number Eighteen: *You know a man is having trouble with his marriage when he starts trying to make friends.* This was accompanied by distraction, by tasks left unfinished. If the employee was female, she usually told her friends and bosses immediately. A man generally waited until a superior called him in and asked if everything was all right at home.

Sometimes—this was the exception—the man would sit down and talk, occasionally even cry. This was understood to be a phase that would pass, but it was a tricky one. If you allowed him to become too intimate or emotional, the guy would forever be uncomfortable with you when he returned to normal. Not that his colleagues wanted to hear much in the way of complaints, anyway. He was entitled to one or two outbursts, but no one wanted to listen to more. If they became a habit, he was encouraged to get help and was accordingly branded as unstable, a more damning development than getting caught cheating old ladies out of their Social Security checks.

But generally, one of the older hands, someone who had been through it, took the latest victim out to dinner and explained how it worked: the sudden depression, the fear, the temper tantrums at work, the lusting after young girls, the legal tangle, the loss of social life. The worst of it usually passed in six months. USB News executives considered themselves highly compassionate and contemporary for having looked the other way during this period. After that, the guy was just another divorced man, joining the overwhelming majority of divorced or formerly divorced men. If he was ambitious—and what would he be doing there if he wasn't?—he never referred to the divorce again, except to bitch about the financial pressures. That was acceptable and didn't count.

Allen's marital troubles were no bombshell. He had been dropping hints for some time that things weren't going well. Adelson was urging Allen to take a leave of absence to try to work things out. That was often part of the divorce ritual—a company-approved week or three in Europe or the Caribbean, where the couple tried to patch things up. Sometimes things got better for a few months, even a year or two, but rarely did the relationship improve permanently.

"Pull over," Allen yelled suddenly. "Pull over here!"

Adelson swerved off the road, nearly into a roadside stand. "Jesus, Buzz," D'Amato muttered, "that truck behind us almost climbed right up our ass."

"Sorry, but I bet there's something great for my kids here," Allen said. The stand called itself Harry's Tropical Souvenir Paradise, and Allen had been thinking the same thing Peter had: chameleons.

Adelson was incredulous. "Lizards?" he asked. "You want to give lizards to your children?"

Barnard was revolted. "You're taking those fucking things into your hotel room? They'll be shitting and slithering around."

Harry came out from a room in the back, smiling. He was wearing sandals, dirt-smeared shorts, and a polo shirt that tightly encased an almost refreshingly old-fashioned beer belly.

"Blondie's right," Harry said to Adelson, immediately sensing who was the boss. "How 'bout I ship the little guys home? The kiddies will have 'em before you get back. You wanna spring the extra eight bucks, I overnight-express 'em."

"Brooklyn?" Adelson asked Harry.

"Bay Ridge," Harry replied. "I've come a long way, baby. How about some oranges and grapefruit?"

"No, no, send the fucking lizards overnight express," said Adelson. "It's on me, a gift to the kids. Everybody gets a lizard, everybody who has a kid. Harry, these aren't going to show up dead and mummified, are they?"

Harry shrugged. "There's a guarantee. If they don't make it, I'll send you another. No grapefruit?"

Adelson took out his American Express Gold Card, as Peter and Allen filled out the address forms. None of them balked at Adelson's buying; they knew the chameleons would eventually appear, somewhat disguised, on an expense account.

"You guys with USB?" Harry asked.

They all tensed. "Why do you ask?" asked Adelson, who pictured the local paper running a feature story, which would be picked up by the wire services: USB EXECUTIVES CLEAN OUT LOCAL SUPPLY OF CHAMELEONS ON WAY TO FAT CAT CONFERENCE.

"One of my delivery guys works on security up at Santo Cristo, and he tells me Jack Thomas might be there." Harry looked foxy. "You're going to tell me to fuck off, but I don't suppose there's any chance he would like to come down here and sign some postcards? Fifty-fifty split?"

"Fuck off," said Adelson.

They sped past trailer parks and roadside stands hawking fruit baskets and suntan lotion. Barnard led them in song—they sang old *Evening News* theme music and played a game they called "Guess the Show," which involved identifying the theme songs from old sitcoms.

After about twenty-five minutes Adelson, checking his printed directions, turned off the main road onto blacktop and drove for several miles through pine and scrub. Eventually they came to a one-story concrete building with a red-tiled roof and a heavy gate posted with stern warnings to stop.

Two uniformed men came out to the car and approached from either side, urban police style, checking each face against the list and photographs on their clipboards, then distributing clip-on ID cards.

"Shit," said D'Amato, "it's easier to get into Damascus."

The Mercedes cruised up the road another quarter of a mile. They could hear and smell the ocean, but they could not see it behind the tall stucco wall and the hundreds of giant royal palms. Then they rounded a turn and came to a rambling, intricately painted Victorian house.

Adelson's secretary, Elaine, and Harriet, Brookings's premier secretary, came out to meet them. They gave each of the men a hug and kiss and a packet containing a schedule, a welcoming letter from Brookings, and directions to their "cabins," spread out below the main house along a hillside overlooking the Gulf. Each had an unobstructed view of the water.

It was as pleasing and restful a retreat as any battered executive could want: dazzling flowers, perfectly trimmed shrubs, flamingos stalking the lawns, the obligatory rows of palms. From each cabin a path led down to a central pier, where a dozen sailboats were moored.

The first order of business was the ritual that preceded every network meeting—the poring over of the packets in search of political intelligence. No Politburo photograph was ever more meticulously scrutinized than the order of events and speakers, the seating plans for meetings and dinners—all guides to the ascent or decline of the participants.

Adelson was pleased to see that he would be seated at Brookings's table as usual. Adelson had a strong working relationship with Brookings, who, after a quarter of a century to-

gether, trusted him absolutely. It didn't hurt, as Adelson was the first to point out, that Brookings loved his jokes. Among his other qualities, Adelson was the person you wanted to sit next to in a room full of people excited about microwaves.

Adelson did not leave this or anything else to chance. He paid an agent he knew $500 a year to pull funny—but not crude—jokes out of struggling comedians. Adelson and Elaine then rehearsed them before they were delivered.

"Go to your rooms, children. According to the schedule, we're due on the dock for the welcoming cocktail reception in twenty minutes," Adelson announced.

Peter walked down the flower-lined path to Cabin 12. No keys were used at Santo Cristo, a confident statement about the resort's security.

The cabin was actually the size of a small suburban tract house. The door opened on a wide, tall living room with a fireplace and an enormous picture window with a palm-framed view of the water. There was a full kitchen off to the right. Peter was startled to see his suitcase already in the bedroom, his clothes hung in the closets or tucked away in the spacious chest. This was a new twist—score one for Elaine and Harriet.

He walked back to the dining alcove and checked the refrigerator. Alongside a six-pack of Perrier was a bottle of champagne with an attached note from Brookings, handwritten on USB stationery.

"Dear Peter," it read. "Welcome to the winter meeting of USB News. These are complicated times and we have a lot to accomplish, but the abortion investigation and the tragedy in Lisbon have again underscored your capacity for hard work and your extraordinary judgment. This is one way of saying thanks." It was signed "Elliott."

Peter glowed. The fact that he never drank champagne, that forty similar notes were being opened at that moment, and that it was almost certain that Brookings had not written any of them, did not diminish his temporary swell of pride and well-being.

He changed into a polo shirt and chinos and hurried down to the cocktail reception. D'Amato came up behind him and clapped him on the back.

"Danny, I know you tough, globe-trotting, do-or-die producers don't like to get sentimental, but that was an incredible

job you did in Lisbon," Peter told him. "The abortion stuff was terrific too. You've made me look like a hero twice."

D'Amato put his arm around Peter and gave him an Adelson-style squeeze. "You didn't do badly yourself. But I admit I'm blessed with a particular talent that has given me a long career and a substantial livelihood."

They walked a few more feet along the shore before Peter, taking the bait, said, "What's that?"

"I get along with customs agents," said D'Amato, and both of them laughed. "Always have. Listen, Peter, aren't we due for lunch? What's it been, a couple of months?"

"Soon as we get back," Peter agreed. "I think we only fit in three in the past year."

"That sets a record for me," said D'Amato matter-of-factly, shielding his eyes from the sun with his hands. "Let's take a boat out tomorrow morning. They provide some kid who can sail, if you ask. We can get an hour in before breakfast."

Breakfast was not optional. It was considered tacky to spend mealtimes playing, even when irresistible toys were provided—which, according to the introduction packet, included scuba diving equipment, chartered boats to nearby coral reefs, clay courts ruled by Santo Cristo's world-famous tennis pro, saunas and hot tubs in every cabin.

As they approached the dock where most of the other USB guests had already gathered, D'Amato squeezed Peter's shoulder.

"This is going to be fun, Peter," he said, "but don't confuse it with real."

"Looks pretty real to me," Peter shot back. "Did you see the view from those cabins?"

"That's what I'm telling you," said D'Amato. "Listen, I'm older than you and a lot wiser, even if I don't read as many books. My daughter, Bobbie, is real. Your kids are real. You still have a marriage, so Barbara is real. This is a mirage—it's water in the desert; it's Candy Land."

Peter frowned. "Sometimes I think they want me to make a choice, you know. I'm good at being a father, when I get to do it. I can make the kids feel better; I can sense when they're in trouble; I love playing their games. In some ways I think I'm a better father than I am a producer. But I don't know how to do both. Sometimes I get the sense that the people at work are

watching me, waiting for me to make up my mind." Ever since his father's recent heart attack, he'd been imagining that thirty years from now, Ben and Sarah might be groaning at the need to visit *their* father in some hospital. The seeds of closeness had to be planted now—he knew that.

"Sure they're watching you," D'Amato answered. "You think they're paying you this kind of money to have ice cream cones with your kids and watch Yogi Bear? They figure you've got a wife to raise your kids, or at least the money for a nanny. They don't figure *you'll* do it."

D'Amato stopped and pointed across the path to a telephone booth nestled discreetly in a corner of the marina. Allen was huddled over the phone, with Brookings standing nearby. That probably meant a big story in the works, or some policy question to be resolved for the *Evening News*. Glad to be uninvolved, they strolled on.

Elaine and Harriet were in their element. Along the length of the dock the h'ors d'oeuvres table, its white linen tablecloth flapping in the evening breeze, was crowded with trays of shrimp, lobster, crayfish, and stone crab claws.

Adelson appeared and put his arm around D'Amato. "Look at all this—what did I tell you?"

Barnard came toward them, walking in a wide arc around Grace Viola. Peter got trapped into an animated conversation with the chronically aggressive New Delhi bureau chief—India was as far away as Brookings could send him.

At the sound of silver tapping on crystal, everyone stopped talking. Elliott Brookings, his silver hair lifting in the breeze, wore a dark-blue linen blazer, tan poplin slacks, and a blue oxford-cloth shirt without a tie, but he was incapable of looking truly casual.

"I would like to welcome all of you to Santo Cristo," he said in his most gracious baritone, "particularly the bureau chiefs who labor so gallantly in distant places for our glory and gain.

"Jack Thomas has asked me to welcome you on his behalf and to promise you that he will be here to help close the bar in a few hours, once he takes care of some minor business—the *Evening News* broadcast. He is flying down on a company plane; you might want to wait up for him."

"There is an order if I ever heard one," Adelson whispered to Barnard.

Brookings surveyed the crowd on the dock. "It is wonderful to see in one place the greatest collection of talent ever assembled in broadcast news. We are here to discuss some pretty damned serious things and to work hard. But tonight I want to tell you how proud I am to be here with you. I toast you—the men and women of the greatest information-gathering institution in the Free World."

An extraordinarily grandiose statement, thought Peter, but he had no doubt that Brookings believed it. From time to time, it might even be true.

The thirty-six men and five women around Brookings raised their glasses in silent tribute.

At first, few people noticed the waiters rolling out a ten-foot-high wheeled scaffold, and pulling the covering off an enormous television monitor atop it. Several technicians clambered over the back, connecting cables from the conference center's main building. At that point the bureau chiefs, whose lives depended on cables and monitors, began to point and murmur. The technicians finished their work, positioning the scaffold toward the end of the dock.

"The feed," Adelson growled to D'Amato. "These assholes are going to make us watch the fucking *Evening News* feed. Get a drink fast, if you want one. Stock up on food." He jerked his head to Peter, who nodded and scurried over to the buffet to pile on shrimp and crabmeat paté.

Suddenly—7:00 on the dot—the monitor popped to life and there, looming in color above his colleagues like the God of News, was Jack Thomas, anchoring the first of two "feeds"—or newscasts. "Good evening, this is the USB *Evening News,* with Jack Thomas reporting from New York."

Elaine let out a sigh of relief when the picture appeared, then looked mortified and clapped a hand over her mouth. The bar remained open, but no one dared approach it.

They called it "The Broadcast," the only one of USB's many programs that could be so named. Everything else was just a program. At 7:00 every weeknight, no matter what else might be happening, fifteen people gathered in Elliott Brookings's conference room and sat in absolute silence, broken only by commercial-break chatter, for the first of two feeds of the *Evening News.*

At 7:30 Brookings would critique the broadcast from his notes. He would complain about incomplete pieces, lack of balance, a feature that didn't quite work, or pictures that were badly shot. Jack Thomas was never criticized, by anyone.

Brookings had not missed a broadcast in more than twenty-five years. Neither had any major executive working for him, vacations excepted, and the truly ambitious made it a point to vacation near a television set. Brookings even refused calls from the Chairman while the *Evening News* was broadcast.

So it seemed a trifle to arrange for the early feed to be beamed by satellite to a dish set up on the roof of Santo Cristo's main house and wired to a giant monitor. Elaine really needn't have worried. Network technicians airlifted from the Miami bureau three days earlier had been testing the equipment all day.

The lineup seemed routine, although Brookings looked unusually sober. Then, in the segment usually reserved for the offbeat pieces of Americana with which Thomas loved to conclude the broadcast, the anchorman paused. "And now, a story about us, one that we will strive to report as fairly and accurately as we do any other. United States Broadcasting's board of directors will hold an emergency meeting in New York on Tuesday to respond to several reported takeover efforts.

"The latest bidder, according to the Associated Press, is industrialist David Nab, the forty-four-year-old chairman of Nab Enterprises and developer of more than one thousand real estate projects from Maine to Florida.

"Nab's attorneys filed notice with the Securities and Exchange Commission this afternoon that he intends to purchase up to forty percent of USB stock at one hundred and seventy-five dollars per share. Attorneys for Nab said the industrialist wished to acquire controlling interest in the network.

"USB stock, which yesterday closed at one hundred and twenty-four dollars a share, shot up to one-sixty today as rumors of Nab's SEC filing swept Wall Street. It was not immediately clear—and Nab's spokesman refused to say—how the takeover bid would be financed.

"Minutes ago, USB released the following statement: 'It is USB's intention to remain under the control of its current management. We believe we have the resources to challenge successfully any takeover effort. We consider such an effort to be hostile and against the best interests of the company and its stockholders.

" 'United States Broadcasting—particularly USB News—is an important American institution. We feel the nation's interest will be best served by the company, and its news division, remaining independent.' "

Thomas paused, nodded to the viewers as he did every night, and the giant monitor went black. Brookings turned to Allen and shook hands, an oddly formal gesture.

"Professional job," he said. "Please pass on my congratulations." He might as well have been Mountbatten, saluting the Queen's Lancers and ordering them onto the last ship home to England.

Before the shocked group could erupt with questions or speculation, a hundred-foot yacht came gliding toward the dock, the USB blue eagle waving from its mast.

Adelson's jaw dropped. Elaine, he thought, could come out of this conference a vice-president. The boat slid alongside the dock and tied up.

"Ladies and gentlemen. As a welcome prelude to what I know will be several days of hard work, Elaine and Harriet have arranged a ride into the famous Gulf sunset," Brookings announced, imperturbable as always.

The executives and producers, lining up to board the huge white boat, turned to one another in agitated confusion. The situation had suddenly gone way beyond rumors.

"Is this it?" asked the Paris bureau chief. "Is this the takeover?"

A colleague posted in Hong Kong shook his head in uncertainty.

Some, like Adelson and Brookings, were subdued. The national editor pooh-poohed the reports. The company had more than enough resources to fight off a takeover attempt, particularly from someone like Nab, he said. But nobody really knew much, a strange situation for so many reporters and producers.

Still, the news report, as dramatic as it was, receded a bit when they slipped out into the Gulf, with the captain pointing out the occasional dolphin. The breeze encouraged some people into the cabin, where still another bar and more food awaited.

Adelson noticed Grace Viola standing by the bow, her hair tied back in a ponytail because of the wind. The newspeople had ignored her as usual. Even if she hadn't been on the warpath about expenses, even if she'd been sexy and single instead of buttoned-down and a mother of two small children, they still would have ignored her. They always ignored people who fussed about money.

Adelson came up and offered her some shrimp. "You don't look like you're having a good time," he said. "Are you bothered by the Nab report? Or are you adding all this up? You can take some time off from worrying about the cost of things, you know."

She smiled briefly. "I know what this costs."

"And is the company paying for it the usual way?" he asked, looking around to make sure no one was within earshot, then glancing down at the briefcase tucked under her arm.

The briefcase had drawn snickers at the dock, wisecracks about Viola being so straitlaced she couldn't even have a drink without bringing along some paperwork, but Adelson knew what it was for.

"Yes," she said. "There's a hundred and twenty-four thousand dollars in cash and cashier's checks in here, and I have to carry the damned thing around for two and a half days, and I feel just like the asshole everyone thinks I am."

Viola carried the cash to pay for goodies like the yacht, the helicopter that Brookings and Thomas and some of the others had chartered to take them fishing farther up the Gulf the next morning, the fifteen-piece jazz band that would play at the reception later that night. She had already paid for the Lucite blocks with the network eagle and for the blue satin jackets with the words SANTO CRISTO WINTER MEETING: USB NEWS, for each person attending and for every spouse and child left at home.

These were not things it would do to have stockholders fussing about. So Viola wrote a check for the conference center rooms and food. Everything else was hidden in various bureau and program expenses. The Cairo bureau, for example, was a great place to bury expenses, because the Egyptians rarely used receipts and the bureau chief's word had to be taken for everything. The bureau chief would be surprised when the $15,000 bill for this little cruise showed up on his monthly expense budget, but he would never say anything about it.

"Sam, don't give me your sanctimonious look. I'm not such a prig as to mind fudging a party. I just don't think Brookings is facing reality. Or anybody else around here that I can see."

Adelson looked around again to make sure they were out of everyone's hearing. Most conversation was drowned by the cries of the seagulls divebombing the bow, trying to catch the shrimp the Warsaw bureau chief was tossing to them.

"You can't expect guys like Brookings, or Barnard for that matter, to change overnight. This is the way they've been doing things for a long time."

Viola shrugged impatiently. "My problem is, I have to tell the truth, and no one is listening. Numbers really don't lie— that's why I chose this for a living. Network revenue isn't rising this year for the first time in forty years. Competition from cable and the independents and VCRs is hurting us. We're a perfect target for a killer like Nab, a flabby company worth four times as much sold off as we are intact."

Adelson tried to sound soothing. "Don't overreact. It isn't clear that Nab has the backing to take us over—"

Viola jabbed a finger into Adelson's chest. "I listened to these worldly bureau chiefs getting on the boat, putting this guy down. Nab can get the backing to take over a place this fat and slow in ten minutes, and you know it. He is smart and tough and credible. I don't understand how these people can travel the world and cover everything and know so little about what's happening to them."

Adelson held up his hands in a conciliatory gesture. "I know, I know. They can't face it. I know."

"The network wants cutbacks in operating costs," Viola said. "We need to show we can manage this company. That means fifteen-thousand-dollar yacht rides in Florida are not necessary. It means Barnard ought to get more than a naughty-boy memo for stealing twenty thousand dollars. It means we can go inside and watch Jack Thomas on the color set in the lounge, and not order six thousand dollars in satellite time and equipment just to pull in his early feed. Every time I try to tell Brookings this, his eyes glaze over."

Adelson had come to like Viola, to spot the humor just below her sometimes forbidding surface, to appreciate her directness, although he knew the egos around her were too enlarged and fragile to take much of it.

Initially, she'd loved the idea of being around creative people, of helping them figure out what things cost and coming up with the money to get them done. But lately she had begun to wonder about these people; if they were cavalier, even dishonest about money, maybe they dealt with stories and reputations and issues the same way.

"So maybe you didn't go to Harvard Business School to carry around a briefcase like some Mafia errand boy," Adelson sympathized.

"That's why the Mafia is in so much trouble," she retorted. "They don't let women run things. If they did, they'd be a lot richer and would stay out of jail. Ahhh, let's get a drink. If I have to listen to any more talk about the finest news organization since prehistoric man discovered fire, I'm going to lean over the side and feed the seagulls myself."

The chopper thumped in so low that Peter thought it was going to lop off the mast as the sailboat slid into the dock.

It wasn't one of the four choppers maintained by the news division—this one, with the blue eagle across its belly, was twice that size. It was part of the corporate fleet that ferried the Chairman and senior corporate executives to and from USB's domestic and foreign properties.

A Santo Cristo attendant ran out to guide it onto the heliport, tucked invisibly beyond the bougainvillea-lined tennis courts less than a hundred yards from the dock. McCallister and Adelson peered through the dusk, McCallister declaring that this had to be the Chairman—no other USB executive would arrive with such intrusive flair.

McCallister was right. He and the others smiled knowingly when they recognized Harry Sommers's shock of gray hair as the door opened. Sommers emerged waving, as if he were returning to the White House from Camp David, then stepped aside for the patrician figure of the Founder, who regally descended the pull-down staircase.

"Surprise," Adelson muttered sarcastically.

"Showing the flag, I imagine," ventured McCallister. To see the Chairman remained a rare experience for most of them.

The Chairman made it a point to keep his distance. He

claimed that this would maintain the news division's independence, but in fact he was only too happy to give a wide berth to the unkempt and uncouth people in news, the least predictable division in the company. Harry Sommers was a rare exception.

As Brookings walked over to greet the Chairman, Sommers bounded over toward the cluster on the dock, ignoring, as usual, lesser executives and functionaries.

"Long way to come for tennis, isn't it, Harry?" popped Adelson, who remembered Harry fondly from the days when the *Weekend News* producer actually worked for a living.

"We're on the way to Cancun. The wives are on board," said Sommers indifferently. "He thought, in view of the stories going around, it would be nice to stop by and rally the troops."

The Miami technicians were scrambling to activate a sound system, and as the USB executives reassembled on the dock, the old man walked up to a microphone, as comfortably as if he were sitting in one of his many living rooms scattered around the world. He deserved them, thought Peter; the old bastard had practically invented modern broadcasting.

"Men," he said, and Peter caught the tail end of Viola's grimace. "I am on my way to Mexico and a tennis clinic, where I hope I will not embarrass myself. But I wanted to stop by and to reassure you that USB will never be taken over. Not by a condominium builder, not by anybody. The company has retained the best legal talent in New York and has arranged for a line of credit that could buy Japan." He chuckled.

"You are the proud symbol of this company. You have been since it was created. Nothing should spoil the opportunity you have to relax in this charming setting. Thank you for listening to an old man who hopes he was able to cheer you all up."

Brookings led the applause, which continued as the Chairman took Sommers's arm and climbed back into the helicopter, which whined into the air and veered south.

"If he says to relax, then I'm going to relax," D'Amato announced as the sound of the rotors faded. But Peter, watching Brookings, noticed that he looked anything but relaxed.

CHAPTER ELEVEN

LAVA ROCKS

*T*wo charter buses had lined up in front of an unmarked office building on East 18th Street. They looked like the hundreds of coaches that poured out of New York each day taking old ladies to their favorite casinos in Atlantic City.

But it was a bit early for the slot-machine runs, and the men and women milling alongside the buses would never be mistaken for gamblers. The men wore dark-blue blazers; the women, severe suits. Nobody looked particularly old or particularly young, but all were clean-cut, chatty, and a bit edgy at the same time.

David Nab and Harold Wallace stood in front of the second bus, chatting. They looked both eager and at ease, like buddies about to go fishing.

A police car passed and kept on going, the officers taking in the sight of the one hundred or so private security guards from an exclusive and discreet firm that hired only former state troopers. Some were in plainclothes, some in uniform, and the city cops and the private guards acknowledged one another through almost imperceptible nods and half-waves.

All of the men and women boarding the buses carried clip-boards with checklists of names and wore ID badges clipped to their jacket lapels or pockets. The badges identified them by name and by transition team—eleven teams in all, each with a different color.

At 7:50 A.M. the lead driver honked his horn, and everyone climbed onto the buses. The team leaders—identifiable by small pins in their jacket lapels—hung back while Wallace gave some last minute instructions.

"The command center number is four-four-six-nine," he said. "Five people from my firm will be there, along with a security coordinator. There are two things I want you to remember and to emphasize to your people. Unlike some of our previous acquisitions, which no one on the outside really cared about, there will be a lot of press swarming around by mid-morning. I don't want one employee of this company to say one quotable word to a single reporter.

"Secondly, this involves a large number of people. The people on the red-lined lists are to be out of the building immediately—or not allowed in if you get there first. You are to refer any arguments, disagreements, problems, or glitches to the special hot line. That couldn't be simpler or clearer, right?"

The team leaders nodded. Privately, they'd already figured this one as a piece of cake. The instructions were quite simple. Other than the media presence, this wasn't as difficult as some of the takeovers had been: the lumber company in Washington State that covered forty square miles, for example, or the steel plant in Pennsylvania where the wives and kids showed up to block the entrance. One thing *was* special: This was the first time Nab himself had ever come along, and his excitement was infectious.

Nab and Wallace walked down the street toward the dark-blue Chrysler sedan waiting for them, and the team leaders boarded their buses. It was only a ten-minute ride to the network building.

David Nab had, at Harold Wallace's suggestion, considered three options. He could have launched a proxy fight, persuading stockholders to replace the existing members of the USB board with new directors who would vote in new management.

He could have tried to take over USB directly, through a tender offer for all or most of the outstanding shares. He had lined up financing to offer $175 a share, $50 above the average recent price.

He could also have opted to persuade some other corporate giant to buy USB and install him as the new chairman.

Nab had hired Izes & Reynolds to prepare a workup of USB's worth—its real estate and publishing divisions, television and radio networks and stations. The stock was deliciously undervalued, a reflection of sluggish advertising revenues for the first time in USB's existence, and of Wall Street's increasing disenchantment with the way the company was being run. It had proven relatively easy to borrow money against the potential worth of the company if chunks of it were sold.

Nab's bankers had also been happily surprised to discover that four members of the board and the Chairman's nephew—who owned 18 percent of the company's stock—were known to be disgusted with the decline in revenues and the overfed management. The dissidents had discreetly but enthusiastically joined forces with Nab.

It turned out, too, that given the Chairman's advancing age and a feeling that a takeover was inevitable anyway—perhaps by someone even less appetizing—Nab's offer was viewed as too generous to refuse. His pledge, at a secret board meeting, to keep the company intact and the news division independent was welcomed, even believed.

Nab was also helped by the sudden and mysterious rumors—completely false, as it turned out—that a giant Hollywood studio, famous for successful shlock, was amassing funds for a takeover effort. The rumors panicked USB's directors, some of whom reasoned that Nab looked like Andrei Sakharov in comparison.

So USB was taken over during the second week in April, on the first really warm day of spring, just weeks after the last out-of-town winter meeting in the news division's history had concluded in Santo Cristo.

The takeover had been something of an anticlimax, given the company's storied history and everyone's assumption that it would go down fighting. In the news division, producers watched in astonishment, as much at the things that weren't happening as at the things that were. Congress was not rising up in protest, government regulators were yawning, stockholders were salivating, and the public barely seemed to notice.

Peter claimed later that he was the first person in the news division to learn of the landing, since his broadcast was on the air when the buses arrived and unloaded a squad of uniformed security guards, who hit the lobby like the marines taking Okinawa.

Peter's discovery had nothing to do with his news acumen; it was due more to the last desperate act of a loyal employee. Sanjih, the ambitious Sri Lankan security guard, had time to call him, as he always tried to do when some network VIP popped into the building for a surprise visit. The kid was remarkably calm under the circumstances, given that virtually his only security training had been posing for his ID photograph.

"Mr. Herbert," he said, "this is Sanjih in the lobby."

"Yes, Sanjih," said Peter irritably. This had better be pretty serious, for a security guard to use his direct line during a broadcast.

"We are now taken over," said Sanjih. "There is an army coming in and they are all headed straight toward my desk. Busloads of them. And they have real guns," he added. "I wanted to warn you."

"Good luck, Sanjih," said Peter. "I expect you not to be taken alive. If you get out, make your way to CNN. They're making money now." Peter laughed, until an unnerving image flashed in his head of Sanjih charging Nab's troops with his Fordham backpack. "Sanjih, you know I'm just kidding, don't you? You should do what they tell you to." But Sanjih had already hung up.

Peter yelled to Patel and Webb and the control room techs: "Mr. Spock, the Klingons have beamed themselves into the lobby. I'm afraid our phasers are not powerful enough to stop them. Remain at your posts; I'll try to reason with their commander."

Peter called Adelson at home.

"Yup," answered Adelson, who never sounded surprised.

"Sam, it's Peter. They're here. They are probably heading

for the control room. This is the last transmission from me you will ever receive. I want you to know that I love you and have always loved you. Whatever happens, you have always been a blood-sucking management leech anyway, so this will make no difference to you and your kind—"

Adelson laughed. "I'm coming in," he said. "I can't leave you alone to be violated. I'm bringing in some doughnuts."

"Great," said Peter. "I'll squirt jelly at the bastards."

"Peter?"

"Yes, my leader?"

"Remember the show. You still have forty-five minutes of airtime to go. I don't want anyone in America to notice from the show that anything is going on. And Brookings will be watching, even if they come through his apartment door with attack dogs. I mean it."

"You got it, chief," Peter growled, trying to sound Bogart-like. "Over."

You sort of had to love men at times like this, Peter thought. These were the times they had been so well prepared for: standing tall on the bridge, showing poise, wit, and camaraderie under fire. They fantasized about such moments their whole lives, read about courage starting with the Hardy Boys, imitated John Wayne and James Bond.

To Peter's left, Patricia Flannery was on the telephone with a Cincinnati fireman who had crawled on his belly into a one-hundred-foot tunnel to pull out a kitten—the beloved pet, as it happened, of an eleven-year-old boy with cerebral palsy.

"Chief, all you have to do is go to our Cincinnati affiliate. We'll send a car to pick you up and take you back to the firehouse. You're not the chief? Well, you ought to be, probably will be once your picture is on national television. Anyway, all we're going to ask you about is rescuing the kitty. And the boy's—Kevin's—parents have said he can come on with you, and think what that could do for cerebral palsy research."

Flannery grabbed for a cup of coffee, turning to Peter and rolling her eyes. She suddenly brightened.

"And, Chief, Don Leeming is an *old West Ohio boy!*" Peter shook his head. Leeming, as Flannery well knew, was a Toronto boy, but in the course of her guest-getting efforts he had been declared a native of towns from Tacoma to Tuscaloosa.

Flannery blinked suddenly. Her exquisite radar had just sensed a change in the control room atmosphere. "Chief, can I put you on hold for just a second? The White House is on the other line."

She swiveled toward Peter. "What the fuck is going on?"

"Patricia, we are taken over." He was smiling calmly. "The new owners are in the lobby and heading right for us, I would imagine."

"Shit," said Flannery. "I gotta wrap this cracker up." She picked up the telephone. "Look, Chief, I'm a little rushed for time here, you understand. I don't think it's fair for the police to be the ones to appear on national television when they weren't the ones who crawled into the tunnel. . . . Yes, they have agreed to, but I just don't think it's right. . . . I couldn't agree more. . . . All right, it's done. My assistant, Janice, will be on the telephone to work out the details. We'll send a nice big car for you. Thanks."

Flannery handed the telephone to Janice and bolted out of the control room toward her office. It was unusual—unprecedented—for Flannery to leave her desk during a broadcast, and Peter realized, looking at her empty desk, that he had rarely been in the control room without her.

She was back in seconds, clutching her book of names and numbers, her enormous Rolodex, and several plastic shopping bags. She began ripping cards from the Rolodex, pulling them out in fistfuls with no regard for their order, stuffing the cards into the bags, then tossing the Rolodex case into a trash can. She crammed the plastic bags into her canvas tote, and strapped the tote over her shoulder.

She looked up at Peter, who was staring at her, bewildered.

"These numbers," she announced, "are the rest of my life, and anybody who tries to keep me from getting them out of here will have his face rearranged."

"Patricia, calm down," said Peter. "This isn't the Gestapo coming. I'm sure they'll let you keep your personal telephone numbers. No one's going to bother us. We have to keep our cool, you know."

Flannery turned back to the phones. "You and your pals can be good Jews, Peter. I'm not a gentleman. I'm not going quietly."

Peter thought Flannery was overreacting. What you did was cooperate. USB producers had discussed this over the preceding few days, among themselves and in phone calls with Adelson. They had known for days that the takeover was likely, and they had all decided to show that they were professionals and team players; under no circumstances were they to reveal anger or fear.

Peter's red phone began flashing, which meant Brookings. Oh, shit, he thought; do I have to do this all over again?

"Peter?"

"Yes, sir."

"I just got a call from security. They're here."

"Yes, I know that."

"I'm going to tell you something that is very important, and I want you to pay close attention to it."

Jamie Webb, the director, had turned around and was watching Peter with a puzzled look on his face. Peter made a fist and jerked it up and down, the universal male symbol for masturbation.

"Yes, sir, I'm listening."

"I don't want one single viewer even to suspect from watching your broadcast that anything out of the ordinary is happening. We will maintain our usual standards and decorum. Can I rely on you?"

Peter rolled his eyes and mouthed the expected reassurances.

He would not have treated the call so lightly if he had known that he would never see or speak with Brookings again, but that did not cross his mind, and he would not have believed it if he had been told.

Nabih Patel first saw the three men in blazers come into the control room carrying thick leather folders. They were youngish, mid-thirties, and quite at ease, with the unmistakable look of people concerned with handling money—shortish hair, white shirts, tightly knotted ties, jackets buttoned to project authority. They introduced themselves as Transition Team Five. Would it be all right if they watched the broadcast? Observed the staff? Visited later in the morning to go over the budget?

Patel brought them to Peter and scurried off to tend to the feeds coming in from the Persian Gulf. "Of course I'll cooperate," said Peter. "The only thing is, there's a strict rule in the news division against outsiders coming into control rooms during broadcasts for any reason. I will need a higher authority, and you'll have to wait outside until I get it. You understand, I'm not

questioning the takeover—it's just that you aren't news people. . . ."

The team leader, whose badge identified him as Jarett, said
he understood perfectly. No problem, he said. He just had to
make a telephone call or two and would be back shortly.

Within two minutes one of the news assistants came up to
Peter and told him that Julian McCallister was on the telephone.

"Peter?"

"Yes, Julian."

"Look, sport, give these transition people every cooperation, you understand? They can come into the control room.
They can come into your office. They can come into the bathroom and hold your wee-wee while you piss if they want to. Am
I clear?"

The three—whom Peter immediately tagged Transition One,
Transition Two, and Transition Three—split up and fanned out
into the control room. They asked a lot of questions. What were
all the monitors for? How were satellites ordered? What did they
cost? How far in advance did they have to be ordered? What bloc
of time did you have to purchase them for? What shifts did the
techs work? The stagehands? For how many broadcasts? How
long did it take to fire up a studio? To close it down?

Transition Three approached Peter. "What is that monitor
for, please? The third one down?" he asked. Transition One had
drifted into the studio and was staring at the floor manager.
Transition Two was watching the technicians behind Jamie Webb.
Transition Three smiled encouragingly.

"It's the Mideast satellite," said Peter. "We order satellite
time every morning for the first hour of the broadcast. There are
so many stories from the Mideast that you use it most mornings,
but the big problem is, if you don't bloc-book, order well in
advance, then when something big happens—hostages, embassy
bombings—you can't get satellite time and you blow the story."

"So," said Transition Three, "you order it every day of the
week?"

"No," Peter answered, "just Monday through Friday."

"For how long?" asked Transition Three.

"For the past eleven months."

"What does that cost?" Transition Three was jotting notes
in his leather folder.

"I'm not exactly sure," said Peter. "I think it's five thousand dollars an hour or something. I can find out."

"No need to bother," said Transition Three. "It's eighty-two hundred an hour." He reached into his briefcase and pulled out a pocket calculator. "That's forty-one-thousand dollars a week, then. You can see it's over two million in the past year," he said, offering Peter the calculator.

Peter looked as if he'd been offered dog droppings. "I believe you," he said.

Transition Three, no longer smiling, quite absorbed in his numbers, looked genuinely surprised, pained, as if a promising friendship had just evaporated.

"Well," Peter added lamely, speaking slowly, as if to a child. "You know, the Mideast has been a pretty hot story. You can't very well not run pictures of the Seventh Fleet off Kuwait; you wouldn't last very long on network television."

The truth was, Peter was shocked to learn that he had spent $2 million in the past year on Mideast satellite time. No one had ever mentioned the amount before. You ordered what you needed, had the stuff fed to London, then into New York. It had never crossed his mind to ask what it cost.

He remembered the Adelson law about no executive producer ever getting fired for going over budget. He thought that was probably not true any longer.

The head of network security had been in the lobby when the first of the new uniformed guards arrived. Unlike the part-timers who had been manning the network barricades, these guys were the real thing: .45 caliber pistols, Sam Browne belts, crisp blue uniforms. They even had badges on their right shoulders: the letters USB below the blue network eagle.

The security chief had handed over a ring of keys and shaken hands with his replacement, Frank Mahoney. They were both former FBI agents and had treated each other with elaborate courtesy. Then Sanjih and the other security guards had been smoothly escorted from the building and onto a Benefits Bus parked outside. When it was full, it would make the first of several trips that day to a special office set up in one of Nab's buildings half a mile away. Each guard would get six weeks' pay, and Nab Enterprises would pay for each to see an employment counselor.

A tall plainclothes detective had taken up his position in the front lobby with a computerized list of all of the division's 1,500 employees.

The transition teams moved briskly and purposefully through the lobby and toward the executive offices. The few USB News employees already at work gawked. Transition Team One hit the press office; Team Two, the computer center; Team Three, the main network control room deep in the basement. Nab's planners understood the power centers of a modern business.

The four employees sitting in the network press office—the people who cajoled television reporters into writing admiring profiles of network stars, who explained what Jack Thomas really meant to say the time he punched a combative viewer in the stomach—stayed in their seats looking shocked but composed when the team strode into their office.

The leader of Transition Team One was Hal Danzig, the distinguished-looking publicist whose L.A. firm Wallace had retained for the occasion.

"Good morning," he told the press office staff. "My name is Danzig, and I have been named acting head of the network's press office, effective immediately. I am sorry to tell you that your services are no longer required at USB. Benefits that we believe can accurately be described as generous will be provided you, as well as relocation assistance. In order to obtain these benefits, we will ask you to accompany this gentleman"—he smiled toward a security guard—"to our relocation offices on East Twenty-Fourth Street. We have a bus waiting outside."

John Burke, the network's chief press spokesman, came out of his office and paused, his mouth open.

"The terminations take place at once," Danzig continued. "Your personal belongings will be packed and sent home to you. We ask that you take any clothing you came in with and leave now."

The phones on the desks began lighting up. Burke, a former *Daily News* reporter, started to move toward one, then hesitated. "Let's do it, kids. It's their ball and their ballpark," he said. One of the secretaries began crying, and one of the press aides muttered under his breath about not even being able to call his wife. The five put on their coats and began filing out, looking back at their desks.

Burke was the last to leave, and as he did he picked up one of the blinking phone lines. "Hello, this is John Burke at USB News. We're being held hostage by Hasidic terrorists. Please notify the NYPD hostage negotiation unit. This is not a joke." He hung up the telephone, gave Danzig the finger, and left.

Danzig and the team members quickly went to their desks and began answering the telephones. To every caller they read the same statement:

"The transition of USB to ownership by Nab Enterprises was begun at eight this morning and is now complete. We intend to maintain the high standards and quality associated with USB, and anticipate no disruptions in the network's normal routines. Beyond that, we will have no comment for at least forty-eight hours."

The strategy was a simple and smart one: Get the network press people out, so there would be no one to talk to the media. The forty-eight hour lid meant the takeover would have long been completed before the new owner had to say a word about it.

The transition team sent to the control center in the basement was unnecessary. None of the technicians working in the dark room had ever met a single executive of USB anyway, and they couldn't care less who was running the place. Their union contract, which Nab had acquired along with the company, looked to be airtight. They offered the guards coffee and cigarettes.

The computer technicians were led from the building right behind the press people. The computer room offered access to all of the network's confidential files, from contracts to payroll. Nab's own computer people had been working with the computer manufacturer's representatives for days and knew the system well. They would be running it themselves by 11:00 A.M. This was another area to entrust only to your own people.

The heavy security turned out to be unnecessary as usual, but Wallace, who had supervised more than a dozen takeovers, felt that it had enormous psychological value. The only trouble they had run into so far had been in the nurse's office, when Elly Edwards, R.N., loudly refused to leave without her personal effects, vowing to carve open the first person who came near the mementos she had assembled over twenty-two years in the news division. These included a Viet Cong knife, lava rocks from Mount St. Helens, a prayer wheel rescued from a Buddhist monastery torched when the Chinese Army invaded Tibet, and a burned British nautical flag from the Falklands, all gifts brought back by correspondents visiting Elly Edwards with headaches, blisters, or need of tender loving care.

When the head of Transition Team Six called the emergency number, Wallace told him to let Nurse Edwards leave with her souvenirs. It took her just a few minutes to stuff them into a box and stalk through the lobby with them, fighting back tears. Not being allowed to say goodbye to everybody was the worst part for her, although she was relieved in a way to be able to retire. Sometimes days went by without anyone coming in, and when they did they were such babies, those correspondents. If someone got a splinter, you'd think he had minutes to live.

Edwards was taken aback by the commotion outside. Vans full of New York City policemen with long rifles were surrounding the building. Some wore vests marked HOSTAGE NEGOTIATING UNIT. Others carried machine guns; a few had dogs.

Nurse Edwards didn't dare pause for a look back at the building where she had worked for so long. The last thing she needed was to be taken prisoner by some terrorist. She boarded the Benefits Bus.

The Occupation, as it came to be known, was still less than thirty minutes old when Transition Team Four walked off the sixth-floor elevators and into the Finance department. Like the press office and computer room, Finance was one of Wallace's most urgent priorities. Three uniformed guards blocked the doors to the department, turning away employees as they tried to come to work. Grace Viola was talking with her deputy, Ron McCabe, when the leader of Team Four knocked on the door. The team leader had been prepared on Viola's background, including her Harvard Business School degree, and he beamed, holding out his hand.

"John McKelvey, '78," he said. "I understand you're '74."

Viola shook McKelvey's hand coolly. "Is all this melodrama

necessary? It's Nab's company. He could just come on in and run it. There is no armed resistance that I know of."

McKelvey stiffened a bit. "Armed resistance is not the problem, Ms. Viola. If you'd seen the computer sabotage, file theft, and vandalism that we've seen elsewhere, you would consider all of this reasonable. I might as well get the unpleasantness over with first."

Viola had already done some calculating and concluded they wouldn't throw her out, at least not yet. But if the Nab people had done any homework at all, McCabe, a diligent but mousey twenty-five-year veteran of USB, had to be up at the top of their list. He must know it, too; he was literally cringing, as if he'd like to back right through the wall.

"So you've come for McCabe, is that right?"

McKelvey looked at his list. Actually, he had come for McCabe and eleven others. By nightfall, all payroll and accounting operations would be merged with the finance staff at Nab Enterprises. For one thing, Nab would never trust these people. For another, he didn't need them.

"Mr. McCabe is on the list of people we're letting go, yes. There's a bus waiting to take him and the others to a benefits and relocation counselor who will explain everything—"

Viola walked between McKelvey and McCabe, reminding herself how ironic it was to put her head on the block for this cipher. She had little use for McCabe herself. He was a caricature of the terrified accountant, meticulous but unable to make a difficult decision, bucking it up the line instead. People ,in Finance learned never to come up behind McCabe without making some warning sound, and never to ask him about anything controversial. But she had tolerated him; he was due to retire in two years anyway. Now, she stepped in before McCabe could respond to the ultimatum.

"Mr. McKelvey, nobody is throwing Mr. McCabe or anybody else out of here this morning. We are all grown-ups, and if there is no employment for these people, we can all understand that. But I'm not going to watch my people bundled onto buses with no time even to call their families. That is cruel and unnecessary, and if Mr. Nab has any illusions about my being a part of that, you tell him to stuff it."

McCabe's mouth fell open, but he said nothing and eventually closed it. This was the worst thing that had ever happened to him, and he just wanted it to be over. He was uncomfortable about letting a woman speak for him, but Grace Viola was his boss. McKelvey had already dialed the special number, explained the circumstances, and handed Viola the phone.

"Ms. Viola? This is Harold Wallace, an attorney working for Mr. Nab. Mr. McKelvey has explained your position to me."

"Mr. Wallace, I will do whatever needs to be done, within certain ethical and human considerations. But if you toss Mr. McCabe and these other people out of here like this, I will, in fifteen minutes, be holding a press conference in front of this building, denouncing Mr. Nab's inhumanity and spilling every financial secret this company has."

There was a pause. McKelvey now looked as pale as McCabe. A press conference like that would not be considered good handling of a tricky situation on his part.

"Ms. Viola," Wallace said. "I know a bit about you, and I don't believe you would reveal any financial secrets. Neither do I doubt that you would hold your press conference and portray us as blood-sucking monsters. Am I right?"

Viola hesitated. It was rare to meet a man who did not at least try to patronize her.

"You *are* right. But if I stay, my people stay, at least until we can sort this out in a professional way. That's firm."

"Agreed," said Wallace. "Please put McKelvey on the line. I will tell him, as I am telling you, that he will report to you and work as your liaison with us until we get properly organized. And, Ms. Viola?"

"Yes?"

"If you fuck me on this, I promise you that the best job you will ever get will be adding up box office receipts for a traveling carnival," Wallace said pleasantly. "Do you understand?"

"I do. But my knees are not shaking."

Actually, not only were her knees shaking, but the rest of her as well. Her voice, however, remained crisply in control.

"If you will get this month's printouts," she said to the still-cowering McCabe, "I'll show Mr. McKelvey around the Finance department. Until we sort out who is working for whom, how about we just pretend we're partners?"

McKelvey nodded.

★   ★   ★

They didn't get to Armand Andreas until noon. There was no boss to stand up for him; he hadn't talked to a boss in months. The door on which Team Seven knocked was unlike any other in the news division, with Andreas's name spelled out in brass letters sculpted to look like musical notes.

Andreas was the news division's musical director, a fixture at the network for thirty-five years. He lived with his eighty-six-year-old mother in an Upper West Side co-op. Elegant and Old World, he always carried himself as if he were about to mount the podium at Carnegie Hall. He looked, not entirely by accident, a touch like Arturo Toscanini, with tufts of white hair sticking out in different directions. He always wore a black suit, whatever the weather. It was not clear whether he wore the same one every day or had a dozen. Few people in the news division saw Andreas regularly, anyway.

As music director, Andreas maintained a musty but impressive library presided over by two assistants. In the network's early days his office and the library were a humming hive. A dozen composers worked for him, hammering out themes to new programs, news broadcasts, and dozens of documentaries. Bands and orchestras were hired by the week to record the music in the studio next door. Most current USB executives would have been surprised to learn that Andreas had once been a guest conductor for the Boston Symphony.

Now, he was beyond being an anachronism. Any practical reason for his existence had long since passed. The new young producers, who favored rock rhythms and driving synthesizers, were not comfortable around someone whose favorite contemporary composer was Gershwin. If anybody in the building was surely doomed, it was Armand Andreas, and he waited to hear the footsteps coming.

He heard them at noon. Judy Goleman, the head of Transition Team Seven, introduced herself and gave him the news that the music unit was being disbanded and that he was being asked to leave, effective immediately.

Andreas felt chagrined. "It must be unpleasant, having to do this," he suggested in his courtly way.

"Very much so," she said, meaning it.

Andreas took Goleman on a tour of the music library—"My pride and joy for more than a quarter of a century," he said. Thousands of record albums—classical, jazz, folk, some rock— were stacked in yellow manila envelopes piled to the ceiling. If Andreas was an anachronism, his assistants were fossils—two aging, arthritic gnomes who had been dusting record folders since the dawn of television. Goleman winced when she saw them, knowing they would never find work.

Andreas turned confidentially to her in the library. "My assistants—they will have to go too?" She nodded. He asked if he could be the one to tell them, and she said yes, but only if she was present. She was responsible. He said he understood perfectly.

Later, as he began layering his memorabilia into cardboard boxes—Goleman had called Wallace and received permission to let him spend the day tidying up—Andreas wondered if he should call someone. He had met Adelson and Julian McCallister only once or twice, and had not seen Brookings for more than a year. The person he knew best was the Chairman, but it would have been inappropriate, even at the end, to call the Chairman.

Elizabeth, his secretary for every one of his thirty-five years, came in, looking, as always, perfectly composed and regal.

"I would have retired, you know, Elizabeth. I wonder why they chose to do it this way? Although," he sighed, "I know I am a dinosaur. Every day for thirty-five years I have come to work at precisely eight-thirty, never sick, never late." His finger was wagging. "Every morning I wore a suit. I have never been seen in this building without a suit jacket on. It is the way I was raised." Andreas took his Grammy awards from their shelf, then put them back again.

Elizabeth smiled and nodded and reminded Andreas that he had only a few hours to get his effects together and asked how she could help. Her own employment, of course, concluded at the end of the day as well. She was seething at the cruelty of the situation, as only devoted secretaries and old-fashioned corporate wives did, but he would never know it.

"Who will take care of the library?" he wondered to her. "Should we call someone?" But she had no ideas about whom to call, either.

Perhaps more than anyone in the building that day, Andreas remembered the network's glory days. He remembered how the

Chairman would send him roses and champagne every Christmas; how, when he wrote a score the Chairman liked, Andreas would get a call the morning after the broadcast aired. The two men would always have precisely the same conversation.

The telephone would ring at 9:30 and he would hear Elizabeth say "Good Morning, Mr. Chairman. Yes, of course, he is here."

Then Andreas would say "Good morning, Mr. Chairman," because he knew the Chairman detested small talk. The Chairman would say "Great job, Armand. Nice piece of music. Is your wife all right?"

Andreas would have considered it unpardonably rude to tell the Chairman that he had never married. He would say "Fine, Mr. Chairman, thank you."

The Chairman would then say "Armand, someday you are going to write a symphony and I will finance you and you will conduct it on the stage of Carnegie Hall."

And Andreas would laugh and answer "Thank you, Mr. Chairman. You are too kind." After the telephone call, he and Elizabeth would giggle like schoolchildren and review every word the Chairman had said as if they were scholars poring over an ancient manuscript.

Andreas proudly considered himself a news musician, not merely a composer. His work had provided a musical backdrop for some of the most turbulent events of the decade, from the Korean War to the JFK assassination to the network's famed Vietnam documentaries. He believed that future composers would listen to his work as a musical history of the period.

He had few regrets, really. Perhaps not having had a family. He had always felt he had to choose between his work, which for years had been intensely absorbing, and a family, and he had made his choice. Although he sometimes had his doubts, by and large he'd had a better and more interesting life than most people have, or than he had expected to.

If there was any other regret, it was that he had never gotten to meet the Chairman. He would have given a great deal for that.

Danny D'Amato declined to ride the Benefits Bus. He decided to walk the half-mile with the twelve members of his Special Assignment Team, who, like him, had just been canned, so that he could buy them all a drink.

He had been stunned when the men in blue blazers with badges—Team Eight—came into his office and told him that none of the other networks had SAT teams anymore, that cheaper satellite technology had rendered them obsolete, that it was no longer necessary to send a plane sweeping around the world every time some terrorist shot up a 747.

It had never crossed D'Amato's mind that he would get fired, now or ever, and it had not yet sunk in, he knew. He was counting on shock and numbness to hold him together until he could get home and think. He hoped to God that Bobbie hadn't heard anything on the radio, that he'd have the chance to tell her first.

From the instant the team leader—a twitchy man in a blazer, with ferret eyes and a southern accent that was just a bit too syrupy—had given him the word, the thought began bouncing around his head, the thought that came back again and again: He was fifty-one years old. No one wanted to hire a fifty-one-year-old man. How could he ever pay the $25,000 a year for the medical school that would make Bobbie a doctor? Adelson had come in to commiserate briefly, shake his hand and pat his shoulder. There wasn't even time to call Peter. There wasn't time to do anything. It almost felt as if he were being arrested; he wanted to throw his jacket over his face as he walked outside.

D'Amato's can–do style had left him unprepared to be on the street, as he thought of it, after twenty-five years with USB News. He had never really wondered why USB alone had a Special Assignment Team. He had always assumed it was be-cause the company was determined to be the best at everything.

Mickey Grodner was deep in her computer, searching the news division library for statistics on child abuse, when Transition Team Nine walked past her and into the office of the chief of Research, closing the door behind them.

The fifteen women and three men huddled in their partitioned research pods began, one by one, to stand up so that they could see what was happening. Grodner clicked her computer off and slipped some personal letters she kept in her desk drawer into her purse. She looked across to Laura Cooper, her closest friend in Research, but Cooper remained hunched, unseeing, over her terminal. It was hard to break her concentration when she was lost in a project.

The chief's doors reopened quickly and a woman in a blue blazer with a badge came out and called Laura Cooper's name. Cooper got up without a sideways glance and walked into the office. The door closed behind her, and soon—it seemed like only seconds to Grodner—Cooper walked out again, shocked, crying.

"Oh, God, Mickey, they fired me. They told me to just take my pocketbook and get on a bus. Call me. Call me later." Grodner put her arms around her friend and gave her a quick, fierce hug.

"Harvey Friedman," the woman in the blazer called out. He had been hired only months earlier. It seemed to Grodner, walking Cooper to the door, that Friedman stayed in the chief's office longer. But he eventually trudged out, took his jacket off the back of his chair, and walked resignedly to the elevators. Grodner's hands were shaking. When you thought about it, it was no great shock that researchers would get it. There were no agents to scream, there would be no publicity, and viewers and critics would not notice the difference, at least not for a while—maybe not ever.

Grodner rushed back to her computer, flicked it on, and called up the Child Abuse folder. The research was for the *Evening News,* and she had located more than fifty newspaper stories focusing on the most serious recent incidents of abuse. She highlighted all of the entries and instructed the machine to print the stories out on the *Evening News* newsroom printer, not on hers.

She pulled on her luminous USB News Research sweatshirt. On an uncharacteristic impulse, she opened her desk drawer and grabbed a dozen ball-point pens, black, with USB News embossed on their sides. Although it made no sense to her later, she was suddenly afraid she would have nothing to remember the Research department by.

She was about to pick up the telephone to call her sister, who was a buyer at Bloomingdale's, when the door to the office opened and the woman called her name.

She sat next to Laura Cooper on the Benefits Bus, holding hands. By the time it left the curb, ten researchers were riding the bus with her.

The second wave of Transition Teams took control of the less critical areas. One went to the cafeteria and posted new opening and closing times. Instead of staying open twenty-four hours a day, the cafeteria would be open from 7:00 A.M. to 7:00 P.M. —two shifts instead of three. The Emergency Omelette, offered in the predawn hours to lobster-shift technicians and journalists, passed unremarked upon, but not unmourned, into history.

The energy carts—the network nickname for the aluminum dispensers wheeled around the building all day to deliver coffee and high-sugar snacks to frayed producers and technicians—made their final run at 10:00 A.M. So did the nine Dominican and Jamaican porters who operated them.

The USB gift shop—where employees could buy USB News mugs, pens, notepads, windbreakers, and sweat shirts for their friends and families—suddenly offered all items at half price, sold out, and shut down.

The news division gym didn't last the day, either. Guards padlocked the basement rooms; rumor had it that the saunas, Nautilus equipment, computerized exercycles, and free weights would be auctioned.

Navy fighter jets were trading fire with a couple of Iraqi gunboats in the Gulf. Distracted, Buzz Allen didn't recognize the well-dressed, corporate-looking type who appeared in front of his desk, waiting politely to be acknowledged. Had it not been for Sam Adelson and Julian McCallister, flanking the man at either elbow, Allen would have told the man to take a hike. Visitors were not allowed anywhere near his program during the day.

"Mr. Allen." The man offered a firm hand. "I'm David Nab."

Allen stood up, mouth open, a telephone—an open line to Kuwait—still cradled in his neck.

"I'd like to meet with Jack Thomas, if I might." Allen saw that Thomas's secretary had already buzzed the anchorman, using the security code that guarded against nuts or terrorists forcing him out of his office.

Before Allen could speak, Thomas, all six feet three inches of him, strode purposefully out to Nab and shook his hand. Allen was befuddled, but Thomas did not unnerve easily. The entire staff was watching and the anchorman knew instinctively when he was a part of history—he had certainly seen enough of it in the making. He had stormed ashore at Santo Domingo, stormed into Hue during the Tet offensive, stormed into the White House during his Washington tour of duty, and he would certainly rise to the occasion now.

"Take care of business, Buzz. Mr. Nab will have to learn, if he doesn't already know, that stories come before chitchat in the news business—the beaver has to find water before he can build a dam, isn't that right?" A slight but clear murmur of admiration swept the room. Thomas had taken the offensive, and the beaver analogy, nonsensical as ever, was the one he often used to make politicians and other targets squirm.

Nab laughed, his white teeth flashing in his well-tanned face. "Jack Thomas, they told me you were a man who talked straight, and I can see that is true."

Thomas straightened, even as Allen groaned inwardly. Nothing pleased Thomas more than being told he talked straight, even as his talk became ever foggier and more meaningless.

"I came to tell you—and I'll say it in front of everybody here—that I am committed to this news division, to its history and its traditions. I promise you that in the hands of my company, USB News will be prouder and safer than it has ever been. And I have come to ask you to join me in walking out front to about a hundred or so reporters while I make that pledge."

Nab eyed Thomas sharply, and Thomas got it. The look said: *Take that, you motherfucking cracker. Say no, and you'll look like a mean-spirited piece of shit.*

Thomas smiled back. "I'll go out there with you, boss. But you may not like everything I have to say."

Nab looked around the newsroom, and swept the anchor desk with his arm. "That's what this is all about, isn't it, Jack? The freedom to say what you want."

He shook the hands of several shell-shocked *Evening News* writers and producers. Then he and Jack Thomas, who possessed one of the most famous faces in America, walked out through the lobby and into the shrieking, snarling, and jostling that was increasingly the signature of the American press en masse.

Over the babbling and shouting, Nab spoke from memory, talking slowly until the crowd quieted somewhat. "I am here with Jack Thomas to assure you—in the presence of our anchor, our stockholders, the employees of USB, and the nation—that I am totally committed to the traditions that have served this company well. While we must manage the company effectively, there is no question that USB News will be given the resources, the support, and the freedom to continue doing what it has done so splendidly for forty years."

Thomas, still in shirt sleeves, waited a moment before speaking. He and the other television types were impressed with Nab's comfort in front of the cameras—the confident delivery, the emphasis on every third or fourth word, the nearly invisible pancake makeup. Thomas waited while some of the crews switched cassettes.

"I and all of us at USB News appreciate Mr. Nab's assurances. I learned when I was a little boy that promises are like the fall harvest—you don't spend the money unless you see the corn. Mr. Nab knows that we will be watching the harvest closely to see what it brings. He has assured me that I am free to say what I wish here, and I do appreciate that. What I want to say is this: Mr. Nab, we're a little nervous today, and a little sad. But we're also fair. If you keep your word, you'll have the same loyal employees doing the same damned fine job that USB News has done since the beginning of broadcasting."

Allen, back in his office, watched the two men on a monitor hooked into the news division's closed circuit system. He thought two things as the phone rang: that Thomas never had to worry about having plenty of corn, and that Nab was a pretty smart fellow to know that few people watching the news that night would remember anything but the two men standing together.

Harold Wallace walked into the USB News conference room at 7:30 P.M. on the button. The team leaders were all accounted for, although markedly more disheveled than they had been eleven hours earlier and more relaxed as well. Eleven boxes of Domino's pizza lay opened down the center of the long rosewood table, edged with six-packs of Coke and Diet Pepsi and a stack of Styrofoam cups from the cafeteria.

Wallace's tie was in his pocket. He sat down at the head of the table with a sigh and an enormous smile.

"I've just left David and he's jubilant," he told the men and women around the table. "He wanted me to tell you all that he never imagined the transition would be so swift or smooth."

Wallace popped open a soda can. Behind him, a communications aide plugged his emergency telephone into a wall jack, a reminder to everyone—not that they really needed it—that total relaxation would be premature.

"The key," Wallace mused, allowing himself an expansive moment, "is to replace their culture with our culture." He was entitled to gloat. By morning he would be the hottest takeover attorney in America. By summer he would own the sloop in Key Biscayne he had been drooling over for five years.

"What *is* our culture?" asked Judy Goleman, leader of the team that had sacked the music library, leaning back in her chair and kicking off her flats beneath the table.

"Our culture is no culture," he said, smiling. "Our culture is efficiency and moderation. And class," he added. "If I may say so, I think we demonstrated considerable class today.

"The first step is always to remove, immediately, the quirky, old-fashioned, economically unjustifiable parts of the company, the things everybody inside associates with it. By removing those, we remove the old identity. As for the security—while melodramatic, the security is important; it buys cooperation in ways you can't see. Even though you know you'll almost never have to use it, it says this is our company now, period."

The team leaders paid close attention. Harold Wallace did not often philosophize in their presence, and they were flattered and excited, eager to learn. He snapped out of the mood quickly, though.

"So let's have the reports," he said, reaching for his clipboard. Everyone at the table straightened.

"Security?"

Frank Mahoney, once the head of the FBI's prestigious New York field office, cleared his throat and read from a short list.

"Well, there was the hostage hoax," he said. "The NYPD

was plenty pissed about that; they wanted to file charges against Burke. Per your instructions, we declined to cooperate. They were gone in ten minutes. Turns out there were also bomb threats against the Syrian Mission to the U.N. this morning, so they were especially jumpy. There were three bomb threats telephoned to USB headquarters, none of them deemed serious enough to act on.

"There was the incident with the nurse—I believe her name was Edwards—who threatened to stab one of my men unless she could leave with her souvenirs, but that was resolved. And there was one reported incident of a man urinating on the Benefits Bus—we don't know who. The only other incident involved the Finance office and Ms. Viola, where she declined to cooperate at first. But she worked it out with you, I guess, and my men are guarding the files."

Wallace nodded. "And the major facilities are secure?"

"Yes, sir. The computer room, the broadcast center control room, Finance, and the press office are all secure and quiet. Our people are at all the entrances and exits with lists of terminated people to make sure they don't come back in.

"We also have computerized the security desks and linked them to the personnel office and the telephone system. Our new badges will be issued to employees tomorrow. There were no serious problems, unless you count the hostage hoax, and I personally think the guy had to have been drunk."

Wallace smiled, nodding again. "Okay, Frank. Well done."

He turned to Hal Danzig, whose forelock of brown hair was now hanging over his forehead. "Publicity."

"I'm happy to say it went a lot better than we had any right to expect," he said, leafing through his notes. "The Burke episode worked in our favor, in one way, because the media hadn't known about the threats to the Syrian Mission until then, and that distracted everyone a bit. The Nab-Thomas meeting got the lion's share of publicity, led all three of the other networks, and certainly occupied the print people as well—"

"If I may interrupt," Wallace purred, "that was brilliant, Hal, absolutely brilliant. I initially opposed it because I was sure Thomas would make some pompous self-serving statement, and he did. But it made us look all the more tolerant and credible, and Nab showed that he could handle this crowd—"

"And then some," finished Danzig. "Thank you for the compliment, Harold. It did work out well. I was more concerned about the nurse, given her age and history, if the reporters had seen her popping off. But she was out of the way before they even got there. The other press people all signed silence agreements; they're getting severance by the week for a year and if they talk, or if little snippets start appearing in the papers, we'll cut them off fast and they know it.

"I'd say we're in good shape for now. Nobody is going to write stories about cafeteria workers, souvenir sellers, or security guards. If and when the cuts go deeper, that will be another matter."

The people around the table chuckled appreciatively.

But Danzig frowned. "I have to prepare you, Harold, and I would hope you would prepare David, for what will come. He has not been through this sort of takeover before. You and I know that hundreds of thousands of people have lost jobs like these all over the country, and except among a few rock musicians, they haven't generated much attention. But if this isn't handled just right, the media will never forgive Nab for taking over this company. There will be book after book and article after article; they will never stop coming. From now on, he should never say or do anything to anyone that he wouldn't want to read about."

Wallace nodded, although he thought Danzig was being a bit melodramatic. True, the USB takeover was a little stickier, but barring a stupid move—and so far they hadn't made any—the image to which most people would return was of David Nab and Jack Thomas working uneasily but together to keep the traditions of USB alive. The bloodletting could wait, although it couldn't wait too long. Wall Street was watching too.

As for the other employees, it was so rare for white-collar types to make a fuss that Wallace could not remember anyone having done so in the dozens of takeovers he had consulted on.

Wallace believed that women, like this Viola, could be less predictable. It wasn't because they were emotional, although in older women that was something to watch for. It was because they hadn't been in management long enough to have absorbed the code.

According to the few studies he'd seen on the subject, in

recent years hundreds of thousands of middle managers, virtually all of them men, had gone with dignity to their professional deaths in takeovers, mergers, and "downsizings." It was Wallace's business to know that almost all of them had gone quietly.

"What about this SAT unit?" Wallace asked. "That was the only editorial cut we made. Wasn't that unit well known? You expected some flak about that."

"Well, I did," said Danzig. "That's why I joined Barry and his team when they went in. But this D'Amato, who heads the team, is absolutely a perfect gentleman, stiff upper lip. He'd never make any trouble or bitch to reporters. Definitely not his style. And it's easy enough to point out that none of the other networks has such a unit. There's just no need for one anymore. In any case, there's not been a single question from the press about it. And tomorrow Nab is going to Washington to meet with the New York congressional delegation and assure them that the news operations will remain independent. He's slated for a *Time* cover and for stories in *Newsweek* and *New York*. Diane Sawyer may do him for ABC."

Wallace looked up to make sure the door was closed. He had something confidential to say, and it was a mark of his trust in this group that he didn't bother to caution them about discretion.

"One more thing, Hal. Elliott Brookings has just told David he's going to resign as head of USB News. He's given Nab a one-sentence note saying his resignation is effective immediately. In fact, I believe"—he looked to Mahoney for confirmation—"that he's already gone. It was inevitable, I think, and maybe it will make the next couple of months easier."

Mahoney volunteered that Brookings had left with his personal belongings at 5:00 P.M.

"Will this be a problem with the press, Hal?"

Danzig knew that Brookings could cause a lot of trouble if he chose to. But he doubted that Brookings would criticize the institution he'd run for so long.

"I'm glad you told me," said Danzig, mildly irked at the delay in information. "My advice would be to lie pretty low for a couple of days; don't do anything to ruffle his feathers. If he doesn't see a massacre under way, he'll disappear from memory pretty quickly. I feel confident he will do nothing to hurt the organization if he isn't unduly provoked. Is there a successor?"

"Not yet," said Wallace. "Nab is meeting Jack Thomas for dinner. Some of the senior correspondents are coming; he'll sound them out. He knows that he could blow it on this one, and he won't." Wallace checked off another box on his list and turned to Judy Goleman. "Any problems?"

She shook her head. "Armand Andreas, the music director, was hard. His job was completely indefensible, and even he knew it, but he was sweet, and he went on and on about Gershwin and how nobody appreciates that kind of music anymore. I had the feeling that if I told him we all appreciated Gershwin, he would have gone happily. There were no problems."

Wallace nodded appreciatively. "McKelvey?" he continued. "How is our courageous friend Ms. Viola tonight?"

"She's wary and in shock, I think," said McKelvey, "but she's certainly a professional. I was much impressed. I wish she were on our side."

"Any chance of getting her there?"

"Absolutely not," McKelvey said firmly. "She'll always hate our guts."

CHAPTER TWELVE

THE NUT

*A*fter several attempts, Peter got through to D'Amato at 8:00 the next morning. D'Amato's speech was distinctly slurred, as if he had just been awakened or had been drinking.

"Peter, my man," said D'Amato jovially. "You're all right, aren't you? They didn't get you, did they? No, of course not, they're not so stupid. You're a brilliant newsman, an intellectual. They need you, at least for now."

Peter had no idea what to say. Everything he thought of sounded empty or banal. *I'm sorry. Is there anything I can do? Try to look ahead. You deserved better.* He cleared his throat.

D'Amato filled the strained pause. "Peter, I walked over to this office—I refused to get on the fucking bus—and I met with a counselor, some little girl who talked to me like I had a drug problem or was pregnant or something. I don't think she was old enough to vote, Peter. She smiles and hands me this envelope of stuff—tells me what I'm entitled to, you know, what pay and health benefits I can get for three months or whatever the fuck it is. Then they take my ID and my keys and I sign this form so they'll send the stuff in my desk over to my apartment, like when you get out of jail and they give you back your belongings."

Another silence.

"And you know what I'm thinking, Peter? My passport is so full of stamps there's no room for another one, and I've been in every kind of scrape you can be in for this company—my ass kicked by the IRA, the Polish riot police knocking me senseless, napalm from Russian helicopters popping around me, and I'm sitting here like a jerk and I don't know what to say to this kid who's my daughter's age. And I'm thinking that I can't say what I'm thinking, which is that I'm too old not to know what I'm looking at. Which is, that I've just lost my first and last job."

"C'mon, Dan," said Peter, "that's just the shock talking. With your experience—"

But D'Amato cut him off. "Don't stroke me, Peter. I've been around a lot longer than you. Nobody's going to hire a fifty-one-year-old man whose specialty is getting tape in and out of foreign countries. Nobody needs that. All the networks are cutting back, and they wouldn't hire someone my age anyway, 'cause I'll be drawing a pension before I know where the bathroom is. I'm an old man in this game, Peter, you know that. And I'm looking at twenty-five-thousand-dollar-a-year tuition for Bobbie. I *promised* her I'd pay for her to become a doctor, Peter. I *promised* it. Am I supposed to tell that to little Miss Knowlton, my benefits counselor?"

Peter jumped in. "Dan, look, Bobbie's not going to get kicked out of medical school. And you can't possibly know so quickly what the job prospects are for you. You've been all over the world for the best broadcast news division in the country; I don't believe all that experience counts for nothing. You need perspective. You need to get away and clear your head and think about—"

D'Amato sighed, and spoke more calmly. "I'd like to have lunch, Peter. You're the only person there I can talk with. I can't talk with Adelson—he knows that I ain't ever going to work in television again. But you could cheer me up, because you probably don't. Besides, you're a family man, like me. Remember down in Santo Cristo, I told you none of that was real. And wasn't I right?

"But I'm just hung over, Peter. I'm not going to do the

bitter thing. I'm not going to stalk around. I'll face what I have to face. That's the way I was raised and that's what I'm going to do.''

Peter fell silent again.

"At the end of the session, Miss Knowlton says, 'Mr. D'Amato, do you have any questions I can answer about your termination?'

"And I thought about it, Peter, and I said, 'Yeah, I do have a question.' And I picked up the phone in front of her—the way she jumped I thought she was going to call a security guard. I said, 'Miss Knowlton, I have a father who's somewhere in his seventies and has been working in the Italian Market in South Philadelphia as long as I have been alive, and the best thing in his life is that he can brag to all the old geezers he hangs around with about his boy Danny, who runs a television network. Now my father, he stops whatever he is doing—*whatever* he is doing— at seven P.M., and he turns on the TV over the meat counter, and he points out to everybody in the place that the best pictures on the program are from his boy Danny, who is in charge of all the pictures USB News runs.

" 'And, Miss Knowlton, nothing I can say will ever con- vince him that I'm not responsible for the whole damn show. He thinks I'm just being modest. So I want you to call him up at the store and tell him that after so many years of running around taking pictures and giving up everything else in life, his son Danny just got canned, and there'll be no more pictures for him to look at. And when you're finished telling him—here,' I said, 'I'll write the number down—I want you to call my daughter, Bobbie, at NYU and tell her that her father is going to have to break the promise he made when she graduated from Silver Spring High School that no matter what else happened in her life or in mine, I was going to see her through medical school. Believe it, I told her, build your life around that promise from your dad.' "

Peter wanted the conversation to be over. It was possible that just talking helped D'Amato, but it didn't seem that way.

"And she smiles at me and says, 'I'm sorry, but that's a personal matter. I can refer you to psychological counseling, which Nab Enterprises will pay for, if you need additional help.' "

D'Amato hung up, mumbling about Bobbie making breakfast for him.

Most of Harold Wallace's predictions were already proving accurate. Peter and Flannery chuckled bitterly over the fact that Nab got lots of attention when he went to Washington the day after the takeover and pledged at a press conference that he would not allow USB News to be destroyed. In fact, he reassured New York's two senators that with the company more efficiently managed, USB News would be safer than ever.

The senators were further reassured, as was the Washington press corps, by Nab's intelligent demeanor and lack of any overt political ideology. "I believe," he said over and over again, "in hiring good people and leaving them alone to do their jobs." Peter decided it could have been much worse.

Even Wallace's staff was startled at how little furor had been stirred up over the takeover. There'd been more attention given a fistfight on a *Geraldo* show.

What surprised Peter particularly was the way Nab's image was being burnished by the satraps of the news division, led by Jack Thomas, who said in the *Times* that he had been truly worried that some right-wing oil cartel might try to buy the network and that Nab was a long way from that.

"But," said Thomas, "we'll be watching him like a horned owl watches a mouse at night." Jack Thomas himself, he pledged, would be the first to sound the alarm if anything went awry.

Harold Shurken, the quote-happy Wall Street analyst, sounded ready to burst with joy. "Although there are questions about his knowledge of broadcasting, David Nab is a proven manager," he exulted in the *Times* business section. "His properties yield high returns to investors. This was a company in desperate need of tough leadership, and it seems likely to get it."

Harold Wallace put into effect Phase Two of the takeover plan, which was to pretend for several weeks that the company hadn't been taken over at all. Wallace had always been mystified by the clumsy, self-destructive way so many companies completed acquisitions, crashing in and immediately decimating payrolls. Despite all the squawking on Wall Street, USB was expected to turn a $420 million profit that year. Nab could afford to defer

further downsizing until the fuss died away. There would be
time enough to consider which of USB's many profitable assets
should be sold off. Meanwhile, Wallace could use the time well,
working in a few key dinners and some tennis matches to smooth
the way.

It was three days post-takeover before Adelson could call Peter
and Phil Barnard and summon them to a Sanity Lunch. He
invited Buzz Allen as well. Barnard wanted to switch the site to a
swell peach-walled bistro down the street, in an effort to boost
sagging spirits, but Adelson and Peter demanded a return to
Tony's Pizza.

There was some discussion about calling D'Amato and cajoling him into coming, but they decided against it. Peter said he
doubted, from his telephone conversation, that D'Amato was in
the mood for a chatty lunch. Besides, Adelson cautioned, D'Amato
was now a security risk; the Sanity Club couldn't talk freely in
front of him.

So they were four, comfortably sprawled in a corner at
Tony's, Adelson ordering four pizzas, two pitchers of beer, and
several baskets of fried onion rings on their behalf.

Something about the place encouraged candor. "Let's get
down to business," Barnard said abruptly. "How long can each
of you hold out? If you get fired or run out, how long can you
survive?"

"He means the nut," said Adelson. "How big is your nut?"

"Is that a dirty line?" Peter asked. "Another excuse for your
tit jokes?"

"I'm serious," Barnard said impatiently. "If push came to
shove, how much time would you have? Be honest."

In his awkward but earnest way, Allen seemed almost relieved to discuss the question. He had obviously been giving it
some thought. "Well, I think about three months, if you figure
pension plan, savings, selling the vacation house—"

"Hold it," said Adelson. "You can't get your pension money
out for six months after you leave, and then you'd have to give
half of it to the IRS, so your calculations are off. Let's figure it
out," he said, pulling out a small notebook. "How much have
you got in the bank?"

It was odd how easily they immersed themselves in their intimate, gloomy calculations. A few months earlier, such a conversation would have been unthinkable, as well as inappropriate. Now no one seemed hesitant about revealing his financial secrets, except, of course, for Adelson, who had mastered the art of seeming to confide while keeping a comfortable distance.

"Well," mused Allen, "you probably all know by now that we've decided to get a divorce, and since it's a long way from being final, I've got about twenty-five thousand dollars in bonds. And there's the summer house upstate, which we think is worth a hundred and seventy-five thousand, and I could go to my dad for ten or twenty thousand if I had to. That's against six thousand a month in child support, combined with the mortgage on the Westchester house, and just about two thousand for my new apartment. Plus tuition and expenses, which I haven't figured out. But I figure I'd get severance. I've been with the company ten years, so that's at least two weeks a year. . . ." Adelson and Allen were both scratching figures down now.

"But it would take you some time to sell the cottage," Adelson pointed out, adding and subtracting. "And your wife would get half of that anyway, and you have two kids. Very little of what you have is liquid. If you didn't get a job right away, you'd be in trouble in four months at the outside, with expenses like that. I think if push comes to shove, you'll end up at a welfare hotel with your kids playing with crack vials in the halls."

He meant it as a joke, but it was in fact a recurring nightmare of Allen's.

Buzz shook his head. "I read this men's column last week about how this guy decides to spend more time with his kids and he quits his job and stays home. But the column didn't say how he pays for it."

"Maybe his wife makes decent bucks," said Adelson. Carol did.

"Well, mine doesn't," said Allen. "Four months. I better make sure to put more of Jack Thomas's fascinating ideas on the air."

It occurred to Adelson that what he had suspected about Allen was almost certainly true: He was not going to make it. His slight whine was a tip-off, and the revelation that he'd already been thinking about his own ruin. Adelson noticed again that Allen seemed to lack the predatory instincts his job required.

As for Adelson, the discussion was academic. With his company stock and nearly $3 million in Manhattan and Berkshires real estate, plus his wife's earnings, Adelson was long past working for mere money. He was in it for the sport and for the glory.

He turned to Barnard. "What about you? You got a trust fund?"

Barnard normally would have fired back some insolent answer, but he nodded, a bit sheepishly. "But my ex-wife gets a third. That was the deal before she remarried. I could always go hole up at the family estate in Maine, but that's a long winter up there. Still, I could probably hang on. My uncle has an apartment in London, in Knightsbridge. I could spend a few months playing court tennis." No one pressed Barnard. He was in a special category, not so wealthy that he never had to worry about money, but with resources to turn to if necessary.

It was Peter's turn. "Three, four months, depending on severance. Is it true that if you get them to fire you, you get a better deal?" he asked Adelson.

Adelson shrugged. "Depends on how much they want you out," he said.

This particular tack was a specialty of Adelson's, Peter knew. People went away from conversations with him feeling grateful for his attention and empathy and wondering at his having remained one of the guys. He always referred to himself as if he were in the same boat as everyone else, although he was careful never to be. His ultimate loyalties lay, always, with the people he worked for.

"So, let's see," Peter calculated. "We have two cars, although one is paid for, and we have a twenty-four-hundred-a-month mortgage. You have to give me one thing—better to make a stand in Jersey than on Park Avenue."

"Please," said Barnard. "I'd rather be homeless in Manhattan than comfortable in New Jersey. At least you'd have a good social life."

Peter gave him the finger.

"How about D'Amato?" Peter asked Adelson. "How's his nut?"

"I don't know," said Adelson. "He's scared about his daughter's medical school tuition—that's what he kept talking about when they threw him out. Being single, he could probably hold out a long time except for that."

Allen poured everybody another beer. "A toast," he commanded. "We're all still employed—that's something."

"Yes," said Barnard, raising his glass. "But will the living envy the dead?"

The conversation sagged, each man mulling over his resources.

"You were there when D'Amato got it?" Peter asked Adelson.

"Yeah. Elaine heard they were hitting Research and the SAT, so I went over there. D'Amato was completely shell-shocked. But Nab's people had done their homework, you know," said Adelson. "The SAT unit has been unnecessary for years."

"That's not fair, Sam," Allen argued. "His unit got us some of the best pictures the division has ever run. He got to the hijacked seven-forty-seven in Cyprus first, and got pictures of them shooting that hostage; he had the first pictures out of Afghanistan when the Russians invaded. And they tell me his stuff out of Vietnam was unbelievable. It wasn't a technical unit—it was more like a commando team."

"Look at the stuff he just did for my show on the *Providence* sinking, and the infrared pictures he got on the Ponzio abortion stuff," Peter put in.

Adelson nodded sadly. "I know. I know better than any of you what D'Amato did for this company over the years. I just meant that Nab's people had sniffed around. They knew the unit was redundant now that you can practically carry a satellite dish in a briefcase. So it was an instant eight-million-dollar hit."

"Is there anything we can do to help the guy?" Peter wondered.

"You ought to stay in touch with him," Adelson said to Peter. "He thinks of you as a close friend."

Peter recoiled. "But I don't really know him that well," he protested. "We have lunch once in a while and I like him, I like him a lot, but I wouldn't say we were close."

"Well, maybe by D'Amato's standards, you're close," Adelson said. "He sure isn't very intimate with anybody else. You ought to keep an eye on him. We all should."

Barnard snorted. "What is this, group therapy? Don't you know that men are loyal to other men only in war and sports?

Otherwise, you're on your own, isn't that right? What about Adelson's Law Number Whatever: *Never bandage a leper?*"

"What're the odds of his ever getting a broadcasting job?" Allen asked Adelson.

"Zero to none."

"You're kidding," Peter objected. "The guy's got more than twenty-five years of network television experience. And he has a great attitude—he's loyal, enthusiastic, not a troublemaker."

"Look, nobody wants to hire somebody that age. You end up paying more in benefits than you get in work. Besides, the networks are all cutting back," Adelson said. "Nobody needs what D'Amato does. I think he has to get out of the business."

Now Allen was shocked. "Out of the business? What would he do? Go to real estate school?"

Adelson looked tired. "Reality may have just struck you guys," he said, "but people like D'Amato have been getting whacked by the hundreds of thousands for almost ten years now. I don't know what the fuck guys do when they get the ax. Just don't be one of them, okay?"

CHAPTER THIRTEEN
SEVERANCE

*A*delson had gotten the first phone call from the New York bureau at 2:30 A.M.; by 5:30 he was at the Connecticut State Police barracks in Mystic, and on his umpteenth cup of muddy, bitter coffee. The sergeant was finally finished with his paperwork and ready to talk, and Adelson shook his head to jolt himself alert. He took his notebook out, thinking about the grilling Brookings would subject him to. Then he remembered that Brookings was gone. There would be a lot of questions nevertheless.

The car—a rented import—had been towed to the back of the barracks, a blackened lump. Nothing could have walked away from it. Adelson had stopped at the accident scene on the way. The wires on the guardrail were torn open; the car had shot down a thirty-foot hill onto a concrete underpass below and exploded, according to a truck driver who'd witnessed the accident. He'd been there still, watching the emergency crews work in the darkness; he told Adelson that he'd pulled his rig over but had seen only a fireball. The driver had to have died real quick, the trucker had said.

The sergeant, thought Adelson, was the size of a small tractor-trailer himself. He looked uncomfortable.

"Mr. Adelson, you've been waiting to see me? I'm here. How can I help you?"

"Thanks for seeing me, Sergeant Kass. I'm here as a representative of USB News and as a friend and employer of the victim. I'm not here as a reporter." He had interpreted the sergeant's uneasiness as suspicion of the press, and he wanted to reassure him. "What you tell me is for the company, not for publication. I just want to know what happened."

Kass took out the accident report from a folder on top of his desk and sat down, gesturing that Adelson should do the same. He gratefully accepted a doughnut Adelson had picked up at a diner down the road.

"I'll tell you what I can, Mr. Adelson. The accident investigation isn't complete yet, so it's unofficial, but pretty straightforward. From the tire marks and eyewitness accounts, he was going at a pretty good clip—looks to be about seventy to seventy-five—when the car suddenly swerved sharply to the right. The guardrail there is just some cable between posts—wouldn't stop a motorcycle really—and he popped through that. On the way down, the car overturned, and gas from the tank spilled into the engine and ignited, we think. In that situation a car is like a Molotov cocktail, although I'll tell you frankly, I don't think he could have survived that crash even if the car hadn't blown up. It's a sheer drop of thirty feet onto concrete, and with the car being upside down and all, it folded in on him. The medical examiner will be able to tell whether it was trauma or fire that killed him, although I don't suppose it makes much difference to you."

Adelson was scribbling notes. He looked up at the big trooper. "Sergeant, was there any evidence of alcohol, anything like that?" It had been years since Adelson had asked a cop that question, but it was coming back to him.

"The lab at the hospital says preliminary blood tests show alcohol in the blood at three times the legal limit. But even that wouldn't satisfy me as to why he made such a sudden turn. You'd have to pull the wheel sharply to the right to go through the rail there, and we know from people behind him that he was traveling straight, up to that point."

The sergeant picked up a clipboard, and sat back in the chair. "Maybe you can help me a bit, Mr. Adelson, as long as we're all being so cooperative here—"

"Anything I can do," said Adelson.

"You know the next of kin?"

Adelson handed him the emergency personnel folder USB News kept on every employee. Network security had driven it to Connecticut. Kass leafed through it, jotting notes down on a pad, pausing as a whining teenager was led down the hall in handcuffs.

"Well, Mr. Adelson, there's a question I would like to put to you. You were his boss. Do you think he might have killed himself?"

Adelson shook his head. "No, absolutely not. He wasn't the type. It just didn't seem in his nature to do something like that. I mean, he had good reason to be worried lately—he lost his job about ten days ago. But I can't see him killing himself."

Kass's eyebrows shot up at the mention of the job, and he made some more notes on his pad and tapped his papers neatly into a stack. "Well, Mr. Adelson, I couldn't make a guess about it until I know more. I can tell you suicide has to be considered a possibility. Even at two A.M. on a Saturday, cars don't just suddenly make one hundred-degree turns to the right at seventy-five miles per. Maybe he was driving along the road with a few pops in him and suddenly saw the rail and figured, hell, at least there's the insurance. Who knows? I'm not a mind reader, but we'll try and sort it out." He stood up. The interview was over, and Adelson went to the pay phone to call in the news alert.

The alert was sounded at 6:30 A.M. on Saturday and Peter sprang up, ready to hit his ice-cold shower. He gave his code to the network operator.

"Good morning, Mr. Herbert. This message was authorized by Mr. Adelson, and was transmitted by the New York bureau. . . ." The pause was to make sure the caller was awake and armed with pencil and pad. "Dan D'Amato was killed early this morning in an automobile accident on the Connecticut Turnpike, according to the Connecticut State Police. His car broke through a guardrail near Mystic and crashed down a slope and burned.

Mr. Adelson is at the scene. Coverage is being coordinated out of Boston. That's the end, sir."

"That's it?" Peter repeated dumbly. The deaths of executives and key producers were traditionally announced over the NAPS system, like stirrups reversed in the saddle for army heroes.

"Yes, sir. Good day." The click snapped him out of it, and out of his self-absorption over his own mounting career difficulties. He turned instinctively to Barbara to tell her, but paused. My God, he thought, we ran as far away from him as we could get. We didn't even want him to come to lunch.

He put his head in his hands. Barbara was awake and up in an instant, her arms around him. There were telephone calls and telephone calls, and she knew the difference.

"What is it?" she asked. "Is it your father?"

"No. D'Amato's dead, killed in a car crash in Connecticut, near Mystic. Burned to death, maybe."

Barbara held him for a moment, then got up and put her robe on. "I'll get some coffee," she said. "I'm so sorry, Peter."

Peter walked toward his children's bedrooms. Eugene lay in his customary post in the hallway between Ben's room and Sarah's, and even though he did not open his eyes or stir, his tail thumped softly when Peter approached.

Peter sat on the edge of Ben's bed and stroked his son's face, pushing his brown hair back off his forehead. He went into Sarah's room and kissed her cheek. Then he sat down on the floor next to Eugene and was not able to hold back a few tears.

It wasn't, he thought, as if Dan D'Amato had wanted to run USB, or even a part of USB News. He just wanted to take pictures of big stories and send them back to the network faster than anyone else, as he had done for years and done well. He had not asked for much in return. It was a reasonable enough contract, thought Peter.

CHAPTER FOURTEEN

WAR

*H*arold Wallace had gotten rid of Elliott Brookings's leather chair and replaced it with David Nab's own newer, more streamlined version. Wallace had the old chair sent to Brookings's New England house with a small silver plaque attached to the back, engraved TO ELLIOTT BROOKINGS: A PIONEER IN BUILDING USB NEWS.

The new chair was installed at Brookings's old spot at the head of the rosewood conference table, where Nab and Wallace were addressing their first major task involving USB News: the selection of a new president.

Nab had let it be known that Harold Wallace would choose Brookings's successor, allowing Nab to set himself above the fray and avoid responsibility for whatever blood might be spattered in the ensuing brawl.

The next USB president had to come from within, both men had agreed. That would calm the forces in government and the press who might sound the alarm about the takeover. If USB News veterans were still running the place, critics could hardly claim that one of the nation's sacred institutions had been defiled.

While the news division's vast staff was busy speculating and trading shreds of gossip, Wallace had quietly taken steps to ensure that USB News's most prominent veterans would cause no trouble. Like the truly best lawyers, he was not boastful by nature, so few others ever knew all the details, but it had required only three tennis matches, one dinner party, and four new contracts to complete, discreetly and carefully, what he thought of as the Second Takeover—the secret one. Other top-ranked lawyers preened at their clubs and angled for gushing press profiles. Wallace was more than content to know that his homework had paid off, that his strategy had been perfect, his service to his client brilliant. He earned his staggering fees. It was always the details, he told his associates whenever he could, the little things that separated the excellent from the mediocre.

He never underestimated his prey. If anything, he felt a bit disappointed at how cowed these self-styled lions of broadcasting had been. He had thought they were in for the fight of their lives, Wallace mused as he and Nab settled in for their strategy session. But these people went belly-up like a bunch of St. Bernards wanting to have their tummies scratched. Once their own contracts were secure and those skyscraper egos fed, there was no more whining about USB's public trust.

So far so good, he thought. Now to help Nab negotiate the last treacherous shoals. Once past the appointment of Brookings's successor, Wallace would gratefully head back to the Street, where there were just as many cutthroats but less need for pretense. His role in the USB takeover had not gone unnoticed there, despite his discretion, and his appointment book was filling up; some important names in American business wanted his counsel.

There would be an ugly little war within USB News now, he knew, between Julian McCallister and Sam Adelson and their respective supporters, but that would be an internal conflict, fought far below Nab. It would be brief. And there would be, Wallace knew, distractions.

"You know, David, we're in a pretty fortunate position, because either man could run the news division perfectly well."

A few days earlier Nab had offhandedly asked Wallace whether he was interested in running USB News himself, especially now that he knew so much about it. Wallace had been surprised to find himself momentarily tempted. It was an extraordinary job, there was no doubt about that.

The president of USB News would never, for example, have to negotiate the city's subway system, hail a cab in rainy weather, walk down a dark street, lick a postage stamp, miss a Broadway opening, stand in line at a movie theater, spend an entire dreary winter in freezing New York, drive himself through Hamptons traffic, or ever worry again in his life about money. When his time ran out, if he chose, he would retire to a powerful foundation or a prestigious journalism school, becoming one of the wise old men who harrumphs about the decline in journalistic values. In the meantime his social calendar would be filled with important names. But it wasn't the personal perks that attracted him: Wallace had his own.

The president of USB News, however, sat in the control room at presidential conventions, helping to shape the nation's agenda, signaling with a nod of his head whether to leave the air or stay on. The morning after each nomination, one of the new candidate's first actions would be to meet with him, chatting respectfully about the campaign, perhaps tactfully seeking his advice.

The heads of some of the world's most powerful entities—the CIA, the State Department, Defense, the United Nations—would be constantly on the telephone, pleading with him to cover this or that story or to withhold this or that disturbing report.

His office would be among the required stops for visiting heads of state. He would receive a personal tour of the Forbidden City, be known at his favorite hotels in London and Paris, watch baseball games in the network box. Professors and authors, judges and newspaper columnists, actors and directors would all want to meet him.

It had been a prospect tempting enough to discuss with his wife, whom he never ordinarily consulted on professional matters. But Wallace had dismissed it. These peacocks with their vanities and illusions would drive him crazy, and no matter how many perks they threw in, USB couldn't meet his salary demands.

★   ★   ★

"Everybody's betting on McCallister," said Flannery. "But Adelson is not someone I would underestimate. I bet he learned a few moves back in Brooklyn he might pull out of his pocket about now."

Peter and Flannery traded kernels of information on the phone several times a day, preparing in their own way for the blow everyone knew was coming.

Peter tried to hold his conversations out of earshot of Barbara, who was growing increasingly edgy about the turmoil. Preventing Barbara from overhearing wasn't difficult, since he'd spent much of his spare time holed up in the bedroom, brooding, since D'Amato's funeral.

Barbara's inclination was to give him lots of room when he needed it, and in any case she was not into gossiping about USB News. She hadn't seemed to want to know much about the takeover, either, at least not until something concrete happened. It wasn't indifference, Peter thought; it was denial. Too many questions about maintaining their life in Glen Ridge and her existence as a writer, the novel that seemed to be taking shape so well, would suddenly arise if the company blew up. Barbara's prediction was that the new owners wouldn't ultimately prove that different from the old—they were all white, middle-aged male capitalists, she said, with more or less the same goals. Peter believed that, too, or wanted to. He hadn't mentioned the ominous request he'd received this week, a memo from Harold Wallace asking for the names of staffers that *Morning in the U.S.* could function without, "in the event that financial pressures caused USB to reassess its personnel needs."

But Flannery permitted herself no such reassurance, and she wasn't inclined to let him keep his illusions, either. "Peter, you just don't want to deal with the fact that you might lose your big backyard and your summer swim club and your stupid, smelly dog lounging by the hearth," she scoffed, when Peter weakly tried to pooh-pooh a *Times* story quoting a "USB source close to David Nab" as saying USB News's next president would be chosen from within by Harold Wallace. The choice was between two veteran USB vice-presidents, Julian McCallister and Sam Adelson, the source said. In either case, the *Times* pointed out, the new regime would likely pursue staff and budget cuts.

"Patricia, you're getting yourself in a lather. You ought to jump into that car wash you built in your bathroom and cool off. Sure, there will be some cuts—there are cuts everyplace. But nobody thinks Nab is going to chop up the whole company. He wants to be a *player*; he wants the prestige of owning a television network. Nobody was interested in what he thought about condo development. Now he gets to go to cocktail parties with Linda Burns gasping in wonder at his brilliance and Harry Sommers ready to drive him to the tennis court and Jack Thomas calling up to chat and the best box at the Kennedy Center Honors show."

Peter heard, in reply, the whooshing of the water in the tub. Flannery, from her aquatic command post, knew more about what was happening behind USB's closed executive doors than many of the vice-presidents who were behind them.

"I'm already *in* the tub," she protested. "It gives me perspective. You executive producers can deal in wishful thinking. It's my business to know how people like Nab think. There's no mystery about him or what he will do—he'll do what he did to every other company he's taken over. He'll take control of the pressure points, make a deal with the key players, and then in six months, when nobody's looking, he'll go through the place like a crackhead through a BMW. He'll hack the budget with a cleaver, sell off half the company, put a few billion in the bank, and you know what, boss? He'll *still* be a major player and *still* get to go to cocktail parties and have Linda Burns look him deep in the eyes and say 'Ooh, Mr. Nab, what do you really believe about Third World debt?' "

Peter was irritated now; this was not what he had been telling Barbara, or himself. "You honestly think Nab'll pillage the place? They'll tear him to pieces, Patricia, if he tries to do that."

Flannery bore down. "*Who'll* tear him to pieces? Elliott Brookings, who ran off to Vermont without a peep? Jack Thomas? He'll stomp around about the cuts all right, but you won't see his behind going out the door. Adelson and McCallister aren't going to stalk off in a huff; one of them will be president of the news division and one of them will be gone. I haven't noticed Congress calling a special session about the takeover, have you? And I'll give you a dollar for every letter USB gets from a viewer about this great institution being taken over by Condo Man.

Forget it, viewers won't notice anything different. In television you never know what you *aren't* seeing. Nobody knows that Mickey Grodner isn't there anymore fussing with her little computer to check the extra fact, and nobody gives a damn. Jesus. Men! It's the Empire to the end, no matter what you see in front of you."

Peter heard a splash, as if for emphasis. The fact that Flannery's voice was echoing off the tile walls of her supertub made her typically direct analysis more eerily unsettling, like the Wizard thundering at Dorothy. But dawn after dawn in the combat conditions of morning television, Peter had learned to trust Flannery's judgment.

Flannery immodestly agreed that her judgments were piercing and her record accurate. This was how she lived, she said. She didn't have a husband to please or children to soothe. She lived or died by her ruthlessness and her ability to see clearly.

He would do well to think more clearly himself about what was coming, Peter realized; if Flannery was even close to being right. For one thing, McCallister was almost sure to win a corporate bout with Adelson. McCallister was markedly more smooth and had been networking day and night for years. His Park Avenue duplex had become a favorite salon and watering hole for influential journalists, fellow executives, and celebrities of various sorts. There was hardly a major newspaper editor left in the country whom McCallister didn't call regularly to exchange witty little anecdotes and barbs.

Before, when it all seemed so abstract, Peter had often lectured Flannery on the medieval quality to the office wars that erupted inside USB News. Unpopular or overly ambitious executives often came under siege, harassed and attacked until they fled or were thrown out. Correspondents, executive producers, and vice-presidents were always forging alliances with one another, or with unlikely combinations of agents and reporters, to bring people down. On-air princes and princesses, kept in palaces and surrounded by doting attendants, lost touch with reality and made foolish errors in judgment, often paying with their professional lives. Reporters covering television became proxies in these struggles, trading access and information for character-assassinating or image-building items.

But now Peter felt less pleased with his historical analogy.

This was Adelson on the line now, and Peter winced at the thought of his friend in the arena.

Adelson was a superior newsman, but Peter had no illusions about the weight that carried. Adelson was too much the corporate outsider. He worked like a dervish and knew every nut and bolt of USB News, but a maestro was what they would choose, not a mechanic. And McCallister, Peter had to concede, had a tough and creative vision of where television had to go, whereas Adelson tilted a bit toward the Old Guard, whose religion was Keep It The Way It Was.

"You know, Patricia," Peter said, after one of the pauses that the two allowed each other, to ponder this news or that strategy, "I can't help thinking what a team they would make. McCallister and Adelson, Mr. Outside and Mr. Inside. They would have it all. I mean, I have to root for Sam, but imagine the two of them together."

Flannery hooted at the idea. "Out of the question, Peter. Big Players do not link up or submit to one another." And as she said it, Peter recalled one of Adelson's own favorite laws—*Pick your fights carefully: All battles are to the death.*

"You're not sounding optimistic notes about my own career, are you?" Peter asked Flannery. "Maybe Nab won't be so tolerant of my ratings just because I nail a congressional aide now and then."

Her tone changed, from wisecracking corporate realist to a gentler one. "I don't know, Peter, but I think we should both be prepared. Every producer in the place got one of those just-in-case memos from Wallace. There's an ill wind blowing, eh, Watson? And I think it could blow us away with it."

Peter heard the whooshing again, which he guessed meant Flannery was warming up the tub.

"Listen," she said, "can we go friend-to-friend for a minute? I know how dicey men are when it comes to talking about anything that counts."

"Go ahead," he said. "We're old pals, aren't we? We'll even be talking sports one of these days, if this keeps up."

"I don't want to add to your mounting middle-aged woes, but are you okay about D'Amato? You haven't said a thing about it since the funeral. I can tell you're down."

"I don't know, Patricia. As long as we're puncturing illusions, don't let me hold on to any about Dan. I don't believe he just went over an embankment at that hour of the morning by accident. And we didn't do a thing for him. We didn't even want to invite him to lunch. I called him up, but it never crossed my mind to go see him or anything. Maybe our friendship was just a mirage, not only D'Amato's and mine, but all of ours. I have to wonder, I guess I'll always wonder, if it would have made any difference if we had let him know we were there, let him know there was a group behind him. Although I guess the idea of us being a group at all—Barnard and Adelson and Allen and me— that was bullshit. We even said so, but we've sure proven it, haven't we? Probably *I'm* on somebody's we-can-do-without-him list. So now I figure, this is all I did for him, and this is all they'll do for me."

Aside from the splashing water, there was silence on the other end of the telephone.

"Patricia. You know the abortion story?"

"Of course I know it, shmegeggy. I got it. Why do you bring that story up now?"

"D'Amato, I guess. He worked on it and he's gone. So is the Special Assignment Team. Adelson says they're going to whack the Investigative Unit too. *Adelson* may be gone himself, soon. Brookings is gone. Will it count, that story? Will it count for anything?"

"What story?" she said, and laughed.

CHAPTER FIFTEEN
DOS AND DON'TS

*T*he layoffs were the only thing he would have done differently, Harold Wallace later decided. Perhaps he should have spread them out over a longer period, perhaps given the employees more notice so they could find other jobs. It might have even made sense to allow more of the longer-term employees to stay on for a while.

He had considered it more humane to get the layoffs over with, instead of leaving an ax dangling over everyone's head. But that, he had realized over time, was not the way the employees saw it.

It had begun at nine on a blustery but brilliant May morning, when Harold Wallace stood up and opened the meeting, the first of its kind in USB's long history. Wallace had planned the meeting with painstaking care, as he planned everything. He wanted the meeting held in USB News's conference room, around the great rosewood table where almost every major decision involving the news division had been made for forty years.

He was adamant about there being no food or drink, not

even coffee, the austere atmosphere befitting a meeting called to plan the logistics of dismissing 475 people. A lot of money had been spent at that table, he'd told Nab; now they were going to save some there.

Besides Wallace and David Nab, who was sitting behind him, the group encircling the vast table included Adelson, McCallister, the news division's eight operating vice-presidents, the foreign and national editors, the Washington bureau chief, and the division's executive producers. Grace Viola was one of three women in the room.

Arrayed in a row of chairs set up behind them were litigation, labor-relations, and benefits specialists, looking like federal agents in their black or navy suits with tightly knotted ties. Hal Danzig, the public relations expert, sat armed with a note pad and tape recorder.

Rafael Miranda, the steward whose domain the conference room was, had been puzzled to learn that a meeting had been scheduled without refreshments, without even coffee or juice. He stopped by to make sure there hadn't been some mistake. Miranda, who often joked that he had dined with more members of Congress than any illegal alien in history, edged into the room, noticed the grim-looking strangers, and caught Adelson's frown. He turned on his heel and left. Had he lingered he would have learned that dining services were to be contracted to an outside vending company and that his days of mingling with the famous and powerful were over.

"I trust everyone has received a packet," Wallace began. Peter looked down at his, a gray envelope with the network logo and a computer-printed label: HERBERT, PETER—EXECUTIVE PRODUCER, *Morning in the U.S.*

He unwound the string that fastened the envelope and looked inside. An instruction sheet on top listed five procedural steps, each a paragraph long. Behind it was a "Do Say" and "Don't Say" sheet. The third sheet was a computer-printed list; his had twenty-two names, all of editorial or technical employees working on his broadcast. Alongside each name was the employee's Social Security number, his or her starting date at the network, and contract status or base pay.

Peter looked up from the list and sought Adelson's eye. Adelson caught the look, then smiled sadly and leaned back. He and McCallister, Nab and Wallace and Danzig had been up half the night plotting strategy. Wallace had argued forcefully, and without much resistance, that he should play the heavy, since he would shortly be returning to his law firm; Adelson and McCallister should remain absolutely silent, and Nab should say little.

Most people at USB would want to forgive their new owner and boss, Wallace had explained, whereas they were quite free to hate *him* forever. Danzig had agreed, advancing what he liked to call the notion of "nonquotability": If you said nothing—not even "no comment"—you could not only avoid being quoted by the media, but no one would retain any memory of your even being present at the event. In the next day's stories, no one would be able to credit Adelson or McCallister with a single word, either insensitive or sympathetic.

Wallace sipped from a glass of water and cleared his throat. "Please open your packets if you have not already done so. The names on the third sheet have been selected from recommendations and staff evaluations you submitted to us last week.

"The final selections were made on the basis of an independent audit, by a private accounting firm, of the division's needs and of staffs at enterprises of comparable size and function."

Indeed, the independent accounting firm had sent its auditors swarming through the news division like DEA agents on a dope raid, redefining broadcast journalism in seventy-two hours by concluding that a third of the division's staff was no longer necessary. Using a statistical computer analysis, which totaled the numbers of producers and correspondents, divided them by the number of pieces aired from each of their bureaus, and factored in length and shooting and editing hours, the auditors had immediately red-flagged Bangkok, Paris, Bogota, Toronto, Warsaw, and especially London. The same analysis drew attention to the division's much-acclaimed Investigative Unit, to all the entry-level news assistants and pages, and to the clusters of aging producers parked in the public affairs unit.

To his credit, Adelson had battled furiously with Nab and Wallace, arguing eloquently that a news organization was like a firehouse: It looked as if lots of people were lying around, but when a tenement went up, you needed every one of them. McCallister also demurred, but halfheartedly and clearly for the record. It was an argument Nab and Wallace both said they respected them for making, and they made sure that Jack Thomas, key producers, and favored reporters knew that Adelson and McCallister had "gone to the wall," as they put it, on behalf of their people.

Once the decision had been made, Adelson avoided complaining and threw his considerable energies into helping to plan how the cuts would be carried out. He was a corporate adult, a quality he prized over almost all other attributes, especially in a world he believed was peopled with spoiled and naïve adolescents. You got paid to do the rough stuff with grace and loyalty. He was willing to go to the wall, but he wasn't about to go over it. McCallister simply made himself scarce.

So, a month after the takeover, Harold Wallace was giving the division's skittish middle managers their marching orders. "The employees on your lists, as I am sure is obvious to you, have been designated for termination. These names have been reviewed by our legal staff and are final and non-negotiable. I will outline and review the procedures you are expected to follow, which are listed on the first sheet inside your packet. Mr. Bedell from our legal department will be available after the meeting to handle any questions. So will I—"

"Needless to say," Nab interjected, "we regret these steps. I can only tell you that they are necessary to ensure the company's healthy future and to meet our responsibilities to our stockholders. This is not being done callously or without genuine regret."

Wallace nodded. "Thank you, David. Now, here are the procedures to follow. These are not, repeat not, guidelines. They are not optional. Each of you will be held responsible for seeing that every one of these steps is faithfully executed.

"Number One. These are not firings. You will note on your 'Don't Say' sheet that the terms *firings* and *fired* are not to be used. These are positions being eliminated, not people being fired. The distinction is an important one, as well as one which should considerably ease the discomfort of the affected employees. When you summon an employee into your office, *Do Say* that you regret having to terminate his or her position, that he or she is not being released for incompetence or any other reason having to do with his or her work. Be sure to emphasize that; it greatly diminishes the possibility of a lawsuit.

"In other words, this is an economic situation. There are no grounds for dismissal, thus no grounds on which to challenge the dismissal."

That would certainly make *me* feel better, thought Peter.

"Number Two. Please tell the affected employee that a special counselor from the personnel office will be standing by at headquarters for the next ten days to explain the benefit situation, the separation procedure, and relocation assistance.

"Number Three. Notify the affected employee that he or she must surrender company identification to you immediately, as well as all company credit cards and office keys. Collect them and place them in a manila envelope. If an employee refuses, notify building security immediately and a security guard will come to your office and escort the employee from the premises. In our experience, that will probably prove unnecessary.

"Number Four. Please notify the affected employee that he or she must check in at the lobby from that moment forward, like any other visitor to the building. Employees will be given twenty-four hours to clean out their desks, and boxes will be provided by building security for that purpose. If an employee's personal affects are not out of the building in twenty-four hours, security personnel will remove them and ship them to the employee's home at the company's expense.

"Number Five. Please advise affected employees, should they bring it up, that the company's revenues are down by twenty percent this year and that we project a greater decline next year. Since these employees are likely to be interviewed by the news media, we believe it is important for our side of the story to get out.

"*Do Not Say* that someone upstairs made these decisions. You are management. *You* supplied the lists of candidates for terminations. Blaming the company only encourages anger and suggests arbitrary behavior on the company's part.

"Questions?"

Harry Sommers had one. The *Weekend News* producer's friendship with the old Chairman and, if rumor had it right, the new one as well, permitted him to be blunt. He reportedly had already spent a weekend at Nab's Connecticut estate.

"Mr. Wallace, you mentioned benefits? What benefits exactly will these people have?"

"Good question, Mr. Sommers; but I can't give a single answer. That depends on salary level and length of service and contract obligations. These questions should be referred to the relocation counselor at extension seven-six-six. Please, for legal reasons, do not attempt to answer questions about benefits yourselves, as noted on the 'Don't Say' card."

"But, these people will be given some benefits and protection, won't they?"

"Please, Mr. Sommers, I can't generalize. Some of these remarks are sure to be repeated beyond this room, possibly even to the media."

"We are the media!" Sommers insisted.

"Are there any other questions?" asked Wallace.

"Why do they have to be out in twenty-four hours? Isn't that a little cruel?" asked a voice behind Peter.

Wallace frowned. He reminded himself that he was not dealing with his own well-trained team but with a group of journalists. He had always assumed they would be worldly and savvy but he had been amazed, as Hal Danzig had predicted, to discover that they were as naïve as grade-schoolers. Wallace had found himself stating the obvious all day long for weeks and was by now desperate to get back to Wall Street, where, whatever else you could say about the financial community, delusion was simply too expensive. He was thinking, even as he simply and patronizingly answered the question, that people on the Street might be sharks, but at least they didn't pretend to be holy.

"Ladies and gentlemen," he began, choosing his words carefully, aware that if he were to step in it, this would be the place. "I am special counsel to your new chairman with regard to these terminations and am, unfortunately, quite familiar with economic retrenchment and restructuring.

"These procedures may seem abrupt to you, but quite frankly, this is not the first time our company has assumed responsibility for new properties. Our experience has been that when middle managers are asked to make reduction decisions, there is less likelihood of legal action than if senior management makes those choices. Our position is that you know your own employees best and can best defend your choices concerning necessary and unnecessary—or less necessary, if you prefer—positions."

Peter was impressed by how much smarter Wallace was

than most of the fairly bright people sitting around the table. He wouldn't fire anyone himself. Neither would Nab. They could— and would—say with complete sincerity that it was USB News executives themselves who had made the selections and handled the executions. And why should Wallace care who got thrown out anyway? The lawyer's tone was soothing, suggesting that *we sophisticated sorts with heavy responsibilities understand what we have to do.* It made everybody seem, and presumably feel, a bit more important.

"We have reviewed your choices as to legal concerns, particularly age, sexual, or racial discrimination. Some of you will find names on your lists that you did not put there. That is simply because we felt the need to balance the overall employee reductions and eliminate any pattern that could provide the basis for legal action.

"Even when such reductions are justified, some employees will consider themselves the victims of arbitrary and unfair practices. These individuals may agitate or spread malicious rumors, damaging morale and spreading resentment toward management. Judging from past experience, we feel that the sooner the employee is gone, the better for him or her—and for you, by the way."

Peter again looked across the table at Adelson, who was staring straight down at the table. Wallace had deflated the group. His sense of authority was daunting. He was too smart to lie, too clever to tell the whole truth. He spoke as if what he was saying were obvious and inevitable, and in assuming the cooperation of everyone in the room, he had somehow guaranteed it. Obviously, Wallace's previous experience had included handling managers as well.

Peter looked for Barnard and found him. Barnard looked bored. Allen, however, was serious, attentive. You could count on Barnard to ignore the Dos and Don'ts and on Allen to follow them to the letter. Peter was also watching Grace Viola. She had been a prophet, Adelson had told him, almost the only one clear-eyed enough to see precisely what was coming and what was at stake. She was right about something else, too, Peter conceded, something he could never say aloud: They had brought so much of it on themselves.

But this could still be stopped, he found himself thinking. If we all got up and said, "Wait, this is the wrong way to handle this"—the way Viola had for that mouse in finance—if we didn't go along, they couldn't do it, could they? We are the machinery they have to use. Why should we do their bloody work? We could scare them off, or at least slow them down. If just one of us balked, maybe the others would join the resistance.

Peter looked around the table, wondering whom he could count on if he said something. Not Adelson. And Barnard would never do anything so brazenly idealistic—it wasn't his style. Allen? Peter didn't know. Publicly challenging authority was not the way Buzz had been trained, but then, who in this room *had* been trained that way? Viola, he thought. Her standing up to Nab's shock troops that first day had astonished and embarrassed every executive in the division, all of whom had watched like Cub Scouts at a baseball game as people they had worked with for years, sometimes decades, were tossed out of the building like sacks of trash.

But Peter sagged, because he knew better. A revolt by middle managers? Unthinkable. A contradiction in terms.

"Last caution," said Wallace. "You may reasonably expect that reporters will be coming around looking to interview the terminated employees or yourselves. We ask that you discuss nothing that happened in this room. Included in your packet is a number to call when your terminations are concluded, or if you run into unexpected questions or challenges. We know this is unpleasant for you, as it is for us, but we also know your professionalism will enable you to carry out these instructions precisely."

Nab stood up. "What Mr. Wallace is saying, in case any of you require interpretation, is that you are all grown-ups being paid a lot of money, and this is one of the things you get paid a lot of money to do." His bluntness was almost refreshing after the velvety attorney. "If any of you have problems, this is the time to raise your hands. Otherwise, I'll expect you to do your jobs as instructed." He sat down.

It was a straightforward warning. Nab was preempting any rebellion that might be simmering below the surface in any of the sullen people around the table. He didn't want to be blamed for the layoffs, but he wasn't sitting there like an invited guest either. Peter thought he caught an admiring look from Adelson, who approved of people who took responsibility for what they did. Wasn't that what had driven Adelson himself up and out of Brooklyn to Princeton and to the top of USB News?

This was one of those watershed moments, Peter thought. He was responding differently from most people at the table; he had someone else to answer to, someone whose disapproval he was coming to fear more than Nab's.

The big difference in having kids, he thought, is that you know in the back of your mind that someday they'll look back at your life and judge you. They'll want to know where you were when important things happened. Ben and Sarah, he imagined, might want to know where he was when USB News was taken apart. And what was he going to tell them? That he helped do it, because he was so frightened that if he opened his mouth he would be tagged a troublemaker and never have a big job again, that he'd lose the secretary and the trips to Europe and the sense of making a difference in the world? That Barbara might lose her novel? Or that he had stood up and said no, this is wrong; I won't be a part of it.

For a second, Peter again felt a stirring, as if everyone would get up and protest if just one person did. But no one at the table moved, including him, and he realized that if he hadn't done it then, he never would, and his noble place in history had been lost.

Harold Wallace rose and buttoned his jacket. "Since we expect these terminations to be completed by the end of work today, this meeting is concluded. Thank you."

Peter stood up with Allen, and the two edged over to Adelson as they neared the door. "Sam, this stinks," Allen whispered. Peter nodded.

"It's got to be done," Adelson said grimly.

"But why are they making us do this? It has nothing to do with us."

"They are us, pal. This is what you get paid to do in the big leagues. So do it."

The editing room was so dark that at first Allen couldn't find Bill Siegel. The producer was staring at the small monitor as the tape editor fast-forwarded past pictures of snarling dogs, and Siegel pointed out where to make the cuts.

Siegel was features producer for the *Evening News,* working for twenty-four years on some of the strangest stories in the country. His beat included chickens that water-skied and watermelon-eating contests—the point being to end the *Evening News* on a lighter note once a week.

The month before, Siegel had profiled the Potato People, a cult of sorts in Maine whose members devoted their lives to growing, eating, and extolling potatoes, which they believed had spiritual qualities. He had reported on the sisters who had stitched the largest quilt in the world; on the dancing pigs of Hyacinth, South Carolina; and on too many UFO kidnap victims to count. Jack Thomas loved Siegel's pieces; he thought they captured the fabric of America. This one was about junkyard dogs and their owners.

The tape editor turned and saw Allen come in and jerk his head; without a word, the editor stood up and left the room. Siegel, absorbed as he was after two hours of looking at tapes of dogs, was not as quick.

"Hey, Buzz," he said, "I think we've really got a winner here. You know, there are probably fifty thousand junkyard dogs in America. Not a group much written about, yet they're very much their own breed." Siegel cackled, then took in that Allen wasn't laughing and that the editor had vanished.

Allen let the room remain dark.

"Bill, I have some terrible news, some of the most awful news I've ever had to give anybody."

"You mean my piece isn't getting on tonight?" Siegel laughed. His wife had died years earlier and he had no children, so the possibilities for bad news were few.

Allen tried to smile. "Bill, I don't know any other way to do this but to straight out tell you that I am letting you go. We're cutting the staff back by a dozen people, and yours is one of the positions I and—well, just say I—have decided is not as vital as others."

"You're telling me you're firing me?" said Siegel slowly, in disbelief.

"I'm telling you we're laying you off for economic reasons. Bill, this is difficult for me. You've been one of the mainstays of the broadcast for years. I can't believe it myself, but we were told to make choices and we had to make them—"

Siegel walked over and switched the light on. "And the choice you are making is that the pieces I do are less important than stories from Washington or reports about presidential primaries, is that right?"

Allen felt himself near tears. He had said what he was supposed to and now he didn't know what else he could say. He nodded.

"I've been here for twenty-four years, Buzz. It's my whole adult life. You can't just walk in here and throw me out. It's outrageous. This company has a responsibility to me; I helped build it. I've had a thousand pieces on this broadcast. If mistresses can sue their boyfriends for palimony, what could I get for what I've contributed to the billions of dollars this company has made in the years I've been here? I don't believe this."

A picture of a huge, Doberman-like dog with its mouth open in an angry growl was frozen in the monitor behind Siegel's head. Allen could think of no proper answer. He couldn't tell Siegel how miserable he was, how lonely he was adjusting to his single life, how much he missed his daughters, how constant the battling with Jack Thomas was becoming, how dreadful the meeting had been that morning. There was nothing he could say that would make Siegel feel better, so what was the point of saying anything at all?

Let Siegel sue, Allen thought. He almost hoped he would. It was David Nab's money anyway.

Siegel suddenly came forward and offered his hand to Allen, who flinched before recognizing it as a friendly gesture.

"I'm so sorry," said Siegel. "I apologize for the outburst. I feel like a fool."

"No," stammered Allen, "there's no reason to apologize. You have a right to feel bad."

"Please," said Siegel. "It's their company and it's your show and you have the right to have anyone you want on it. I just thought after twenty-four years . . . Well, I never expected to have to leave this way. Please, Buzz, don't tell anybody about my outburst. I'm mortified."

Allen stood up. "Don't apologize, Bill. You *should* be angry. But I promise, this is just between us."

"I mean it, Buzz. Don't mention this in notes, to Adelson, to Thomas, to anybody. Swear it."

"I swear."

"Thanks. I appreciate that. Buzz, how much time do I have?"

Allen hesitated. For some reason, this was harder than breaking the original news.

"One day. You have to stop working on your piece now. We'll send your things to you."

Siegel looked as if he had been struck. "You don't even want me to finish the piece? I went to junkyards in four cities! What are you going to do with all these cassettes? You're killing the piece?"

Allen nodded, put his hand on Siegel's shoulder, and went out, leaving the name and number of the benefits counselor on a piece of paper. As he walked down the hall, he encountered the tape editor, reassigned him to another piece, and looked to see whose name came next on his list.

Peter walked upstairs to his office, cutting through the newsroom littered with papers, coffee cups, magazines, phone message slips, and cans of stale soda. Everyone in the room looked at him quickly, then away.

"I have some rough stuff to do," he said to his secretary, Marie, of the suede miniskirts and spiked hair. "I need your help, and I need you to help in just the way I ask. No jokes, no improvisations, just the way I tell you. Okay?"

Marie nodded.

"I'm going to start calling people in here. When you see each person leave, call the next person on this list and say I want to see him or her. Tell people to wait here outside the office. If anyone sees any name on the list, or if you show it to anyone, your name goes on it. This is going to be lousy, so it's very important that you take it seriously."

"Okay, Peter, I know what this is about."

"So do the people I'll be calling in, so let's make it as decent as possible by not keeping anybody waiting any longer than necessary. Give me a few minutes. When I buzz you, let's go."

Peter took a couple of moments to rearrange his office, which suddenly looked inappropriate. One wall displayed a poster from an old movie called *Deadline U.S.A.* He lifted it off and turned it around; it seemed in poor taste.

He switched off the table lamps. His office was in a corner of the news division basement, unpenetrated by natural light. When Peter had taken over the broadcast, he had brought in antique lamps to soften the room. Now he turned on the overhead fluorescents, avoiding any suggestion of intimacy.

He buzzed Marie, then waited.

The first name on his list was Cynthia Zuckerman's. She appeared almost immediately, her eyes wide, like a deer trapped in the headlights of a car.

She was in her fifties, single, promoted to producer from secretary in the early '70s when the company had discovered feminism in a hurry. She always projected a cheerful, enthusiastic bubble-headedness, but she had never known an easy day since. When she and twenty other secretaries had been promoted one Monday, in the heady days when such expenditures were considered worthwhile to avoid lawsuits and bad publicity, there were no intermediate steps. They were secretaries one day, producers the next. Some of them had made it. Others seemed doomed never to catch up with their colleagues, never to stop feeling insecure, never to believe everything wasn't going to evaporate suddenly.

Cynthia Zuckerman could break your heart, Peter thought. A valued and savvy secretary, she had none of the quickness, brass, and energy that went into producing, and years of trying had turned her edgy and neurotic. She was frightened almost all of the time, in the way of someone perpetually in over her head.

Her worst problems had come not from the men so much as from newer female producers, the ambitious, bright young women who had fought their way into the company from Ivy League schools. They were openly contemptuous of the "secs," as the former secretaries were called. They bristled at the suggestion that the women's movement had anything to do with their own success. Women like Cynthia were trapped in the middle, ignored by the men, put down by the younger women, likely never to make it to the next rung. They existed to flesh out the stat sheets of the company's lawyers, and a new management would give them no quarter.

Companies don't do well with memory, thought Peter as he

got up to close his door behind her. USB's new owner had made it clear that he came in with a clean slate. If there had been a union contract, Nab would have had to honor it; people like Cynthia thought they had contracts, too, unwritten but nevertheless binding and long-lasting. There ought to be a vice-president for Memory, an Office of Previous Understandings, someone to go to and say "Wait a minute, this wasn't the deal. You're breaking the bond."

"Cynthia," said Peter, his voice cracking a bit, as it always did at first when he fired someone. "Sit down, please." He paused to control his voice, then continued. "I'm afraid I have bad news for you."

He had learned never to show fear or hesitation when he fired people. If you didn't seem sure about it, they sure as hell wouldn't accept it. Women, at least of Cynthia's generation, were still the most likely to show emotion. Men almost always tried to show how well they could take it: No matter how much they might hate you, the men invariably stiffened, nodded, shook hands, and left.

"As you must know, the company is eliminating four hundred and seventy-five positions today," he said quietly. "I'm afraid yours is one of them."

Cynthia closed her wide eyes. A tear was already sliding down the right side of her face.

"I also have to tell you that you are to surrender your ID, credit cards, and keys to me by the end of the day and have your office packed in twenty-four hours."

Peter paused. Her eyes were tightly closed. He didn't know if she could hear him or not, but experience had taught him to finish. You had to finish; then you could let up.

"A special counselor will explain your benefit situation, your severance, all the details you are probably wondering about and I don't have the answers to.

"Cynthia, I am sorry about this, but I have to tell you that this decision was mine. I decided that if cuts had to be made, your associate producer position was one the broadcast could function without."

He waited again. "Cynthia, have you understood everything I've told you?"

She opened her eyes, bit her lip, and nodded.

"Do you want me to leave the room for a minute? Do you want some privacy?"

She shook her head, then ventured "Is there someone I can appeal this to?"

"No. I'm afraid it is final."

"But I know a lot of people here. I have a lot of friends. Does anyone else know about this?"

"Cynthia, believe me, it's irrevocable. It's been approved all the way up. Accept it. If I can help you in any way—references, suggestions—please let me know."

She was speaking just above a whisper now. "Peter, I like you. You've never complained about my work—"

"This isn't a firing, Cynthia. I have no complaints about your work." Slow down, he thought. Let her have her say, let her get it out.

"Peter, I don't have anything else in my life. I don't have a husband or kids. I have a Manhattan apartment, I pay sixteen hundred a month for two and a half rooms. I can't live for two months without a job.

"The younger ones, they can get other jobs. Can't you take some of the younger ones? I'm not going to beg, but I have never worked anywhere but this company. The other networks aren't hiring. . . ." Her voice trailed off.

"Cynthia, some of the younger ones are going to get it. Some of everybody is going to get it. I was told to pick a certain number of names. I picked them. I wouldn't have chosen to throw you out, but the company is different now. Before, you had to set the Chairman's Lincoln on fire to get the ax. Now, you just have to add up to the right number. I'm sorry, but it's final, and I have a lot of other people to talk with."

"I guess I knew you never really liked me. I never played up to you, or told you how brilliant you were. Is that it?"

"Nobody told me how brilliant I was. Believe me, this isn't personal. I don't dislike you. I honestly believe your position is among those the broadcast can best exist without; that was the framework of the choice I had to make. If you feel easier making me a monster, do it. But all I can do is tell you the truth."

Cynthia stood up, walked out, and slammed the door. Number one. By the end of the day he would have twenty-two fresh enemies, he thought. And the truth of it was that he didn't need any more enemies; he had plenty already. People you wouldn't hire or promote or give raises to, people whose work you criticized, and, especially, people you fired; they were instant enemies and they were forever. A firing was always personal to the one getting fired.

Peter winced when he thought of how many people he had fired since he had become a producer. Twenty or more, he guessed. But then, there had always been a reason. In this case, the company seemed anxious to emphasize that there *was* no reason.

He wasn't surprised by Cynthia's fear or her bitterness. What else did she have but this job? He thought one of the reasons he might have chosen her was that she didn't have a family, didn't have kids depending on her. Would it be worse if she did? he wondered. It was probably illegal even to harbor those thoughts.

The next one was worse, in a way. Jim Axelrod, a young assistant producer. Like any other successful company, this one had attracted scores of bright, intense kids who worked all the time. They were the future of the place, any place. The kids were like bees, always buzzing around, always looking for work. They had the energy to make the extra phone call, do the extra scutwork, come in on weekends; the more you asked them to do, the happier they were. They were fun; they lifted him out of his advancing cynicism and fatigue. He knew there would be hardly any of them left by the end of the day. No responsible manager would toss out thirty-year veterans if there were a choice.

But no one had a choice. So they were throwing out both, the young and the old; the young because they had the fewest obligations and the shortest history, and the old because they had already been shunted aside, most of them.

Think of it, Peter thought as he waited for Axelrod to bound in. These days a company gets to destroy its past and its future, all at once. He wondered if the stockholders, whoever they were, or the new owners of the company had any inkling of what this would really cost them.

Young Axelrod bounced into Peter's office in the midst of his little reverie. Outside, Peter saw Patricia Flannery peering into his office to see if he was free and then, spotting Axelrod, move away.

"Peter, what's up? What can I do for you?"

Axelrod did not cry or get angry. He was too young not to believe there must be some reason, too young for it to dawn on him that there were not numerous possibilities elsewhere. He thanked Peter for his encouragement, asked his counsel on where to look for work, and said he hoped he would have the chance to work for him again one day.

Axelrod was in and out in less than ten minutes and Peter stuck his head out of the office to see Flannery waiting off to one side. She was clutching her huge Rolodex under one arm, looking pale and angry.

"Peter, I gotta talk to you. Now. Before you hear this from anyone else."

He waved her in, closed the door, and sat down. He allowed himself a long sigh.

"I'm glad to see you. This is awful," he said, growing more concerned as he saw her eyes reddening.

Flannery smiled weakly. "This is pretty awful for me, too, Peter. I hope you know that," she said hoarsely.

"Patricia, what is it? Why do you have your phone numbers? Nobody's going to lay you off. We still have a show to do tomorrow, you know." He should have known, of course, as soon as he saw the Rolodex.

"Peter. I just talked to Cynthia."

He remembered that the two women had become good friends. "I feel bad about that. I should have called you and asked you to stand by. I didn't have much of a choice, but I'm glad you're there to help her. Is that what you want to talk to me about?"

"Sort of. Peter, I want you to be the first to hear it. I quit. The exec producer on *Good Morning America* heard about the layoffs and called and offered me a job. Just now. I took it."

Peter was astonished. "Patricia, what the hell are you talking about? You're not getting laid off. You're the only thing that keeps this show together. What are you doing?"

Flannery shifted the Rolodex to her other arm.

"I don't want to be here anymore, Peter—it's just that simple. This place is already dead, they've already destroyed it, and they haven't even ordered their own stationery yet. My life is fucked up enough without this."

Peter came out from behind his desk and sat down next to her. "Is this about Cynthia? This is crazy, Patricia. I just wrote a commendation letter for you a couple of weeks ago and put you in for a raise. Brookings was dazzled by your work on the abortion story. You made this big breakthrough from booker to somebody they know can report a story. You'll be a full producer in a few months. You're golden here."

Flannery looked at him, drying the tears from her bloodshot eyes. She waved her hand to dismiss what he was saying. "Peter, I thought you were a person who had some values beyond this place. I've seen you with your kids and your wife. How could you—all of you—take part in this? My God, this isn't managing. This isn't leadership. This is like slaughtering chickens at the butcher's. Dan D'Amato is *dead,* remember? Doesn't that make all of you stop and think that there has to be a different way to do this? Don't you know you just killed another person, just as if you'd taken a gun and put it to her head? Cynthia has no life left; you've destroyed it. She told me the bullshit you gave her about not firing her, about economic reasons. She's my *friend,* Peter, and I have to respond somehow, okay? I can't just pretend nothing happened. I couldn't face her.

"How do they get you to do it? Don't any of you have the guts to say no? I can almost hear you all going on with your macho crap about responsibility. How can you *do* it, Peter, and still go home to Ben and Sarah and read them your precious award-winning children's books about honor and heroes and kindness? They're turning you into their whore, Peter, don't you know that?"

Flannery's voice had risen almost to a yell and she had begun crying again. He opened his mouth, then closed it. He almost told her how close he had come to being a hero.

But she spit at him. Not in his face, but on his shoe. He had been spit on only once before, by antivivisectionists at a rally he was covering in Asbury Park, and he considered it one of the most humiliating moments in his life. He reached for his handkerchief to dab at the spittle, as Flannery, suddenly calm, got up and left.

It took six hours for him to fire all twenty-two.

His speeches got quicker, more abrupt, frighteningly more comfortable and rote. His voice no longer cracked. The older men were the angriest, the most bitter. The middle-aged men were the most frightened; the "secs," the most emotional.

After the last, he went to the command post the lawyers had set up in a converted studio upstairs and reported to Wallace that all twenty-two terminations had been completed.

Wallace smiled. "Any problems, Mr. Herbert?"

"No," said Peter. "Not unless you count the best producer on my show quitting. Or unless you want to count blowing twenty-two lives all to hell a problem. You don't usually get to do that outside of war, do you? But don't worry, nobody's going to sue you, Mr. Wallace. There'll be no bounce-back on my list." Despite everything, he could not help feeling a twinge of pride. He had not whined, or slopped it up; he had done what he had to do as professionally as it could be done.

But Peter's hands were shaking as he drove home. He wasn't hearing the radio, wasn't hearing anything but the hum of the Toyota moving through the Tunnel. So he missed the announcement that, today, the White House had announced that David Nab had been appointed to the President's Select Commission on a Competitive Economy.

CHAPTER SIXTEEN
NEW AGE

*T*he New Age Coffee Shop, Adelson's favorite dining spot after Tony's, was a shared joke. It was an appalling place, typical of the city's hundreds of coffee-shop dives. No matter what you ordered, the waitress shrugged as if you were a fool and the food arrived within seconds, shining with grease. The check, always tucked under the sandwich, was so oil-slicked and ink-smeared that only the cashier could decipher it.

Adelson loved the place. For one thing, though it was less than a block away from USB News, no television person, not even a tech, would be caught dead there, so the New Age was safe to talk in.

For another, it could not muster the pretense and snippiness epidemic in the city's expense-account restaurants. Adelson had allowed several such Yuppie passions to pass him by, including fitness and fiber. He made it a point never to eat a salad in any form.

His favorite on the New Age menu was the Walter Cronkite Deluxe Cheeseburger Platter. All the lunch and dinner specials and desserts had been named after television journalists, in the vain hope that New Age would become a favored hangout of broadcasters. This did not seem imminent, but Adelson had ordered a Cronkite with extra slaw anyway.

It consisted of two burgers with lettuce, abundant mayonnaise, and tomato slices, on a roll grilled in butter, served with a half-pound of limp fries, the wet cole slaw oozing into the burger and the fries. Underneath the soggy mess the check stuck out.

"No matter what you pick up, it drips," said Peter with some disgust as Adelson held the burger sideways to let the grease drain off onto the plate.

Adelson leaned over to tell Peter confidentially: "I have this theory that they take all the checks at the end of the day and boil them to make the soup." Peter had ordered the Bill Moyers Dieter's Delight—a plain greasy burger with cottage cheese and potato salad—passing up the Dan Rather Fruit Salad.

"How down are you?" said Adelson. "You sounded pretty grim on the phone last night. That's not surprising, is it? But I still don't believe it was suicide—no way. D'Amato was no coward, and he wouldn't have lost all his faith in ten days. Suicide just doesn't add up."

He could be right, Peter thought. But in the weeks since the funeral he had stopped talking about it with Adelson. Like other successful managers, Adelson sometimes reordered the world to fit his own reality; that was how he got things done. He tolerated no suggestion that D'Amato's death was anything but an accident.

"I feel bad about Dan, sure, but that isn't why I wanted to talk," Peter said. "I guess I'm sort of unsettled all of a sudden. I haven't had a chance to catch up with things. I mean, a few months ago we were wondering how many people in the world were as important as we were—"

Adelson laughed. "What did we decide? About twenty thousand, when you throw in CEOs and generals?"

Peter laughed back ruefully. "Yeah, but that seems like another century to me. Since then we've gone through the takeover and D'Amato's death, and the layoffs yesterday were brutal. I told you on the phone—didn't I?—that Flannery quit. And *spit* on me."

Adelson waved his hand, as if to brush away such talk. "Aaah, she'll stay. You'll see. You want me to call her?"

"No. I think if she says she's going, she's going. She carries that Rolodex around the way Moses must have borne the Ten Commandments through the desert. She's been a good friend, you know. Her asking what had happened to me, as if I had turned into a child molester—it was pretty jarring. Besides, I know the show's in trouble. Shurken's singled it out ten times as the leading example of what has to change. I have this weird feeling that everyone else knows that I'm not going to make it, but I haven't caught on yet."

Adelson put down his disintegrating sandwich and wiped his hands. He swallowed his food and took a sip of Classic Coke. Peter recognized these gestures as the prelude to a lecture, which was fine with him. He wasn't sure anymore what he was supposed to be feeling, and he would be relieved if someone could tell him.

"First off, *fuck* Shurken and *fuck* Flannery, okay? Shurken doesn't make personnel decisions around here. I do, and I will continue to, believe me. And as long as I do, you will have a job. It would be inconceivable to let somebody as smart as you go. Secondly, Flannery is a friend of yours and she's a great booker but she doesn't know fuck-all about responsibility. She's never been in charge of anything. We're managers; life isn't so simple for us. Flannery doesn't know about managing."

Peter waited while Adelson's Brokaw Pudding arrived. "Maybe not, Sam, but she knows a lot about being a human being, and I'm not sure she's off by that much. Up until a month ago I thought I would retire or die at USB News. Now, I can't imagine being here another twenty years. During the layoffs I wondered, what was I doing all this for? If the company is no longer loyal to us, and we are no longer loyal to it, why am I slashing through my own staff, chopping people into little bits? I mean, isn't it a manager's job to protect his people, to do what Viola did for that little jerk?"

Adelson lapsed into what Peter called his Kim Philby routine. No matter where he was, Adelson would pause for sixty seconds or so before he said anything sensitive, eavesdropping on adjoining tables and booths to make sure no one was talking television. Satisfied, he turned his attention back to Peter.

"What you're going through now—it's almost a midlife thing, isn't it? Until a few months ago you're cruising happily along, and all of a sudden shells are exploding all around you and you're freaked out. And you're thinking maybe you ought to bolt before you take a direct hit. But let me tell you something that you'll soon figure out one way or the other—you're over the Responsibility Line, you know that?"

Peter had grown accustomed to Adelson's street-corner philosophizing, but this was a new one. "What the hell is the Responsibility Line?"

"It's simple," said Adelson. "When you're Flannery, and you live in a fucking bathroom and you have no house, no kids, no responsibilities to anyone but yourself, you can be concerned with purity and righteousness. When you're an executive and you have a family and a mortgage and a couple of cars and a wife who's a writer and brings in—what, fifteen thousand dollars every two years or so?—then you're over the Responsibility Line. It means you have to proceed cautiously in life. That's why nobody stood up yesterday and said 'Fuck you all, I'm not laying anybody off,' even though I could see that you and a few others were thinking about it. Because everybody in that room was over the Line, either with families or alimony or life style.

"We have good lives, and we work hard for them. Me, I have a house in New England, a co-op with stiff maintenance, and a passion for wine tasting in Europe. But I have a wife who brings in a nice income, and I have enough company stock to last a long time. You're in a worse pickle. How many lessons does Sarah take? Dance, riding, what? What about Ben? Isn't he going to some sailing camp—"

Adelson froze. Peter was startled, thinking at first he was choking or having a seizure. But Adelson lowered his head, whispering, "Those two girls behind us just mentioned Jennings." Peter looked over to see two young women giggling over their salads.

"For God's sake, Sam, they're probably just talking about how sexy he is or something. You ought to be in the KGB." But Adelson held up his hand and the two sat in silence for nearly two minutes until it became clear that Mr. Jennings was an accountant in the firm the two women worked for.

Peter shrugged. He knew that, if pressed, Adelson would

just have cited his well-known Law Twenty-Eight: *Corporate history is littered with the corpses of careless people who made a little mistake.*

"I don't really need to be reminded about my responsibilities," Peter said wearily. "They're much on my mind. Sometimes I wish I didn't have all this baggage trailing me—the kids, the house, all that. When I was in school we thought we had more choices than anybody ever had. Sometimes I think we pissed them away.

"I have this funny feeling, Sam. I have this strange sensation that I'm not going to make it the way I thought I would. I wonder if I should refuse to wait and be a victim, if I should start rethinking my life, my work. There are things I could do—maybe teach, do some consulting, maybe even go back to reporting. I'm young enough to go to law school, if it came to that. I don't want to be D'Amato, sitting there minding my own happy business until one day a tank rolls over my back."

Adelson looked mildly annoyed, as he always did when there was too much introspection or it had gone too far, a luxury he thought important and successful people did not have need of or time to indulge in.

"You're not hearing me, Peter. You want to teach? Fine, go teach. If you're lucky you'll end up in a one-bedroom apartment in Jersey City commuting to Fairleigh Dickinson every morning. No more vacations in Bar Harbor, no more sailing camp for Ben, all because we're going through a rough patch? You going to go back to being a reporter? Cover the cops in New Haven? You couldn't do that. You don't have a lot of options, pal. You're an executive now—that's what you are.

"Let me ask you something, Peter. You know what a postage stamp costs? Tell me."

Peter was startled by the question. He had no idea what a postage stamp cost.

"You see? You haven't mailed a letter yourself in ten years. You don't know what real trouble is. Your wife or kids get sick, you're completely covered, every cavity, every hit of cough medicine. You've got twice your salary in life insurance; you never have to worry about college for the kids if you keel over, or about retirement if you don't. In fifteen years you'll have enough money to retire early while most poor bastards will run until they drop. You live in a nice big house with—what is it? three bathrooms? And you go soak your ass at a swim club when it gets hot in the summer. How many times have you been to Disney World? Two? Three? You thinking of quitting? You can wipe all that away—it's all gone. So what is there to rethink? You can do it here or you can do it at one of the other networks, and they're going through the same thing. Anything else is bullshit."

The New Age had begun to empty out and the waitresses sat down to rest, determinedly ignoring Peter's attempts to get a cup of coffee. Adelson's bellow rang out across the small restaurant. "Joanie! Have we done something to offend you, like not finishing all of our food? If we're good, will you bring us some coffee?" The waitress rolled her eyes and struggled to her feet.

"Well, Sam, you have certainly reduced my life and my options to a sweet thirty-second spiel, haven't you? You're telling me I have no choice but to do what I'm doing, in one form or another, for the rest of my life, especially with two kids and a novelist wife, so I should quit sniveling and get on with it."

Adelson nodded. "Yes, that's about right."

"And what if I get thrown out?"

"Then you wipe off the blood and do it somewhere else."

"And that's all the choice I have?"

"That's it, the way I see it."

Joanie arrived with two cups of coffee. "So what's the difference between living here and in Yugoslavia? What did my grandfather walk across Russia for so he could get to America?"

Adelson stirred two packets of Sweet 'n Low into his coffee. Peter thought that by now chemicals were probably vital for Adelson, as vitamins were for other people. "There's a big difference. In Yugoslavia, you're guaranteed a job and food and medical care. Here, you give in to a midlife crisis and quit without another job, with two kids and a mortgage, and you fall into a big black hole. In this country we walk the wire with no nets."

There was a long and awkward silence. Peter thought, for the first time since he had known him, that Adelson could grasp none of his feelings; he had no idea what Peter was talking about. Peter felt more depressed and uncertain than he had when lunch began.

But Adelson, his bluntness notwithstanding, possessed a

great capacity for compassion if he felt someone's wounds were genuine, though none at all for pain he viewed as frivolous or self-indulgent. He was beginning to see that Peter was going through something he had witnessed before but, blessedly, never experienced: the feeling that the ground beneath your feet was suddenly in motion.

"Look," Adelson said finally. "You seem pretty low. Maybe I'm not really being responsive. I understand you've been through a rough time, I really do. And since we're being honest, there is a fair amount of grumbling about your show's ratings and there is pressure to make a change—I'm not going to bullshit you. The layoffs, well, you just don't get a lot of sympathy from me there. You make almost a hundred and seventy-five thousand, and it isn't just to go to lunch and talk about how important you are or to go to Santo Cristo and take a sunset cruise. You get the money to ride with the good and the bad. You're a manager, you're responsible for other people, and you're also a father and a husband and you have things you have to take care of. But D'Amato checking out like that, sure, that was a jolt, I see that.

"So here's what I think you should do. I talked it over with McCallister and he's agreed—you should take a few weeks off and cool out, get over this hump, okay? Spend some time at home with Barbara and the kids."

Adelson could maneuver with the best—Peter had seen graphic evidence of that. But he also knew that when it was really important, when you sat down face to face with him, Adelson told the truth, a rare trait. And Peter understood the truth that Adelson was reluctantly disclosing: that Peter wasn't doing nearly as well as he thought; that not only wasn't he one of the 25,000 Most Successful People on Earth anymore, he had become A Problem.

Take a few weeks off. That was what Adelson told recently divorced men. Peter felt a chill.

"I'm going to get tossed off the show, aren't I, Sam?"

Adelson fiddled with his coffee spoon, pondered, and looked him in the eye. "In a word, yes. There's going to be a change. I didn't want to tell you until after your time off, but since you asked, I don't want to lie. So now you have something else to worry about. But, Peter, I can tell you straight—and I mean this—there's no talk of firing you. Julian and I both agree we'll sit down with you in a couple of weeks and go over your options. You should be using the time to think about what else you'd like to do at USB News. That's as honest as I can be.

"There's no question that you're a terrific journalist—smart, good instincts. But these days, life is more complicated. You have to be a good manager, too, and you have to be a great television producer. The show has to work a different way. Frankly, sometimes we have to send a message that there's going to be a change."

Peter felt as though his lawyer had just told him that the governor had commuted his sentence from the chair to life imprisonment; he reminded himself that this wasn't precisely comparable.

Though in a sense it was. Peter had reached the point where he felt his ambitions and his expectations quietly expiring. In all the times he had avoided failed colleagues or helped to demote or exile others, it had never occurred to him that he could join their ranks. Now it was a difficult prospect to ignore.

The brave team player in him rose, the reflexive male response. "Well, Sam, I guess this just isn't going to be one of those great weeks, is it?"

Adelson smiled and slid the check from under the Cronkite burger and got up.

"You know what Murrow used to say, Peter. 'Tomorrow's another ball game.' "

CHAPTER SEVENTEEN

GOOD WISHES

*P*eter began his leave of absence wondering why Patricia Flannery was in his backyard shrieking with laughter and joining Ben and Sarah in a wild chase after Willie, their lop-eared rabbit, who was hopping erratically around the forsythia bush. Eugene gaily joined in the chase, unaware that among his genes were a few belonging to a hunting breed.

Peter thought the scene too treacly even for a Kodak ad, but the laughter and barking and bright May sunshine would etch themselves in his mind. Wasn't this, he thought, exactly what a father was supposed to come home to, what a father was supposed to be working toward? He was haunted now by Adelson's warning, for wasn't this exactly what was at stake?

He sat in the Toyota unnoticed for a minute or two. He thought he could hear the sound of Barbara's typing wafting out of her study and across the yard. Barbara had rejected any technological advance past the electric typewriter, and her clunky old Smith-Corona could be heard well down the block on spring and summer mornings and evenings, handily beating out sprinklers and rustling leaves, losing only to lawn mowers and motorized shrub-cutters. The thumping sound of her work vibrated throughout the big old house and seemed to him the comforting background of their thirteen years together.

Barbara had ferocious discipline about writing. With the aid of a nanny who lived in the small attic apartment, she wrote from 9:00 to noon and from 2:00 to 4:00 P.M., unplugging the telephone, locking the door to her study, training her family and friends to consider her absent.

Once, Sarah had fallen at school and split open six stitches' worth of forehead, and the teacher, unable to raise Barbara at home, had called a neighbor. The neighbor, hearing Barbara's typewriter thumping, hammered on the door for ten minutes before they all gave up and called Peter at work. To survive, Barbara said, she had to pretend she really wasn't at home, and after years she had come to believe it. Peter was incredulous when he heard the story, but Barbara had maintained that no kid had ever died for want of six stitches. If it were really bad, she said, they would have found a way to get to her.

Peter walked into the backyard and yelled hello, shocking Eugene, who yelped happily. Sarah shrieked, "Daddy," and rushed toward him in their familiar ritual. Of all the things he did in the course of a day, he was proudest of Sarah's unwavering certainty that when she leaped at him, he would catch her. Even though the two of them sometimes went down in a heap, he always had. He loved this scene, the dog waggling against him, Sarah yelling, "Daddy, Daddy, Daddy." He was about to spend more time at home with his family than he ever had, and he was determined to forestall his depression until he had enjoyed it a bit.

Ben, older and conscious of his status in the family, waved and smiled, which was the most Peter could hope for these days, and grabbed the rabbit, who had stopped to nibble on a dandelion.

Flannery walked over. She knew he wouldn't be impolite to her in front of the children.

"Didn't expect to see you here in the evil slime's backyard," he said grimly, putting down Sarah, who ran to her playhouse.

"I came to see my kids," she shot back. "Not you. I got scared, after what happened, that I wouldn't see them again."

"Patricia, how can you come here?" he said, when the kids

were out of earshot. "How can you just show up at my house like this, after what you did at the office?"

"Let's go for a walk, okay? I understand how you feel. You've got to understand how I feel."

Peter reached into the back door for Eugene's leash, and the two of them walked out the gate and toward the park two blocks away.

"I'm sorry for spitting on your shoe, okay?" said Flannery, glancing nervously down at Peter's brown loafers, as if to see whether she'd inflicted any permanent damage. "But I'm not sorry for what I said."

"Patricia, I don't need you coming here to shit on me. What I had to do in the office was no fun. It wasn't something I wanted to do, and I didn't need your self-righteous outburst. Adelson is right about you: You've never managed anything, including your own life. You think life is about getting guests on the show, but it isn't. It's about balance and responsibility, maintaining a fucking house, giving Barbara the chance to work on her novel, and it's about my kids' futures—"

Flannery, hands in her jeans pockets, gave a gray pebble a kick. When they walked they took turns kicking a stone to the park, like little kids. The effort reminded Peter, and Flannery as well, of their long history. With her antennae and her sources, she must have heard that he was in trouble, he realized. Whatever had happened between the two of them, it was typical that she would be the only person in the news division who would come out to his house, and right away.

"I didn't come out here to replay the Civil War," she said, her voice softening. "I meant what I said. We just agree to disagree. I love you and your family and let's just make it something we put behind us. I'm sorry about your shoe, is all."

"Aww, spitting on me isn't so harsh. Just an unusually intense way of expressing your feelings."

He sent the stone into the street, but Flannery kicked it back onto the right track.

"I'm glad we can at least talk," he said after a minute. "Although, if you want to come crawling back, it can't be to me. I'm off the show."

Flannery winced. "I'm sorry, Peter. I don't want to crawl back, as it happens. But I'm probably not going to ABC either.

I've decided I'm running out of time to construct the other half of my life, and I know I'll never do it unless I get off the train awhile."

Peter put his arm around her shoulder and kissed her on the cheek. The two of them headed back toward the house, waving at Carmen, the nanny, who had come out to watch the kids carefully but discreetly from the corner of the yard.

"You'll stay for dinner, right?" Peter asked.

"I *brought* dinner, dummy; it's in the fridge. So they dumped you off the show? Interesting that they waited until you did their dirty work. It makes me even more determined to do what I'm doing."

They came into the wide, cool kitchen and Peter poured himself a diet soda and Flannery some bottled water. "What *are* you doing, Patricia?"

She sat down at the wooden table strewn with homework, colored drawings from school, 3-D "G.I. Joe" comic books, and the odd Rice Krispie.

"Well, it isn't definite, but I'm thinking about spending a year in Boston. I'm going to take some history courses at B.U., not because I give a shit about history, but because I want to live in Cambridge and hang around with people who aren't jaded yet. And maybe look real hard for some slightly younger, intense and sensitive man who never watches television and is desperate for a slightly used, almost middle-aged woman to share a life with. I decided that I'll approach it as if this guy, whoever he is, is Gorbachev and I'm going to land the first interview with him for the show. That way, you *know* I'll find him. Then I may come back to television, if anyone will still have me.

"I don't want this whole thing," she said, looking around the kitchen and gesturing toward the backyard. "But I want some of it, and I just don't think I'll ever find it living like I do." She looked anxiously at Peter. "What do you think?"

What Peter felt was envy, not so much of what she was doing but of her determination to seize the initiative. It seemed so straightforward. "That's a terrific philosophy," he said, nodding warmly. "I admire you. That's neat, going up to Cambridge. I wish I could think of something like that, that would work for me."

Flannery smiled gratefully at the encouragement. "Why can't you, if you want to?"

"You know what they say." He shrugged. "I've got a hot-and-cold running mortgage here."

After dinner, after Flannery had hired a car to take her back to New York (she prided herself on not having ridden a bus since high school), and after the kids were in bed, he sat down with Barbara.

The nights were still cool enough for a fire. Like many of their suburban neighbors, having a crackling fire before which to drink tea and talk was the essential reason they'd bought the house. The retriever dozing at the hearth was required as well.

He dreaded much about the coming weeks, but mostly he feared disturbing Barbara's peaceful regimen. She was making good progress on her book, about a feminist heroine in occupied France, and she was in the fugue state she always drifted into when the writing took her over. He worried that he would disrupt her concentration with his news, and worried more that he would no longer be able to provide her with the security and comfort she needed to continue her work.

Not being able to support your family, or failing to support it in a comfortable way—that was the ultimate failure in a man's life, so he had been taught. He often thought of his Uncle Max, a perpetual stumbler unable to keep a job, reduced to borrowing money from wealthier relatives to rent the ground floor of a grim triple-decker in New Haven. A week had not gone by in the first half of Peter's life without hearing Max's name raised, a dread specter of what happened if you didn't go to school, didn't work hard, didn't remember to keep fear close by. Or if you lost your job.

"So," Barbara said carefully, once she was satisfied that the fire was blazing satisfactorily. "Looks like some changes coming. How are you feeling?"

"Surprised. Scared," he said. "I have to face some big things I hadn't even thought about a few months ago. I don't want to lose all this. The kids are happy here. We love the house. After six moves, this is the place I can see us staying for good. But everything's turned so quickly. USB is so every-man-for-himself now.

"Sam swears they won't fire me, but I might not like what they want me to do. And I haven't a clue as to what I would do if I should suddenly start to hate my work and feel frightened and pissed off all the time. I don't want to live like that. I guess, to be honest, I have to at least prepare for the possibility that they won't keep me on, no matter what Sam says. Hell, I don't know for sure that *he'll* even be around."

Peter paused to see how Barbara was taking all this. He was usually more guarded in talking with her about work. He didn't want to put too much pressure on her, for while Barbara had always been intuitively independent, she had always been a writer. It wasn't as if she could return to Wall Street or join a law firm, even if she wanted to. He didn't really know if she'd ever thought about doing anything else. And there was the flip side as well: He wanted to be closer to the kids, but if Barbara took on a full-time job, he might have to get more involved with the shopping and the car-pooling than he really cared to.

Barbara sipped her tea. "Patricia thinks you should get out. She told me while you were doing the dishes that unless you can do something for them, they won't care about you. That the old notion of the company is gone, and that you should get out before you become one of those bitter, defeated, middle-aged men." She laughed at the thought of Flannery's impulsiveness. "Of course, she doesn't have two kids, a dog, a rabbit, a nanny, and a novelist feeding at the trough, does she?"

The smile vanished, and she put her hand over Peter's. "But you know, after what happened to D'Amato, I'm taking your work a hell of a lot more seriously."

Peter squeezed her hand, shrugging off the reference to D'Amato. "Patricia doesn't have a mortgage," he said, "but she's taking a risk. She's giving things up too."

He stood up and walked around the living room, too restless to stay put. "Let's be honest, Barb. I have to start thinking of options. This all costs a lot of money. If I left USB, I don't know if I could find something else that would pay as well."

Barbara and Peter rarely quarreled. They were both from particularly quarrelsome families, so they tried to avoid sparring, and besides, they tended to see the world the same way. Barbara sometimes suggested to Peter that he had wandered too far from the idealistic young reporter she had married. She was bewildered by the energy and time he put into his television job, and occasionally resentful of how little time it left him to spend with the children. She had very little understanding of what went on at a place like USB News, what it took to land and hold a job like Peter's.

She was nevertheless conscious of the kind of life his income allowed them to lead. It was like being on a continuing fellowship, she told him. Carmen appeared at writing time. Barbara could take as long as she needed to finish her research and writing, something almost none of her author friends could claim. She had to look no further than Hannah, her closest friend, who called herself the oldest waitress in Berkeley as she struggled to keep a roof over her head to keep her ever-in-progress novel dry.

So Barbara had not pushed Peter much about the direction his life was taking. He had never seemed quite as happy since leaving behind reporting to become an executive, and his time had increasingly been spent on things that had little to do with journalism: hiring, firing, politics, agents. But she had kept her doubts largely to herself.

She wondered now if she would have to start thinking about taking a magazine job or even writing a historical romance, a potboiler. A poet friend in Glen Ridge wrote copy for an advertising agency in Princeton four afternoons a week. The thought made her chest contract.

She knew that Peter felt occasional twinges of resentment about her life and her attitude toward his, though they were usually offset by the satisfaction he took in being a provider. He didn't expect her to join in the politicking and ass-kissing at USB, although many wives did, but he wouldn't have minded if she'd taken a bit more interest. On those nights when he'd dragged in the door, exhausted from the long hours, the arrogant executives, the insecure staff, the temperamental anchors, he felt that she could never understand his previous twelve hours. He had wished she wanted to know more; now she might have to.

"Peter, I don't want you to be unhappy. But I'm not sure I understand what you mean. We have a nice life. We're all very content here. Do you mean you'd move to another network?"

Peter shook his head. "Kid, I think you need to understand what's happening. They're throwing people out of windows all over USB. Thy'll soon be doing the same thing at the other networks. I don't know if I'll have a choice."

She was puzzled. "So what do you mean by options? I'd be willing to get a job, of course, but I'm not sure what I could do that would pay for the house and Carmen and all. Are you talking about some other kind of work?

"We do have responsibilities. There's your father's health to keep in mind; what if he needs to go into a nursing home eventually? That could eat through our savings pretty fast."

The men at work used to joke about the 6:30 Friday Blues, when the housewives would start calling their husbands to demand to know how soon they were going to be home. That had never happened to Peter; he knew that the freer Barbara was, the more freedom he had. Now that was beginning to appear to him an illusion—like his own success. He wondered if he had any freedom at all.

"I'll call my agent this week; we can set up a lunch to talk about money," Barbara was saying, without much enthusiasm. "I'll try to find out what the possibilities are, if there are assignments I could get that would bring in more. Meanwhile, we have to think through what choices you have that would keep our lives together, all of our lives, and I'm speaking for Sarah and Ben as well."

Peter's annoyance intensified. "You know, I don't understand why all of a sudden everybody's telling me what my responsibilities are. I know what they are. I'm not going to leave you all high and dry. I'll take care of my family, believe me. Let's not panic, okay?"

"Peter, I don't mean to put this all on you. I think these people are dirtbags, you know that. Aside from Flannery, there isn't one of them I trust. You had this notion of making it in the big time, but I don't like them. I don't want to watch them, party with them, or know them. But I'm scared. I just want to picture how we're going to eat, that's all."

That, he thought, was a reasonable concern. He couldn't quite picture it himself.

"Well, I've decided to give broadcast journalism a last, desperate shot. I hear they're looking to give Linda Burns her own show, but they don't know what it should be. I've got a neat idea, I think, for a traveling issues show. I'm going to write it up and take it to Burns. It's worth a try."

Barbara shook her head skeptically. "Not if it's going to make you crazy. I don't want a nanny that badly, or a novel for that matter."

Peter smiled and hugged her. The thought of hammering out a new pilot cheered him. If the right idea was paired up with the right superstar on the move, then all bets were off. Careers in deeper shit than his had been revived.

Just before nine the following morning, watching his own show, he heard Don Leeming announce that *Morning in the U.S.* would soon be welcoming its new executive producer, Lee Laybourne, who would begin work in a few weeks. Peter felt the cold sweat almost immediately, on his neck and on the palms of his hands.

"The staff here would like to thank Peter Herbert, whose hard work and terrific news judgment helped us through many a big story," Leeming intoned. "He has our gratitude and good wishes." By nightfall, Peter knew, a large basket of flowers from Leeming would be delivered, a gesture of thanks and condolence, at company expense, but there was a good chance he would never speak to Leeming again unless they ran into each other in the hallway.

The sudden eulogy meant that management had been planning this change for some time—perhaps even before the takeover—and that his conversation with Adelson had provided a fine excuse to move more quickly. He blushed when he realized that Nabih Patel would be yelling his traditional "Flameout!" at the end of the show and rolling the tape of the plane hitting the ground.

He drove the kids to school, to their surprise; even Ben showed delight. When he returned home, Barbara was thumping away. Peter felt reassured that her writing was unaffected, although mildly irritated that she wasn't being more wifely in his time of crisis, perhaps brewing him a second cup of coffee.

He picked up the *Times,* but felt too unnerved to concentrate. The anxiety was beginning to build. What should he do? Whom should he call? He was not prepared when the telephone rang and

it was Eddie Cohen, the television reporter for a weekly broadcasting trade magazine. Peter had liked Cohen when they had
first met, introduced by Adelson. Cohen had been an eager young
reporter then, harassing Brookings and the other brass with
scoop after scoop, but years of being fawned over had made
Cohen lazier and more arrogant.

"Pete? That you? Hi, babe. How's Barb, and little Benny
and Sarah?"

"Everybody's fine, Eddie." No one ever called him Pete or
his son Benny. "What's up?"

"Well, Pete, I was surprised to hear the announcement on
the show this morning. I mean . . . you weren't surprised, were
you? You knew, didn't you, you and Sam being close and all?"

"Yes, of course I knew. Why?"

"Well, I thought I'd do a little item on it, you know,
especially after that story today in the *News*. You've seen it,
haven't you?"

"No, Eddie, haven't seen it yet."

"Oh, that's right. I forgot you live in Jersey. Well, let me
read it to you. The headline says 'Morning Show Producer
Dumped in USB News Shuffle.' The story says: 'Peter Herbert,
for two and a half years the executive producer of *Morning in the
U.S.*, the struggling and perennially bottom-rated morning news
program, has been removed from the program, according to
USB News officials.

" 'The decision, greeted with jubiliation by the program's
demoralized staff, was followed by rumors that Herbert's replacement will be the respected Lee Laybourne, executive producer of *Sunup*, the syndicated morning show aired on more than
one hundred independent stations.

" 'One USB News executive, who asked not to be identified, said that "it was certainly time for a change. Herbert lacked
the leadership qualities and the vision for a successful morning
show. Now we all hope we can bring some excitement and
competitiveness to the morning. Being last isn't good enough
anymore." Laybourne is expected to report for duty in two or
three weeks.' "

Peter sat down hard at the kitchen table, angry and humili-
ated. Fuck you, McCallister, he thought. And fuck me. The
biggest story in my career and I blew it.

"Pete? I wanted to ask you if you had any comment on this, how you feel about it."

He kept his voice neutral. "I . . . I enjoyed my two and a half years at *Morning in the U.S.* and look forward to my next assignment. That's all the comment I have."

"Pete, what is your next assignment? There will be one, won't there? I mean, they'd *never* let a terrific producer like you go, would they?"

"I can't say any more, Eddie. I've got to run, got an appointment. Thanks for calling." Herbert hung up before Cohen could ask him anything more. Shakily, he dialed Adelson, who was just getting to work. Adelson answered the phone himself.

"Sam, what the fuck is going on? And why did you have to announce this on the show before I even had a chance to tell my secretary or say goodbye to the staff? And who's mouthing off to the *News*? Nobody ever told me everyone was so unhappy with my work, or that the staff was demoralized. What the hell is this? I lose my job and they have to go after my reputation as well? I have to hear about this from your little toady pal Cohen? It's McCallister, isn't it? He'd sell his whole family up the river to ingratiate himself with some fucking TV reporter—"

"Peter, calm the fuck down. I'm just as pissed off about this as you are. I don't know where this came from, although I would bet a month's pay that you guessed right. It's vintage Julian—once he hears you're off the show, he figures he can at least plant a little item and lick Cohen's earlobes, and who gives a shit about you? Look, I'm going to talk to him as soon as I can. But don't take any more calls and don't talk to any reporters. You got that? And keep cool. You know I would never let anything happen to you."

"Why shouldn't I talk to reporters if I'm going to get skewered like this?"

Adelson sighed. "Don't be a baby, Peter, okay? We'll find you a new job. Everything will be fine. Just keep your cool. I'll get back to you later."

Peter decided this might be a good time to broach his new idea. "Sam, hang on a second, will you? I've got this idea for a new show, a broadcast that goes out into the country where there are controversial issues—abortion, labor trouble, racial problems. It would be exciting: live television, real people as opposed to experts. I want to propose it for Linda Burns."

There was a pause on Adelson's end. "Well, Peter, you know the drill. Put it in writing and bring it to her. Send me a copy, okay? I got to run." Typically, Adelson was non-committal, especially over the telephone. But he hadn't said no, which meant that if Peter could sell it to Burns, he had a shot.

He would write the proposal today. This was a time to be professional, to be cool despite the attacks. This was the time to move ahead if he had any thoughts of salvaging his career.

He was heading upstairs to break all the news to Barbara when the phone rang again. He hesitated, then picked it up.

"Peter?" He recognized his mother's perpetually anxious voice.

"Hi, Ma. How are you?"

"How are *you*? There must be something wrong—you're home. I'm sorry. I wanted to wait until I stopped crying. Your Aunt Rose called me. She read in the *Register* that you got fired from the program, from your job. It says in the paper that the program wasn't doing well with the ratings and that everybody was happy that you got fired. Are you all right?"

He spoke slowly. "I'm sorry, Ma. I would have called if I had known it was going to be in the paper. I am not producing the show anymore, but I haven't been fired. I still have a job—"

"Did those new people do this to you? This Nab?"

"Ma, it just means I'll be getting another job at USB News, but I haven't been fired—"

" 'Cause Rose, she says she's never watching USB News again if it's true, and I'm sure that goes for the whole family."

"Look, Ma, I'm still with USB News. I just don't know exactly what I'll be doing."

"You don't know what your job is? Oh, God. We're going to have to tell your father. Billy or somebody will tell him. Why don't you come up here?"

"Well, maybe. I'd like to come up with the kids, maybe over Memorial Day."

The phone began ringing again as soon as he hung up. Peter grabbed Eugene's collar and headed out to give them both some exercise.

*   *   *

He couldn't tell whether it was his imagination or whether he was indeed being stared at. He felt strange, a middle-aged man walking through town in mid-morning. You saw some salesman types in suits bustling around, but you almost never saw men his age strolling.

After he'd circled his block a time or two, he brought Eugene home and walked to Susan's Restaurant, a neighborhood coffee shop up the street. He stopped at the newsstand to get the morning papers, picked up some aspirin at the pharmacy, then bought some shears at the hardware store. The young trees he had planted in honor of Ben and Sarah three years earlier needed some pruning.

He decided to skip the offending item in the *News,* feeling embarrassed and cheated more than anything else. Why were they treating him like a thief? Why couldn't he at least have gone in for a last day of work, had the chance to say goodbye before it popped up in the papers? Fucking McCallister! Why did his points always have to be scored at the expense of somebody else's reputation or peace of mind? And, added Peter, why am I whining so much?

When a man he took to be roughly his age came in wearing jeans and sneakers and sat down two stools away, Peter felt better. He wasn't the only male under forty walking around Glen Ridge. The man ordered some toast. He was thin—a runner, Peter guessed. After a few minutes Peter turned to reach for the sugar, and two of his papers slid off the counter and into the man's lap.

"Sorry," said Peter, turning to pick them up.

"It's okay. I was thinking of asking you if I could borrow one," the man said shyly. He shook hands and told Peter his name was Joel Fields, and that he came to Susan's three times a week now, once the kids were off to school and his wife had left for work in New York. The unspoken part of the statement was that the house was lonely, and he came to the restaurant to be with people. There was no mistaking Fields's sadness and embarrassment, although, since Peter was feeling much the same way, he might have been unusually sensitive to it.

They both scanned their papers, and then Peter asked Fields

if he wanted to move to a booth, where they could spread the papers out and have a second cup of coffee.

He was nervous, immediately regretting the suggestion; Fields was nice-looking, and maybe he would think Peter was trying to pick him up or something. But Fields agreed, almost enthusiastically, so they moved to a vacant booth.

"You on vacation?" Fields asked tentatively.

Peter nodded. "Sort of a forced one. But I guess you could call it a vacation."

"Me too," Fields said, "I was with Eastern Airlines, marketing supervisor. Laid off three months ago. I've just started telling people. It's odd to tell a total stranger when I haven't told my oldest friends."

Peter smiled. "Maybe we both sensed we're in the same spot. When you see men our age walking around this time of morning in the suburbs, it usually means unemployment, doesn't it?"

Fields smiled back. "Yes, I guess it does. The women keep looking at me like I'm a child molester, although the truth is there are hardly any women our age around either. Just old people and nannies and kids, mostly. The first two months I hardly left the house at all, so coming here is actually a big step forward." He flushed, as if he expected Peter to grab the check and run.

"I must seem strange to you," Fields apologized. "I never had problems like this before. I was shocked when I got laid off. I just couldn't believe it. A few months ago I was playing doubles at the Glen Ridge Tennis Club and now I don't dare renew my membership. My wife has gone back to work and no one seems to be calling me. There are so few jobs in the airlines now. But this is more than you want to hear."

Peter, trying to be reassuring, felt he needed to reciprocate. He imagined this was what an AA meeting was like. "I'm a television producer. I haven't actually been laid off. I'm supposed to be awaiting reassignment. But maybe it will come to that, I don't know." There was a pause. "What do you do all day—if you don't mind my asking?"

"Well, for two months I watched television and slept and did some housework. Then I started going for walks and mailing out resumés and now I've started coming here. We're not the only ones, you know," Fields confided.

"No?" said Peter, deciding not to point out again that he had not been laid off.

"No. When you're around awhile, you'll spot the others. None of us talk to each other, but of course, you can tell. There's a guy at Seventy-nine Bainbridge who walks this white German shepherd every morning at eleven; he's about our age. I met him through the kids' soccer league. And there's a guy on Glen Ridge Avenue who spends all day in the garden in back of his house, planting and pruning and setting mole traps. I see him going over the lawn blade by blade, looking for crabgrass and stuff. I do some running, but I don't have any other hobbies, so I'm trying to catch up on a lot of years of reading. It's like a secret fraternity—we glance and nod at each other sometimes but we never meet." He laughed. "There's a bunch of us now. You know who's really benefited the most?"

Peter shook his head.

"The dogs. We all have the healthiest goddam dogs in town. You have a dog?"

Peter told him about Eugene.

"Well, he's about to be your best friend. Take good care of him," said Fields.

A few mornings later Flannery called Peter just after dawn and told him to go outside and pick up his *Times*. There was surprising news, she said coyly. Peter went out in his slippers and bathrobe and retrieved the paper. He made himself a cup of coffee, mentally braced himself, then looked.

The news *was* surprising. Julian McCallister had admitted that the mortgage on his new Nantucket home had been co-signed by a defense contractor who was now under investigation by both the federal government and USB's own Washington Investigative Unit for supplying the navy with cheap, cracked engine casings. The story, said the *Times,* had first appeared in the trade magazine Eddie Cohen wrote for.

While McCallister had done nothing illegal, his actions had violated USB News's own code of ethics. McCallister conceded using poor judgment, but reminded everyone that his friend had

UPS guy knocks on his door up in Westchester and the wife gets hysterical, refuses to accept it, and all this shit. The UPS guy has to haul it back to the garage and back out again. You wouldn't believe how many times we show up and it's the first time the guy knows. Anyway, we got four more to do today, so we'd like to get started."

Peter nodded and left the office, his face burning. Struggling to look normal, he walked into the lobby and tried to call Barbara from a pay phone. But he got only her message machine; it was writing time. Then he called Flannery, who, he could tell by the echoes, was in her fabulous tub.

"Patricia, it's Peter. I'm at the office."

"You don't sound wonderful," she said, to the accompaniment of sloshing water.

"You taking a bath at nine-thirty in the morning?" The thought aroused him. He had not thought of Flannery's body much before, probably because he had not permitted himself to; now the thought of her long legs stretched out in a bubbly tub stirred him. It felt so much better than the humiliation and fear that he allowed the thought to linger.

"Why not? I had the morning shows on. We got clobbered. I hate to sound self-serving, but you guys miss my Rolodex."

"Not us guys. I don't even have an office anymore."

"They moved you out already?"

"Four guys in jumpsuits just walked in on me. My name was on a clipboard. Nobody even called me."

"Oh, Peter. Those motherfuckers. You want to get together?"

"Yeah. Actually, I was thinking about dinner. I'm going to be in town."

Flannery paused, sounding suspicious. "You're not the type who hangs around the city when you can play daddy. What's going on?"

"Look, I'm calling from a phone booth. How about we talk at dinner? I'll see you at seven," said Peter, hanging up.

He walked out of the USB News lobby and into the Public Projects annex, an aging apartment building into which the news division had dumped all its special programming years earlier—documentaries, children's news, religious affairs, and *Infinity,* the weekly science program that was so boring Adelson swore it was a KGB plot to kill off Americans' brain cells.

co-signed the mortgage before the investigations began. Still, the *Times* reported, highly placed sources at USB said it was now inconceivable that McCallister would become president of USB News, and that the job would almost certainly be given to Sam Adelson within the next few days. The weirdest part for Peter was reading about it all in the papers. If not for Flannery, he might have heard about it from Joel Fields.

He supposed it was good news for him that Adelson appeared to have a lock on the top job, although he was puzzled that it didn't feel like such good news. He wondered whether Adelson had had anything to do with the Cohen story about McCallister, but figured that was too rough for Sam. Six months earlier, the news about McCallister would have seemed the most important story in the universe. It would have been cause for celebration. Now, it seemed almost beside the point.

Adelson had yet to call him back. Barnard had not called him at all, but Allen had, to say he was sorry to hear the news and read the nasty stories and to say he was trying to set up a Sanity Club lunch for the next week. Peter's phone was certainly not ringing off the hook. Maybe the stories were true; maybe he *was* ill-suited for his job and disliked by his staff.

He laughed at his first impulse, which was to call McCallister and wish him good luck. What a chump I am, he thought. McCallister hadn't called him, and if Peter was dumped from USB News, he could bank on never hearing from McCallister again. Besides, thought Peter, let Julian see what it feels like to try to keep credit card salesmen on the phone a few extra minutes, just to have the company.

The difference, he figured, was that Julian would have another major network job inside of a month. Peter would be reading glowing profiles of him again in six months, none dwelling on his unpleasant departure from USB News. Six months was more than enough time—more than enough brunches, dinners, and Hamptons barbecues—for McCallister to have his history rewritten. Tsk, tsk, Peter scolded himself, let's not be a bitter former executive producer.

Enough moping. He would volunteer to work in a church soup kitchen. He would meet Joel Fields in the morning for coffee and plan a New York excursion with Ben and Sarah that weekend.

Peter went up to his word processor to begin putting together a resumé, just in case. He had not been encouraged by his call yesterday to Chuck Claffey, a headhunter he had used in the past when he'd been the hirer, not the hiree. Claffey warned that it was pretty grim out there. He had never, in his twenty years, seen so many people looking and so few people finding.

Peter sat on one side of the booth in Susan's Restaurant, Sarah and Ben on the other. In the manner of fathers who drifted in and out of their kids' daily lives, he had a difficult time enforcing, or even remembering, the myriad rules surrounding vegetables, fruits, and junk food. He found it impossible to keep track from week to week of exactly what his children would deign to eat, a narrow list to begin with.

His time at home was reinforcing his belief that while he'd been away working, the children had seized power—in child-obsessed Glen Ridge at least—in a bloodless coup. They told their parents when they would go out, which restaurants they would patronize, whether they would go on vacation and where. Frantic parents rushed their children from camp to camp, lesson to lesson, baseball diamond to soccer field, in an almost desperate attempt to ward off boredom.

Peter guessed his own two children to be somewhere in the middle range of obnoxiousness, but he wasn't sure. If he had spent too little time with his own children, he had spent almost none with others.

His schedule had forced him up and out in the early morning and didn't permit his return until their bedtime. He worried that he knew his secretary—his former secretary—better than these two people.

The kids could easily have been models for Norman Rockwell. Sarah, in her russet pigtails and freckles, was cheerful and adventurous. Ben, with his tousled brown hair and slightly pouty manner, reminded Peter of the painting of the runaway having a soda with the policeman who'd found him.

Peter was pleased to have two such all-American-looking kids, but he wondered what was churning below the surface these days. He told Barbara that with the adults in the household feeling the turbulence, the kids must be too. He didn't want to get into the habit of hiding things from them. He wondered if they'd noticed that he was not working. He had decided to take them to lunch to make things perfectly clear.

Ben seemed to know there was business afoot, and had the slightly revolted look that kids his age wore around their parents and their parents' friends.

"What's up, Dad?" asked Ben, tracing designs with ketchup on his burger.

"Yeah, Dad, what is up?" said Sarah, who could be counted on to echo her big brother.

"Well, I wanted to have lunch with you, that's one thing. But I also wanted to talk with you about something that's happening. That's why I took you out of school. I want to be honest with you."

"Did you get fired?" asked Ben impatiently.

"What's *fired*?" asked Sarah.

"How about being still until I get the chance to tell it, all right?"

Sarah shrugged, eyed her French fries covetously. "How many bites of the hot dog do I have to eat before I can start the French fries?" she asked. Peter had little experience at this kind of negotiating, which could rival the most intense contract dispute at USB. Barbara always seemed to know precisely how many bites of chicken or slices of carrot were required before dessert could be considered.

Not knowing the rules, Peter decided to be decisive. "Four," he said.

Sarah's whine went off. Even in a crowded restaurant it could rise above every other sound, like an air-raid siren. "Mommy only makes me eat three! It's unfair."

"Fine, fine. Eat three pieces, okay. There's no reason to whine. We can just talk about it." He cleared his throat and waited for Sarah to wind down. "I'm not on the morning program anymore," he told them gravely. "I've changed jobs."

"We know that," said Ben with disgust. "Harvey Bronstein showed everybody in class the story in the paper about how you got taken off the program because it was boring and nobody was watching it, and how everybody who worked there was happy about it." He was not being unkind—just impatient to get to the new stuff.

"Oh, Daddy," said Sarah, more sympathetically. "The same thing happened to me when I was—what was I last year? Five?"

"I didn't know you were taken off a show," he said, bemused.

She nodded sadly. "I was taken off the girls' soccer team," she said. "I hate soccer, but I was still very sad."

"You were on a soccer team?" he asked.

She shrugged.

He turned to Ben. "Well, Benjamin, why didn't you say something if you knew all about this? I mean, why didn't you ask me?"

"Old news, Dad." Ben shrugged. "Why didn't you tell me?" he finally asked. "Harvey knew."

Now it was Peter's turn to shrug. "The truth is, I am no longer on the show. I don't really know if the people on the show were happy or not—I haven't talked to any of them. I am thinking about doing a different show, a new idea I'm going to suggest. The point is, Mommy and I are thinking hard about what we want to do—"

"Are we going to move?" Ben asked.

"I am not going to move," said Sarah definitely.

"We don't want to move. But I may be taking a different kind of job, doing something else. I expect we'll be able to stay in Glen Ridge; the worst that could happen is that we live in a smaller house. That's the absolute worst."

Sarah began to sniffle. "I don't want to move, Daddy. I don't want to and I won't."

Ben rolled his eyes, perpetual disgust for his sister mingling with extreme boredom. "Can we talk about something else?" he asked.

Peter sat down in front of Ben's computer and opened a file he called "New World." He remembered Adelson's Law regarding written story proposals: *Brief, shallow, and snappy.* Always remember that the people who read them think getting through a by-line is tiring, he'd said. Peter wrote:

TO SAM ADELSON/LINDA BURNS

This is a proposal for a pilot for a new weekly news broadcast called "Your World." Simply, the idea is for me to produce and

Linda Burns to anchor a weekly broadcast that originates—live when possible—from different communities across the world.

Television news is filled with a tired crew of experts—Kissinger, Haig, members of Congress, think-tank blah-blahs. These people do not have fresh points of view and do not, in my opinion, allow television news to capture new ideas. Immigration, AIDS, the urban health-care crisis are just a few examples of American stories the media were slow to pursue, partially because journalists don't get out often enough and talk to ordinary people in ordinary places. We have even less understanding of other countries. We know now that we have understood little of what has been happening in the Soviet Union. We know even less about Latin America, even though it is certain to affect us significantly in years to come.

We should break away from old strictures and from narrow definitions of news and do what television has always held the promise of doing: bring the world into American homes. Famine and political struggles and the legacy of colonialism have overwhelmed Africa; poverty and rebellion threaten Central and South America; Eastern Europe has been liberated. We shouldn't be reacting to these stories long after they have emerged; we should discover them.

My proposal calls for eight production teams on the road simultaneously; five of them scouting, shooting, and reporting, and three of them in production. With the proper promotion and commitment, countries and communities would come to anticipate our arrival, even solicit it. If a community refuses to allow a child with AIDS to attend school, we should be there.

A second unique element: we wouldn't tell the story in terms of bureaucrats and windbags; we'd tell it through real human beings. We wouldn't talk with AIDS researchers—we would put the infected child together with the chowderheads who won't let him or her into their school. For that matter, we could broadcast from one of the African communities that spawned the first known AIDS case. That would generate an extraordinary amount of drama, it seems to me, as well as understanding. And we would accrue the added benefit of opening up network airtime to ordinary people, something that virtually never happens anymore. You both know that it is possible to go through an entire political campaign or major primary night without seeing any voters on television.

This would be somewhat expensive, but it would cost less than a prime-time entertainment hour, and it could be bold and exciting enough to break through the public's skittishness about watching serious news in prime time. In any case, I would like the opportunity to put a more detailed proposal together.

When Peter finished, he printed three copies and addressed one to Burns and one to Adelson. The other he filed. Writing the memo gave him a distinct lift. It was a good idea, he thought, one that might be timely. And it gave him something to look forward to. It would be exciting to have a shot at the ultimate television producer's fantasy: a hit show in prime time. Linda Burns was hot enough to pull it off, given the right producer.

In his second week at home he met Joel Fields at 9:15 at Susan's Restaurant, as they had taken to doing after they had walked their dogs and driven their kids to school. They shared coffee, the news, and a little of their humiliation and fear. It was at Susan's that Fields told him casually—the way no newsperson ever would—that the television pictures from North Philadelphia were the grisliest he had ever seen.

"What pictures?" asked Peter.

"Didn't you know? This jumbo jet crashed in a neighborhood in Philadelphia. They said three hundred people on the plane alone are dead, and that it blew up an entire block of tenements, and the toll might be up to six hundred. It's the worst air disaster in American history, according to the announcer."

"Which announcer?" asked Peter.

"Gee, I don't know." Fields shrugged. "They all seem the same to me."

Peter made it to the USB Building in a half-hour flat. It hadn't occurred to him that he would have lost his executive parking space already, but that was not the sort of detail the new management overlooked, and the guards turned him away. He parked the Toyota in a private lot, astonished to learn it would cost him $14 for the day, and sprinted toward the building.

The red light was flashing inside the building entrance. So

was the blue one, though there was no longer any SAT to send. Peter guessed they would rely on the Philadelphia affiliate.

He hurried down the second-floor hallway to studio 100, which opened up on his right. The enormous special-event anchor desk had been hastily assembled, Jack Thomas atop the odd-looking throne.

The studio was the usual madhouse, lighting techs crawling on walkways twenty feet up, electricians frantically laying cables, the buzzer signaling an impending special report. Peter ducked into the control room, looking for Adelson.

Adelson had appropriated the executive producer's chair, bellowing orders to Tommy Coakley, USB's most experienced and favored director. "Let's go," he bellowed. "We got two minutes. Get the script to Thomas. Is the tape ready?"

Vice-presidents lined the back walls, making what producers called "importance calls"—grave, hushed phone calls to their secretaries, to their wives, sometimes even to their own private lines, to demonstrate that they, too, had crucial messages to relay. Peter noticed David Nab and Harold Wallace sitting quietly in one of the producers' booths. Wallace looked uncomfortable, out of his element, unnerved by the chaos. But Nab glowed with excitement; Peter imagined he felt happy with his purchase.

Among newspeople, the most hardened cynic usually turned into an idealistic kid again when a story as big as this erupted. To be in the middle of it, to keep your cool and your judgment and get the story first, that was the apogee. To be outside it was to bear the stigma of expendability.

"I'll kill the motherfucker," Adelson suddenly shrieked above the babble.

The remote producer in Philadelphia, visible on one of the monitors, had set his earphones down while he grabbed a cup of coffee, breaking a cardinal rule in such situations: Keep a line open and stay on it.

Poor bastard, thought Peter.

"The son of a bitch is toast," Adelson was howling. "He's dead. I'll personally maim the fucker. Pick up your earphone! We're coming live to Philly, you cocksucker. Look, he's right in front of a Burger King." He swiveled in his chair. "Somebody call the fucking Burger King! Get me the Burger King in North Philadelphia."

An assistant producer vaulted the console and found a free telephone. She dialed the network operator and screamed at her: "Get the Burger King on Broad Street in North Philadelphia, and get it now! This is a news emergency."

Wallace, detached from the hubbub, wore a slight smile. Nab sat riveted.

In less than a minute, the producer handed Adelson the telephone. "Hello? Is this the manager of the Burger King? Look, pal, this is USB News. Do you see a camera and lights out in front of your place? Great. There's two hundred dollars for one of your teenagers if they get to the asshole in the brown coat who's drinking coffee and tell him to put his goddam headset on. You got that? And a hundred bucks for you if the kid gets to him in thirty seconds."

About twenty anxious seconds passed until everyone could see, in the Philadelphia monitor, a teenager in a Burger King cap grabbing the producer and pointing to the earphones, see the producer jumping up and snatching up the headset, yelling, "Yes, yes, yes."

Peter thought Adelson might ignite.

"Ken, I want you in my office Friday morning, and you bring with you ten good reasons why I shouldn't blow your ass into the next century. We're going on the air in thirty seconds, and Jack Thomas is going to go live to Philadelphia a minute after that, and if great live shots of burning buildings don't appear on that screen, don't show up at all." The producer leaped off camera.

Seconds later, the special-report graphic duly appeared in the central monitor, followed by Jack Thomas's reassuringly grave face. The firestorm caused by a jumbo jet's crashing into the densely populated North Philadelphia ghetto had spread to eight blocks of rowhouses, he reported. Conservative estimates were that more than five hundred people might be dead. The gruesome pictures that replaced Thomas's face on the monitor showed block after block of smoking rubble and flame. Fire engines, ambulances, National Guard trucks, and police cars raced back and forth as the sky above the buildings glowed eerily orange. Adelson nodded, snapping his fingers to relieve the tension.

Thomas signed off, promising to return as further details developed, and the tension began to ebb from the room. Stress-paks would not do for this crowd. Some of them, Peter knew from previous experience, would go into the bathroom and vomit.

He walked over to Adelson, who had just accepted a congratulatory handshake from the departing Nab.

"Great stuff, Sam."

Adelson sagged. "Yeah, great. Only we were the last to get people there, the last to get pictures on the air, and we've already had to correct ourselves three times. The map showing North Philadelphia had errors, we ran a file photo of the wrong aircraft type, and we were way off on the casualty projections. I told them a seven-forty-seven didn't carry that many people, but we couldn't get a researcher on the phone until nine. We got wiped. It's a new experience for me—getting my ass kicked on a story."

For the first time, Peter registered the difference in atmosphere: There was no Mickey Grodner flanking Adelson, no aviation expert standing by. And no Flannery, who would have had a gaggle of eyewitnesses tucked away somewhere by now. Her staff was struggling to fill in, but finding a top-notch body snatcher could take months.

Adelson turned to make sure Nab and Wallace had gone. "I complained to Frank Nitti with the white hair," he muttered about Wallace. "I told him we were getting creamed and we'd had to correct a special report, and do you know what that son of a bitch told me?"

Peter waited.

"He told me he'd give me a hiring slot for every viewer who called and complained." Adelson shook his head and gave Peter a weak smile. "So I had Elaine call the operator, who told her that Wallace had just called with the same question. No one had complained. Naturally."

He swiveled to one side as an assistant producer handed him the phone. Coakley was waving a lineup sheet in front of Adelson to get his attention.

"Well, I heard about the story. I thought I could help," said Peter when Adelson had hung up again; he was too embarrassed to speak loudly, but he was finding it difficult to keep Adelson's attention.

Adelson nodded, distracted by a monitor showing new pictures from the crash scene, from another network's satellite feed.

"Yeah, well, we're pretty well staffed up here," he said vaguely, reaching toward a call from Philadelphia. "Why don't you go into the studio and ask the National Desk? Maybe they're short-handed."

Peter walked out into the studio, where the national assigning editors were jammed around a makeshift desk. Two of the three men had phones at each ear; the third wore a headset that Peter guessed connected him to someone in Philadelphia. As Herb Bowden slammed one phone down and stretched for another, Peter reached forward and grabbed his arm. Until Peter had been taken off his show, Bowden had reported to him and the other executive producers.

"Herb, I'm loose. You need any help? I can work the phone—anything you want."

Bowden, starting to scream into the receiver at a correspondent who didn't know how to get from Atlanta to Philadelphia, waved him away. The gesture shocked and stunned him, even though Peter knew that at that moment Bowden was no more able to focus on who he was and what he was asking than he could recite a passage from the bible.

Peter saw one of the national editors looking at him sympathetically. This was a scenario Peter had seen played out more than once in his own control room during a big story, when an out-of-favor vice-president or deposed producer came in for a piece of the action, a last pathetic attempt to demonstrate his brilliance. His own reaction had generally wavered between contempt and impatience. He'd had no more time than Bowden to run a last-chance clinic for sinking executives. He turned away, almost colliding with Adelson coming out of the control room.

Peter grabbed him by the shoulder. "Sam, you've got to give me something to do," he hissed, mortified.

"We're getting murdered, Peter. We haven't sent enough people down there. There's nothing you can do—it's not your turf. What we need, if you want to know the truth, is somebody to look after the reporters. Why don't you go talk to them, maybe take them under your wing?"

"The reporters. You mean the television reporters?"

Through a window in the studio he could see Eddie Cohen and about a dozen others drinking coffee and bottled water and taking notes from a glassed-in reception area. It was a strange part of the big story ritual in television: reporters covering re-porters covering stories. But network press departments loved to invite them along, and they loved to come. It was usually a given that USB News was first; the stories always focused on how USB had done it. Adelson was clearly worried about what they would write this time.

Peter felt stripped. But Adelson, rushing off, turned palms up. His face and his shoulders said, *Look, you asked me what there is to do and I told you. Don't blame me if you don't want to do it.*

Peter stumbled out of the studio, tripping over cables and trying to get out of the way of scrambling technicians, wanting desperately to be seen by as few people as possible, to escape the building and to get home.

How could he have become, so quickly, one of those people he used to duck?

In the lot, he put his face against the wheel of the Toyota and closed his eyes. After a few minutes he drove home in time to pick up the kids from school. What a fool you are, he thought. Not embarrassing enough to get dumped in public, you had to go roaring in like some dumb-ass Boy Scout and let them humil-iate you all over again.

CHAPTER EIGHTEEN
PERSONALS

*B*arbara took one look at Peter and decided it was time to start talking, for both their sakes. So that night the two of them sat across from each other at the kitchen table, each armed with a felt-tip pen and a yellow legal pad. The kids were asleep. Carmen had taken the hint and retreated to her apartment. Even Eugene seemed to sense an important occasion and drifted off into the living room. They each wrote the word *Options* at the top of their pads and underlined it.

It was Peter's idea. It helped thin his fear to start thinking ahead. He had always prided himself on his ability to see clearly, once he was focused on something. As he figured it, he would either be tossed out of USB or forced to labor on some low-budget public affairs raccoon show. But he clung to one of his own Adelson-style laws: *He who believes he has no choices is a drone.* He and Barbara were going to discover whether he had become one or not.

The electric coffeepot was plugged in between them, their battered old KLH tuned to the reggae hour on the local college radio station. Barbara was wearing a U2 sweatshirt—for inspiration, she said—and her hair was pulled back in a bun.

There was nothing the two of them associated more with their marriage than the kitchen table, with an FM radio playing rock 'n' roll and mugs of coffee steaming. Even after they'd had the kids, they always tried to find a half hour or so to spend there at the end of the day, to exchange news, catch up on gossip, and endlessly analyze how Ben and Sarah were doing as children and how they, consequently, were doing as parents. *Morning in the U.S.* had made that difficult.

Their yellow pads had three subheadings. The first was POSSIBILITIES, a list of things Peter and/or Barbara might want to do. By mutual agreement, the list could include long shots, wild-eyed schemes, and utter fantasies. The middle column was labeled BARBARA/KIDS; here they would put a rating (on a scale from one to ten) of how dramatically each option Peter chose would affect the rest of the family.

The third heading was PRACTICAL—how much money the option would bring in, and how far short it fell of their current obligations. There was little question in Peter's mind that aside from selling drugs, anything he might choose would fall short. He was making $175,000 a year, and the only jobs open to him that could match that were other executive producer positions. By now he had a folder of press clippings in which unnamed sources charged that Peter's program was a wasteful mess, boring as well as inefficient, and that the staff was as excited at the prospect of change as Wall Street was. Whether the stories were true or not, they were not likely to inspire other news divisions to knock down his door.

"Okay," said Peter, uncorking his pen and turning the radio down. "Let's make a new life! Could be a great quiz show."

Barbara didn't laugh. It was in her nature to be organized. It was also in her nature to eschew most upper-middle-class comforts. Ten years earlier she would have told him to give them all the finger; her reluctance to do so now spoke forcefully about how much she wanted to write her book.

He certainly understood: It had taken her years to reach the point where a serious agent was willing to handle her stuff, years more before they were stable enough for her to write fiction without worrying about money.

"Let's put down *teaching*—probably aren't a whole lot of executive producers available to teach broadcasting to college kids, right?" he volunteered. They both wrote it down.

"Let's put down *going back to school*. Maybe to law school. Maybe to learn retailing so I could start my own small business— that's always been a fantasy," he went on, scribbling. "Also, write down *newspapers*—I could go back to being a reporter. I was good at that. And independent production companies; there are some good outfits doing documentaries, decent stuff, for cable and public television."

"And," Barbara interjected, "couldn't you do some consulting? Maybe evaluate local stations and tell them how to improve their journalism? Wouldn't that be a possible intermediate step?"

Peter shook his head skeptically. "Maybe, although I wonder why anybody is going to want to pay for the views of a failed producer."

"And there are the other networks . . ." she began, without much conviction.

"Well," Peter said, "I feel a bit down on networks these days. I want to be as independent as I can. There's cable, but that doesn't move me, either. I want to be the only asshole I work for."

Barbara put her pen down with a hopeless-sounding sigh. "Peter, don't we all? This is what scares me about what you're doing. We can talk all we want about the kinds of lives we want to lead, but Jesus, honey, we all have to do something. I know academics; you don't. You don't have any advanced degrees; you haven't published long scholarly essays about the media. You would make thirty thousand, assuming you could connect with a major university, and you could never get tenure, so you would never have any security. That would drop our combined income from almost two hundred thousand to under fifty thousand dollars. And you think USB News is rough—it's a church choir next to most academic departments.

"We'd be out of this house in a month. There would be no way for us to stay in Glen Ridge. I could give up the house if I had to—I grew up in one smaller than this. If there's a good reason, I could handle it—we started out with a lot less—but I wonder if you've thought any of this through."

Peter, irritated, fiddled with his felt pen. "Look, that's why we're doing this. I just want the right to think out loud. I'm not losing my marbles; I just need to explore things. I need to feel that I'm not left, even before I'm forty, with no choices. It's like a blow when other people say it, and it hurts especially when you say it, even indirectly. And frankly, as long as we're being honest with each other, you sound pretty whiny."

Barbara was scribbling on her pad. "Well, let's just look at the numbers. On my chart, when you factor in me and the kids and money and all, I cross off teaching, going back to school, starting a small business—unless you dump me and marry somebody with real money—and newspapers," she said briskly, tight-lipped. "I don't see moving to Orlando so you can cover City Hall and bitch for the rest of your life about some asshole managing editor, which is why you left newspapers for TV in the first place, remember?"

Peter flushed. "Well, what exactly do you see us doing? How about *you* go and get a fucking job that keeps us in this house, now that you're crossing off things I might want to do with my life."

"Please," she snapped back. "Don't make me out to be some kept housewife. We have kids, responsibilities, and yes, I want to do my book, I admit it. But you were the one who wrapped yourself in USB News, like some marine wrapping himself in the flag. *You* were the one who came home every night with your damn mugs and pens and sweatshirts, talking about what a great boss Sam was and how much integrity Brookings had. You went on about how you felt part of the team. Well, where are they now, Peter? I'm not the one who bought into all of this bullshit."

He slid his pad toward the far end of the table, his voice quieting—as it did, she knew, when he was angriest. "No, Barbara, you didn't buy into USB News bullshit. All you did was buy into having a nanny and a study and chuckling about all your old Breadloaf buddies having to write computer programs to pay their rent. You didn't have to make any compromises. You weren't going to lower yourself to go to parties or be a corporate wife or fuss over my career. All you had to do was hide behind it. And now that you can't, you want to make me out to be some selfish irresponsible bastard."

★ ★ ★

Peter waited the following morning for the 7:50 commuter bus to the city, the first time in years he had taken the bus to work. He had walked past Susan's Restaurant—a couple of local cops were having breakfast in what had become his and Joel Fields's usual booth—then stopped at the corner stationery store and newsstand to buy a bus ticket. He had no idea what one cost. It turned out that a book of twenty was $70, and the newsstand proprietor glowered when Peter asked if he accepted credit cards, so he wrote a check.

He had left without waking Barbara or even kissing the kids. His fight with Barbara the night before had been the ugliest of their married life, culminating in the kind of door-slamming and name-calling that they had always prided themselves on avoiding.

Barbara had been stunned. She recognized his eruption as fear more than anger, but it was still frightening. She was not an ostrich by nature, but she hadn't had to face too many harsh realities in recent years. She wasn't so simple-minded as to think she had it all, but she knew she had a lot of it, and the notion of risking, losing, or even changing what she had, rattled her.

She had gone up to the bedroom and closed the door. For the first time in thirteen years he'd slept on the living room couch, just like all the hapless jerks he had comforted over the years when they came slinking into his office to explain why they were late or tired or missing in action.

Now, as he fidgeted awkwardly on what he hoped was the corner where the bus would stop, he thought that catastrophe loomed at home as well as at work. His career had gone off the tracks; his company had been taken over by androids; one friend was dead; another had informed Peter that he was a whore; a third had told him he had no choices in life. Now, was his marriage starting to wobble as well? And the final insult was that he had become one of the bus people, stuffed in a seat like a fucking hot dog in a plastic package, breathing revolting fumes and grinding slowly along Route 3 with the accountants and salesmen. Crammed into a seat, he leafed through the *Daily News* and spotted a picture of David Nab and Harry Sommers arm-in-arm at a celebrity tennis tournament to benefit the Metropolitan Museum. He put his Walkman on, closed his eyes, and half-dozed through the forty-minute ride.

The most depressing part of the trip was getting through the beggars and the homeless in the Port Authority Bus Terminal. Peter strewed quarters and dollar bills on his path from the foul upper levels to the street.

"First-timer, eh?" said a fellow commuter traveling down the escalator with him. "You'll ignore them after a while."

He got to his office at 9:00 A.M., half an hour later than he'd planned. He knew people would be surprised to see him—there were still several days of his leave remaining—but he'd had no choice but to come in. He had to clean out his desk and files, something he had forgotten and his secretary had neglected to remind him about. Lee Laybourne, the new executive producer had graciously telephoned him, wished him luck, then worked his way around to asking when he would be able to move into Peter's office.

So Peter had planned to come in while his former staff would be upstairs in the studio and therefore easy to avoid. But he was not early enough to remain unnoticed. As he worked his way through his desk drawers, several of the show's producers smiled and waved, then quickly looked away. Peter closed the door.

Marie was already gone—Adelson had quickly reassigned her. There were few executives, he knew, who would have bothered to save a secretary. She had left a stack of blue memos from the new Budget Oversight Committee on his desk. One memorandum said that effective immediately, newspapers and magazines would be shared. Each *Time* and *Newsweek,* each *Los Angeles Times* and *Boston Globe* would be distributed to a dozen people who would read the publication, cross their names off the list, put it in the out basket, and send it along to the next reader. Peter knew that most of the producers read the newspapers and magazines at home, as he did, and probably in the same place— the bathroom. Now, no one could bring them home and nobody would have time to read them at work. What could you do? he wondered. Write Nab a memo telling him that the new system was a mistake because people had done some of their best re- search while taking a shit?

Another blue memo said the library would be open from 6:00 A.M. to 6:00 P.M. instead of twenty-four hours a day. Re- searchers, said the memo, would no longer be available around the clock; research requests, planned in advance and relayed by phone, would be coordinated more efficiently.

Still another memorandum prohibited USB employees from taking other USB employees out to lunch without vice-presidential approval. The sending of flowers for any reason was forbidden. All travel had to be approved in advance by the Finance office.

A pile of other blue sheets prohibited the hiring of porters to haul camera and lighting equipment through airports. One said the company was considering urine tests for drugs. Another required techs to carry a special blue ID card, with a yellow one for producers, red for other executives, white for all other workers. Paychecks would no longer be deposited automatically. The company would no longer permit executives to draw cash advances larger than $300 without prior approval. Outside experts and consultants, academics and specialists, could no longer be paid for their expertise on breaking stories. Any conferences involving the news division would henceforth be held at USB News in New York. Producers could no longer use two camera crews without a vice-president's assent. Any story requiring more than four shooting days also had to be approved by a vice-president. In advance.

Peter decided to take home the folder of letters Marie had marked *personal,* which meant they were addressed to him by name. It contained the usual felt-pen scrawlings from God, from Judge Crater, and from Lee Harvey Oswald (who insisted he was alive and living in a suburb of Denver); a couple of others needed answering. One from the Israeli-American Friendship League accused Peter's program of bias against Israel in its reporting on disorders in the occupied territories. Another came from a Mrs. Wuraftic, who claimed to be a former president of the Rye, N.Y., chapter of the League of Women Voters, now living in a condominium just outside Boca Raton but obviously still civic-minded—she headed the homeowners association. A longtime loyalist of USB News, she was disappointed that David Nab had acquired the network, since there were strange goings-on at his condominium complex in Florida, including the sudden death of a parrot or two and odd maladies among certain tenants. So, thought Peter, Nab was a parrot-killer as well.

Peter also laughed at a letter from a job applicant that began: "I am no less than the most promising producer in Biloxi, Miss., and I am ready for network television. Is network television ready for me?" Peter stuffed them all in his briefcase. He would have plenty of time to answer his mail at home.

He was beginning to put his files into the cardboard boxes that had been conveniently stacked behind his desk when there was a knock on the door and four men in black jumpsuits walked in.

"Oh, sorry," said the squad's beefy leader—JIM, according to the letters embroidered in white on the front of his uniform. "Didn't know anybody was here." He looked down the list of names on his clipboard. "You Reynolds? Jackson?"

Peter shook his head.

"Look, give me a clue, will ya?" said Jim. "Herbert? Oh, yeah. You weren't expecting us?"

Peter shook his head again.

"Shit, I'm sorry, pal. You know, we're always the ones who have to break the news. It's the worst part of a job that ain't exactly like Lee Iacocca's to begin with, you know what I mean?"

"What . . . what do you want?" Peter asked, stammering. The men in jumpsuits had become a chilling but familiar sight at USB News since the takeover.

"You really don't know? Well, we got orders to pack up all your stuff and move it."

"You're sure you got the right guy?" Peter asked as the men in the jumpsuits looked around the dingy basement office, sizing up how long it would take to pack up and trying to avoid Peter's gaze.

Jim offered to show Peter the clipboard, but Peter waved him away.

"Does it say I'm being moved to another office?" he asked.

"Yeah," said Jim, sounding relieved. "You're going down the block to Public Projects, floor nine, room one-oh-four. Doesn't look like you're getting fired, does it? Or they wouldn't be moving you. Although I gotta tell you, we moved a bunch of people outa that floor; I think you're the first one we moved in. We're like the Grim Reaper, you know—nobody wants to see us coming. The fired guys' stuff, we pack it all into these corrugated boxes and then put it on a UPS truck and send it home. The UPS guys hate it—it's a worse job than ours. This guy over in the *Evening News,* he hadn't told his wife he got canned, so the

During the layoffs the twenty-two-person religious programming unit had suddenly become a five-person unit; *Infinity,*
one of the division's resting places for burned-out field producers, had seen its staff and budget slashed by two thirds; the
documentary unit had been merged with the news staff, in effect
killing it without having to say so.

Peter showed his ID to the guard and went up to the ninth
floor. There was no receptionist; all the receptionists but the one
at USB's main entrance had been let go. Security guards could
direct visitors, according to the Budget Oversight Committee.

The ninth floor was huge; it stretched the length of a city
block. It was also eerily quiet. Peter heard a phone or two
ringing somewhere, but there were no sounds of typing or
conversation and he couldn't see a soul. For almost as far as he
could make out, open doors led into vacant offices.

Room 104 was palatial, although nearly empty because the
crew hadn't arrived yet with his things. Its corner windows
provided a terrific view of the East River and it had an impressive-
looking conference table, four television monitors, and a long
beige sofa. There was also that extraordinary luxury, for anyone
not at the very top, a private bathroom. All to the good, thought
Peter: I'll have plenty of time to read in there.

The office reeked of importance, it depressed him to acknowledge. It seemed to cry out: Look at this silly man. He's
like some banana republic bureaucrat with a gold-trimmed uniform and a vast office and nothing to do in it. The ninth floor
was so far from where decisions were made and from the people
who made them that the President could get shot and he wouldn't
even know it for hours.

Deciding to explore the floor, he strolled gamely past darkened offices and unused desks for long spooky moments, then
almost collided with a coffee cart pushed by a startled, Latin-
looking man Peter couldn't place at first.

"You're Rafael, who used to serve in the conference room,"
Peter said.

The man, flattered to be recognized, nodded. He explained
that his position had been eliminated, but that the man who ran
the cart in this annex had retired, leaving the job open. Miranda
shrugged, and so did Peter.

"Well, I'm Peter. I guess we're in the same boat. Is there anybody on this floor to sell coffee and doughnuts to?"

Miranda shrugged again. "Downstairs in the library there are people in the daytime. On this floor, there are only three other people: a secretary who is taking apart the religious offices and two people in Constitutional Minutes. But they are not really newspeople," he added derisively.

As a welcoming gesture, he presented Peter with a free Styrofoam cup of coffee. They sat down on the sofa in his office. The room felt stuffy, and Peter, still flushed from his encounter with the men in jumpsuits, looked for the thermostat.

"Don't bother," said Miranda. "There aren't enough people left on this floor to make it worth their while to pay for air conditioning, so they've turned it off. There's air downstairs. Upstairs, there's nobody at all, so there's no electricity even. Tell me," he said wistfully, "what is the big news now?"

They chatted pleasantly for a few minutes; then Miranda looked at his watch and hurried off, hoping to peddle some sandwiches to people who didn't go out for lunch.

Peter walked outside. The day was gray and melancholy and Peter had an overpowering feeling that everyone rushing past was more successful than he was. He was the only one of all these thousands who did not have a thing that needed to be done or a place he had to be. If he didn't return to his new office, no one would notice for days.

He walked four blocks to a newsstand and flipped through the news weeklies, searching for something appetizing to read. His eyes skipped over and then returned to a copy of *Coupling,* a raunchy weekly sex magazine; techs on his show were always reading the personal ads aloud, whooping and woofing.

He walked past the newsstand, then circled back, checking to see that no one he knew was nearby. He felt a surge of panic when he saw Bill Siegel, an *Evening News* producer who had been laid off, walk past, recognize him and turn around to shake hands.

"You look lost," said Siegel. "You all right? Listen, I'm on my way to the dentist so I can't stop, but I'd love to have lunch. Please call me." He handed Peter his new card, with his home phone number. They had worked together when a few of Siegel's pieces didn't make the *Evening News* and wound up on Peter's show. Peter liked Siegel's passion for oddballs and his relentless cheerfulness in a business where most people seemed to grow harder by the day. But he couldn't imagine that Siegel would have been amused to see him browsing through pages of soft-core porn.

He later recalled the feeling as trancelike.

He rounded the block, then came back to the newsstand. Again making sure no one was watching, he handed the attendant six singles, folded the magazine twice so that no part of the cover was visible, and stuck it into his jacket pocket. He walked down the street to a park bench and, carefully folding back the cover, turned to the personals.

His eyes came to one that said simply: "Safe, gentle young woman. Sensitive and friendly. Upper East Side. In or out. $300." And a phone number. He assumed the "safe" was to pacify fear of AIDS.

He was surprised by the price, and surprised to be sitting on a bench with a dirty magazine on a cloudy spring lunch hour. He didn't have $300. He went to a phone stand, dialed USB, and asked for his former secretary, Marie.

"Peter? I understand you came in today. I'm sorry. You know, I guess, that your office—"

"Marie, look, I need a favor. Fill out a cash advance form for three hundred dollars. That's the most you can get without a vice-presidential sign-off, right? Fake my signature and meet me outside USB in ten minutes, okay?"

Marie hesitated. "Peter, is this kosher?"

"Look, my signature is on it, okay? I'm still an executive producer. Do this for me, will you? I'll explain later. The cashier's office probably doesn't even know yet that we've been reassigned."

Before the takeover, executive producers had used cash advances for pocket money, fudging expense accounts to cover withdrawals of anything up to $500. Larger amounts could cause raised eyebrows at Finance, but if you stayed within $600 or $700 a month, nobody ever said a word. But that was before.

He felt excited, aroused, and nervous. He had never had any kind of sexual encounter with someone he didn't know. But he did not hesitate, or think much about what he was doing. He knew that if he gave himself time to reflect, he wouldn't do it, and he wanted to do it. He was relieved, when he walked up to USB fifteen minutes later, to find Marie anxiously standing in front of the building with an envelope.

"Any trouble?" he asked.

"No. They just said from now on you would have to come get advances in person, but it was okay this time. Are you all right?" He nodded, kissed her on the cheek, and walked up the East Side for a mile or so, trying to calm himself. He was going to do it.

Near Gramercy Park he stopped at a pay phone and dialed the number in the ad. A woman answered: "Hello?"

"Yes . . . hello. I'm calling about the ad."

"Where was the ad?"

"In this magazine called *Coupling*." He was stammering. "I'm sorry, but this is the first time I've ever done anything like this and I'm a little nervous."

The woman sounded skeptical but welcoming. "And what are you interested in?"

"Well, I don't know. I don't know what the choices are, really."

She suddenly seemed to relax, as if he had passed some secret test. "Well, I'm Sandy. I'm friendly and I'm safe. You can watch me with a friend if you'd like, or we can have a good time together. Why don't you come over and we'll talk about it? If you're not comfortable, you can leave."

Peter said no, he didn't want anyone there but her. She sounded young and appealing. He felt detached from himself, as if he were watching from across the street, but he also felt a powerful erection, more intense than he could remember having in years, the kind of aching that tormented teenage boys. "I wouldn't ask you to do anything strange," he added, thinking it an odd reassurance to offer a prostitute on the telephone.

She told him to come to Third Avenue and 76th and call her from a phone booth on the uptown corner. He reasoned that she probably could see the phone booth from her window and would still have time to bail out if he looked threatening. He thought he could do the same—he could just turn and leave if it felt wrong. Did they arrest people for this stuff anymore? He doubted it. The greater danger, he calculated, was in being robbed. He wasn't really likely to call the police, was he? Yet every time he thought of the risks, he felt even more aroused. He hailed a cab.

There were huge apartment towers up and down the avenue, with boutiques and restaurants on the street level. He had expected her place to be tawdry; maybe it would be, in spite of the Upper East Side address. He dialed the number again.

"What's your name?" she said.

"Steve."

"Okay, Steve. You see the tower right behind you?"

He turned and saw a yellow brick apartment house with a doorman. "Yup." He was trying to sound tough, but his heart was racing.

"Just come on up, then." She gave him the apartment number.

"Can you see me?" he asked.

He was so aflame he was afraid the bulge in his pants was showing, a fear he hadn't had to contend with since high school.

"No, Steve, I'm up in the sky. I can only see the clouds. Come on up."

Peter expected the doorman to sneer or tell him to get lost when he gave the apartment number, but he merely called the apartment and told whoever answered that there was a Steve in the lobby. Then he nodded and told him to go on up. Peter imagined it wouldn't be a big deal for Sandy to bring the doorman in on the whole thing.

In the elevator he took his wallet and cash out of his pants pocket, put both in his inside jacket pocket. For the first time, he wondered what Sandy would look like and what he would do if she was homely or unappealing. He decided he would just bail out.

He was perspiring heavily now, a cold, dank sweat that he knew would soon soak through his shirt. Down the hall an elderly woman came out of her apartment with a yellow trash bag and looked at him with unmistakable disgust. She knew.

The woman who opened the door was in her twenties, with long, curly black hair; she was wearing abbreviated running shorts and a T-shirt that said SHIT HAPPENS. She was athletic and wholesome-looking and reminded Peter of Debra Winger, a pleasant surprise. She smiled and offered her hand. "Hi, Steve," she said. "You want something to drink?"

Peter mumbled yes, and followed her into a dark bedroom

with drawn curtains. He heard talking in another room and, he thought, the coos of a baby. The bedroom, the only room he could really see, was furnished in contemporary Yuppie, with a queen-size platform bed, an oak dresser, and a metal lamp turned almost all the way down. Opposite the foot of the bed were a television and a VCR. Sandy asked Peter to sit on the bed and take his clothes off if he wanted, and she switched on the VCR. It was disconcerting: His penis did not seem nearly as unnerved at being there as the rest of him did.

The image on the TV screen showed an attractive, fit young man and woman in a claw-footed old bathtub. She was sitting astride the tub while he knelt on the bottom, his mouth carefully brushing its way up her thigh. The last time Peter had seen such pictures, back in college, the lovers had been a fat man in socks and shoes mounting a tired old hooker, both of them groaning loudly and insincerely. The two kids he was looking at now showed no such artifice; they were both laughing. He was impressed by the tape's lighting and color. This was no cheap home job; this had production values.

When the man, who kept pushing his longish blond hair back out of his face, had worked his way up to the top of the woman's thigh, he cupped both hands behind her buttocks and plunged his tongue into her. She smiled and groaned softly, shifting her hips.

Peter took his shoes and socks off, then his pants and shirt, carefully piling everything where he could see it. He looked down self-consciously at the slight swelling around his waist and the more pronounced one below.

The man in the video had leaned back in the tub, and the woman had lowered herself on top of him. Peter wondered at the size of the organ she was climbing onto; self-conscious about his own erection a few moments ago, he now felt ridiculously inadequate.

Sandy returned and handed Peter a Coke, which he drank gratefully, since he didn't know what to say.

"You want this on or off?" She pointed to the VCR.

"Off is okay," he said.

"So this is really your first time at this?" she asked, perching next to him on the bed. "You know everybody says that."

He blushed. "It's true. I never thought of it before."

"I'm not prying, but you're probably going through some kind of trouble. That's how it usually happens. I'll only ask you two favors," she said.

"What's that?" he asked warily.

"Don't ask how a nice kid like me could get into this. And don't pretend that you're going to come back again, because that would be a lie. I don't want you to, anyway; if customers start coming back, people will get suspicious. Okay?"

She rested one hand on Peter's bare left thigh, brushing her fingertips in circles. Peter had never been with a prostitute. He knew it ought to seem sordid. But he found himself intensely drawn to Sandy; she seemed so young and sweet.

She pushed Peter slowly down on the bed. He closed his eyes, felt her licking the inside of one thigh. After a minute or two he began to breathe heavily, partly out of deepening arousal, partly to signal her that he liked what she was doing, that she shouldn't stop.

It took nearly five minutes for her to reach his testicles and for her tongue to inch up the sides of his penis. He cried out, something he never did at home.

Suddenly the licking stopped. She cupped Peter's balls in her hands, massaging gently, stroking his penis faster, pressing harder. He felt ready to burst, but when he came, his only concession to the dizziness and relief engulfing him was one surprised and appreciative gasp.

Sandy giggled. "You were ready," she said. "More than ready."

She got up, saying she would give Peter a minute to get dressed and then come back for her money. She handed him a towel, warm and damp.

Down on the street, Peter looked at his watch and was amazed to see that he had been in the building no more than twenty minutes. He thought this must be what a nervous breakdown was like, and that he was clearly having one. Surely he must be going mad, to pay money like that to bed down with a stranger. He took a taxi back down to USB, wondering if his furniture had been moved yet.

Climbing out of the cab, he noticed Flannery's building across the street and thought there was really no point in going back to the office. He crossed the street and leaned on her buzzer.

What he had done suddenly seemed so enormous, so out of character, that terror overwhelmed him. He had just been made love to by an attractive young whore, even though he had a wife he loved and two children he was crazy about, and he had stolen $300 of the company's money to do it. At least it was away from home, with someone anonymous. At least he'd kept it far away from his family and Glen Ridge.

What did you do? he asked himself over and over again. What the hell did you do?

Flannery's voice blared over the squawk box. "Hello?"

"It's Peter. You alone?"

"No. Tom Cruise is in the bathtub with me. As soon as I get rid of him, you can pop on up."

Flannery was in sweat pants and a T-shirt, on the verge of a midday run. She was studying him intently. "Weren't we supposed to have a dinner date?"

He nodded, sweating again, his legs trembling.

"Peter, what the hell is going on? You call me up and invite me to dinner like you're a divorced man on the loose; then you show up seven hours early looking like you just murdered somebody. What is wrong? My God, you look like death."

Her stare was merciless. She brought him a scotch and water and watched the ice cubes rattling against the side of the glass as he tried to hold it steady. She was quiet for a long minute. Then her voice turned soothing. "Peter," she said softly. "Tell me what's wrong."

His sobs were the only sound in the room. "What's wrong? Barbara and I had the worst fight of our married life last night. All of a sudden we're a thousand miles apart. I was booted out of my office this morning and the floor I've been moved to isn't even important enough to have air conditioning. I have no job. My company is in the hands of aliens and I'm up to my elbows in blood myself. And, Patricia? You've got to hear this, because there's nobody else in the world that I dare tell this to. I think I'm cracking up. I just slept with a whore. I just paid three hundred dollars to sleep with a whore. Is that enough?"

Flannery poured a second scotch, for herself. "Three hundred bucks for a whore?"

He nodded, wiping his eyes with a handkerchief, swallowing the sobs.

"Three hundred for how long?" she prodded, when he was quiet again.

Peter snorted. "Fuck you," he said. "This is serious. Twenty minutes."

"Maybe I don't have to go back to television after all," she said. Both of them were laughing now.

"So," she said, finally. "You came here to fuck me, right?"

"It had crossed my mind," he said.

"But you see that would be a mistake, right?"

He nodded.

"Peter. Lord knows I could use a jump. But you know that I love you and your family much too much. And you also see that I know you don't want to sleep with me because of me, but because of all this stuff landing on you. You see that, right?"

"Right."

"And besides, I would want at least five hundred bucks." She took a slug from her drink. "So maybe we can find some alternative to your problems other than falling apart and wrecking your marriage."

"Like what?"

Flannery poured him another drink. She asked if she could be honest, in the way even close friends do when they want to preempt an explosion.

"Yes," Peter said, "of course you can be honest. It would be delightful if somebody would be."

"There's one thing I just don't get about all you guys. I didn't get it during the layoffs and I don't get it now, listening to you snivel."

"What's that?" he asked cautiously. Flannery knew how to be too honest sometimes.

"How come you guys don't get mad? These assholes come in and they railroad all of you, they trash the company, and they slime your shows. They disregard everybody's understandings and expectations, they scare the shit out of even the people who *don't* lose their jobs, so no one ever feels safe in their work again, and you guys just roll over.

"Look at you—you're an ever-loving mess. I've never seen a human being lose it so damn fast as you have, Peter. Three months ago you were a functioning adult—a good husband, a great father, an intelligent, hardworking boss—a little dull maybe, but solid. You had the whole picture: the dog, the rabbit, the pretty kids. Now, I feel like I'm watching one of those movies where Jack Lemmon or someone becomes an alkie and loses everything he has.

"You're bawling like a baby; you don't understand that your wife is scared shitless; you can't tell her that you are too. You're screwing whores like some drunken miner on payday, you want to desecrate our friendship by turning *me* into a whore, and all you can do is sit there and boohoo. I'm looking at a screwed-up pervert whose entire life is going down the drain because some asshole took over the company and is slapping everybody around." Flannery shook her head.

Peter had finished his drink and gone to pour another. "What are you saying, Patricia?" he asked dully. "That I'm a coward? What do you want me to do, assassinate Nab? Nobody fights back against these people—they don't lose. This is the fucking real world. You're talking gibberish."

"Well, I don't know," she drawled. "You used to be creative. And you're always telling me how you used to be idealistic. Maybe you'd feel better if you stopped sitting around blubbering and went to bat for your friends instead of pretending you don't know them, like you did with D'Amato."

Peter whirled, infuriated, gripping his glass. "That's cheap shit, Patricia. That's going too far."

"Bullshit," she yelled back. "I have the right! I paid the dues for my friend; what dues have you paid for yours? You lost your precious show? Is that what all this is about, that the superproducer has hit the wall? Isn't that really it? When what it should be about is getting mad at those bastards. You know, if you ever decided to stop slinking around, you might do something useful. It doesn't matter to me—I'm out of there. You just might try getting mad, doing some damage. You might not feel like the piece of shit that you are."

Peter sat down and took a long pull of scotch.

"Get mad," he repeated finally, after a long pause. "Do some damage. Interesting idea.

"I like it," he said. "I like it a lot."

Ben was draped over the sofa watching Nickelodeon—it sounded like one of the kids' quiz shows he loved and was always badgering Peter to get him on to. Sarah had her block castle set up in the corner.

She got up and flew into his arms, squealing "Daddy." Eugene grabbed Pegasus, Sarah's favorite My Little Pony, and presented it to Peter as his nightly offering. God's sweetest creatures, thought Peter. If people were only like retrievers, it would be a dumb, safe world in which everyone spent all day bringing everyone else gifts.

Seeing his children brought home the shock of what had happened. He said little, dashed upstairs, where he stripped off his clothes and stuffed them into the hamper and hurried into the shower. He could smell Sandy all over him, and he was terrified that Barbara would. He had rarely felt so frightened. He made the water hot, almost scalding, trying to boil her scent away. He heard Eugene's tail thumping against the bathroom door, and looked out to see the dog bringing him another of Sarah's ponies.

Peter, dripping wet, knelt down and hugged the dog. *It's just one time,* he thought. *I won't do it again, and it doesn't mean anything, except that I am near the edge. If I feel the urge again, I'll get help. Don't overreact,* he cautioned himself. *You didn't hurt anybody. Yet.*

Before he could go back downstairs, Barbara came hurtling out of her study and threw her arms around him. They kissed for a long time, and held each other.

"Are we still married?" she asked.

"You have to allow me more dream time," he said, a bit shakily. "You gave me too much reality too soon."

CHAPTER NINETEEN
DESPICABLE

$\mathcal{T}$he producers of *Morning in the U.S.* had debated for nearly an hour about whether it would be appropriate for David Nab to appear on the broadcast. As a member of the President's Select Commission on a Competitive Economy, he was certainly news-worthy. Besides, none of the other members was available, and the latest scary balance-of-trade figures had propelled the econ-omy onto page one of every paper in the country. So the bookers called Nab's office and arranged for him to appear. He declined the limo—he always traveled in a luxurious but unostentatious Chrysler with a nonuniformed driver—but he agreed to be early enough to be made up and briefed. His appearance would be followed by a discussion between a former Secretary of the Treasury and two former chairmen of the Council of Economic Advisers.

Nab and Harold Wallace spent several hours in a hotel suite the night before, kicking around questions. Hal Danzig, the public relations specialist, played the interviewer. As Wallace pointed out, the appearance was worth preparing for. It was

Nab's public debut as CEO of United States Broadcasting, the first time any major news organization had sought his views on a subject dear to his heart.

It was crucial, said Danzig, that Nab be forceful, statesman-like, and articulate. The best in this business of "seersmanship," as he put it, was Kissinger. Haig was promising, but sometimes he got too angry; Kissinger was what you aspired to. An accent was helpful—Americans thought anyone who spoke with an accent was a genius—but in the absence of one, you needed a clear, forthright opinion on any question you might possibly be asked.

Danzig tossed Nab some questions, then cautiously but honestly critiqued his responses. Nab had to remember he was talking to housewives and to people rushing off to work. He reminded Nab to save some of his points for other times. Be more statesmanlike, Danzig pressed. Call for consensus. Be conciliatory toward Japan. Demand more creativity and leadership. You'll make it onto the bookers' Rolodexes: *Nightline, Today, GMA.* You'll hit the business columns of the *Times,* the *Journal.* These were America's town meetings now, explained Danzig; once you made it there, you were one of the nation's most influential people.

Harold Wallace agreed. This was important. This was, after all, why Nab had bought USB, wasn't it? Because he had things to say, contributions to make.

Bill Siegel climbed out of his cab four blocks from USB News, at a corner where Peter was waiting. "I feel like a dope dealer," Peter whispered hoarsely.

They looked warily at a police cruiser, slowing as it passed them. The young cops paid them no attention, and both men giggled like kids trying not to get caught on mischief night. Still, they were more than a little nervous.

"Here it is," said Peter, handing Siegel a small plastic case.

Siegel slid the case into a jacket pocket.

"So you can get in?" Peter asked.

"No sweat," said Siegel. "They don't have a guard at the back door, and a friend of mine from Videotape will push the door open in twenty minutes. An alarm will sound, but by the time anyone gets there, I'll be in my editing room, which is a hundred feet away. I have a copy of the key because I was always losing mine, and I didn't turn the copy in."

"They don't even have guards anymore?" Peter was surprised.

"Just on the main entrances since the layoffs," Siegel said. "And Steve will be alone at the console. His last day is Saturday. He loves the idea. You're sure Nab is on in the first half hour?"

Peter shrugged. "As sure as I can be without calling. Patricia got hold of the show lineup. Anyway, the second half hour on Tuesdays is always a Hollywood report, and the last hour is for the housewives—everybody else has gone to work."

"Good," said Siegel, "because Steve goes off at eight, right in the middle of the show, and we're fucked without him. Afterwards I'll just walk out the main entrance."

Peter walked Siegel to a deli that was just opening and bought two cups of coffee. "You don't have to do this, you know, Bill."

"Are you shitting me? I would have given my left nut to do this. Are you planning anything else? I want to be in on it if you are."

Peter shook his head. "Look, I've been up all night scheming. But it's smarter and safer if all you do is this. It's plenty, believe me."

Siegel was understanding. "Right, that's what they say in the World War Two movies. You can't tell what you don't know. So you'll be at home?"

"Yes," said Peter. "That's where I'm supposed to be. Besides, I want to see it. Going against the traffic, I'll be home before the show starts. Try not to let anybody see you. You scared?"

"Just a bit. This is a little out of my line. But what can they do to me? I'm already fired."

At almost the same moment that David Nab's Chrysler pulled up to the USB News entrance, a back door near the loading dock popped open and Bill Siegel darted in.

Nab had in recent weeks received more than a dozen

phoned-in death threats, the callers ranging from people claiming to be Libyan terrorists to what he guessed were disgruntled employees. He was taking Harold Wallace's security concerns more seriously, so two young men in well-tailored suits and discreet earpieces bounced out of the Chrysler to scan the empty sidewalk before he emerged. Nab and Hal Danzig waited ten seconds, then bounded out of the car. Lee Leybourne, the show's new executive producer, was waiting in the lobby to offer his hand and escort Nab to the greenroom where guests were powdered, fed, and kept alert until it was time to go on.

Emma, the program's makeup czar, strode into the waiting room at 6:45 and ordered Nab to sit down. She bluntly told him that he needed to counteract the shadows under his eyes, and that he would look like a horse's ass if he started sweating on his own network. He climbed into the raised chair and, as Danzig continued to pepper him with questions about the economy, took a good-luck call from Harold Wallace. One of the cafeteria attendants brought in a pot of fresh coffee and a tray of iced pastries, which Nab eyed with distaste. Flannery would have called Nab's office to find out in advance that he preferred fresh fruit.

Laybourne came in to be sure that Nab understood the procedure: that a producer would come fetch him at 7:15; that after the news headlines Leeming would introduce the segment; that the questions would focus on the trade deficit and on possible solutions; and that, given time, Leeming might ask him a question about his plans for USB News. Journalistically speaking, said Laybourne, the show might come under fire if it didn't at least reflect the fact that Nab owned the network and that there was considerable speculation about his plans. Nab nodded. He wanted nothing more than to do the proper thing journalistically, he said.

The segment, said Laybourne, was scheduled for five minutes. He hoped Nab would understand the need to keep his answers short and responsive. Nab nodded, and something in his eyes made Laybourne see that it was time to go away.

★　★　★

Bill Siegel watched the early morning news on the monitor in his old editing room. He kept chuckling to himself, thinking that he'd become as strange as all the people he had done pieces about over the years. He had never imagined being involved in an escapade like this, yet he marveled at how much fun it was turning out to be. Shit, he thought again, what can they do to me? He looked at his watch, slipped out of the editing room and down the deserted hallways. No one in the *Evening News* area would be at work for hours yet.

He walked through the emergency fire exit, downstairs into the basement and the sub-basement. The network control center stood off to his left, a red sign above the door flashing KEEP OUT: ON THE AIR. This was the nerve center of the network, the computerized controls that determined what was transmitted from network headquarters to the hundreds of local affiliates. To get inside, you had to pass an armed guard and insert an ID card—changed weekly—into a machine by the door.

Siegel turned right, away from the control center and the security camera that swept the hallways, and toward the men's room. He looked at his watch: 7:00 A.M. Producers tended to have expensive watches and reliable ones, and he was sure the time was right. He saw that the men's room was empty except for a pair of feet below a stall door.

"Steve?"

"Bill?" said the man in the stall.

Without saying anything more, Siegel took a cassette out of an envelope and slid it under the door.

He left the men's room and walked two flights up to the main lobby, praying he could get to his apartment in time. He chose the north entrance, the one used by accountants, because it was closer to the Finance and Computing offices. One of the accounting clerks recognized him and waved, but that was all right; she probably didn't even know he wasn't with the company anymore. He walked out past the guard, who was checking the IDs of people coming in, and grabbed a cab that was dropping somebody off.

Peter made a pot of coffee and sliced some peaches into his Cheerios, then sat down in front of the television set in the family room. Upstairs, he heard Barbara sounding the first wake-up call in the kids' bedrooms; it usually took three tries to rouse them.

She came down in her bathrobe and the bunny slippers he had given her for her birthday years ago, looking haggard. She sat down next to him on the battered brown couch. Eugene, eyes still closed, thumped his tail in welcome.

"Hi," she said.

"Hi."

"Where the hell have you been? I mean, I appreciate your calling to tell me you wouldn't be home last night, but I am a bit curious about where you stormed off to."

He took her hand. "After the kids are off to school, let's go out for breakfast and have a walk and a talk, all right?"

She nodded and started to get up, but he pulled her down. "You ought to watch this next segment. David Nab is going to deliver his insights about the economy."

Barbara looked amazed. "Why should I watch that?"

"You should get a look at him," Peter said, getting up to pour another cup of coffee, his fourth of the young morning. "He's an important figure in our lives now."

Lee Laybourne settled into the executive producer's chair, Nabih Patel alongside him in the deputy's spot. Laybourne's style was different from Peter's, and while Patel wasn't crazy about any executive producer, he especially disliked Laybourne. He already looked forward to the day he could play the "flameout" cassette on the control room monitor.

Laybourne, undertaking to spice up the show, had made Patel come to work two hours earlier and scramble up to the last minute to land a wider variety of topical guests. He had demanded the biggest, newsiest names first and, to prove his point, had already fired two of Flannery's top assistants. He condemned the show's graphics, camera angles, and lighting, as well as the atmosphere in the control room, which he found lazy and unprofessional.

Laybourne had threatened the producer with particularly horrible destruction if anything screwed up David Nab's maiden appearance on his own network. He had also personally briefed

Don Leeming. The segment was quite straightforward: what should be done about the trade deficit and how could the country become more competitive? Hard to botch that up, thought Laybourne, watching the clock.

It was 7:12 when Nab slid into the guest chair. A cool one, Laybourne thought; if Nab was nervous he didn't show it. A tech attached a microphone to his tie and ran the wire under Nab's jacket and down the chair to the floor. Emma came by and repowdered Nab's forehead and cheeks to guard against perspiration. Laybourne pressed the button that connected him to the floor manager and suggested more makeup under Nab's eyes; the shadows were still too deep.

He watched in the monitor as Leeming came up and shook Nab's hand. The news headlines were over; they had gone to a commercial. When they returned to the air, viewers would see Nab and Leeming chatting together. Laybourne flipped the switch that allowed him to listen to their conversation.

"It's great to meet you," Leeming was saying effusively. "Congratulations are in order, I guess. I hear you're a Yankees fan; we should take in a ball game sometime. Say, did you hear the one about the kid in the wheelchair?"

Laybourne's hand shot out at the button connecting him to Leeming. "Don, why not ask Mr. Nab if he's comfortable and let him know what your first question will be?"

Leeming smiled and did as he was told.

"One minute," yelled Jamie Webb. "Let's settle down, everybody. One minute to air." Nab looked composed and serious.

"Announce," yelled Webb at 7:16. Leeming and Nab appeared in the monitor as Harry Ebener announced the return of the program.

"Good morning," Leeming said. "I am pleased to welcome David Nab, the new chairman of United States Broadcasting, a well-known businessman and a recent appointee to the President's Select Commission on a Competitive Economy.

"First of all, congratulations and welcome to your first appearance on USB News. I trust there'll be many more. Mr. Nab, I'll get right to the point. The latest trade figures were announced yesterday, and they were a shock even to veteran economists. According to the government, our trade deficit rose to twenty-seven billion dollars in April, the largest in history. I'll ask you straight out: What can we do?"

Nab nodded and smiled and looked into the camera, as Danzig had instructed. Laybourne sat back in his chair. Leeming would fit in only three or four questions, at best.

Nab opened his mouth to speak, and the loud, distinct lisp of Daffy Duck seemed to issue from it. "That," said the voice, "ith dethpicable, I tell you, it'th dethpicable!" Webb looked at the monitor and lifted his headset off. "And I'll tell you thomthing elth," Nab seemed to be saying. "I'm not going to thtand for it anymore."

"What the fuck?" said Webb, a look of horror on his face, turning from the director's console to look at Patel and Laybourne.

"That's Daffy Duck," Patel gasped. "That's Daffy fucking Duck."

"Oh, dear God," yelled Laybourne, jumping to his feet. "That isn't going out over the network, is it? Tell me, dear fucking God, that it isn't going out over the network." God did not answer, but the telephone lines lit up. There were twenty telephone lines on the control room console, every one of them warbling softly, until the sound was like a flock of pigeons. The producer mouthed prayers silently and crossed herself.

The control room assistant struggled to get Laybourne's attention. "Mr. Laybourne," she yelled. "Mr. Adelson is on line one, Harold Wallace is on another line, network operations is on four—I haven't gotten to the others. They all say Daffy Duck's voice is coming out of David Nab's mouth."

Laybourne punched up Adelson. "Sam?"

"What the fuck is going on there? Do you know that Daffy Duck's voice is coming out of my television set? Both of them, the one in the bedroom and in the kitchen. Who is doing it? Is it everywhere?"

"I don't know," Laybourne said, gulping. "We're trying to find out."

"We're humiliating the guy. Get the fuck off the air. Get off! Do you hear me?"

Laybourne didn't really have any idea what to do. He ordered Patel to call network operations, then flipped his mike switch to the channel that let him hear the New York affiliate. He hoped against hope to hear David Nab's voice, but the duck was talking there too.

Leeming sensed something was wrong. The floor manager, whose earphones were connected to the network line, was frowning. In Leeming's earpiece, connected to the executive producer, he could hear the most frightful yelling.

The duty officer in the network control center jumped out of his chair as if he had been ejected. "What the hell is going out?" he thundered. "It sounds like a duck."

The six technicians on duty in the climate-controlled room all stared incredulously at the monitor. The officer raced across the room to the main console, even as his emergency telephone began to honk.

He looked toward the telephone, then at the cassette slot under the main monitor control panel, and lunged toward a red button. An unmarked cassette shot out. The duck's voice disappeared. David Nab was explaining why a free market was essential to the American economy.

The *New York Post* was out before lunch with a front page that consisted of five enormous letters—QUACK—in bold black type and a picture of an angry-looking Nab getting into his car. Underneath the picture was the caption: DETHPICABLE? More than fifty reporters were waiting for Nab when he emerged from his office to go to lunch. NAB CRIES FOWL! thundered *Newsday*.

Even the unflappable Hal Danzig lost his cool, testily suggesting to the reporters that there must be something more important happening in the world than a practical joke involving a duck.

Frank Mahoney waited for Harold Wallace to cool off.

"Goddam it, Frank"—Wallace's voice was tense—"what kind of craziness is this? I want you to who find out who did this goddam thing and bring me their heads. I want them caught and prosecuted. Do you know that the whole country is laughing at Nab? The man looks ridiculous. What the hell happened?"

"Well, Mr. Wallace," said the Nab Enterprises security chief, "all I can tell you so far is that someone—we think it had to be one of the techs in the network control center—slipped a cassette into the override mechanism. I'm not an electronics expert, but it's what you do when you want a different sound or picture to go out on the network. This was an audio cassette of Daffy Duck. It was apparently slipped in just as Mr. Nab was about to speak. Since he didn't know he was speaking like a duck, he kept on talking." Mahoney paused to fight back the traces of a smile, then read from his preliminary reports. "There were six techs in the room. Two are scheduled to be let go Saturday—"

Wallace slammed his hand down on his desk top. "Dammit, laid-off people aren't supposed to remain beyond twenty-four hours! This is precisely why we have that rule."

Mahoney nodded. "But these are union people, Mr. Wallace. They have to be given at least two weeks' notice, plus severance. The two who are to be let go deny any involvement. We've called in the NYPD people for fingerprint and audio checks and technical analysis. If one of these guys sweated on the cassette, we have a shot, but it's a long one."

Wallace paced behind his desk. "Are these two cooperating?"

"One, Al Boardman, says he'll take a lie detector. He wasn't anywhere near the control console all morning. The other guy, Steve Toomey—he left his desk to go the bathroom, according to the guard. The guard says he didn't think Toomey was anywhere near the console, but it's possible either one might have been. The thing is, it would have to have been precisely at seven-seventeen, and since the shift changes at seven-thirty, that's when everybody is making up their logs. So it's possible nobody was paying attention."

Mahoney waited for a reaction.

"Look, Frank," said Wallace quietly, "I don't know if this is just a prank, or if there's some concerted effort under way to get at Nab. We need to take this seriously. People will laugh and say big deal, a practical joke, but David Nab looks like a jerk. He's a laughingstock, for God's sake. Whoever did this had some brains and some guts and a sense of a humor, and if they get away with this, they could try something else. I don't want Nab looking over his shoulder every time he makes a public appearance, and I sure as hell don't want him to be Carson monologue material. I want these guys. Got it?"

Mahoney, who'd headed the FBI field office in New York for a decade, nodded. This wasn't exactly the search for Patty Hearst, but he would enjoy being on the chase again. He promised to get back to Wallace as soon as he learned anything.

CHAPTER TWENTY
SECRET AGREEMENTS

*B*ehind her desk, Grace Viola stood up and offered Peter her hand. It wasn't a cold gesture so much as a formal one; she was cutting off a line of conversation she felt uncomfortable with.

"Peter, I like you. I appreciate the instincts motivating you. But I can't imagine what would make you think I would turn over secret financial agreements between USB and its personnel. Whatever arrangements Mr. Nab may or may not have made with key on-air people here are obviously confidential. There are legal questions governing their disclosure, but, more importantly for me, there are also ethical considerations. Nobody who has spent ten minutes with me would think for a second that I would commit so grave a breach of trust."

Peter stood up too. "I understand, Grace," he said. "I respect what you're saying. It's just that if the rumors are true about the contracts, that's a kind of corruption too. If he's buying some people's support and silence with his millions while he's using efficiency as a club to beat others with, well, there's a moral question there also. Isn't there?"

Viola shook her head and pulled on her blazer, as if preparing for a meeting. She turned a framed photograph of her two daughters so that it faced her at a more direct angle.

"And how would slipping you confidential company files help those people? Would it get them their jobs back? Would Nab stand up and say, 'Gee, I've been bad; now I'll rehire everybody'? What's gotten into you, Peter? You're an executive, not some campus radical. Aren't you on leave? Awaiting reassignment? I thought that's what Sam said at the department head meeting."

Peter moved toward the door. "I'm still on leave. I just had to come into the city and I had this . . . impulse. Because of what you did during the layoffs. I thought you might want to . . . I don't know. Forget it. I'm just tired of feeling like a victim, I guess, and seeing victims and creating victims. Doing nothing was making me crazy, so I thought maybe doing something would help me stay sane. This guy has been sticking it to hundreds of people, and somebody ought to stick it to him."

Peter had not harbored high hopes about her helping, but he trusted her to keep his request secret. He'd thought it worth a shot, especially since there were persistent rumors that she was thinking of leaving anyway.

Viola shook her head again. "Come on, Peter. I couldn't look at myself in the mirror if I did something like that. And if it ever got out—and everything gets out—I'd never work for a respectable company again. I'm not ashamed to say I have ambitions. Besides, your outrage is a little selective for me."

He looked puzzled.

"I didn't see anyone here so upset when we caught Barnard and some of the others stealing money from the company. None of you worried much about sending flowers to your friends, eating at the priciest restaurants in New York, drinking yourselves into stupors at fancy Florida resorts. I didn't see anyone taking any moral stands then, did you? And that's really what made Nab possible."

Peter was starting to feel foolish. He should never have expected Viola to get involved in something that now seemed so juvenile. He glanced at the clock over her head, deciding to catch the 11:00 A.M. bus back to Glen Ridge. Taking the bus twice in a day was bad enough—but to do it for nothing was especially annoying.

Viola suddenly stopped. "Wait a minute. You weren't involved in that duck episode yesterday, were you?"

Peter said nothing, seeing her quiver with what he thought at first might be rage. But she suddenly burst out laughing, holding her side with one hand and propping herself against the desk with the other.

"Oh, God," she gasped. "I thought I would die watching that. I spit a whole mouthful of cereal onto the floor when that duck voice came on. Nab looked so serious sitting there and then every time the duck talked he looked like more and more of an idiot. Peter, don't tell me if you did it. I don't want to know." She wiped a tear from her eye, took a breath, and returned to her normal serious demeanor.

"You'd better get out of here," she said, waving him away. "Peter, if you've got it into your head that you're going to take them on, you'd better get on home and take a cold shower and find some other outlet for your fantasies. And no, I will not leak secret contract agreements. Leave now and I'll forget this conversation ever took place—that's the best I can do for you."

Quacking sounds were still filtering through the cafeteria hubbub as Peter, Buzz Allen, Barnard, and Adelson sat around a table, drinking coffee. Peter had run into Barnard in the hallway, and the two of them had cornered Adelson heading for the bathroom. Allen's office was on the way to the cafeteria; he was always happy for a chance to escape Jack Thomas these days, and had come along.

The duck was still the talk of the town. Daffy Duck imitators all over the world were calling Nab's office and the network. Fifty people in different cities had attempted to confess to police. The morning papers were romping for the second day: DAFFY-GATE! cackled the *New York Post,* gleefully outlining details of USB's investigation into the sabotage of Nab's morning appearance.

"David Nab will be hearing duck imitations for the rest of his natural life," Liz Smith purred in the *Daily News.* Peter read that the police and company officials believed disgruntled techs who had been laid off were behind the incident. He also noticed that Hal Danzig had recovered his wits. The P.R. man was now trying to laugh along. "It's annoying," he was quoted as saying that morning, "but we did get a chuckle out of it."

"This beats all," said Adelson. "I've been in this fucking business a long time, and I never heard of anything like this. Even the guy at the station in New Orleans who had the gerbil stuck up his ass wasn't this weird."

Barnard gagged on his whole-grain toast. Allen practically knocked the table over, pounding. "You mean that rumor is true? That's unbelievable! That can't be for real. Are you shitting us?"

Fortunately, the cafeteria was fairly empty in the pre-lunch lull. The story had been sweeping the network for days that a sexually adventurous employee in New Orleans had placed a live fieldmouse in his rectum, a sexual kick sweeping the town's kinkier quarters, and the mouse had become trapped there during a party where coke and mice were being passed around in large quantities. Peter hadn't believed it; even by television standards, it was too bizarre.

"It's true," Adelson confirmed. "The guy was taken to the emergency room of New Orleans City Hospital last week in a high state of inebriation, sexual ecstasy, and physical discomfort, complaining of a rodent in his most private of parts. Doctors removed the rodent—a mouse—causing only minor damage. The mouse, unfortunately, had succumbed. This guy told the police—I got this from a high authority in the network legal department just this morning—that he was assaulted by the mouse while sitting on the john. Not only did the police not believe him, but the ASPCA is conducting an investigation. The newspapers—keep your fingers crossed—have not yet figured out how to report such a gross story."

They sat gasping with laughter.

"Sam, Jesus!" Barnard protested. "We're eating. Cut it out."

"But the duck stuff is even stranger," Adelson mused. "Only somebody with a devilish sense of humor would do a thing like that. It's too sophisticated in its way—that's what I told Wallace this morning. No tech pulled that stunt."

"Why not?" asked Peter, casually stretching his legs out beneath the table.

"Because it's more vicious than shooting the guy," Adelson said. "This is a man who wants more than anything else to be taken seriously. That's why he bought the damn network. You fire a few hundred people and it's forgotten in two weeks. But this—he'll never be able to go anywhere without somebody quacking at him. This will follow him to his grave. It's about the worst thing that could've been done to a guy like that; that's why they're so pissed."

Peter felt a quickening of the fear he had been fighting off. He expected a SWAT team to crash into the cafeteria any second, surround the table, and drag him away. Allen, he noticed, was looking a bit grim, too, staring morosely at his coffee, saying little.

"Buzz," he said, "you look awful."

"Yeah," said Allen. "Is it okay if I tell them, Sam?"

Adelson nodded.

"I'm being reassigned to Washington. Deputy bureau chief. Thomas wanted me off the show, so I was told yesterday. It's take the Washington job or leave by the end of the week—those are the options."

Peter and Barnard both looked at Adelson angrily, but Adelson just watched Allen.

"But you have your daughters up here with your ex-wife," said Peter. "And your girlfriend is up here, isn't she?"

Allen nodded. "And I hate Washington. I've never wanted to go there. I hate everything about the city—the journalists who think they're royalty, the politicians, the bureaucrats. It's just not a place I would ever want to live. And I'll never see my kids."

"Then tell them to fuck off," said Barnard.

"Everybody doesn't have a trust fund," Adelson shot back. "He's got two households to maintain, plus child support. Be careful with your advice, Phil. This is a better alternative than getting fired, which was the other option."

Barnard pushed his coffee away in disgust. "Well, fuck this place. It used to be fun here. Maybe it's time to start thinking about going Hollywood." He got up and stalked out of the cafeteria.

"Could he go Hollywood?" asked Peter.

"Oh, I bet he could," said Adelson. "He has friends at a couple of the studios. The thing is, he *does* have options."

"So how come he's not over the Responsibility Line?" Allen asked gloomily. He'd obviously been subjected to an Adelson lecture too.

"People with trust funds never go over the Line," Adelson said.

Peter, having struck out with Viola, decided to hang some posters in his new office—a hopeful gesture. He saw haulers dragging an enormous copying machine out of an office on his floor toward the freight elevator.

He had come in mostly out of boredom. Hanging around the house was no treat, especially once the kids were in school, Barbara was writing, and coffee with Joel Fields didn't take up much time. Walking Eugene required only half an hour. It was being in limbo that most wore him down. Fired people can look for work, he thought, leafing idly through his uninteresting mail, but stalled people can only sit around and wait.

Rafael Miranda came down the long, dark hallway, ringing the bell on his cart. Peter bought two coffees and a doughnut. He unpacked several boxes of his files, cursing Marie, who had promised to come over that afternoon and help him sort out his office.

It was not until late afternoon that he pulled into his driveway in Glen Ridge. At first, Peter thought the manila envelope in his garage was trash that had blown across the yard, but he could see when he steered the Toyota inside that the envelope was bulging. Were Ben and Sarah hiding some treasure? It was propped on the handle of a rake, tied closed with a yellow ribbon to make it especially visible. Maybe it was a letter bomb.

He opened the flap carefully, not wanting to rip it. Then he stood reading in the dim light for nearly half an hour. It *was* a bomb, of sorts.

When he finally walked through the yard toward the house, Barbara was waiting at the back door. She had switched to her summer writing uniform, since the day had grown warm—a beat-up blue polo shirt and khaki shorts and running shoes—and was holding two glasses of iced tea. He heard a quiz show on

Nickelodeon filtering out through the playroom window, and Eugene came waggling up, offering Peter a tennis shoe.

"I heard the car come in a half hour ago," she said, taking the shoe from the dog and leading Peter to the lounge chairs in the backyard. "What have you been doing in the garage? I was afraid to look."

He took her hand. "Did you think I had run a hose from the exhaust pipe and stuffed it in through the window?"

She nodded. "It crossed my mind. I'm worried about you. I'm worried about us. You spent a night away the other night and I still don't know where the hell you went. We have the worst, meanest fight in our married life and you go spinning off in a rage and come back cackling and plotting. We've never had any secrets and now you're skulking around. So I have to wonder . . .

"Peter, what's going on? The fight woke me up to how beat-up you are. I didn't hear that before—I obviously didn't want to hear it. You know writers can get even more self-obsessed than TV people; they just don't get paid as much. But I'm hearing it now, so I want to know why you're sneaking around like a drug dealer."

Peter drank some iced tea. "I'm going through a lot of stuff, it's true," he said. "I'm pissed about a lot of things. I was pissed at you because you've been happy to sit up in your retreat and not know about my life. I'm more pissed at me, at this craven bureaucrat I've become. I feel as if I'm not even a journalist anymore. I'm pissed at these bastards who have taken over the place, these people who have a logical rationale for everything but always end up reaching the same conclusion—let 'er rip.

"Then we have a blow-up in which you imply that I'm not taking care of my family, either. I just couldn't handle taking any more responsibility or learning any more sad truths about myself."

She was quiet, listening.

"I love you and I love our marriage. What I want is room for a while, some faith and some room. I will take care of us, I promise—"

"No, that's not right," she interrupted. "I don't want you to 'take care of us.' I don't need to be 'taken care of.' We just both have to do our share. You can't duck your part, and I can't duck mine. That's why we fought. You were dreaming of running away from it all, and I already had, in some ways. We just have to come to the middle."

She paused, as if kissing her novel goodbye, then shrugged.

"But whatever happens, you can't do this male thing, this 'it's all on my shoulders.' "

He nodded. Actually, he had been quite proud to have shouldered all the financial responsibility.

"Okay," he said. "I stand corrected. I'm just saying that I won't walk away from my part. I will do something sensible and real—I'm not the type to go to Vermont and open a pastry shop. I just need some time. I'm not involved in anything dangerous. Just trust me, okay?"

Barbara looked skeptical. "How about if I trust you for a week or two, and then I freak out? Will that be enough?"

"More than enough," he said.

"Flannery, you in the tub?" Peter asked. It was 2:00 A.M., and he was sitting in Barbara's study, piles of computer printouts spread before him.

"No, Peter, I'm sleeping with William Hurt. I'll just get him to roll over so we can talk. I'm in bed, shmuck. What do you want?"

"You won't believe the stuff I've got. I've got the contracts Nab and Wallace negotiated with some of USB's major luminaries. It's beyond belief. It's beyond the wildest rumors we heard—"

"Peter," yawned Flannery. "You know all rumors eventually prove true. How did you get it?"

"Well, I can truthfully say I don't know. There was an envelope in my garage when I got home tonight. I had asked Viola for this stuff in the morning but she acted as if I'd exposed myself, so it's hard to believe she did this."

"Typical," she clucked. "Men have the intuition of trees. Of course Viola did it, but she's so professional she even convinced *you* that she wouldn't. It's just like her. Now you can say you don't really know where it came from and even pass a polygraph."

"One sticky problem," he said, "one really sticky problem. There's stuff in here about Barnard. About writing off more than five thousand dollars in clothes as prop expenses for the show and such. It's pretty serious."

She whistled. "Ah, now it makes sense. She's telling you if you want one, you have to take the other, don't you see?"

"I see, but it's a dreadful position to be in. I'll keep you out of this one. Patricia, this stuff is pretty hot. I've got to get it to a reporter, and quickly."

"One of the TV guys?"

"No, they're all carrying somebody's water. There's a guy I worked with back in Asbury Park; he's with the *Times* business section now. I think I can trust him. But I need a big favor from you. I'm going to Florida for a few days, to a development called Key Lime. It's where Nab has his biggest condominium complex. I need you to get on the phone and find out some history on this place, how it was built, what was there before—you know. I need it before I go."

Flannery sounded wary. "This is getting a little spooky, isn't it, Peter? You're not going to do anything dumb, are you?"

"No, Patricia. I'm just going to play reporter. Remember, you're talking to the guy who won the New Jersey Press Association investigative award three times. I've got a friend at the *Miami Herald* who is plenty interested in helping out. But I could use some contacts first."

"How do you know about this place?" she asked suspiciously.

"When Nab first took over the company, somebody wrote me a letter—some dotty old lady who runs the tenants' association. Wuraftic is her name. It could be a wild goose chase, but my gut tells me it's worth checking out."

"Can't your friend do it more easily?" asked Flannery.

"At some point, maybe, but you're the best person I've ever known for getting little old ladies and local pols to talk."

"You got it, boss, I'm getting a little bored anyway. September seems a long way off." She paused. "Peter?"

"Yup."

"You're over wanting to fuck me?"

"Yes. Sorry about that. Mid-career madness. Shrinks call it acting out. I'm sure you're relieved."

"Well, I am, but you should have pretended it was harder to get past. Bill here is getting jealous. I'll talk to you tomorrow."

★   ★   ★

The furor over David Nab's agreements that erupted a few days later drove the duck incident out of the news. The *Times* led its business section with a story headlined INSIDE A TAKEOVER: HOW DAVID NAB SPENT MILLIONS ON SECRET AGREEMENTS. The sub-head said: CRITICS SAY AGREEMENTS MADE TO ENSURE SMOOTH TRANSITION. It began:

> USB's aggressive new management promised Wall Street it would curb spending at the nation's top network, yet agreements made available to The New York Times reveal that CEO David Nab has poured tens of millions of dollars into amended contracts with key USB News personnel that appear designed, at least in part, to ensure their cooperation with his takeover.
>
> The secret agreements reveal that evening news anchorman Jack Thomas has been given a ten-year contract that raises his annual salary from $1.5 million to $4 million a year. In addition, Thomas has received year-round use of a Nab Enterprises sloop, berthed in Bermuda, and a chauffeured luxury car.
>
> Thomas's contract cannot be breached for five years, even if the network fires or reassigns him. The company retains the right to remove him after five years, but if it does so, it is obligated to pay him $2 million a year for the rest of his life.
>
> In the event of his removal, Thomas will be required to anchor one documentary hour a year, retaining his personal producer and secretary.
>
> Thomas's agreement further specifies that USB management will nominate him for the next vacant seat on the USB board of directors and give him more than $6 million in USB stock. Thomas will be given the title of editor of the Evening News in one year, with the right to hire and fire his executive producer. He will also be consulted on major personnel and policy decisions involving the news division. The contract will have an enormous impact on the day-to-day workings of USB's prestigious news division, according to journalism critics and to sources within the division, and represents the greatest degree of authority and editorial input ever granted a television news anchor.
>
> In another amended agreement, correspondent Linda Burns has been offered an eight-year contract raising her salary from $750,000 to $2 million a year. She has been guaranteed her own

prime-time program, key on-floor reporting positions at all presidential nominating conventions, and weekly profiles on the Evening News. A spokesman for Ms. Burns, who asked not to be identified, said he could not comment on continuing negotiations with the network. The spokesman said the negotiations did reflect, however, "Linda's status in the front ranks of broadcast journalism's superstars."

Harry Sommers, producer of the highly profitable Weekend News and one of the news division's most influential veterans, has been given a ten-year contract beginning at $1.5 million a year, moving quickly at annual increments to $3 million. In addition, the contract provides for use of a USB company helicopter to convey Sommers to his Connecticut retreat on weekends, and more than $2 million in USB common stock.

The *Times* story went on to disclose that executive producer Philip Barnard was under investigation by USB auditors for lavish overspending and possible expense account irregularities. While Barnard was being accused of nothing illegal, the story reported, USB finance officers were zeroing in on him as an example of the waste that had preceded the takeover, which management had cited as the cause of more than 500 layoffs and $15 million in budget cuts. Barnard had declined comment.

The uproar was immediate and predictable. Adelson was quoted the next day as denouncing the violation of privacy of USB's management and employees, but otherwise refusing comment. A spokesman for Nab denied that the new agreements had been intended to silence opposition or co-opt influential employees.

Four deans of journalism schools co-signed a letter to several influential newspapers decrying the growing influence of unqualified anchors in editorial affairs.

A lawyer who claimed to represent more than one hundred USB stockholders filed suit in federal court in Dallas, claiming his clients were being deprived of their appropriate dividends by "secret and wanton" agreements. The New York tabloids scrambled to take pictures of Thomas's new sloop and the helicopter that would ferry Sommers to Connecticut. Harold Shurken told the *Times* he was "distressed" at the agreements, calling them a "throwback" to USB's wasteful days.

Of course, everyone at USB News knew that other correspondents and producers would be wild with envy and rage and that every agent in New York would shortly be climbing through USB's windows, demanding more for their clients. Jack Thomas declined comment, other than to say: "There is no amount of money that can buy me. Like a grizzly who's been attacked, I will fight in coming months for my friends and colleagues at USB News."

This time, the group met at Nab's old headquarters, in his own more spartan conference room. Nab and Wallace were sipping Diet Cokes and listening in silence as Frank Mahoney, using a blackboard and a pointer, gave his report. Wallace looked as if he had permanent indigestion, and Nab's lips were pressed together.

"Here's what we know," said Mahoney, unshaken. "This chart shows where each of the employees in the network control room was supposed to be at the time of the tape insertion." He pointed to six X's scattered around a rectangle marked CONSOLE.

"It turns out that each of the employees was in sight of at least one other almost every second. The only one who wasn't was Steve Toomey, the audio guy. He was due to be laid off three days later, so he's a pretty hot suspect to begin with. In addition, he was the only one who left the room at any time in the preceding two hours; he went to the bathroom, the others said. So he could have gone out, been slipped a cassette, and smuggled it in."

"How big is a cassette?" Wallace asked. "Could you hide it?"

"You could hide it in your pants pocket easily enough. If somebody stared at the right spot, he might notice it, but the guard—who's a good man, former NYPD patrolman—didn't check Toomey's pockets. Nobody smuggles things *into* places like this; it's what they take out that you watch for."

Wallace nodded impatiently. He trusted Mahoney, but felt the security chief was showing off for Nab's benefit.

"Also, Toomey refused to go on the box for a lie test. I don't have much doubt that it was him. He refuses to speak with us, even with a lawyer present. We are cross-referencing lists of other people laid off to see if we can tie him to somebody on the outside who might have come in and helped. We know that there was a security breach in the back of the building that morning. Someone opened the fire door in back. Our people searched the place, but didn't find anything. The door led to the tape editing rooms for the *Evening News,* so we're checking any terminations there, seeing if there's any Toomey connection. The guard says Toomey was due to go off-shift in less than an hour, so that he hardly ever went out to the bathroom that late. That suggests he went out to pick up the cassette from somebody who had gotten into the building—probably through the fire door."

Wallace interrupted. "But why would a disgruntled employee need to sneak in? Why not just walk in or leave the tape someplace Toomey could find it?"

"Well, that's a good question. One reason is that we log all entries now, so there would be a computerized record of the employee's coming in. Secondly, it suggests the employee had already been laid off and handed in his ID. So, he would need to sneak in, and he would know how to get in and where to hide until Toomey came out. Then he could hand off the cassette and walk out during the morning rush. We don't make people check out, or at least we didn't. We do now."

Wallace nodded. "Any possibilities?"

"Well, we've got sixty people who worked in that general area and are no longer with USB News," said Mahoney. "We're not wasting any time on Toomey. He's not the type who would dream this up and he'll never talk anyway. He's small stuff. We've got fifteen possibles, when you factor in age, current work status, technical knowledge of the area, et cetera. We'll pare it down. Whoever did this, we're not dealing with pros, so there's a good chance they screwed up somewhere.

"The contract agreements—now they're another matter. All of the original contracts are in place. But we checked the copying machine counters and we found one across the street in Public Projects that was used to copy a hundred and twenty pages of documents, which would amount to four or five contracts, maybe. There was also a computer entry into Barnard's expense account file which we have traced to a computer in the Finance area, four days before the *Times* story. But forty people work in Finance."

"Do you think these two acts were the work of the same person?" asked Wallace.

"No question in my mind. At the FBI the first thing we did

was put together a psychological profile in cases like this. I called my former deputy and he ran it through the computer profiling system. We think we're looking for one person—intelligent, probably a man, because most of the people laid off were men; probably not a kid, because of the choice of Daffy Duck. In fact, the profile points to an executive."

Nab's eyebrows shot up. Wallace looked skeptical.

"I think you'll find our perp is a male executive, gentlemen. No offense, but the duck episode showed a pretty sophisticated sense of humor," Mahoney explained carefully. "That's not the way most people would get even. And the contract agreements show some knowledge of upper-level negotiations and the means of getting them himself or persuading someone in Finance, Law, or Corporate to get them for him. That isn't something you'd do for anybody who walked in off the street. We're dealing here with a middle manager, in all probability a creative person who got laid off and can't get into the building easily anymore. Given those guidelines, the list isn't that long. I've got fifteen people working on it."

"Need more?" Wallace asked.

Mahoney shook his head. "No. This isn't a professional. This is a news type."

"Frank," Wallace said, keeping his voice level with some effort. "These people might have thought they were being cute with the duck, although we didn't think it was very funny. But this contract stuff is serious. They may not be professionals, but they have hurt David, and in very public ways. We'll be cleaning up after this contract mess for years. And Nab can't go out to dinner without somebody making a Daffy Duck noise. It's escalating in seriousness, and they may be planning further escapades. Stop it. Fast."

Mahoney nodded and wiped the blackboard clean.

Dinner was at a French place on the Upper East Side, popular and very public. Nab was a genuine family man, the straitlaced sort, with a wife and three children at home in Connecticut. He anticipated a flurry of rumors about his growing friendship with Linda Burns, but he wanted everyone, Linda included, to understand that there would never be any substance to them.

He need not have worried; Burns had already rehearsed the gracious manner in which she would decline if he came on to her. As a rule, she didn't permit sex with powerful men who could bestow favors; it wasn't the way she wished to be seen. And that was no longer the way to make it in a business like television.

Already seated at his favorite table in the rear corner when she came in, Nab rose, smiling. She had called Marty Hoffman, her agent, for counsel on how to handle the duck business. After the two of them had stopped laughing, Hoffman advised that she not bring it up at all unless Nab did.

As for the contract leak, that wasn't a catastrophe at all from her perspective; she half-suspected Marty might even have had a hand in planting it. However tawdry it might have made Nab look, it demonstrated that she was among the superstars USB News was willing to pay big money to court and to keep. As Hoffman had explained to her, the superstar process in television news worked quite differently from that of movies or publishing or music. You didn't actually have to get people to buy your records or books, or plunk down seven bucks to see your movie. What was most important was to be brilliant at *being* a superstar. You had to look like one, of course, and have the brains to be one, and carry yourself like one, but the most important factor, Hoffman drummed into her, was to be seen as one. If you could manage that, then it was just a matter of time before you were one. Having the *Times* report that you were worth two mill a year couldn't hurt.

"Linda," Nab began apologetically, as soon as they had brushed cheeks and sat down, "I apologize for the leak. We will figure out where it came from. It doesn't have great importance, and—"

She cut him off. "David, in journalism one learns that there are no secrets. And in life one learns that 'the coward does it with a kiss, the brave man with a sword.' Wilde was very wise."

Nab, as always, looked impressed at this glimpse into her intellectual side. "Linda, I'll never understand how you find time to read."

"I read before dawn, as I know you do, when others are sleeping, and I read in the cab to and from work and airports, and I read while the coffee is brewing. And"—she laughed wickedly and tossed her hair off her shoulders—"I read in the tub."

"The tub?" He lowered his voice as if she were saying something wicked.

"I love baths," she confided. "I know they are passing into history, but they are delicious and exquisite. I could never give them up."

Nab cleared his throat. "Can I ask you a question? And get an honest answer?"

"You are that rarest of creatures, a man without guile, so yes, you are owed a straightforward answer," she replied, waving the waiter away. Neither of them ate much at meals anymore; they fought too hard to keep their bodies trim.

"But first"—she raised her glass—"a toast to your stewardship of USB News. And an appropriate salute: 'I pray Heaven to bestow the best of blessings on this house and all that shall hereafter inhabit it. May none but honest and wise men ever rule under this roof.' You seem, if I may say so, an honest and wise man."

Nab raised his glass and nodded.

"Who said that?" he asked, thinking how different this dinner was from the countless ones he had endured with builders, department store executives, zoning attorneys, and mall marketing consultants.

"John Adams, in a letter to one of the women I most admire in American history, his wife, Abigail. Now, what is your question?"

"Do you read all these books all the way through?"

"No."

"How much, then?"

"All of the ones I like. No further in the ones I don't than it takes me to decide."

They each ordered a light salad, and since business was very much at hand, they only wet their lips on the wine.

"Linda, I'll get to the point. You've been a good friend—you've guided me on how television works; you've sought my opinions; you've sent over a trunkful of books that I still intend to read. Our friendship aside, I think you are an extraordinary talent. I know I'm new to broadcasting, but I've been making tough decisions my entire life, and I am willing to bank a lot on your becoming a superstar. I want you at USB News. I know you think we shouldn't talk business, but Harold Wallace and I have been meeting with this guy who worked at CBS, brilliant producer, he used to do their evening news; he's got a whole roomful of awards. He wants to come aboard; he's excited about what we're doing."

Burns leaned back in her chair, as if pondering a great decision. The people closest to Nab, even Wallace, wondered if he really believed that Burns had befriended him for his lively mind and keen economic insights. It was not a subject that could be broached directly, of course, but Wallace had concluded that Nab did believe it—exactly the sort of conceit a good lawyer could never afford. It was an odd thing, Wallace knew, about successful businessmen in America: They had more power and money than anyone else but they were almost always taken for dunderheads, which rankled and left them with enormous crav-ings for respectability. Nothing conferred it more quickly or substantially than owning a piece of the media. Even the Rever-end Moon had started a paper in Washington.

"David, you know I am uncomfortable talking business in this environment. I would never use our friendship that way, and I—"

"Linda, Linda, you've been clear on that. But we have a right to discuss this. I have decisions to make. I want you signed up for a brand new showcase with USB News; I don't care what it costs."

She appeared distressed.

"You know, of course, David, that this puts me in an awkward position. One reason I don't want to discuss this is that I don't want to undercut Sam Adelson, who seems to have different feelings than yours about my career. That's why he means so very much to me. He wants me to progress in steps, slowly, perhaps to a foreign bureau for a few years to get reporting experience."

Nab frowned. "A foreign bureau? He hasn't expressed that to me. And what do you mean he has 'different feelings'?"

Burns paused and stared down at her uneaten salad for so long that Nab became alarmed.

"Linda, what is it?"

"David, this is just the position I wanted to *avoid*. Everyone in the division knows that Adelson thinks I'm too big for my proverbial britches and that my friendship with you drives him wild. I don't blame him. But I don't want him hating me."

"Your friendship with me? That's got nothing to do with him. What are you talking about?"

But Burns refused to go further. After swearing Nab to secrecy a half-dozen times about the little that had been discussed, she excused herself and allowed him to put her in a cab. It was an upsetting evening for the new chairman of USB, and he had Harold Wallace on the car phone even before his Chrysler left the curb.

Wallace had been trying to reach him, as it happened, but not to muse about Linda Burns's future. He had been thinking about the duck incident and the contract leaks and he had an idea, he told Nab. They needed to talk face-to-face as quickly as possible.

CHAPTER TWENTY-ONE
PUBLIC SERVICE

*P*eter glanced at the kitchen clock. It was time for his new 9:30 A.M. ritual—calling Linda Burns about his pilot proposal. He knew she'd received it—her secretary confirmed that—but in two weeks she still hadn't taken his call or returned it.

"How about dropping it," Barbara suggested. "Her nibs is humiliating you, and you keep coming back for more."

Barbara still didn't understand television people, never would. The fact that they didn't call you right back didn't mean a thing, Peter explained. You had to be aggressive—it was that kind of a business. The new show was a good idea, he was sure of it, and he owed it to everybody to pursue it. Unless, he pointed out, she wanted to trade her writerly life for a public relations job with Con Ed.

"Well, what about Sam?" she asked more gently. "Does he like your idea?"

"I haven't heard. I don't want to bug him about it; that would be taking advantage of our friendship."

Barbara laughed wryly, almost bitterly. "And here we have

the male mind in all its glory. Your friend, a person who values you and happens to be in charge, can't be turned to because that might take advantage of your relationship. The superstar who is not your friend—or anybody's that doesn't own a network—*can* be called and allowed to humiliate you daily because that's aggressive. I'm glad you explained it to me."

"You still don't get it," said Peter, with exasperation. "Burns picks her own producer—she's a two-million-dollar monster. Adelson can't tell her who to pick. He's like an NBA coach— he's got the title, but all the people he's in charge of are nine feet tall and earn five times what he does. It's got to go through her. Calling Sam would just embarrass both of us."

He didn't share the other, perhaps more important reason for his reluctance to call Adelson. Facing Sam's notions of loyalty and responsibility, and his trust, seemed unbearable, given the corporate crimes Peter had already committed and the ones to come. The more time Adelson spent with him, the more Peter engaged his friend in career counseling and turned to him for support, the greater the betrayal would seem, if and when it was uncovered. Besides, thought Peter, the less he had to do with Adelson the better, should it all come out. He was giving Adelson those most precious of corporate gifts: deniability and distance.

"Okay," Barbara said, "you've convinced me. Humiliation is preferable." Her response to his troubles at USB News was evolving, he'd noticed. At first she had instinctively moved to protect her novel; now, each day, she seemed a little more protective of him.

They both were startled by the phone's ring, a reminder of how rarely it rang in comparison to his days with *Morning in the U.S.* Barbara used to joke about knowing when Peter was about to walk in the door because the phone would begin ringing fifteen minutes before he arrived: a plane crash in Istanbul, an anchor pouting about the lineup, Adelson fussing over some story. Now it almost never rang, and when it did, three quarters of the time it was Flannery calling.

But not this time. Nor was Burns returning his call. It was Adelson's secretary, Elaine, informing Peter that USB had taken eight tables at the American Broadcasting Awards banquet on Friday and that attendance was mandatory.

"Mandatory," Peter repeated. "That's never happened before."

"I was surprised myself," she said. "All I know is that we're winning the Golden Spotlight Award for coverage of the *Providence* sinking, and at the executive meeting this morning the bigs decided that all executive producers and veeps and major correspondents need to go. With their wives."

Peter groaned. "I can't make my wife go; she doesn't work for USB News. Besides, you are aware—aren't you?—that I'm not an executive producer at the moment."

"Peter," said Elaine in the tired voice she used when dealing with prickly or demanding employees, "just be there with Barbara, okay? Don't kill the messenger. They want managers out full-force, especially people involved in the *Providence* story. Barnard's supposed to be there, your pal Patricia Flannery, and Buzz Allen. Tickets, which are very expensive, will be paid for by the company and left in your name at the USB table in the Waldorf lobby."

The announcement of the Spotlight Award—which had been won mostly due to the Sven crew's quick reaction and D'Amato's stunning pictures after the sinking and the Investigative Unit's follow-ups—had been made the week before. But awards were no big deal usually. USB had regularly won the lion's share of the American Broadcasting Awards for years. Producers sometimes attended the festivities and sometimes didn't, but the event had never been mandatory.

Peter, who'd been otherwise occupied the week before, found it all jarring. The *Providence* had sunk four months ago, and Peter had come to regard it as an almost mystical symbol. At the time, he had seen it as a triumph. Now, the ship seemed to have taken his prospects down with it.

Peter had expected a fight from Barbara, but she seemed almost eager to go, convinced it would be good for him to see and be seen. Besides, she said, she hadn't seen Carol Adelson since Elliott Brookings's fortieth anniversary.

A stream of black-tied television correspondents, producers, and executives were already pouring up the escalators into the Grand Ballroom when they arrived. Seeing everyone preening in evening clothes stirred memories of the good old days, which, Peter bitingly pointed out to Barbara, had been only that winter.

Eight tables—at $3,000 each—were reserved for USB News, all clustered in front of the stage where Guy Lombardo had once ushered in the New Year. Flannery, as was her custom, had arrived early and rearranged all the place cards at their table to her liking. She'd positioned herself next to Peter. To her right she'd seated Barbara, then Barnard and an unnamed friend, Buzz Allen and his unnamed friend, and a cameraman from Dan D'Amato's old Special Assignment Team. It was definitely what was known in the news division as a "C" table—no big-name anchors or correspondents, not even a vice-president for affiliate relations, thought Peter. Most significantly, no one making more than $200,000 a year.

As always, a couple of tables nearby had been made available for the television press; the flow of good wine and famous faces would go a long way toward ensuring that public service would be written about the next morning, not contract leaks.

The flap over the leaked agreements was still Topic A at every table, though, the other networks' as well as USB's. Anonymous USB sources had rushed to respond in ensuing stories that good management sometimes meant spending money as well as saving it, especially to hold on to major talent and develop tomorrow's stars. It had not been an excessive or wasteful effort to lock up the division's most important people, said a nameless official close to David Nab; it was a masterstroke. Jack Thomas was already the leading anchorman in America; Linda Burns was destined to be one of the most successful women in broadcasting. Besides, costs had already been reduced by nearly 30 percent.

But the counterclaims did not seem to have eased the sting all that much, Peter was pleased to see. One producer at a rival network had passed out hunters' duck calls, and every few minutes a loud and surprisingly realistic "quack" erupted in one or another corner of the room. Some prankster had replaced several of the floral centerpieces at USB tables with painted mallard decoys.

Beyond the jokes, several agents were audibly seething. Not only did Nab look ridiculous, they muttered, but their clients were furious. Management had been telling USB producers and correspondents for months that a new dawn had come, that everyone was in for belt-tightening. Then Nab goes off and gives the store away to Jack Thomas and to Linda Burns, a kid who was selling $14 necklaces in North Carolina a few years ago?

After getting an earful from the agent for his ex-weatherman, Peter found Flannery, who was on her third drink with the SAT cameraman and halfway to the floor, he thought.

"There's a lot of sizzling about this stuff," he confided proudly. "This shit has hurt them."

Flannery looked at Peter bleakly. "I'm not talking business tonight," she said. "This is my farewell USB appearance. I only agreed to come for the free scotch and to say goodbye and maybe hustle this guy into bed later on. But in case you're wondering why we have all been summoned here, I will give you a clue." Flannery was slurring some of her words a bit. "The Empire is Striking Back."

Peter patted her cheek. He had not anticipated that it would be Flannery, her loyalty and her unflinching way of looking at the world, that he would miss the most. He was struck again, as he had been too many times, by the things she saw that he didn't. Looking around the room, he couldn't imagine why it had not occurred to him. Of course, this was the counterattack.

It was quite clear, once you looked for the signs. The order of battle was unfolding before him.

He took a stroll around the USB News tables before the ceremonies began, trying not to look too nosy or, God forbid, guilty or apprehensive.

The principals were at the press tables, naturally. Jack Thomas was kidding the reporters about all the money he was going to make and promising everyone sunset sails. He had the television writers from the New York dailies in stitches with his joke about the co-ed and the hibernating bear. Harry Sommers, bringing his favorite white Bordeaux to the second press table, was spinning magnificent yarns about his pioneering days at the dawn of broadcasting.

Harold Wallace had a cultural editor from the *Times* off to one side and was asking her to be blunt about the *Evening News.* How *could* it change in response to cable and VCR technology? Peter saw Eddie Cohen, the trade magazine reporter who'd called him at home only a few days earlier. Cohen looked elegant in a suit from Armani, Peter guessed, with his red curls styled and moussed.

Cohen saw Peter, then pretended not to have seen him while he consulted a small leather book. Then Cohen bounded over to their table.

"Pete," he said, slapping him on the back. "And Barb! Great to see you both. How are little Sarah and Benny? Pete, how about I call you next week and we have lunch? I'd love to catch up on what's going on with you. Hope it's not true what I hear—that you're leaving." Cohen seemed impervious to Peter's unresponsive murmurs or to Barbara's murderous stare.

"Whoops!" he said. "There's an unexpected face. Julian McCallister! Gotta go. I'll be in touch." And he none-too-gracefully darted away.

A number of happy reunions were already under way between reporters and McCallister, who, after a brief sojourn in Tuscany, had swiftly resurfaced as head of a mushrooming cable news operation, his return heralded by an interview in the *Daily News* Sunday magazine, his op-ed column in the *Times* (which called on the industry to fight trash TV), and a lengthy and flattering profile in the *Los Angeles Times*. He had *Newsday*'s television writer scribbling away, noting McCallister's concerns about the future of network television and his feeling that the really creative work would be done on cable.

Peter, catching McCallister's eye, got a nod. Neither man particularly wanted to waste time chatting with the other. McCallister had always had bigger fish to fry when Peter ran *Morning in the U.S.*; he would hardly want to be bothered now. Peter could see, though, that McCallister had used his down time well: He had already acquired a more mature, thoughtful persona; he looked tanned and rested; he was sprinkling his comments with Italian phrases.

"I'm having a few people over on Sunday," Peter heard McCallister telling a *Times* woman. "A couple of people from Paramount; Nicky Bruss, whose new novel is out this week . . ." Peter, walking past, was almost positive he caught his former boss in a wink.

Two tables ahead, he suddenly noticed Linda Burns, whose latest strategy for appearing intelligent as well as glamorous was to daringly flaunt her schoolmarm spectacles along with her low-cut gathered gown. On-air people in television ordinarily would rather be seen naked than with eyeglasses.

Peter couldn't tell if she had seen him or not (there were rumors that the spectacles contained clear glass) and he debated whether or not to break the taboo against conducting official business at social functions. When he was about ten feet away, still uncertain, she stood up suddenly and headed for Don Kristed, the *Television* magazine writer searching for his place card at the press table. Coming up behind him, she shrieked with public delight and led him by the hand to the steps at the bottom of the huge stage, where the two of them sat talking earnestly in view of the entire ballroom.

Peter stopped short and turned back toward his own table, but saw Carol Adelson deep in conversation with Barbara. I'm the Nowhere Man, he thought. Sam Adelson was busy jerking off the network brass, Barnard hadn't shown up, and Buzz Allen seemed so absorbed by his girlfriend *du jour* that he barely noticed the people around him.

Was there really a moment, Peter wondered, when he'd felt they were some sort of community?

He seemed to be the only person there with no game to play. Yet, he did not need to remind himself, in some ways he was playing *the* game, wasn't he?

Linda Burns did not share with Don Kristed her ironic reflection that less than six months ago, in this same room, at the Council on Foreign Relations meeting, she was a budding new television personality who had wangled an introduction to an oblivious David Nab. Tonight she was returning as one of his closest friends and one of the network's brightest prospects.

Kristed, clinking wineglasses, asked Burns how she was holding up after the hoohah about her contract.

"You're not like the others, Don. You know this isn't about money as far as I'm concerned."

He nodded, asked her about the report that she would have her own prime-time interview program that fall. Kristed had not actually seen her since the interview for *Television,* but she had called faithfully once a month, sometimes getting his wife at home and enchanting her by knowing her name and chatting as warmly as a college sorority chum and suggesting that one day they would all have to get together. Kristed's wife had impressed several family gatherings with details of the calls and relayed them to friends and co-workers. The Kristeds were candid now about describing Burns as a friend, though not without reluctance, given Don's feelings about professionalism.

"Don, these rumors aren't what's important. What's important is that I have serious work—I simply have to *fight* for that. I am not going to do a show about the baton twirling champion or that sort of thing. David has assured me that the network is committed to a new program for at least three years—he has personally assured me of it. I feel like Dinesen when she returned from Africa."

Kristed nodded vaguely, a bit distracted. He didn't know how to bring the subject up, but if he was to be her friend, he had to be as candid with her as she always was with him.

"Linda, look, as your friend, I guess I ought to mention—I think you should be aware—that there's a lot of buzzing about your friendship with Nab. I know, any successful woman gets this sort of thing, but your Thursday dinners with him—well, there's a lot of joking, envy and all that—"

Burns stopped him dead with a glare that could freeze boiling water. "Don, David and I are *friends,* close friends. I respect him. He has supported me, that's all. I would never *dream* of mentioning any sort of business to David—how do people *dare?* We talk about *ideas,* about *books,* about *politics,* not about television. Is this the fate of women forever, to be smeared this way whenever they get close to a man? I went through this silliness when I was working with Phil Barnard."

"Linda, the rumors aren't sexual," he said uncomfortably. "Everybody knows Nab isn't that type. And neither are you, of course," he added hastily. "It has more to do with being ambitious. I just wanted to warn you."

"I don't listen to that rubbish, Don. I never will. Would it surprise you to know that there are rumors about you and me; that *we've* had an affair?"

"What kind of rumors?" Kristed demanded, indignant and overjoyed.

Burns waved her hand dismissively. "Forget it, Don. Everyone knows we're close, that's all."

★   ★   ★

Carol Adelson and Barbara were having a fine time muttering, although Carol's official seat was with Sam at the A table with the Thomases and Nabs and Wallaces, and she kept warning Barbara that she would have to return momentarily.

Peter spotted Grace Viola and excused himself to say hello. He offered his hand, and was a little surprised when she gave him a warm, although brief, hug.

"How goes it?" he asked.

"It goes well, Peter. And you? Even though you're awaiting reassignment, I see you've been busy," she said quietly, glancing around. But in the din of table-hopping, no one could hear them. "Be careful, Peter. They will find you out, you know."

"Listen, thanks for what you did," he said. "You caused a lot of agony for me, but I think I did right by the package."

"Package, Peter?" She offered her hand in farewell. "I don't know what you're talking about." She turned toward Adelson's table, hand outstretched.

David Nab accepted the Golden Spotlight Award on behalf of USB News, while Frank Mahoney sat at an adjoining table, scanning the faces of the people at the USB tables.

Nab walked briskly toward the stage, ignoring two quacks, seeming not to hear one soused NBC producer along the aisle lean over and offer himself to USB for a few million bucks, a 747, and the QE II. A few people even hissed, more because of the cuts than the contracts, Wallace guessed from his carefully chosen vantage point.

At the podium, conscious of the blunt coaching he had been getting from Hal Danzig, Nab gazed out at the crowd, made eye contact with several people, paused for about five seconds, took a sip of water, and unfolded some notes. He did not need to read a verbatim text anymore, but he still felt more comfortable with notes. A serious misstep tonight could catapult him right back to what he'd been on the awful Day of the Duck: a joke.

But he had regrouped, thanks to Harold Wallace and his usual brilliant strategizing. This would be a surprise, this speech.

"Ladies and gentlemen, members of the American Broadcasting Awards, fellow broadcasters"—he smiled at that—"and colleagues at USB News.

"First, I want to thank the judges and directors of the ABA for bestowing the Golden Spotlight on USB News for its coverage of the tragic sinking of the *U.S.S. Providence.* This is the thirty-third statue that USB has received and it will join the others in the lobby of USB News. That is where it belongs."

There was a polite spattering of applause and a few whistles from mildly buzzed USB News producers.

"I also want to thank the people who really deserve this award, the people who take the pictures in the dead of night and work long hours and with great care to get the story right: the reporters and producers of USB News!"

The USB tables erupted in cheers and applause. Flannery sat silently, scowling into her wineglass.

Nab waited for the applause to quiet down. "I wanted to accept this award on behalf of USB News because I am intensely proud of this organization. But I had another reason as well. I have something to say, and this is the best forum from which to say it."

The vast room stilled quickly. Something in Nab's tone suggested that he actually might have something important to impart. Nab, glancing at his Rolex, waited fifteen seconds, as Danzig had suggested.

"I won't go into detail here tonight about my motivation in acquiring the controlling shares of USB News. A part of me wanted to help guide this important institution through what we all know is going to be a turbulent time. But I have to confess that in the days after Nab Enterprises acquired the proudest name in broadcasting, I believed that I had acquired a business, an important one, but a business nonetheless."

He timed another pause. "Christ," Barbara whispered, "is he going to declare for President or what?"

Peter looked beyond her to Adelson's table. Adelson sat without expression, occasionally staring down at his lap, careful to avoid eye contact with anyone. He never looked in Peter's direction.

"But I am here to tell you that I was wrong," Nab continued dramatically. "USB is not another company, and broadcasting is not another business. It is special, and it needs to be nurtured and protected in a special way. I know that now, and I'm going to put my money where my mouth is."

The entire room seemed to be buzzing, the applause swelling but uneven, almost confused. Finally, someone at the top was saying what they had all been wanting so badly to hear, but wasn't this the same someone who had cut USB News until it bled, before he even knew where the newsroom was?

Wallace and Danzig smiled and nodded at each other. A bold stroke, but a brilliant one. Wallace felt the familiar glow that meant another calculated risk was about to pay off.

"I am announcing tonight that USB News is launching a new prime-time public affairs broadcast this fall. I am pleased to tell you that *TGIF* correspondent Linda Burns will anchor this program, a series of weekly broadcasts from all over the world. We expect to sign a new producer within a week. All I can tell you is that he will come from outside USB's news division, part of our efforts to strengthen what is already the best production staff in television." The reporters were pushing aside their brimming plates and scrambling for their notebooks and tape recorders. Acceptance speeches normally produced platitudes, not stories.

Barbara reached under the table and grabbed Peter's hand. He stared, unseeing, at Nab. Flannery leaned over and touched his shoulder.

Burns flushed and her eyes widened, but she continued to look at the podium, despite cheers and whoops from the adjoining USB News tables.

"I am also announcing the creation of a new, two-hour USB News series called *The Week in America,* to air on Saturday mornings. These new programs represent one of the most extensive public affairs commitments in modern broadcasting—three hours of public affairs programming every week, with no reruns. This will give network television, and network television's premiere news organization, an opportunity to raise public issues and focus on serious and not-so-serious stories as never before."

He concluded to considerable applause. Even producers from competing networks were tapping spoons against their glasses and cheering; nobody was going to knock new news programming. The one or two duck calls were almost completely drowned out. Nab basked in the approval for fifteen seconds, then left the podium and walked back to his seat, shaking hands en route like the President after a State of the Union address. Wallace and Danzig were moving about, tracking the murmurs, trying to pick up the reaction in the room.

Wallace had little doubt they'd scored a coup. Everyone would be happy. USB would run its hours and garner points from Congress and the critics and the pesky goo-goos always whining about public affairs. But the Wall Street analysts would be just as delighted—they didn't need to be told that news was the cheapest possible programming now. They didn't need to be told that USB had lost money for years on Saturday mornings, either. News was even cheaper than cartoons.

Let the assholes pull all the stunts they wanted. Nab would get strong press in the morning; his gutsy performance and high-profile initiatives would put him back on the road toward respectability and acceptance, toward being a broadcaster of the first rank.

Adelson looked as awkward and uncoached as Nab had looked prepared and at ease. Adelson, the perennial inside man, was never comfortable when he stepped into the shoes of an outside man, Peter knew. And he was going to be in them a lot now. He felt a sharp, melancholic sense of loss watching Adelson. Peter seemed to be losing friends. Some of the friendships weren't terribly deep to begin with, he knew. But he'd felt particularly close to Sam. And the head of USB News could not have friends like Peter—that didn't need to be said. Adelson had gone to a much bigger league.

"Ladies and gentlemen, thank you," said Adelson too abruptly, forgetting to look at the audience.

"That was a hard act to follow. I want to thank the ABA for this award. We appreciate it. It has special meaning for us in what has been a difficult year."

The USB tables quieted again, perhaps instinctively picking up Adelson's subdued tone. "Even though Mr. Nab and I are officially accepting this award, we both know that it belongs to the men and women of USB News who, for decades, have gotten up in the middle of the night, crossed hostile borders, injected themselves into murderous crossfire in Beirut and Islamabad and San Salvador. They suffer from constant pressure and tension, they often sacrifice their personal lives, but they never walk away from a story.

"I am immensely proud to be part of the effort to carry on that tradition, and grateful to those of you who make it possible."

He paused, but no cheers filled the silence; his comments had the feel of an elegy as well as an accolade. He looked pointedly toward Nab's table, then at Peter's, where what remained of the charges he had once jealously guarded now sat quietly.

"I would not sleep well tonight if I did not give special thanks to a producer who cannot be with us tonight, but who certainly embodied the spirit of USB News throughout the years. He was not famous, but he probably did as much as anyone has to bring us this kind of recognition for so long. I would like to recognize Dan D'Amato, formerly head of USB News' Special Assignment Team and the person who, more than any other, should be up here tonight to receive this statue. Dan D'Amato."

Adelson held up the statue. Tentatively at first, the people at USB's eight tables rose to their feet, until a fourth of the room was standing silently. At the table closest to the stage, Nab looked to Wallace and then to Danzig as Jack Thomas and Harry Sommers and finally Linda Burns stood up. Wallace was careful to hide his irritation. He shook his head from side to side almost imperceptibly, and Nab and Danzig remained seated. His look said, "This is their moment. Let them have it. Better to risk looking cold-hearted than hypocritical."

Peter climbed dejectedly to his feet, with tears stinging the corners of his eyes, but without illusions about whom they were for. The evening had spelled the end of his own career as loudly, if less poignantly, as it had symbolized the end of Danny D'Amato's.

CHAPTER TWENTY-TWO

KILLER CONDOS

*I*f he felt at all strange occupying Elliott Brookings's office, Sam Adelson didn't show it. It felt odd to Peter, though. Brookings's presence had so dominated USB News that it had once been impossible to imagine anyone else in that job. Now it was growing hard to remember exactly what Brookings looked like. In the corporate way, he was gone, body and soul.

Adelson had not yet refurbished the office in his own style, a perk intact under the new regime. He would be allowed up to $250,000 to spend on furniture, artwork, and the decorator of his choice. Brookings had actually gone through a number of phases in his career at USB, from Georgian to Japanese to contemporary. When an executive moved on or got canned, he got to take the goodies home. His secretary, who got canned along with him, inherited the silk flowers that decorated the reception area.

Adelson motioned Peter to the plush but temporary beige velvet sofa the network's Transition Office maintained in a basement room for those frequent situations in which executives found themselves between furniture. He buzzed Elaine and asked for two coffees.

"You know Phil's resigning, don't you?" asked Adelson sadly.

"Did he really resign or did you have to throw him out after those leaks?"

Adelson made a what-can-I-say? face. "He had one foot in L.A. anyway. But I warned him; I warned him not to take these changes lightly. He's not a guy who knows how to be cautious. That's what makes him so talented, I suppose. He'll be happier out there.

"But it's driving me crazy, knowing there's a rat in the ranks. Who could it have been? Viola is much too honor-bound. But you know, she's the only one who has the balls, if you'll pardon the expression, and she wanted Phil's head." He sighed noisily. "The agents are driving me nuts—more feuds and pouting and finger-pointing than you can imagine. Jack Thomas is bananas. Who could have done it?"

Peter shrugged. "Could be anybody who got laid off and knows how to open a file drawer. Or anybody who has reason to be pissed off about the takeover and has a brain. That narrows the list to about a thousand. The security around here isn't exactly like the Pentagon."

Peter was enjoying surprisingly little glee after his triumph. With Adelson he felt uncomfortable and more than a little ashamed. Could Adelson possibly understand if he ever found out? Or forgive Peter's compounding the sin by sitting there, nodding, while he ranted on?

"It is now," said Adelson. Then he slapped his palms on his knees, veering away from the unpleasant topic. "I've got something to talk with you about," he said.

Peter thought his heartbeat must be visible through his oxford-cloth shirt.

But Adelson sounded upbeat. "I've got a pick-me-up for you, an assignment that will do wonders for your career and help me out of a tight spot."

"What's that?" asked Peter.

"I want you to go to Washington next week and help prep David Nab for his testimony before Congress."

Peter worked to keep his face noncommittal. He was finding it difficult. "Pardon me?"

"Look, I know you're down. I'm sorry I haven't been a

better pal, but I know we'll work something out; I'll never let you go down. And this could be a once-in-a-lifetime chance for you to let Nab see how smart and useful you are. He needs somebody to help prepare his material and to run him through his paces.

"This is his Washington coming-out party, and it's more important than ever, with the duck stuff and all these leaks. He's cramming like a school kid. His press guy, Danzig, asked for a producer who knows live TV and can set up some Q-and-A drills. These guys don't leave anything to chance. That's probably why they own us, instead of the other way around."

Peter drained the rest of his coffee. "Sam, I don't think I can help you. I'm going away for a couple of days—personal family stuff—so I won't have much time. I'm sorry. Besides, I don't feel comfortable doing it, to tell the truth. I don't like this guy, or what he's done. He's busted up a lot of lives. He's shredded this place.

"I don't like your helping him, either. Look, I'm your friend—I have to tell you: That was a very moving statement you made at the ABA dinner, but people are starting to call you The Slasher. You're chopping bureaus and research and the library. You saw what happened during the plane crash: We couldn't check anything; we didn't have anybody on research; we got killed. People hoped you would fend off these vultures, not do their cutting."

Adelson spoke in the icy, controlled way that signaled he was about to lose his temper. "I'm not running for City Council, Peter. I do fend off these people, more than you or your chatty colleagues will ever know; I just don't go around boasting about it. This is my company, too; I've spent almost thirty years in it. If people like me walk away, there'll be nothing left. We'll just give it to them for free. I do what I can, consistent with my sense of responsibility to the people who pay me and the people who work for me.

"I have no trouble sleeping at night. I'm not of your generation, which believes in loyalty as long as it's comfortable. Nab is paying me, and that means he and I have a contract."

"One he'd tear up in a second if you stumbled or he didn't need you. What kind of contract is that, where only one side has any obligation?" Peter retorted, afraid to imagine how Adelson would judge him. "I'm sorry to be an asshole, but I don't like what these guys did, not just to D'Amato but to a hundred other people we both know. I don't like what they did to me, for that matter."

Adelson struggled to stay calm. "We can't afford delusions anymore, Peter. What was done to you, you did. The simple truth is that you're good, but not as good as you need to be now. That's what you don't want to face, since we're being honest with each other. That's what Allen is facing."

Peter poured himself some orange juice from the pitcher Elaine had left on the sideboard. "It's nice to know what's in store for me. The old no-options routine. Let me ask you something, Sam. Is there any line you wouldn't cross for them, any point at which you'd say 'Sorry, this isn't what I came to the company to do'?"

Adelson stood up coldly. "I don't get you, Peter. It's not like you've just returned from leading Pickett's charge or something. Look, I'm your friend, so I'm going to bring this conversation to an end. Take your couple of family days. But next Tuesday, you be at La Guardia, Eastwind Aviation, at eight A.M. to meet Harold Wallace and Hal Danzig, who are flying on the company jet to Washington, where you will brief Nab. When you get back, I want to talk to you about working on a new pilot, a weekly news show. We're thinking of calling it *Walk Back in Time*—"

Peter stood up as well. "You mean one of those tape shows where you run pictures from fifteen years ago and pretend it's a news program? You don't need a journalist for that."

"Goddam it, Peter," Adelson roared, "you don't have to love everything you do. That's not the promise you get when you pop into the world. I'm sorry that you're not doing as well as you wanted to be doing. I'm sorry Burns didn't think you were enough of a hotshot to produce her new show. I'm sorry that the show you *can* get may not be pure. But not as sorry as I feel for some people.

"Get your ass on that plane, and then we'll talk about the new show. It's temporary, something you can do for a couple of years. Maybe you can get another show after that, who knows? Maybe once this CBS guy gets the show up and flying, you can step in. At least you won't lose any money. It's the best I could do for you—you got that?"

Peter wandered over to his echoey new office in a daze. He thought he felt the water closing over his head, but at 1:00 P.M. he would be putting his no-options ass onto a plane for Florida.

He had two stops to make before he left. The first was Buzz Allen's office, but Allen had already had his secretary ship his things to his apartment and had reported for duty in Washington. Peter went back to his own office and called him at the bureau.

"Hey, asshole, you don't say goodbye?"

"I couldn't bear to go back to the office," Allen said glumly. "Besides, I thought I should get it over with. I have to get used to it. I tried calling the other networks, just for the hell of it, but nobody returned my calls. So now I'm assigning crews to stake out Senate hearing rooms. Not exactly a launching pad for glory, is it? But call me when you get to D.C."

"Which will be next week," Peter interrupted. "I've been ordered to help prepare David Nab for his testimony before the Senate Commerce Subcommittee on American Competitiveness." He ignored the guffaw. "Come to think of it, you can do me a favor. You can ask around and get me the name of an aide who works on the committee, so I can do some research."

"Research? Nab could handle this in his sleep." Allen sounded puzzled.

Lying to your friends was easy once you got used to it, Peter thought. "It's something Adelson wants."

In television, those were the magic words. "Okay," said Allen. "How's Phil? I would have called him with condolences, but I know he doesn't really give a shit. Besides, he never called me."

"He'll love Hollywood," Peter agreed. "What an honor— the first executive producer in USB history to get canned for wasting money. The times really are a-changin', aren't they? I think I'm next, if it's any comfort. I'll see you next week, Buzz. Just call my house and leave the name of the aide. I'll be away for a few days. Vacation."

He walked back down the street into the main building and took the elevator three floors up. Barnard had not slipped away. He was emptying a bottle of expensive champagne, a farewell from his staff, while simultaneously stuffing his favored toys—a wind-up brontosaurus, a Howdy Doody puppet—into a valise. He gave Peter a hug, an uncharacteristically warm gesture.

"Well, the bitch got me," said Barnard jovially. "You gotta hand it to her. Adelson was right: I completely underestimated her. She did me a favor. I would have had to get out of this place anyway—it's on its knees and it's going to get worse. But I never thought she was the type to leak. Just didn't hit me that way."

Barnard handed over some files, which Peter helpfully stuffed into one of the Transition Office's corrugated cardboard boxes. "I doubt it was her," said Peter.

"Oh, I don't know if she was the one who handed it to the reporter, but it was her. She's been after me. She ordered the audits; she got me. I thought women seemed tough these days, but I guess I wasn't ready to believe one could be that tough. Well, if I was dumb enough to doubt her guts, at least I can be gracious enough to credit her with style. It was a clean, untraceable kill. And now she's gone, so we'll never know."

Peter's head snapped up. "What? What do you mean she's gone?"

"It was announced this morning, jerk. She's gone to be senior vice-president of American Telecommunications—they own twenty TV stations. As of tomorrow, she'll be one of the more powerful women in broadcasting. I bet we'll be lunching at Spago in a year or so. Anyway, I've got a line on a rental house in Malibu with a view of the ocean. Good riddance to New York, to USB News, and to the rest of you."

Peter sat down on the edge of the desk. "I always found your sentimentality touching, Phil. I hope we can stay friends."

Barnard looked at him quizzically. "Friends? Come on, Peter, we're both getting too old for adolescent illusions. We were never friends. We can stay in touch, if you'd like to. I would. You're a decent man, and you don't take yourself as seriously as some of the other hot-air balloons around here do."

Peter struggled to think how to say goodbye, but Barnard was having none of it. "Oh, don't start slobbering. I needed a kick in the ass to get out of here. We weren't much good at being friends anyway. Men aren't, you know. We've always set about slaughtering each other in one way or another, and we probably always will.

"But call when you get to the Coast. Like everybody else in this business, we'll sit down and have a drink and pretend we don't even remember how totally inadequate we all were to one another."

Peter called Flannery from Terminal C at Newark airport.

"Peter, I'm glad you called. I've got the telephone numbers you asked for. The lady that wrote to you is Hazel Wuraftic. And John Etheridge, at Biological Research Associates, is the engineer your friend from the newspaper mentioned, the one who used to work for Nab. He wouldn't say much, though, sounded pretty skittish. Mrs. Wuraftic really is president of the Key Lime Homeowners Association, and she has some weird stuff to tell you about. I sort of wish I were there."

So did Peter. Nobody could get people to talk the way Flannery could. He jotted the Florida telephone numbers in his reporter's notebook—the first one he had used in years—and scanned the computerized board for his flight gate.

"You sure you don't want to stop this?" Flannery said suddenly.

"Pretty sure. Why, you think I should?"

"Up to now, I think it's all been good, clean, delicious fun. But there's something smelly down there at Nab's condos. I'm starting to feel a little spooky. I mean, if they catch you, which they very well could, that could be a mess."

"You're right that it's getting dicey," he agreed. "You've been wonderful to help this far, but you should get out of it now yourself. I don't know, maybe it's going too far.

"My friend on the *Herald* does a lot of investigative stuff on real estate and development; he won a Pulitzer a few years ago. He's happy to jump on it if anything turns up, and he says it almost always does in big condo deals. Nab *isn't* in the mob or anything, is he? What's he going to do, put out a contract?"

"No," Flannery laughed. "But watch yourself. We'll get together when you get back, okay?"

"Patricia, I do need one last favor. Anything in your Rolodex that could lead me to anybody on the Senate Commerce Committee?"

"Sure, Senator Zarchin and I are old-time buddies. He's

been on the show a dozen times, and has propositioned me at least as many. Why?"

"I need his home number, no questions asked."

Peter felt oddly lightheaded on the plane down. What he was doing did not feel dangerous so much as oddly familiar. It came to him quickly enough, when he stopped to think about it, that he was acting just like a reporter, which was what he had been for more than five years. And he had done it well, he thought, a lot better than he had done anything since.

He was crossing a bridge; he doubted he would ever be allowed to cross back again. But at least he had stopped feeling as though he were slowly bleeding to death.

He could have become a lawyer or a doctor, could have joined the parade of middle-class kids heading one rung up, he reflected as the plane droned southward. But he had wanted to be a hell raiser, a gadfly journalist with no pretensions to respectability, a tormenter of the mighty—someone whose writing Uncle Nate would send around to promising young friends. Peter had made good on that ambition for a few years at least; he'd left his mark all over Asbury Park. Every now and then he still could; wasn't that the point of the abortion story, he reminded himself?

Such moments now seemed all too occasional, though, even before the takeover. Not much about his work life had to do with covering stories; he hadn't been able to resist his own ambition to be recognized, to move up, to show with one rapid-fire promotion after another how sharp he was, and to be paid accordingly.

He had never meant to be a person who laid people off, let alone fired them for no reason. He had never imagined himself giving briefings to moguls trying to look good or being so cold and fearful a friend as he had been to Dan D'Amato. Now, he felt like a gadfly reporter again. He raised his airline scotch and toasted I. F. Stone, his iconoclastic inspiration. It felt wonderful to be outside the tent pissing in, again.

The bill would come. This had to end soon, one way or the other, he couldn't spend the rest of his life skulking like some celluloid spy. Even if they didn't catch him, how could he return to USB News and develop a pilot?

But he promised himself not to become Buzz Allen. Not

me, he vowed. You just have to keep telling yourself you *have* to have choices. The worst thing about people like Nab was that they not only take away your job and your company, they rob you of your sense of having a future. You must not ever give in to that.

It's not as if they can take everything, he thought. Just your livelihood, your reputation, and your peace of mind.

Key Lime was neither a key nor were there limes, but as condominium developments went, it was pretty substantial. There were more than a thousand units nested amidst the endless and dishearteningly ugly suburban sprawl west of Boca Raton.

Key Lime was a burgeoning community with its own mall, movieplex, restaurants, and health club. From the tasteful architectural details (sloping tile roofs and enclosed courtyards) to the expensive landscaping, it announced itself as an enclave for the wealthy. Any doubts were dispelled by the heavily shrubbed parking area, which resembled a Mercedes-Benz dealer's lot.

Peter checked into a nearby motel, where the air conditioning was so cold it almost stung. It came as a relief; the air outside felt like a bathroom after a hot shower.

Stretched out on one bed, he read through the *Miami Herald,* marveling at routine crime stories that would have set other cities on their ears: a fire fight between federal drug agents and a band of machine gun-toting dealers; drowned Haitian refugees washing up on Key Biscayne for the fourth time that month. Peter fantasized about reporting in Miami. It was the only American city besides New Orleans, he mused, that actually reeked of intrigue. Washington *should* be reeking with intrigue, but instead it was swarming with lawyers and self-important journalists and diplomats. You could do worse, he thought, than to come down here as an assigning editor or feature writer.

Hazel Wuraftic was delighted to hear that his trip had gone well and was eager to see him. Come on over, she said. Peter decided to leave his rented car at the motel and walk across the busy highway and into the Key Lime complex, so that no easily traceable license plate number could be recorded. The guard, obviously surprised to see someone on foot, gave him a register to sign. He wrote his name: E. Murrow. He was making little effort to hide his identity, but why not make them sweat a bit? He easily found Mrs. Wuraftic's apartment, which overlooked the golf course.

Mrs. Wuraftic was one of those people who can make a journalist's life sweet: lonely, snoopy, meticulous. She was all of four and three quarters feet tall, but she could not have taken her position as head of the homeowners association more seriously if she had been running the State Department. Half-expecting to be on camera, she had dressed for the meeting, pearls at her throat, a diamond bracelet over one skinny, sun-speckled wrist. Tea was brewing in an ornate silver pot.

"I'm *so* sorry you haven't brought Patricia," she said, smiling. "What a lovely child. And when she told me she was from Rye, New York, as well—you know, you never get over missing home, no matter how much you enjoy keeping warm. Is she married?"

"Single, but she has several serious prospects."

"Good," said Mrs. Wuraftic.

She was the type who seems to have been waiting all her life for a reporter to knock on the door and ask about her passions. She knew virtually nothing about Peter or what he was doing there, but she knew enough: Someone from a big news organization wanted to hear of her findings and complaints.

"Look, my boy," she said, carrying over a thick manila file, "I am not a scientist or a doctor or anything. I'm just a housewife. But I do have common sense. There have been strange things going on since this place opened five years ago. Young birds die. Mrs. French down in W-Four-oh-one was the first one to get these awful rashes, but there have been thirty or more since then. Here, I took notes the day Mrs. Aker's poodle went out back one day and came back all muddy and got these terrible sores and died within a few weeks.

"And here, here's a survey we did. We found that more than eighty percent of the residents said they had headaches more than once a week. If I had any brains I'd open an aspirin stand at the gate."

Peter took the files, which Mrs. Wuraftic had thoughtfully photocopied.

"What does management say?" he asked.

She poured tea for both of them and smoothed her flowered

dress. "Why, they say very politely that most of the people here are on the elderly side, after all, and that it isn't unreasonable to expect some aches and pains. They even sent some big New York lawyer down here to try to sweet-talk everybody."

Peter nodded. "Have you gone to the county or local health authorities?"

"Only a hundred times," she said, handing him a separate folder with the names of all the bureaus and agencies she had called. "They checked for asbestos, they tested the water for arsenic, and they took an air sample. They never would tell us what the tests showed. They think I'm dotty. I heard one of them joking to the other about the 'Parrot Lady.' "

She leaned her head back and laughed with delight. Peter recalled an old rule he used when reporting: You could generally trust people who had a sense of humor about themselves. Few psychos did.

Mrs. Wuraftic got serious again. "But there's a lot of coincidences in these folders. I'm getting a little old to be running around like Sherlock Holmes. But you look into it, young man. They won't push USB News around so easily."

Despite her bravado, Peter thought she was smoothing her skirt a bit frequently. He waited for her to share what was troubling her.

"Young man," she said. "I wrote you the letter—I have always watched *Morning in the U.S.*—to warn you about Mr. Nab. I thought you people should know what was going on here. But I didn't expect that someone would come, certainly not an executive producer, and especially not after the company was taken over."

He had learned early in his reporting career not to underestimate the elderly, but was surprised nonetheless.

"I watch the credits," she explained, smiling sweetly. "Am I to believe you intend to expose Mr. Nab on his own network?"

Peter smiled back, looking Mrs. Wuraftic squarely in the eye. He paused for effect. "Mrs. Wuraftic, I will be as direct with you as you have been with me. My reasons for being here are really no different from your reasons for writing me. If I can confirm your story, it will see the light of day."

She stared back for several seconds, nodded, smoothed her skirt, and smiled.

The knock on Mrs. Wuraftic's door came a few minutes earlier than Peter expected. He explained to her that he was meeting someone who might be able to help.

John Etheridge was an engineer who specialized in testing construction sites for structural and toxic-waste problems. He had worked for nine years on Nab's Florida construction projects before moving on to other employers.

Peter's friend on the *Miami Herald* had fished his name out of a state computer, and Flannery had worked some of her magic to track him down. Etheridge had at first refused to talk, she said, but had eventually agreed to a meeting. It was a foot in the door, Peter knew. If he was willing to sit down and talk, there was a chance.

Etheridge was short, a bit under five three. He was wearing a bright-blue polo shirt and polyester slacks, and carried some sort of tool in a metal case. He looked intense, distracted, and anxious, and nodded to Mrs. Wuraftic without offering a hand or introducing himself. Peter told her goodbye and thanks, and promised to keep her informed about anything he learned. Then he and Etheridge walked to the back of the complex.

"Mr. Herbert, I only have a few minutes. We can walk right out behind this wing. Just keep an eye out for the patrol," he cautioned, gesturing toward the air-conditioned guardhouse at the Key Lime entrance. "I gave them a phony name."

"Are they real cops or just old geezers down here for a tan?" asked Peter, noting Etheridge's failure to greet him, taking it as a sign of nerves.

"One of the condo's big selling points is its tough security. In fact, if someone breaks into your apartment, the condo association will pay you for what was stolen, up to ten thousand dollars." He said this almost proudly, as if he were selling a unit.

"This guy has something he wants to say," Flannery had told Peter. "But I'm not sure you can get him to say it." We'll see, Peter thought, as they walked into the still-fierce sunlight.

"Let's go around to the back, to the lagoon," said Etheridge, whose shirt had almost instantly soaked through with sweat. They walked more than two hundred yards among the palms and groomed gardens. The condo patios were designed so that none faced directly onto another, affording the residents privacy and quiet. Emerald golf greens stretched out behind the complex;

a lake snuggled almost directly against the side of the course. Etheridge took Peter down a path away from the buildings, past a maintenance shed that was hidden from view by tall hedges. They walked behind it, Etheridge leading, seeming to go in circles until they came to a second low shed, equally well camouflaged.

Etheridge took out a ring of keys, unlocked the two pad-locks that hung on the low door, then hesitated, looking around.

"I knew they wouldn't change the locks. But this cloak-and-dagger stuff isn't my style," he said. "Promise me you won't use my name."

"You have my word on it," said Peter as Etheridge unfast-ened the door.

The two men had to squat to get in. Inside, the air smelled faintly acrid; Peter soon felt a slight burning in his throat. Etheridge pulled open a heavy concrete cover and took the foot-long tool from its case. It looked to Peter like a fat corkscrew, only the tip didn't come to a point. "It's a corer," Etheridge muttered, to Peter's inquiring look. He pushed the tip into the dirt, and turned the wooden handle until a sample of the dark soil came up, then slipped the dirt into a plastic tube which he stashed in a back pocket. He needed only seconds, in the practiced way of someone doing his work.

They walked around to the front of the complex, waved casually to the man in the guardhouse, and darted across the highway to a Pizza Hut next to Peter's motel, choosing a booth all the way in the back. Peter, grateful for the powerful air conditioning, downed a glass of ice water, trying to flush away the bitter taste in his throat and nostrils. Then he excused himself to make a phone call.

"My friend from the newspaper is joining us for a pizza," he said when he returned. "Then we'll go over to the motel and have a few drinks; we deserve them."

"I won't be staying long," said Etheridge. "I'll just have a quickie."

Peter discreetly checked out the adjoining booths. Satisfied that both were empty, he turned to Etheridge. "John, what was in that shack? It's giving me a headache already. I know you don't want to get any further involved, but you obviously showed me that place for a reason. What the hell was that stuff you dug up?"

Etheridge, staring at his watch, looked intensely uncomfortable. Peter, trying to make him feel that the two were a team returned from a dangerous mission, was pushing him a little. But Flannery was right: This guy had something on his mind.

"C'mon, John. Something is wrong there. You've got something you've been wanting to tell; now you've got somebody who wants to hear it."

Etheridge nodded. "That's why I took you back there. That soil is contaminated. Spend more than a few days in there with no ventilation and you could do yourself some serious harm. I'll tell you, but I want you to keep my name out of it. Nab is a powerful person here and I'm no hero—I don't want to apply for unemployment—"

"Well, you're half right. You may not want to get canned, but you could be a hero."

He had overdone it; Etheridge was irritated. "Look, I'm not stupid," he snapped. "This is something that's been bothering me for five years. If you can do something about it, I'll sleep a lot easier. But can the crap, okay?"

Peter told himself to slow way down. He was rusty, and Etheridge was thornier than Hazel Wuraftic. Peter began thinking about his old reporter's tricks, especially the ones he used for men.

Sports was the great icebreaker, the thing you tried first. Find out what the guy's favorite team was and shake your head and cluck about how badly it was being managed. From the desk sergeant to the governor, that worked more often than any other. But this guy might not be a sports fan.

You could also try wives; men loved to bitch about them. Next came the cost of things—anything. And there was always the boss. Nobody in America liked his boss.

Put the brakes on. Let him take his time and get comfortable with you. You're here to find out if this stuff is dangerous and if Nab knew about it when he built the condos. The *Herald* can take care of the rest.

Etheridge gulped his soda down in seconds. Peter ordered another. He would have to get this guy to someplace that served liquor, he thought; he was too tense.

"Five years ago when we were doing the workups for this

project, for Key Lime, I came out and did bore and drill tests on the property," Etheridge began finally.

"I had them sink a drill fifty feet down and we discovered that the Key Lime site is directly over a series of lagoons that flow all around here. We found twenty-six lagoons underneath the construction site. That isn't unusual for this part of the state. But we also tested the soil, and we got ratings that any environmentalist or engineer knows right away mean toxic waste.

"If you get the stuff in this container analyzed, the lab'll find about forty different chemicals from a factory that made industrial paint. The plant went out of business years ago, but everyone in town knew that shit came up out of the lagoons. You'd get dead birds and turtles popping up from time to time. Some of the locals used to call this area Poison Swamp, because nothing lived around it. The stuff only oozes up now and then, when the lagoons swell and rise, but it's in the subsoil all the time. The initial land survey must not have gone deep enough, or maybe somebody was bought off—who knows?

"You can't imagine what goes on in the condo-construction business—a couple of days can make the difference sometimes between making huge amounts of money and going bankrupt. Nab went crazy—he had fifteen million dollars committed to the land and the construction, a lot of it from contracts already signed on condominium units. He never builds until he has the place seventy-five percent sold; it's one way he's avoided the ups and downs of the condo market here. And Nab is one of the better ones. He insists the buildings be well designed and built. Some developers . . . There've been people killed when ceilings fell in on them."

Peter held up his hand to let some tourists walk past the booth. He'd learned from Adelson how to canvass a restaurant for eavesdroppers. Etheridge was further delayed by the arrival of the pizza, but Peter was still slightly nauseated by the smell in the shed, which had lingered and left him with a slight sore throat.

"So the bottom line is this: I estimate there are about six hundred thousand gallons of toxic waste underneath Key Lime. It was sure strong enough to kill off a bunch of rabbits and mice in a lab, and I hate to think what it can do to people."

Peter thought about what he had just heard. "So what

you're telling me is that Nab knowingly constructed more than a thousand condo units over more than a half-million gallons of toxic chemicals.''

"That's about it," said Etheridge, with what sounded to Peter like enormous relief. "The condo market down here is extremely volatile. Removing the soil and draining those lagoons would have taken a year or two, with luck, and Nab would've had to pay off all these contracts. Besides, who's to say people would ever want to live on that site, even if he did clean it up? There's always another development down the road. So it was probably a fifteen-million-dollar decision to Nab at a time when the rest of the company was a little rocky. The word was, it might have done him in.

"And government isn't exactly aggressive down here. Hell, this strip, the mall down the road, it's all come since Key Lime brought a couple thousand people here with money to spend. Instead of a rotting swamp, you have a booming little community here.

"Nab brought in this lawyer, a guy named Wallace, and he spent some time nosing around, making it clear to all of us that our jobs were on the line—without actually saying it. My wife and I were scared. We had two little kids and a third coming. But I tell you, I swore that if anyone ever asked me about it, I wouldn't lie. And I feel like a truck has been lifted off of me.'' He almost smiled, for the first time since Peter had met him. But his face turned anxious again when the reporter from the *Herald* arrived, shook his hand, and got an update from Peter.

By eight, the three of them were at the bar in the lobby of Peter's motel, downing drinks and talking easily. Peter was wrong about Etheridge and sports. He was as fanatic a Dolphins freak as there was on the east coast of Florida, and he and the reporter almost broke into tears over one of the team's recent trades.

Peter struck out on marital problems. If Etheridge had any complaints about his wife, he did not want to share them. But he had plenty about his kids, who didn't seem to recognize the value of hard work. Peter suddenly worried aloud about his own kids, topping each of Etheridge's stories. It would have startled Peter's USB News colleagues, who had long wearied of his incessant bragging about Ben and Sarah.

By ten they had adjourned to Peter's room and ordered more scotch for Peter and his reporter friend, more bourbon for Etheridge.

By eleven Etheridge was bitching to Peter and the reporter about his new employer's incompetence and his own wish to stand up and tell the truth.

Buoyed by the liquor purchased through the reporter's expense account, Etheridge turned to Peter at ten minutes after midnight and announced importantly: "What you have here is a killer condo, and Nab knew it because I told him about it."

Peter and the reporter both reached for their pocket tape recorders and placed them on the coffee table.

"Would you mind, John, just repeating that for us?" Peter said.

Back at home the next evening, Peter felt frightened again, more so than when he was in motion. It was there in Glen Ridge, with the big house and the toys and the evidence of the monthly bills, that he thought he must have gone completely out of his mind to jeopardize everything he had worked so hard for and that his family enjoyed so much. This isn't the way it's supposed to work, he kept telling himself. The father gives these things; he doesn't take them away.

He found a conciliatory message from Adelson on his answering machine: "Peter, it's Sam. I'm sorry I lost my temper. Where are you anyway? Listen, I'll be brief because I hate these fucking machines. I promised Harold Wallace that one of my best producers will be in Washington to help Nab. That makes you one of my best producers, get it? Wallace was pleased, Peter, so don't blow it, for my sake or yours. You be on that plane. When you get back we'll go to the New Age for the Cronkite special, okay?"

Mahoney didn't bother to sit down in Wallace's law office for the now-daily briefing. There was no point pretending to be anything but employer and subordinate, although each had been more impressed than he'd expected by the other.

Wallace once thought that law enforcement people must be

stupid. Why else would anyone voluntarily do that kind of work? But watching Mahoney handle a string of delicate assignments had changed his mind.

Wallace had made it clear how important the investigation was, but he'd given Mahoney complete latitude in pursuing it. The sign of a professional, thought Mahoney.

"Good morning, Frank," said Wallace, in his shirt sleeves, setting down his newspaper. Mahoney's trained eyes took in everything, as usual. He'd been impressed by the fact that there was never anything on Wallace's desk that he shouldn't see. "How's it going?"

Mahoney flipped through his notes. "We're almost certain we know another of the people involved in the duck incident. Here's his ID." Mahoney threw down a photo card laminated in plastic, showing a man in his fifties, with a wide smile, a full head of graying hair, and thick wire-rims. "Bill Siegel. He was laid off in the first wave. He was a producer and worked in the tape-editing area right next to the back door that somebody opened. He also played on the USB News softball team with Steve Toomey, the tech we think smuggled the duck cassette into the network control center." Mahoney took back the ID card. "The question is, do you want us to get formal? I called Siegel's house and he told me to fuck off—those were his exact words. Maybe some city detectives could shake him up a bit."

Wallace shook his head emphatically. "Absolutely not, Frank. This has to be kept in-house. We can't be monkeying around with cops and reporters. We've just got to stop this thing now. Do you think this Siegel is the only one?"

Mahoney shook his head. "The people we've talked to who know Siegel just don't see him as coming up with this by himself. So, going on the assumption that a senior-level producer or an executive is involved, which the computer profile suggests, we're making up lists of other people who might be disgruntled, ticked off about the changes, facing demotion or loss in pay— people like that."

"And how many people would there be like that, Frank?"

"Well, we're at a hundred and fifty and counting," said Mahoney. "And Toomey and Siegel aren't talking. But there might be a faster way."

Wallace looked up inquisitively.

"Technology—the cop's new best friend. A computer phone sweep works like a charm when you're dealing with amateurs. You take the main telephone numbers—Toomey's, Siegel's, the people on our lists—and feed them into the phone company's computer, along with all USB News employees' home numbers and their office numbers. You run them through; you see if anybody on the list called anybody else; you come up with some connections. The only problem is . . ." Mahoney shrugged.

He didn't want to tell Wallace that for a phone check you needed a warrant. He knew if he stopped now, Wallace still could say he had no idea what Mahoney was planning, which was important for a lawyer. Wallace could swear he'd never authorized the plan, or known it would be used. Mahoney was simply giving Wallace the chance to stop him.

Wallace brooded for a minute or two. Mahoney was extremely professional; Wallace trusted him to handle the phone check discreetly. He weighed the potential damage against the mess this person or these people were creating for Nab. Announcing new programming had worked very well, and he felt they had regained the initiative. But that was only a partial antidote. His tormentors had succeeded in making Nab look ridiculous. Now they were making him look unethical as well. Wallace didn't like the progression from ridiculous to unethical and wasn't sure they'd stop there. What was next? Nab had done some pretty rough stuff in the early years, assembling his real estate empire.

He nodded at Mahoney. "Thanks for the technology lecture. Interesting. Let me know if you have any news."

Mahoney nodded and left. His first stop would be the telephone company. One of his closest buddies, the veteran of more than twenty years of elaborate FBI operations, worked in security there.

CHAPTER TWENTY-THREE

MAHONEY'S PROGRESS

*A*s always before reporting to Harold Wallace, Frank Mahoney buttoned his jacket, a holdover habit from the FBI. Mahoney had met J. Edgar Hoover only once, and, like the other new agents, he'd been terrified, having heard dozens of stories about guys with dirty shoes or too much after-shave being summarily expelled from the agency. He still thought Hoover a major asshole, but you had to hand it to the old bastard: No FBI agent he knew ever showed up sloppy for an important meeting.

Wallace came out expectantly from behind his desk and, as usual, wasted no time in small talk. Mahoney took a manila envelope from his pocket and tossed an ID on the desk in front of Wallace.

"We think this is our guy. Here's his resumé and company history."

Wallace stared at the ID, shocked. "I remember him. You're sure?"

Mahoney took his notes out of his pocket. Naturally, Wallace would want to hear the full account, with nothing left out.

"He has been demoted. He made four or five calls to Bill Siegel the day before Mr. Nab's appearance, and he's the only USB person who did. He's smart and fits the profile."

Wallace slipped the picture into an envelope and put it in his pocket. "You'll be accompanying Mr. Nab to Washington tomorrow?" It was an order, not a request. "I'd prefer that you be there. It'll be a zoo in any case, and now we have a new problem."

Mahoney took his notebook out again expectantly.

"A reporter from the *Miami Herald* called this morning. He tried Nab's office, which had the good sense to refer him to me. He's working on a story about the Key Lime condominium development outside of Boca that David built some years back. He says he has evidence that David knowingly built the complex over hundreds of thousands of gallons of toxic waste, and that pets have been dying and residents breaking out in rashes and maybe worse. I've got to stall it past tomorrow's hearing. I told you I didn't like the progression from ridiculous to unethical. Now it goes to the edge of illegal. We don't need this kind of grief now.

"I want to tie up the duck episode and the leaks. Some illegal phone checks aren't enough; I have to have proof. I've got to take what you suspect in to Sam Adelson with hard evidence, enough so that this guy goes away for good.

"And can you check into this Key Lime thing? Somebody must be down there snooping around. Maybe somebody saw something. Can you get your Florida people on it quickly?"

Mahoney finished scribbling in his notebook. He might just take a Florida trip himself.

Peter had just yelled upstairs for the kids to be quiet and go to sleep. Barbara looked up from her doodling, capped her pen, crossed her arms, and stared hard at him across the kitchen table. She had on her Serious Talk look. "Peter, you did the Daffy Duck thing, didn't you?"

Peter gaped. Her remark had come completely out of the blue. She had said nothing that indicated she had connected him to the duck incident or the contract leaks. Finally he nodded.

"You ought to be embarrassed at having married somebody you obviously think is dumb as a tree frog. Did you think I didn't notice that you made a point of having me watch David Nab that morning? Do you think I am unaware of your slinking around, whispering on the phone with Flannery, going out at night with a plain brown envelope three days before contract leaks make the papers? And the trip to Florida—that's related too. Part of your little Maoist counterattack, isn't it?"

He nodded again.

"I can't believe you didn't talk to me about this, Peter. I can't believe you didn't say something. This is why you've been disappearing and not telling me where you were going, right? Dammit, Peter, I had a right to know about this."

Peter was unprepared for her anger. He had felt so guilty about the curly-haired young woman in the building on Third Avenue that he hadn't wasted much time feeling guilty about also hiding his anti-Nab projects from Barbara. His rationale, which suddenly seemed flimsy, was that she was always so involved with her own work that it had been easy to find reasons not to bring her into things. But then, he had never had anything remotely like the last two weeks' escapades to bring her into.

He toyed with his coffee mug. "Sorry. Maybe I should have talked with you about it. I honestly didn't think you should know. I wanted it to be only my problem, so nobody else had to be touched by it. I guess there's another thing, too: I'm ashamed to be *having* problems. I'm supposed to be the rock. I know it's an old-fashioned notion, but that doesn't make it disappear. I'm out of a job; Adelson tells me I have little to say about the next one; I'm supposed to be grateful and accept whatever turns up. Everybody I know, including you, is telling me how few choices I have in the world. Ben's classmates razz him with newspaper clippings about what a turkey I am. Now I'm into this James Bond stuff—"

"Is this legal, Peter?" she interrupted. "Are you doing anything they could have you arrested for?"

"No," he said vigorously. "I suppose they could charge me with malicious mischief or something on the duck thing, but they'd never go through a trial, even if they could tie it to me, which I'm not sure they can. And the rest is just old-fashioned reporting, which isn't against the law yet. These aren't just college pranks, but they're not the Lindbergh kidnapping either. I'm acting like a reporter again, and I can't begin to tell you how great that feels."

He looked at Barbara for some reaction. She seemed to be steeling herself for more questions. "Patricia's into it with you, isn't she?" she asked, looking down as if she dreaded the answer. Peter sensed the question had more import than leaked contracts and ducks.

"Barbara, I'm not into anything with Flannery; that's not what this is about. She has helped me, but it's my neck on the block."

"And are you into anything with anyone else?" she went on quietly. "It sounds like some B-flick, but the week before last I swear I smelled perfume on your clothes in the hamper. And you took a shower when you got home from the city the day after we had that fight, which you never do."

Peter never hesitated, and later recalled his response as the best and smartest lie of his life. "No," he said. "I swear it."

Barbara's sigh this time was of relief. "Okay," she said. "If you're lying, never tell me. But, Peter, they're going to get you for this. You must know that. They're going to fire you at least."

He opened his mouth to respond, but she went right on. "So what we have to do is, we have to sit down again and talk this all through until there's nothing either one of us has to say that hasn't been said. And we'll keep going through this exercise until we're sure we've come up with every idea that heads you in the direction you want to go and doesn't wipe out the rest of us. See, I think this is one of those moments in a marriage, one of those milestones where you move together or you move apart. I say we move together, okay? You did what you had to do. At the moment, the most important thing to me isn't what you're up to with Nab. It's us.

"Just tell me one thing, Peter. All this—the duck tape, the contracts, whatever you're into in Florida—I've never known you to get caught up in anything like this. It's so out of character. Why?"

Peter unplugged the coffeepot and carried it over to the sink.

He clicked off the radio so that he could think more clearly, because he wanted to know the answer as much as Barbara did.

"That's why," he said. "Because it's out of character, and it shouldn't be. I shouldn't be on their side. I don't expect I'll win or anything like that, although there's some chance that I'll get away with it. I know there's no way Nab will ever give the company back, and the people who ran it before probably don't even deserve to have it back.

"But Nab should pay. He should pay in some way for breaking the contract we all had with an institution that wanted to be great, and even was, once in a while. He should pay for D'Amato. Those people have the power, I know that, but they don't have to use it the way they do. They have the money to do it differently. I didn't get off my ass when I should have. At least I'm getting off it now."

He looked to see if she understood, but found it hard to read her face. "You know, maybe I'm most pissed off at Nab for what he taught me about myself, about us elite managers. We could have slowed it or softened it, but we didn't. We didn't even try—it didn't really cross our minds. He made me see how weak I am. He made me see how little community we have, how little help we give each other. He made me understand how quickly we roll over and hide behind our families and our mortgages. For all our pretensions, he made me realize we're ciphers and drones.

"It's hard to leave it at that. You know, it's strange, but going up to New Haven last time my father was sick reminded me why I got into journalism in the first place. It sure wasn't to lie by the road and rot like some raccoon hit by a car on I-95. Somewhere along the line my gyroscope broke and I thought I got into journalism so I could be a big shot."

"Well, you *were* one," she said, almost proudly.

"Maybe, I don't know. And maybe we can keep all this. I like it here too. But I ought to tell you before we get our notebooks out that I called Chuck Claffey, the headhunter, and I told him I might become one of his clients. He's a pro, and a smoothie. He said he would be tickled to represent me, but to keep my expectations low. He said he had more clients than he's ever had."

"And fewer jobs?" asked Barbara.

"You got it."

The expression on Barbara's face seemed strange to Peter, thoughtful and amused at the same time. She didn't look as shaken or frightened as he'd been sure his confession would make her.

"You look weird," he said.

She looked at him. "You really did the duck thing, eh?"

"Yup."

"And you leaked the contracts? You really did that?"

"It's not something I would lie about. Why?"

She held her hand up in the air and smiled. "Congratulations."

He slapped his hand against hers.

"Wanta talk?" he asked, putting his arms around her, grinning.

"No," she said. "Let's go fuck."

Peter had taken the train to Washington the night before the briefing so that he could have dinner with Buzz Allen. Allen seemed almost desperate to see him, and Peter was determined not to avoid him.

They met at the bureau, which had always resembled a cramped beehive.

Peter walked up to the second floor, pausing to stare at a row of empty cubicles lining the wall to his right. They had housed Zeke Christian's Investigative Unit, a collection of older reporters and specially trained producers who nosed around the Pentagon and government agencies rooting for juicy tales of waste, corruption, and intrigue. The unit for years had served as an honorable resting ground for tired Washington correspondents who knew something about the city but no longer had the energy for breaking news or the looks for appearing on the tube; it had also served as the source of much of the news division's prestige.

The Denial Wall was still intact: Several dozen black-and-white glossies of some of the most powerful people in postwar Washington were mounted there amidst appropriate bunting and patriotic hoo-ha, along with their printed denials of USB's damning stories about them.

Absolutely false, said a former Speaker of the House. The

high-salaried woman on my staff payroll was merely an invaluable political confidante.

Libelous and scandalous, declared a former chairman of the House Public Works Committee. My wife and I would never dream of using public funds for our private parties. And the trips to Cannes were legitimate committee business—we were studying traffic flow in and out of a busy resort.

Absurd, bellowed two members of the Senate Armed Services Committee. The cash we received from the defense contractors was never meant to win them favorable treatment with the Pentagon; it was just a coincidence that we pushed for these companies to get military contracts.

And near the end of the Wall was Senator Ponzio's outraged denial of any links to abortion clinic bombers. A "left-wing fantasy," he called it. Peter had to blink to remember that that story had broken only a few months ago. Indictments against Ponzio's aide Jack Fox and several members of the Sanctity group had been handed down within weeks of the USB News story, and there had been no abortion clinic bombings since.

He had heard that the Investigative Unit was being disbanded, its members retired or scattered to other jobs. Christian had been transferred to the assignment desk, but quit instead. No one seemed to know where he had gone, which was characteristic. No one wrote about the dismantling of his unit, either. At first Peter had thought that the new management wouldn't dare tamper with USB's traditions; the outcry would be enormous. He knew better by now, recognizing his optimism for the conceit it was. There never was an outcry, from within or without, as long as famous faces weren't involved. The reporters who covered television seemed more interested in the memos Jack Thomas was writing to David Nab. The people at USB News were clinging to their jobs like drowning sailors to driftwood. All kinds of horror stories were floating around. The current story was that Kevin Messinger, an *Evening News* producer, had quit in protest over the two-day shooting limit recently imposed on stories, and a month later had been forced to take a job as a public relations man for Johnson & Johnson.

As he rounded the corner Peter was relieved to see some activity, signs of the manic scrambling evident in almost any newsroom. It was 7:30 on the dot; Allen would be able to back out of the nightly postmortem to join him. Peter was hoping to avoid the other people in the bureau. It would be too depressing to compare this battered outpost to the old days—just a few months back—when they would all have gone out to one of Georgetown's perenially sprouting new restaurants to gossip and drink until midnight. Peter cautioned himself not to get maudlin; old days were not necessarily better days.

Allen popped out of the meeting early. He looked fit as always, but to someone used to seeing him lope through the halls in New York, he seemed deflated.

"You look good," Peter said anyway, as the two of them headed out of the bureau and into a cab. Allen had suggested an Indian restaurant on Connecticut near his new apartment.

"Well, I'm in good shape," said Allen. "This is a great town for runners, I'll give it that. And at the apartment later, I hope you can meet Sally."

"Sally?"

"Yeah. She's a producer for PBS. We've had dinner a few times. She's going to come over for drinks. I think she'd like to meet one of my friends."

Peter laughed. "It's the first time I'll ever have seen any place you lived."

Allen got the irony. "Well, it's easier now; we're not competing. I don't know anybody much in Washington yet, and I'd like her to meet somebody from my glorious past, to convince her that I had one and to remind myself.

"You all set to brief Nab? Pretty fast company you're keeping now, Peter. Maybe there'll be a new contract in it for you. We're going to have two crews at the hearing. Nobody's worried about spending too much money on that, are they?"

Dinner was edgy at first, Peter realizing that the two of them had never even had lunch alone.

"The bureau looks pretty grim. Is it as depressing as it seems?"

"Just about. They had to chop away a fourth of the correspondents and producers. That pretty much leaves the major beat people—State, Defense, Justice, Capitol Hill, the White House. There was no choice, really, but to cut out the special unit; it was either that or not cover the news every day. Adelson told the bureau it was up to us; he'd never presume to dictate what the cuts should be—"

"I know, I know," said Peter. "These are *your* choices, right?"

Allen instinctively lowered his voice. "I know he's a particular pal of yours, Peter, but Sam seems to be wielding a pretty sharp ax these days. His name does not bring smiles and warmth down here, even if he does remember Dan D'Amato."

"Up there either," said Peter. "You know Sam. Mr. Corporate Loyalty. If he gets paid by somebody, he does what he's supposed to do. I hope it doesn't take over his soul."

"I think maybe that battle's been lost," Allen said cautiously.

"Buzz, that's not fair. He's from a different generation; he has his whole life tied up in USB. Somebody else might be a lot worse. You don't know what he's stopping them from doing."

"Right," said Allen. He ordered a lamb curry for both of them.

"You actually seem in better shape than I'd expected," said Peter. "Girlfriends and all—you obviously don't find Washington that horrible."

Allen stirred his scotch and soda and looked into his glass. "Nothing could be as bad as I expected. And I was taught not to complain. But we can be honest with each other, Peter. I'm not kidding myself, either. I've got two little girls up there who will grow up strangers to me.

"A few weeks ago, I had a thousand people all over the world waiting for me to tell them where to go. Now my day consists of sending the crews we have left to the White House and the State Department and to whatever agency is holding a press conference. I suppose I should be grateful to Adelson for getting me a job at all; otherwise I'd be up the creek without a paddle. But this is not a job I'll ever climb out of, I know that. And you? You're in a transitional state, as they say?"

Peter decided not to widen the number of people involved in his little project. Allen was not a rule-breaker; the pressure of knowing would be almost unbearable for him.

Peter shrugged. "Adelson says I might have to work on this new nostalgia show they're planning. Near as I can tell, they go through the tape library, find good pictures of stuff from fifteen or twenty years ago, hire some voice to narrate it, and run it in some prime-time slot they know they can't win. I don't think I can do that."

Allen ordered another drink. "You can do it, Peter. What else can you do? Welcome to the world of radically adjusted expectations."

CHAPTER TWENTY-FOUR
TESTIFYING

When Peter returned to his hotel, he had three messages. One was from Harold Wallace's secretary telling him not to appear at Nab's suite the next morning for the planned briefing. Nab was well prepared, the message said. Peter was free to attend the hearing, of course, if he wished.

The second message was from Adelson, asking Peter to come to his office at ten the morning after Nab's subcommittee appearance.

The third caller left no name; the message read simply: "Going with Key Lime tomorrow."

At first Peter felt a rush of jubilation. He'd had no idea how he would ever have gotten through two hours of briefing Nab. Then the relief was overtaken by a dread that would not rise or fall but lodged in his chest. He did not even try to go to sleep, staring instead out the window of his hotel toward Constitution Avenue and the Capitol dome.

The phone startled him shortly after midnight. It was Buzz. "Jesus, Peter, has anybody called you about Nab? The *Miami*

Herald is reporting in tomorrow's edition that Nab built a ritzy condominium project on a zillion gallons of highly toxic chemical waste, even though an engineer warned him the glop was there and was potentially dangerous. The paper says dogs and cats and birds have been dropping all over the place, and there's a ten–times–higher than usual rate of respiratory infection and rashes and all. It's unbelievable that they're breaking this the morning of his Senate appearance. Every reporter in North America will be there—"

Peter expressed shock. "How did you hear?"

"The bureau just called. We're sending an extra crew to catch Nab outside the Senate. We've obviously got to cover this. Meanwhile, the bureau's having a secret champagne party down in the basement right now. They're calling it a "There Is a God" party. The idea is to get drunk and celebrate all night. Want to come?"

Peter did not feel festive enough for champagne. He was too afraid. He lay in his clothes on the bed until seven the next morning, when he switched on his old show and fondly remembered the days when he was doing nothing more complicated than running a two-hour news program every morning. He listened as Don Leeming dutifully reported the *Herald* story several minutes into the 7:30 newsbloc, which was precisely where Peter would have run it. He kept glancing toward the door, steeling himself for the moment when it would surely come crashing open and a dozen men brandishing shotguns would order him to freeze and would read him his rights.

He ordered a sumptuous room service breakfast worthy of a condemned man, then called Flannery. She called back within minutes with a copy of the *Miami Herald* and read the story to him. When she was done, he felt almost as elated as he was terrified. The paper had gone well beyond the account of Etheridge, the twitchy engineer; reporters had pored through local medical records and building reports. The story was solid.

He reminded himself to enjoy the moment. Soon it would be their turn to have some fun.

Peter went to the Capitol with plenty of time to spare, watching as the gaggle of reporters swelled to a growling, cursing pack. At ten, a huge gray limousine pulled up in front of the Capitol's Senate entrance and Nab—flanked by Wallace, Mahoney, and Hal Danzig, the public relations expert—hopped out. His four plainclothes guards were augmented by a dozen uniformed Capitol police officers. Peter watched from one side.

It was the journalistic equivalent of the kill. With so many papers, local stations, and foreign news organizations in Washington, with so many of them lugging around microphones, tape packs, cameras, and audio recorders, the mob resembled a swarm of heavily laden bees. And they stung.

Peter, taken aback by the sight of his colleagues from this perspective, felt a momentary twinge of sympathy for Nab. Politicians had gotten used to it, but to new initiates, the assault was horrifying, a literal attack by a screaming mob. Even the normally collected Nab could not mask a look of consternation and fright as the horde shrieked questions at him and his entourage.

Alongside the entrance, the People's Committee for the Environment was picketing in a circle, chanting, *"Quack! Quack! The people attack! Nab took the land, now give it back!"* A dozen or so cameras had obligingly broken off from the media crush around Nab to pay attention. One woman, wearing a sandwich board saying THERE'S NO PLACE TO DUCK NOW, NAB, was being interviewed by local television reporters from San Diego, Denver, and Philadelphia.

"Mr. Nab, Mr. Nab, a moment please." The correspondents from competing networks were circling like sharks. "Is it true that you deliberately built your condominium over a site so poisonous that birds fell from the sky when they flew over it? Just stop for a minute. Why are you hiding? Why won't you answer us?"

One correspondent, wisely despairing of catching Nab, was doing a stand-up in front of her crew, holding the latest edition of the *New York Post,* just in on the air shuttle. KILLER CONDOS! roared the headline.

Nab was carried along by his guards into the building, through the halls, down the aisle of the conference room. He had regained the calm mask he had briefly lost outside. If he heard the questions hurled at him every step of the way, or was bothered by the flashing bulbs or the microphones thrust toward his mouth, he did not reflect it. Wallace paused briefly to shout that he would make a statement about the *Miami Herald* reports later in the day, once he'd had an opportunity to study them.

Inside the hearing room, Senator James Zarchin and his colleagues were momentarily taken aback by the media swarm, but quickly and happily recovered. This was the sort of publicity that cost a lot to buy at election time. And as luck would have it, Senator Zarchin was a Democrat from New Jersey, where toxic waste issues were not merely theoretical. He had lots of constituents clamoring about cancer clusters, lots of sites awaiting cleanup. And reporters had filled virtually all of the seats in the gilded chamber. Zarchin beamed, then looked serious and senatorial.

Nab faced the raised tiers of senators calmly, his statement on competitiveness, trade, and tax reform ready in front of him. Hal Danzig circulated desperately and hopelessly among the reporters, pointing out that this appearance concerned trade, not toxic waste. Three reporters in the front row held up their middle fingers and laughed.

Peter, seated at the edge of the chamber all the way to Nab's right, watched his face and Wallace's. Frank Mahoney, from the back of the room, scanned the faces in the crowd, stopping frequently at Peter's.

Zarchin, waiting to be sure that the cameras were up and working, and mindful that all the networks carried news breaks at noon, gaveled the session to order; the television floodlights sent the temperature rocketing in seconds. A dozen still photographers crawled on the floor in front of Nab, their motorized cameras whirring and clicking. Zarchin gave them almost a minute to work before he gaveled them away.

"We have called these hearings," he said without fanfare, "to help find ways to increase America's economic competitiveness. We have asked David Nab, chairman and chief executive officer of USB Incorporated, to lead off this session, to present his views as the head of a major American corporation and a member of the President's Select Commission on a Competitive Economy. I would be derelict in my duty as the elected representative of the great and much-maligned state of New Jersey, however, if I did not first call the attention of my colleagues to a development reported by the *Miami Herald* this morning. I have distributed copies to my fellow committee members. . . ."

Peter could not suppress a smile. Isn't democracy grand? he thought. Adelson would love this scene. No, he quickly corrected himself, Adelson would not, not anymore.

The voice interrupting Senator Zarchin was Harold Wallace's, as confident in a Washington hearing room as in a Wall Street board room. "Mr. Chairman, with all due respect," he said, "unless I misunderstand the rules of this body, the purpose for which Mr. Nab was invited to testify was to address issues he is prepared and eager to speak about—namely, America's ability to compete economically with the rest of the world. We have not had an opportunity to study the story you're referring to and are not able to respond to it. I can assure you, Mr. Chairman, that Mr. Nab has never knowingly engaged in any behavior—"

Senator Zarchin knew, as did Wallace, that the scores of reporters hovering behind Nab were not interested in economic competitiveness. In the two weeks the hearings had been under way, no more than a dozen of them had deigned to attend.

"Mr. Wallace, excuse me, but I don't need you to tell me what the rules of this committee are. We are here to talk about the American economy, but ethics and responsibility and operating within the law are a part of business, too, wouldn't you agree? I would hate to have to subpoena Mr. Nab to testify, especially since you say he has nothing to hide."

Wallace and Zarchin bickered for nearly twenty minutes. Both men knew that Wallace was perfectly correct about the rules, but few forces were as implacable as a Senate committee chairman in front of a hundred or so reporters in his own hearing room. For Wallace, there was the problem of how to get Nab out of the room without touching off a riot. So an odd spectacle occurred, a nightmare compromise for the new chairman of USB, Inc. His statement on the American economy was first read into the record of the proceedings. Then he joined the long, notable line of bootleggers, mobsters, and presidential aides who'd taken the Fifth Amendment before the Congress of the United States.

CHAPTER TWENTY-FIVE
BETRAYAL

*T*he U.S. Army executed one soldier for desertion during World War II, to make an example of him, remembered Peter, who'd seen a movie about the guy. Maybe USB would make an example of him. Perhaps they'd lock him in a room with a dozen anchors. No, that would be inhumane, even for them.

He was surprised to hear himself laugh out loud, a nervous chuckle as he paced the hall outside the conference room.

He missed Brookings. When you faced a court-martial, Brookings was the person you wanted to be running it. He would invoke the death penalty as quickly as anyone, perhaps more quickly, but he would respect your dignity and, being a gentleman, would insist on the minimum violence necessary to do the job. Although he wasn't facing a court-martial, Peter knew, but a firing squad.

He was sweating, which bothered him. He wanted to be cool, to keep his wits about him. Say as little as possible, he thought, glancing down at his penciled list of Dos and Don'ts for the meeting:

Answer yes or no.
Look them in the eye.
Volunteer no information.
Make no jokes or wisecracks.
Admit nothing; deny nothing.
Protect your family. Fight for severance.
Avoid self-righteousness.

Peter had thought about hiring a lawyer to represent him, as Flannery had strongly advised, but had decided against it. Lawyers just bred more lawyers. His strategy was to get out of this quietly, with enough money to buy some time while he sorted his life out. He wanted a truce. He wasn't constitutionally suited to being a Maoist; if he could never be a player again, at least he could be a noncombatant.

The conference room door opened; a grim-looking Elaine emerged and waved him in. Like other veteran secretaries, Elaine had come to assume the characteristics and values of her boss. She looked angry, which meant Sam was. No pleasantries, none of the usual queries about Ben and Sarah; she stood back and held the door open.

Peter felt three pairs of hard eyes on him. In Brookings's old place at the end of the table sat Harold Wallace, in his shirt sleeves but perennially poised. Adelson was on Wallace's right; Frank Mahoney on his left. Mahoney appeared slightly bored, like someone who'd finished his job and was just mopping up. The other two looked like a vigilante jury that had already reached its verdict. Peter instinctively looked around for the coffee, almost expecting Rafael Miranda to provide it, then remembered he wasn't even really entitled to sit down unless asked.

Elaine stationed herself at the rear of the room with her steno pad. A microphone was attached to a tape recorder in the middle of the table, but it was not switched on.

"Peter, please sit down," said Wallace with studied pleasantness, waiting for Peter to settle himself into a chair at the opposite end of the rosewood expanse. Peter took out a pen and notebook and placed them on the table in front of him.

"There are two ways we can do this," said Wallace, "formally or informally. Formally means turning the tape recorder on and putting ourselves in an adversarial situation. You would probably want to get an attorney. The other option is to settle this informally among ourselves. To be frank, the latter course will cost you a little money—a good lawyer could probably get a bit more out of us. But it will get you out of here quickly and at least leave open the possibility of your resuming some sort of television career, although I assume from your behavior you have decided to forgo that. I prefer the latter nonetheless; this has been messy enough, and you know we would just as soon avoid any more publicity. Your call."

Adelson watched Peter carefully, as if he were half-expecting him to jump up in outrage and demand to know what this was all about. Mahoney fidgeted.

Peter put the notebook back in his pocket.

"I obviously prefer the latter as well, which is why I came alone. But I have to be frank: My family is entitled to be protected, and if you impose any sort of arrangement that puts them in jeopardy, my first call when I leave will be to Melvin Belli. I promise you, I'll go down like the *Titanic,* lights ablaze and band playing."

Peter's voice had cracked only once, on "latter." He cleared his throat and felt somewhat closer to comfort than panic.

Wallace nodded, as if to say he understood perfectly. "You were, I take it, responsible for the duck incident, for the leaked contract information, and for the stories about the Florida condominium?" asked Wallace quietly.

Peter said nothing for what seemed to him a long time. "I am partially responsible for the reports about the Florida condominium, which is the only part of all this that I will discuss, because it involves no employees of USB other than myself. I have nothing to say about the other two episodes. I assume you have descriptions of me from Florida. You could easily enough have checked the visitor's list; I made no attempt to disguise myself—"

"Do you always go by the name E. Murrow?" asked Mahoney matter-of-factly but with a touch of sarcasm. Peter smiled, but said nothing.

Mahoney leafed through the papers in front of him. "We also know that you attended Boston University with the *Miami Herald* reporter who wrote the condo story," he said.

"I suspect you know a lot more than that. But that's all I'm going to talk about without an attorney here," said Peter.

Adelson, deflated but silent, looked sadly at Peter. Wallace doodled a bit, then resumed talking, a bit more impatiently.

"Peter, here's what we're getting at. We're not playing cops and robbers. We know you were responsible for all three incidents. We're not here to try to trick you into implicating anyone. That would obviously save us time and trouble, but we're adults. We don't underestimate people—certainly not anymore. What we want are two things: a clear sense that this spree is over now that you feel you've made your point, and a way of separating you from USB that protects us in the future. Do you understand? We have grounds for prosecution on several fronts, I believe, from slander all the way down to trespass and malicious mischief. I won't insult your obvious intelligence by pretending we could make all those charges stick, but we do have considerable resources, and I doubt you want to spend the next ten years in court."

Peter pushed his chair back. "Mr. Wallace, you *are* insulting my intelligence. If you'd planned to prosecute me, you would have. And if you think I buy for one minute that you're going to drag me into court and air all this in the media for years, with depositions and all, then you obviously do underestimate me. I'll just go call a lawyer and we can all hack it out. I can sort of picture a class action suit, about five hundred former USB News employees seeking damages for breach of contract, loss of income, emotional damage. I can even see Bobbie D'Amato talking about the years her father sacrificed for USB before he killed himself—"

Wallace flared. "You do that, Peter, and the only job you'll ever get is at a—"

Adelson suddenly slapped his hand down on the table. "Cut it the fuck out, Peter. What do you want? Now that we've all whipped our dicks out and put them on the table to see whose is longest, can we get this over with? We need to know that there are no more dimes dropping. That you'll go away and shut up—no articles, no books, no off-the-record interviews about USB News. Just silence. Now, what do *you* want?"

Mahoney slid his papers into his briefcase and fiddled with his nails. Wallace looked slightly bemused, as if he had been put in his place, but liked it.

"I want what you should have given everybody: I want a year's pay with benefits. I have to rebuild a life, and I want to know my family is protected while I figure out how to do it. I think that's fair; I've put in some hard years here and I want time to make the transition."

Wallace interrupted, showing some anger again. "You understand, I am sure, that that is out of the question, Peter. Under your contract, you are entitled to four months of severance. If we give you a year, we will be sending a dangerous signal to every employee of this company: that they can do anything they like—leak confidential files, sabotage an on-the-air news program, attack the company's leaders—and the response will be to hand them a year's vacation. I can't accede to that."

They went back and forth for fifteen minutes or so, ending up with a severance package that was the equivalent of eight months' income. Peter consented to sign a silence agreement, which meant that the weekly checks stopped if he spoke or wrote publicly about the company. He didn't like that provision, but he wanted to go home and tell Barbara that this part was over, that they had some breathing room and could get serious about finding alternatives.

When they reached agreement, Wallace and Mahoney stood up and walked toward the door. Wallace shook Peter's hand. "I'll need a resignation letter addressed to Sam," said Wallace, "and I would prefer it by tonight."

Mahoney walked past as if Peter no longer existed.

Adelson remained behind, moving down the long conference table to sit next to Peter. Peter had dreaded this moment the most.

"They could've at least given us some coffee and doughnuts, the cheap bastards," Adelson muttered.

"That's right," said Peter. "The condemned should go out with a flaky croissant and fresh-squeezed juice. Or possibly shrimp."

Adelson grimaced. "There's a silver lining in every cloud, pal," he said.

There was a painful silence.

"I'm sorry, Sam. I hope this hasn't hurt you much," Peter said.

Adelson looked down at the table, casting about for the

right words, the discomfort evident in his voice. "Aaah, it's hurt me a bit, Peter. I fought for you. I kept them from throwing you out in the first place, and that hasn't done me any good, I'll tell you. I fought to get you a spot on this new retrospective show. I tried to take care of you. Now when I try to save somebody else, they'll throw this in my face. And I gotta tell you, I can't believe you sat in my office chatting about this with me like I was some kind of jerk, never saying anything." Adelson shrugged. "But they'll get over it.

"I couldn't believe it when they came to me. I couldn't believe you'd be behind this. I don't think you have a clue as to what you've done to yourself. These guys aren't Boy Scouts. You'll never work for a network or a major company again, never. Why did you do it? You're an executive, an adult. Why?"

Peter patted Adelson on the arm; then he leaned back in his chair. "I don't know that I can come up with one sentence that makes sense. Not here. I hope we can spend a drunken evening together sometime and I'll try to explain."

Adelson's eyes reddened. He shook his head. "I don't think so, Peter. You've crossed a line with me—you gotta know that. You were taking money from these people, you worked for them and for me, and you betrayed all of us just so you would feel better about yourself. I can't admire you for that. I'm sorry. Maybe you were right, but we sure come from different places on this one.

"I'm trying to protect the biggest investment I have—my work life—and I am honestly trying to protect this place and the people who work here. I'm doing the best I can to keep these guys from blowing it all away. You know what, Peter? I'm making some progress; they're starting to listen to me. I've stopped them from doing some things, and I'm convincing them to start moving in the other direction, to make money by doing some new stuff. I know what they are, I know what people are saying about me, but I'm not running away. I don't believe deserting this place—or sabotaging it—is the answer."

Adelson suddenly seemed to run out of words, at least words that would make a difference. They realized how far apart they had grown from each other, or perhaps always had been; it was a shock to both of them.

Peter smiled wanly. It didn't sound as if the drunken evening would come along too soon. They stood up and, impulsively, embraced. Peter thought he could feel the wetness on Adelson's cheek; his own eyes moistened too. Adelson patted him on the shoulder and turned back as he left.

"But good luck, Peter. I mean that. I hope you get what you want. I love you, you know. I want you to be happy, no matter what. We'll never be enemies. Maybe in a few years we can get together, but not yet."

"No," said Peter, his voice quavering now. "I wish you well too, Sam."

Adelson left Peter alone in the room.

CHAPTER TWENTY-SIX
THE CASUALTY LIST

*T*echnicians were unscrewing the four-pack bank of monitors in each suite, replacing them with cheaper communal monitors in the hallway, as Peter walked back down Executive Row. Two vice-presidents heading toward him saw his face, panicked, and darted into the men's room as he approached. He had the curious sensation of feeling simultaneously like a man condemned and like a prisoner who'd just been freed. It was all over; at least he did not have to wonder anymore what would happen to him.

He crossed to his own building and took the elevator up, conscious that he was seeing almost everything for the last time. It was unlikely he would ever set foot in a USB News building again, or in any other television news division. The elevator door opened, the sound bouncing around the empty floor. The two aging men down the hall who produced *Constitutional Minutes* had not yet come in; Peter wasn't sure if they ever came in, but the rumor was that *Constitutional Minutes* was the one unit at USB News that was sacrosanct, per orders of David Nab.

Rafael Miranda was sitting outside Peter's office patiently, his cart laden with plastic-wrapped doughnuts and Danish, ready for morning rounds. He stood up and shook Peter's hand and asked if he had a moment.

Miranda came into the large office and sat down on the sofa. Peter sat across from him, puzzled. Although Miranda had dropped by a number of times to discuss news coverage, he spoke with particular formality this morning.

"Mr. Herbert, I wanted to tell you myself, before you heard it elsewhere, that I'm quitting the company. I'm moving on."

Peter waited, but Miranda said nothing more, so Peter said, "You're leaving the news division?"

Miranda nodded. "Yes. After fourteen years it's difficult, but you can see there isn't much future for me here. The conference room doesn't need me, and there is no longer anyone here to sell coffee to. It is time to think of my future. In the afternoons, on my own time, I've been investigating the prospects at other office buildings. I've decided to get into publishing—run the coffee cart at Farrar, Straus. Their offices are all full and I feel it would be interesting to learn about books. I thought I should tell you."

"You mean, you're giving *me* your resignation?" said Peter.

"I have no one else to tell. There is hardly anyone else left on my floors. This place isn't the same. The barbershop is closing up. . . ." Miranda shrugged and stood up.

"Well, good luck, Rafael. You have a lot more common sense than the rest of us. We all waited to get thrown out." Peter accepted a complimentary cardboard cup of coffee and a jelly doughnut, and the two shook hands again.

He called Barbara at home to relate the denouement. He tried to reach Buzz Allen in Washington, but Buzz was in a meeting. He thought briefly of calling Barnard and decided against it. He called his mother, told her that he was leaving, and warned her not to be surprised or upset by anything she read in the papers. She broke down and sobbed. He felt bad that she would not have much to brag to her sisters about, at least for a while, and she urged him in a hushed voice to be careful how he told his father, who had seemed weaker lately.

After his father there was no one else to talk to, which he

thought was a sorry record for more than fifteen years in the news business, most of them at USB.

Without air conditioning, his office was warming up. He wanted to complete his letter before the day got too steamy. He flicked on his IBM Selectric, braced himself with some of Rafael's coffee, and wrote:

Dear Sam,

I offer, with deep regret, my resignation—my sign off, you would say—from USB News, effective today, June 20.

I realize, of course, that I'm supposed to leave it at that. But I know that for legal and other reasons, you will have to file this letter, forward it to lawyers and personnel people and such, and that presents an irresistible temptation. I love the idea of this letter bouncing around corporate files and computers forever. "Look," some vice-president will say in 2025, "this is the guy that pulled the duck stunt." Bureaucracies being what they are, it will make me immortal.

I am truly sorry if I caused you any personal embarrassment. I know you were fighting for me and I appreciate that. I hope that one day, when we're old men sitting on some veranda in Florida, we can at least read the papers together every morning and bitch about how lousy the coverage is. I would like that.

Among the things I have learned in the past few months is that clichés are true. Don't bite the hand that feeds you. You're the last to know when you're in trouble. Money and success aren't all they're cracked up to be.

I'm sorry that I couldn't come to it on my own, but the takeover and the collapse of my own previously promising career have combined to remind me that I got into journalism in the first place because I wanted to stick it to people like Nab, not work for them. I started to get the feeling that I was playing for the wrong team.

As long as I was helping to make the rules, they didn't bother me. I didn't get religion until someone was making rules for me. But the change made me see that I had sold out in bits and pieces—a month in Bar Harbor here, a reliable nanny there, a good health plan. Over time, I got so far from what I started out to do that I couldn't even remember it anymore.

I find that I am haunted by the people at USB News, some-

times obsessed by them. I wake up and go to sleep with them—
not just the people swept away by Nab but those swept away by
us, by me. Do you ever think much about them? I don't imagine
you can, compassionate though you are, because it would be hard
to do your work if you did. That's why successful executives don't
tend to introspection, isn't it?

There's a list of names that keeps running through my mind,
a casualty list.

Dan D'Amato's is the first name on it, of course. If he had
died in a plane crash over Kuwait, USB News would have mounted
a bronze memorial plaque somewhere in the building and somebody would have endowed the D'Amato Chair at Columbia. This
will not happen, although he clearly died in the service of his
company. Your tribute at the ABA Awards was surely the last
time any executive here will mention his name. I assume you
aren't kidding yourself about him; you must know that he killed
himself. I wish I had been a better friend; I should have done
something. Some poor shrink will be hearing a lot about it from
me.

Remember Elliott Brookings? Forty years running USB News?
He's sitting on some farm in New England, quite brokenhearted,
I am sure, although I don't really know because I haven't had the
guts to call him and neither, I imagine, has anybody else. Hard to
believe Brookings doesn't have a single thought the company
could use anymore, that he would be chucked into the backyard
like an old sofa with sagging springs.

Did you hear that Armand Andreas moved into one of those
death complexes in the exurbs, where you give some church
everything you own and move into an apartment and they are
obliged to take care of you until you die? I'm told they make you
share meals with people so you don't get cranky and weird. I only met
Andreas once or twice. Certainly fodder for Harold Shurken there.

There's Bill Siegel, who's typical, it seems to me, of the
people who have been hit the hardest. For a generation or so he
wandered around the country, one of those rare journalists who
delight in oddballs. I always found his pieces hopeful, because
they told me that when all was said and done, you could find your
own sort of glory and honor by going off into the hills somewhere and building the longest barn in the state. Those people

don't usually get on television. Siegel seems unable to do that himself, though. He's desperately looking for another job in the industry. At fifty-two, he'll have trouble landing anything.

And what can I say about Cynthia Zuckerman? I probably have wrecked a life or two before hers without feeling the impact of it quite so much. The thing is, I always fired somebody for what I thought was a reason. When Harold Wallace made such a big deal out of telling us there was no reason, that is what triggered the beginning of my own mid-career crisis.

Cynthia went to restaurant school—she had a fantasy about running a café—but she dropped out. She applied to a university program in family counseling, but I hear she was not accepted. Now, Patricia Flannery tells me, Cynthia is working as a receptionist at an independent production company. Flannery says the whole thing has damn near done Cynthia in, that she can't get past the shock of having been a USB News producer who's wound up answering telephones for twenty-seven-year-olds.

Flannery assures me that Cynthia will get over it. I don't know. People do get help and get past trauma, but D'Amato has made me wary of taking that for granted.

If you had told me six months ago that I would be putting Buzz Allen on a casualty list, I would have said you were bananas. A college football star, still young and still handsome, nothing flashy but absolutely dependable and conscientious—boy, did his life fly apart in a hurry. His marriage hits the rocks, Jack Thomas suddenly discovers Buzz makes him as twitchy as a tick on a hound dog, and bam! he's in Washington assigning camera crews to the Food and Drug Administration.

Buzz believes everything you tell him. He doesn't think he has an option in the world, so he has dug his foxhole and jumped in. It is a terrifying thought—twenty-five years or so in a foxhole—but it is his life, and as we all know, what choice does he have?

There are, of course, the lesser figures. Nurse Edwards and her lava rocks; Rafael Miranda, who knew more congressmen than Walter Cronkite; Jared Weld, who has four kids around college age and broke down and wept when I threw him out; Emmy Thayer, the tape editor and recovered alky who will never get another job.

Am I being preachy here, or sanctimonious? I imagine that if we were lunching at the New Age, you would be puncturing my balloon, saying something like, "C'mon, Peter, this isn't the United Way. Times change."

I agree. I wouldn't have had the guts to make a change if I didn't have to. I suspect men need to take a beating—a divorce, a heart attack, job trouble—to force them to think about this stuff. For me, there were just too many casualties, myself included.

But I don't mean to seem confident, either. I'm scared to death of the future. The loss and pain are quite real. I'm used to being surrounded by scores, sometimes hundreds, of people, and to making dozens of decisions each day. Now, the loneliness can be overpowering, especially when the kids are at school and Barbara is working and the phone does not ring. I worry a lot about money. I keep telling myself that I will certainly survive—I can piece together a living one way or another—but can we stay in the big house? We'll see.

Along with career, though, there is a more poignant loss— that notion of success that was so sweet and that we all shared for some years. I never dreamed that I would become the pariah we all kidded about and avoided in the hallways. I hope we can both remember that success wasn't only a mirage. We *were* successful, weren't we? And you will still be one of the 25,000.

The big problem I've had, and it almost sunk me for a few weeks, was that I was simply unprepared to fail. You never warned me— nobody did—that the day might come when I would have to face up to the fact that I just wasn't as good as I thought I was or wanted to be. Was I ever any good? Would this have happened if I was?

I'm taken aback by the number of men who've warned me recently about my mortgage and my obligations. I don't need to be reminded; they're much on my mind. It sometimes seems unlikely that these men are all wrong, but I sure hope they are. Where does this strange conviction come from that a forty-year-old man with experience and brains and half a life to live has no choice but to accept this *lack* of choice; this judgment of him by other people? I understand why they want us to think it's true; that's why we all sit in a room and nod when handed our layoff packets, I guess. But I don't know how we're supposed to be loving husbands and fathers when we think that leaves us no choice but to hang on to jobs we abhor, or that abhor us, because the bills are due by the tenth of each month. That's what my father did.

Speaking of fathers, I have to tell you—as Dan D'Amato told me—
that it ain't easy calling up your father and telling him you're on your
ass, that you didn't make it after all. My father was pretty supportive,
for him, especially considering that the Red Sox are in the toilet again.
He said that I made it once, and he was sure I could do it again. That's
an endorsement of sorts, isn't it?

Okay, for the last time—the score's at 7 and 2—who said this?
I've been carrying this one in my blazer pocket for months. I always
meant to save it for the capper, but I had no idea how much of a capper it would be.

> ". . . human beings are not born once and for all on the day
> their mothers give birth to them . . . life obliges them over and
> over again to give birth to themselves."

Gabriel Garcia Marquez. You would have guessed wrong, I
know it, so I'll mark it down as 8 and 2. Down the road, I'm sure
we'll get to 10 and I'll pick up the free lunch, which I'm sure I'll
need.

Now, without being sentimental, which we would both hate, I
will miss you. We were a great team, and I hope neither of us for-
gets that as we justify the choices we made. I think I understand why
you made yours. You seem to me the personification of responsibility; walking away is unimaginable to you, cowardly.

Fair enough. Staying would have felt the same way for me.

Best,
Peter

Peter smiled at the security guard who had appeared in
the doorway of his office. He smiled and raised his hands
in the air. "I'll go quietly, officer," he said. The guard laughed
back.

Peter lowered his arms and put the letter, along with his
USB ID cards and his office keys, into an envelope, licked the
flap, sealed it up. He did not need to be told that his personal
belongings would be packed into cardboard boxes and shipped to
his house.

He scrawled Adelson's name and office number on the envelope and handed it to the guard. He waited while the guard

locked the office with his master key and walked him to the elevator. They descended; the guard smiled but did not speak when Peter said he had heard it would rain. Then the elevator opened in the lobby; the guard waited for Peter to go first.